I0534868

Bright Spark

Psions of SPIRE
Book 1

Alex Silver

Copyright

This is a work of fiction. Names, characters, places, and incidents either are the product of the author's imagination or are used fictitiously. Any resemblance to actual persons, living or dead, events, or locales is entirely coincidental.

Copyright © 2019 by Alex Silver

All rights reserved. No part of this book may be reproduced or used in any manner without written permission of the copyright owner except for the use of quotations in a book review. For more information, address: asilverauthor@gmail.com

First paperback edition 2019

ISBN (paperback) 978-1-9995310-5-8
ISBN (ebook) 978-1-9995310-1-0

http://alexsilverauthor.wordpress.com

Table of Contents

PART ONE

6 Years Ago

Chapter 1

Jake

"Ten, nine…" I tuned out the crowd's chant as I ran up the field, pivoting around one of the opposing defense-men. Garrett was to my left, bringing the ball up the field. He crossed the ball over to me and I dribbled past the last opposing player. Only me and the goalie now.

"Three, two…"

I took the shot. The goalie leapt for it, his fingers brushed the ball, but it flew past him and into the back of the net—goal.

"One," said the crowd. The buzzer blared as the timer hit zero. I threw up my arms in celebration. We won, three to two. Garret plowed into me and we were both whooping with joy. Soon the whole team was on the field hugging and cheering as the spectators applauded.

It was epic. The perfect beginning to the elite soccer season, and it was my goal that put us there. My junior year was off to an awesome start.

I floated through the wrap up, a quick pep talk from our coach, and congratulating the other team on a good game. The locker room had a jovial air as we all changed out of our uniforms. We horsed around and joked. It was a heady feeling, having all my teammates' admiration.

"Great goal," Paul said from beside me. I grinned at our newest rookie player.

"Thanks, couldn't have done it without Gar's epic last minute steal," I said. As team captain, I needed to share the glory. And Garrett had made my goal possible. "You played great defense in the first quarter, that's the way to keep the pressure off Smithy."

Paul flushed at the praise and Smithy, our goalie, made a teasing remark about it. Hanging with my team was one of my favorite activities. Good thing too, considering how much time we spent practicing and working out together. It took commitment to reach peak performance. And it all paid off on game day. Today was a great day.

The only missing piece was my best friend at my side. Aaron was not athletic, but he often came to my games to support me. I wasn't sure if he had made it tonight though because he'd been having awful headaches the last couple of weeks.

My phone buzzed, rattling against the metal of the locker.

"That your girlfriend?" Smithy asked.

"Aaron," I said. I knew he was teasing because he thought it was funny to refer to Aaron that way. I chose not to play along and instead I read the text from Aaron.

Aaron: Epic goal Jake! Gonna be the best season yet!!!

Jake: U here?

Aaron: Like I'd miss it. Meet you near your car?

Jake: B out soon.

"So, it *is* your girlfriend then," Smithy said. A few guys laughed. Garrett caught my eye and gave me a sympathetic look. Smithy had played on our team for the past three years and his 'jokes' about me and Aaron had worn thin. And this year I had authority to put a stop to his comments. It was a big responsibility. At least I knew Garrett and the other guys from my school would support me. They'd all known since middle school.

"Nope, see, Aaron's a dude, so he would be my boyfriend. If we were dating, which we aren't."

The atmosphere in the locker room had gotten tense, conversations died as everyone listened in on me and Smithy.

"Could have fooled me."

"He's my friend," I said. I was a little surprised at how calm and level my voice sounded. Much more confident than I felt. Out of the corner of my eye I noticed coach poking his head out of his office to check on the sudden change in the team's mood.

"Whatever, f—"

"Smith!" Coach said over the rest of the slur. He stood in the doorway scowling at Smithy. "We have a zero-tolerance policy on intolerance here, that language will get you benched, you get me?"

"Yes, Coach," Smithy said. His eyes dropped to his bag. He finished stuffing his belongings inside, then he stormed out of the locker room, grumbling under his breath.

"You good, Moretti?" Coach asked.

"Yeah, Coach," I said. It was nice to know the coaching staff enforced that policy. That I had support. Coach stepped back into his office. Garrett gave me a playful slap on the back.

"You know, you could do worse than Aaron if you dated a dude," he said in an undertone. It startled a laugh out of me.

"I don't think he's interested," I said.

Paul gave me a wide-eyed look, but there was no malice in it, so I didn't comment. Anyone else who overheard said nothing.

"Well, who is up for a celebration? Let's meet at Shakes and Stuff in an hour and get our grub on," I said, trying to recapture the jovial mood of our victory. Smithy's outburst had put a damper on my excitement. There was a general rumble of assent to my suggestion. Banter picked back up as we finished in the locker room.

I helped to coordinate rides for everyone and then left with Garrett and Paul after most of the team had already departed.

"Is Aaron coming for burgers?" Garrett asked, pointing toward where he was waiting by my car, fiddling with his phone.

"I'm not sure," I said. I couldn't help admiring him as we approached though. His unruly copper curls made him unmistakable even at a distance. The glow of his phone screen cast his features into sharp relief.

"Hey!" I called to him as we approached, so we wouldn't startle him. He was standing alone in the corner of the deserted parking lot.

"Great game you guys!" Aaron said. He lit up when he saw me, or rather us.

Aaron tucked his phone into his pocket and I gave into my impulse to sweep him into an embrace. I figured it would be the same hard

7

backslapping congratulatory style of hug I had shared with my teammates on the field. All muscles in a display of strength. It wasn't.

Aaron melted into me, soft and inviting. Taken by surprise, I held him tighter than I had intended. Supporting both of our weight as he stood on his toes, chin tilted up, lips parted. Uncertainty clouded his features before the familiar stubborn determination overtook his face. And he reached up to press our lips together.

I stood there like a lump. Aaron's hands on my face were unexpected, but welcome. It was a clumsy kiss, our noses bumped, and ours cheeks rubbed together for a moment as he figured out the angle. He tasted like mint gum and his lips against mine were soft and perfect.

When I felt him go from pliant to tense in my arms, I realized I was analyzing the kiss instead of returning it. With a muffled moan I kissed him back, deepening it a little. I wanted to convey I was fine with this new development in our friendship. I wanted to touch him, to let my hands drift from his back, but Garrett broke into our private moment with a wolf whistle.

Aaron pulled back, his fair cheeks burning with embarrassment. But his bright hazel-green eyes danced with good humor..

"Way to go, get the game winning goal and the guy, huh, Jake?" Garrett said. He gave me a playful shove and then gestured at the car. "Now unlock the doors."

I kept an arm slung around Aaron's shoulders as I unlocked my tiny sedan for my teammates. Garrett popped the trunk and tossed his duffel on top of our school bags. Paul dumped his in next and I followed suit, only releasing Aaron with reluctance.

"You have a ride?" I asked as Paul and Garrett scuffled over who got to sit in front. Garrett won, putting Paul in a headlock.

"Took the bus," Aaron said, shivering in the autumn chill.

"I can give you a ride home, you want to come out with us for burgers?"

Aaron bit his lip, considered for a moment and then shook his head. "Nah, it's team stuff, right? Have fun and text me later?"

"Sure, but, we can kiss again, right?" I asked. Garrett and Paul were already buckled into my car. I took advantage of our brief privacy to figure out Aaron's intentions before I got in the car to go out with my team.

This was big. Our first kiss, it was special. I had convinced myself Aaron didn't see me that way. Not that we ever discussed that stuff. We didn't talk about sex or sexuality. Aaron hated it when people made assumptions about him. And he hated talking about it. So we didn't.

"If you want to," Aaron said then grinned at me. "I've fantasized about doing that for ages, and since I'm on a roll, I guess I'll come out and say it, do you want to go out?"

"Like boyfriends?" I asked.

"Yeah."

"Yes."

"Good. So, we're boyfriends then," Aaron said, and his satisfied smile mirrored mine.

Aaron looked so happy that I couldn't resist leaning in to give him another quick kiss. Which led to a longer kiss. And if Garrett and Paul weren't in my car, I would have ditched the team dinner to see where things might lead. But then Garrett was leaning on my car horn and Aaron was grinning at me, his smile inches from my face.

"Maybe not the ideal location for getting physical," he said.

I had to agree that a public parking lot was not the best make out location. Even if we were the only people in sight. Aaron went around the car. That forced Paul to slide into the middle seat since my little brother Luca's booster seat took up the rear drivers' side.

The drive to Aaron and my neighborhood wasn't far out of our way to my chagrin. As much as I loved my team, I would have preferred more time with him. I regretted having to drop Aaron off instead of spending the rest of the evening together. Still, I had obligations to my team and we would text later.

After we dropped off Aaron, Paul and Garrett teased me about being besotted, but their ribbing remained good-natured. The same joking hard time they would give any of our teammates about a new relationship. So I took the teasing and tried not to obsess over rehashing the kiss.

Chapter 2

Aaron

"Jake and I are going to a movie tonight," I told my parents over breakfast.

Jake had been my best friend ever since my family moved in next to his when we were both in kindergarten. But things had changed last night. After Jake's soccer game. I was glad I hadn't let my headache keep me from being there.

It wasn't the first time Jake had scored the game-winning goal, but it had still been fun to watch. His excitement must have been contagious because when he swept me up into a hard, sweaty hug I had taken it as an invitation to kiss him. And he kissed me back. So this movie differed from the countless others we had seen together over the years. It was our first date.

I wanted my parents to understand how important it was. After close to seventeen years, I should have known better. Hope springs eternal I guess.

"That's nice, dear," my mother said as she poured coffee and buttered a stack of toast.

I fidgeted in my seat and fiddled with the fraying edge of my place mat. Aware of the nervous twitch, but unable to sit still. If I planned to make this my big coming out moment, then I would need to spell it out for them. I figured they would take it in stride, but there was still a part of me that worried.

"It's a school night, make sure you come right home after," my father glanced up from his cell to level a stern look at me. I repressed the urge to roll my eyes when his attention returned to his phone. I had envisioned this conversation going a different direction.

"No, I mean, yes, I'll be home by ten, but it's not just a movie."

"Are you boys getting dinner first?" Mom asked as she sat beside Dad with her breakfast. Dad stole a slice of her toast and they exchanged smiles before he turned back to his phone, already absorbed in work drama.

"We are, but that isn't what I meant. I'm trying to tell you something important. Would you guys look at me for a minute?"

Mom smiled at me, one of the big fake ones she used when she was humoring me, "what's the matter, dear, you seem flustered."

"Make it quick, I need to get to a meeting this morning, son," Dad frowned at me, but he turned his phone face down on the table.

I took a deep breath and blurted out, "it's a date. Jake and I are dating."

There, I'd done it. The words were out, on my terms. I grinned at them because I wanted them to know how happy that made me. I guess a part of me thought I could alter their reactions by the sheer force of my will. It didn't work, but it was a nice thought.

"That's unexpected," my mother said.

She glanced at my father like she was waiting to take her cue from him. He stared at me for a long time, his mouth full of toast. Then he frowned, chewed, took a large gulp of coffee, and acted as though I had said nothing. His undivided attention back on whatever was so important on his phone.

"Uh, Dad?" I asked. My mild anxiety that my parents wouldn't be excited for me turned to fear I had misjudged their level of acceptance.

"What?" he said, distracted, "you're old enough to be dating, but your curfew is still ten. And we expect you to keep up with your studies and extracurricular commitments."

Then he finished his coffee and stood. He tucked his phone into his pocket before donning the suit jacket he had draped over the back of his chair while he ate.

I gaped at him. That was it? I almost had a heart attack over his reaction to my coming out and he told me he didn't care?

If I was honest, I was indignant. How dare he not care about something so significant? But, that was typical of our relationship. My anger faded to a familiar disappointment.

Dad and I never seemed to relate. He was glad to support me with his checkbook, paying for everything from skating classes, to soccer camp and guitar lessons when I was younger. Last year he had donated to the theater department at my high school to buy costumes for our annual play when I became involved with the drama kids.

His only requirements for me were that I earned good grades and that I have at least one extracurricular activity during the school year. He wanted me to go to a prestigious university. I wanted to be close to Jake, I figured the rest would just fall into place.

"I'll be home late tonight, I'll text when I'm leaving the office. Aaron, make sure you get your homework done before your date."

"Yes, Dad," I told him, suppressing an eye-roll. I understood where he expected my priorities to be.

"Have a wonderful day, dear," Mom said, following him down the hall away from the kitchen. The sounds of their voices receded. I didn't bother eavesdropping. If they spoke about me I didn't want to hear it, anyway.

I set the spoon down in my soggy cereal, giving up on eating it and taking care of my dish. Too nervous and excited about seeing Jake again to waste more time on breakfast. We had stayed up for hours texting last night. But seeing him in person was different.

Jake sounded enthusiastic about our relationship too. But what if he got cold feet when faced with everyone at school knowing about us? He was more popular than me. Hanging out with a scrawny theater nerd already got him teased over our friendship. I worried about what our classmates would say about us. He had brushed off other people's opinions before, but would it be different now?

I turned from the sink to find my mother had returned to the kitchen and was staring at me.

"What?" I asked, swiping at my face, thinking I had gotten food on myself without noticing somehow.

"It's nothing, dear," she said, but her voice sounded all choked up like she wanted to cry, and that scared me again. Until she added, "you know your father and I love you, no matter what, right?"

"I know, Mom," I said. And I recognized it even if they didn't always do the greatest job of showing it. They tried their best.

I couldn't help a lingering resentment at how little they cared about the details of my life though. Like it didn't matter who I was, they had a contractual obligation to love me. So they did, for a value of love that translated to meeting my material needs more than being present in my life.

"Good," she said before resuming her seat at the kitchen table. She took a sip of her lukewarm coffee, then continued, "your father has a business trip out of town this weekend, I had planned to go with him. Do you think Jake's parents would mind if you stayed over there like usual, considering your relationship?"

"I can ask."

"You do that," she said, "have fun tonight."

"I will, thanks, Mom."

"Now, get ready before you're late."

I took the dismissal and went to brush my teeth and pack up my school bag.

Jake met me at his door, he drove his siblings and me to school whenever he didn't have a morning practice. Before I psyched myself out and made things awkward, he pulled me into a hug and gave me a peck on the lips. Right there at his front door, with his younger brother and sister both getting ready behind him.

Jake's mother knelt beside Luca helping him into his shoes while he did his best impression of still being asleep. Sofia was fussing with a scarf in front of the hall mirror.

"Jake and Aaron, sitting in a tree," Sofia singsonged, erasing all doubt she had seen us. Jake smiled, inches from my face, his bright smile drawing my eyes to his mouth. Those full lips made me want to kiss him again even with his family right there. I restrained myself, taking in the easy affection that his family always seemed to have for each other.

"Sofia," their mother chided, "don't taunt your brother, or he won't give you a ride to school."

"But you and dad said he had to drop us off if he got a car. How else am I supposed to get to school?" Sofia protested.

"You can always take the bus," Jake pointed out. He stepped away from me and gave his sister a playful nudge as he walked past her to get his gear for school and soccer practice.

"Here, go unlock the car while I grab my stuff," Jake handed her the keys.

"The bus is for losers," Sofia whined, sticking her tongue out at Jake's back as he disappeared around the corner.

"I like the bus, my friends ride it," Luca mumbled rubbing sleep from his eyes. "Do I have to go to school today, Momma?" he asked, plaintive.

"*Sì, amore*, you all have to go to school," she finished tying her youngest son's shoes and helped him into his coat. Even though he flopped around like a rag doll, she made it appear effortless.

I knew from experience with helping Jake babysit that dressing Luca to go outside was harder than it looked. Their mother kissed Luca's forehead before handing him his bag. He gave his mother a big hug and a sloppy kiss on the cheek.

"You have your homework, Sofia?" Mrs. Moretti asked.

"Yes, Momma," Sofia gestured with her schoolbag. She tolerated a quick hug and a kiss from her mother before taking Luca's hand and leading him out to Jake's car.

"Have a great day at school," she called after them before she faced me. "Good morning, Aaron," Mrs. Moretti smiled at me as she watched Sofia help Luca into his booster seat.

"Good morning," I said, smiling at her.

"Jacopo tells me you two are an item now," Mrs. Moretti said, using Jake's full name. She was the only one who called him that. Her full attention fixed on me now that Luca and Sofia were in the car.

"Yeah, we're, uh, going on a date tonight," I said, my smile big enough to split my face in half. She chuckled.

"So I've heard. I wondered if he would make a move."

"I kissed him," I told her, still wearing a goofy grin.

"That does not surprise me," Mrs. Moretti told me. "Jacopo has a hard time asking for what he wants *non è vero?*"

"Yeah," I agreed, then it occurred to me that she had implied that she saw this coming, "wait a minute, you knew about him?"

"He told us he might like boys when he was twelve, yes," Mrs. Moretti agreed.

"About us?" I clarified, even though her response surprised me. I hadn't known Jake wasn't straight until last night, we didn't talk about that stuff. And I'd seen him checking out girls with his soccer buddies.

"That you boys were flirting for years? Yes, Aaron, I have eyes."

"How didn't I know?"

She patted my arm in comfort, "you aren't the first person to be oblivious to a close friend having a crush on you. It took Giancarlo and me ages to date."

"Hey, Aaron, you ready to go?" Jake asked as he came around the corner loaded down with his backpack and a duffel bag full of his soccer gear.

"Yeah, just chatting with your mom," I said, "oh, right! Mom wanted me to ask if it was okay if I stay here this weekend, my parents will be out of town."

"It's fine," she said, "we trust you boys."

Jake groaned, "oh my god, Mom, really?"

She shrugged, "I was seventeen once too. Tell me if you need me to pick up condoms."

"I can buy my own stuff, Mom," Jake covered his face with his hands, mortified.

I could empathize, but I felt more comfortable discussing this topic with Jake's mom than my own. Maybe because I could always count on her for a hug when I needed one. I was close with Jake's whole family. To where they brought me on family vacations with them for the past few years.

"Let's go before I die of embarrassment," Jake said. He grabbed my hand and dragged me out the door. "Bye, Mom."

"Bye, second Mom," I quipped, twisting around in Jake's grasp to favor her with a cheeky wave.

"Have a good day," she called out with a return wave.

Jake held me until we got to the passenger door. Sofia had already buckled herself into the front seat, Jake opened the door and glowered at his sister, "that's Aaron's seat, Sofia."

"I got here first," she said, crossing her arms over her chest.

"You're not even supposed to ride in the front," Jake protested.

"I'm old enough now, Mom says twelve is old enough."

"It's fine, Jake, I don't mind sitting with Luca," I offered, not wanting to be the source of conflict between Jake and his sister. Jake scowled.

"Just this once, Sofia? I want to sit next to my boyfriend," he said.

"Fine, but you owe me," Sofia huffed.

"Sure, I'll bring you home sour patch from the theater."

"Sour patch and a bag of popcorn. You know how I feel about the movie theater popcorn."

"I know," he said, aggrieved.

"And make sure you get extra butter this time," she added, eyes narrowed before she unbuckled and climbed over the console into the back seat. Jake looked on the verge of protesting about her hurting his car with her dirty shoes, but he bit his tongue to avoid further conflict.

"I'll remind him," I said, "thanks, Sofia."

"Whatever, let's go," Sofia said.

Jake leaned in and kissed me again, quick and chaste in front of his siblings. The way he eyed me let me know he wanted privacy as much as I did though. I smiled. Jake shut my door for me, which was silly, but I would have been lying if I said I didn't like it.

"So, you two will be even more lovey-dovey now, huh?" Sofia said, sounding sullen.

"We aren't lovey-dovey," I protested.

"Whatever," Sofia said, and I heard the eye-roll in her voice. I craned around to look at her, I hadn't expected it to bother Sofia that I was dating her brother. We usually got along. We were quiet as Jake opened the trunk to stash our school bags.

"Sofia's just upset because she owes mom twenty bucks," Luca piped up as Jake slammed the trunk shut.

"Huh, why?" I asked, confused.

"We had a betting pool," Luca said, "I bet you would ask him out on your birthday because everyone knows you get a wish on your birthday."

"Um, your whole family bet on when Jake and I would become a couple?"

Luca nodded, all earnest and matter-of-fact, "well, yeah, Nonna bet you asking at Christmas, Zio Gregorio said—"

"Oh my god!" I exclaimed, cutting off Luca's list.

"What? Is everything okay?" Jake asked as he folded himself into the driver's seat. He was too tall to fit in the compact sedan with any comfort, but it was what he could afford, and he was ridiculously proud of the car. His pride was justified since he bought it with his own money.

Jake was always the responsible one. When he wasn't busy with school and sports, he worked. He babysat his siblings and little cousins, tutored at the middle school and did lawn care for most of the homes in the neighborhood during the warmer months. And he got a job bussing tables as soon as he was old enough to work a real job.

"Your entire family had a pool going on when we would get together," I said. Jake gave a rueful shake of his head.

"I should have known," he said, and then after a moment of thought he guessed, "Mom won, didn't she?"

"Yep!" Luca said from the back seat. Jake laughed as he started the car.

"That explains why she was so excited when I told you guys last night," Jake twisted around and narrowed his eyes at Sofia. "It also explains why you were so insistent hinting that I should ask Aaron to homecoming, right, Sofia?"

"Hey! That's cheating, Sofia, no trying to influence them," Luca protested.

Sofia did her best to look innocent, "Jake was talking about homecoming and I only asked if he had a date. And if Aaron was going with anyone."

"You guys are unbelievable," Jake said, though his affection was clear.

"You love us," Sofia told him.

"Yeah, I do," Jake said, smiling at his sister. "All right, time to go."

Nothing would dampen my mood today. Not showing up late because Luca forgot his bag in the car and Sofia called us halfway to the high school. We had to turn around, but it was fine. And Jake held my hand as we rushed through the halls, he didn't care who saw us.

My spirits were too elevated for anything to bring me down. Not a pop quiz in algebra I was unprepared for, or Noah York shoving me into the lockers between classes. Everything was fine because Jake texted me throughout the day.

Lexi Hammond mangling her lines at rehearsal couldn't ruin my buzz. Even though we ended up taking twice as long as we should have to run her scenes. God only knew why she insisted she had the script memorized after only a week despite all evidence to the contrary.

And okay, eating dinner alone before the movie because Jake got called into work to cover for a sick co-worker sucked. But he apologized, and he guilt tripped his supervisor into giving me free cheese fries. Plus, it was a partial shift so we could still make it to the theater on time.

Well, to a later showing of the movie, after I negotiated a one time extension on my curfew with my mom. Sure, I agreed to extra chores for a week, but the time with Jake was worth it.

And it wasn't ideal to have a date who smelled like the industrial cleaner they used in the kitchen where he worked. But it was Jake, and I didn't care how he smelled, I liked spending time with him.

When the employee at the ticket counter told us the movie we wanted to see was sold out, it had me on the verge of tears. But only because nothing went right today. I was emotionally exhausted from maintaining my good mood. None of that mattered though, not really, because I was dating Jake Moretti. My best friend.

"I'm sorry. I should have bought our tickets online, new releases are like that sometimes," Jake turned to face me outside the theater. He juggled the treats he had promised his sister to dig out his keys.

"It's okay, we'll try again another night," I said. I took Sofia's popcorn so he wouldn't drop it and Jake gave me a grateful smile.

"It's not okay. You had a rough day. I am taking you on an awesome first date if it's the last thing I do," Jake insisted.

"It's getting late, we don't have to," I said. But I flashed him a genuine smile,

"I want to," Jake said as we reached his car. After I stashed Sofia's bribe in the back seat and buckled up, I angled myself toward him.

"Where are we going now then?" I asked as Jake pulled out of the parking lot.

"You'll see," he said. It surprised me when he parked at the grocery store. I waited in the car while he bought supplies. Then he drove us out to the lake where his parents owned a camp.

Without his siblings in the car, he was more relaxed about driving. He kept one hand on the wheel, and twined the fingers of his other hand with mine, resting on the console. I had no complaints, I enjoyed the freedom to touch him.

Jake didn't have the keys to the camp. So we skirted around to the narrow strip of beach behind the building where there was a fire pit. We stumbled in the dark with only the glow of our cell phones to light the way.

Jake brought his purchases from the grocery store and we roasted hot dogs since he hadn't eaten earlier. I found ingredients for s'mores when I dug further into the bag. My favorite.

We chatted and laughed and I sat pressed against his side because I could. And when we got around to dessert, I might have accidentally on-purpose smeared melted marshmallow and chocolate on his face while I fed him a s'more.

That led to us making out. Until we heard a neighbor calling to their dog, and it reminded us we were in public. I climbed off his lap at that point even if I would have preferred not to stop.

We sat cuddled together in the crisp fall night, with a blanket from Jake's car wrapped around us. Watching the dying flames reflect off the gentle waves and blend with the silvery moonlight until my curfew forced us to head home. It wasn't the first date we had planned at all, but it was still perfect.

Chapter 3

Jake

After our disaster of a first date, I resolved to ensure our first night together as a couple went to plan. I wasn't sure if we were ready for sex yet. We were only dating for two days.

We had also been best friends for years though. After how our make-out session last night had gone, I figured that I should prepare myself. I thought we would have gone further than second base if the neighbor's dog hadn't interrupted us on the beach. I felt comfortable doing more with Aaron. Mostly.

Aaron deserved romance. Everything had to be perfect. The problem was I had only the vaguest notion of what I was doing. So I cut my last class of the day on Friday. Which I didn't even feel bad about since it was a study hall. I headed home to prepare.

In times of uncertainty, I preferred learning as much as possible about the topic in question. So I conducted research. Lots of research. Then Mom walked in on my research. And we had a super awkward conversation about how porn did not qualify as sex research.

She offered to answer my questions. I was reluctant to ask my mother about sex though. We compromised. Which amounted to mom lecturing me, again, on safe sex.

As a nurse, she reminded me she that she knew what she was talking about. She also showed me some websites that had good information. The talk ended with her offering to answer questions after I read through the resources she provided.

Mom made a point of affirming she and Dad loved me. No matter who I loved. My sexuality had been a non-issue since I hadn't dated until now.

But they had known for years now. And considering Zio Gregorio and his husband attended all our family gatherings, I never doubted my family accepted me.

It only came up in a conversation once when I had been twelve and getting ready for a school dance. Dad had teased me with one of his stock lines about breaking all the girls' hearts. He always used to say stuff that assumed I would grow up to be a casanova.

I had snapped back at him, annoyed, 'who said I even like girls?' He had given me the strangest look, startled, like he needed a moment to recalibrate how he looked at me. But he had recovered fast said I would break the boys' hearts too, if I preferred.

When I got home from the dance, Dad had made a point of telling me he loved me. And he was proud of me no matter what. That ended the conversation.

So I never had a big scary coming out moment like Aaron had told me about with his parents. Other than that one flippant remark before the dance it hadn't been worth mentioning. I figured that they had forgotten about it.

The biggest change afterward was that Dad switched to using gender neutral language when he teased Sofia, Luca, and me about crushes. It was an improvement if he must tease us.

Except they had understood what my throw away comment had meant. They had read Aaron and my interactions better than we had. And started their ridiculous pool about me and Aaron months ago.

I guess I understood that on some level though. Since I had announced that Aaron kissed me when I got home from celebrating with my team and no one had batted an eye. And now Mom was lecturing me with a blithe air as if it wasn't awkward.

Just when I thought the mortification was over, she handed me a bag from the pharmacy. It was a relief that the bag contained only condoms and lube. But then I saw that she had also included a package of baby wipes. And a box, which on closer inspection contained an enema—gross.

Which showed she had put far too much consideration into my sex life for comfort. It was almost enough to make me reconsider having sex this weekend. Or ever. Contemplation of my mom thinking about me having sex was a total boner killer.

But it was Aaron, sleeping in my bed. Spending the entire weekend together. I figured it would take something catastrophic to keep us from at least experimenting.

The website Mom had shown me helped. The rest of my afternoon passed in a flash as one topic led to another. Armed with my new knowledge, I gained confidence I wouldn't screw up everything.

Around supper time I climbed upstairs to wait for Aaron and check in with my family. It surprised me when Mom was the only one around. She stood in the entryway getting ready to leave for a shift at the hospital.

"Oh, good. I wanted to chat before I left," Mom said. "Did you find everything you needed earlier?"

"Yeah, thanks, Mom."

"*È Bellissimo*. And is Aaron still staying the weekend while his folks are out of town?"

"That's the plan."

"Okay, you two will be alone for dinner tonight. I have to get going, but there's lasagna in the oven for your dinner. I already turned off the heat so it should stay warm in there until you're ready to eat. Your dad is out with his bowling league until late and Sofia and Luca both have sleepovers."

"Uh," I said. The dawning realization that my mother had orchestrated a night alone for me and Aaron was surreal. "I didn't realize you all had plans."

"Funny how these things work out. Sofia took the bus home with her friend and your dad dropped Luca off on his way to bowling. I hope you don't mind it's only you and Aaron tonight?"

"No, not at all. We'll be fine," I rushed to assure her. My voice only squeaked a little.

"Be safe, Jacopo, *amore mio. Ciao*."

Mom patted my cheek before she put on her jacket to leave. Aaron arrived as she walked out to her car.

"You boys have a good night," she said as he passed her on the front walk with his overnight bag.

"Thanks, Mrs. Moretti."

Aaron grinned at her. I hurried him into the house, shutting the door behind him.

"Hey," I said, super awkward about being alone with him now. Which might have been Mom's plan all along. It was also possible she wanted to make sure we had a safe space to experiment. Or some combination, my mom had a diabolical streak like that. With Aaron standing in front of me I pushed aside thoughts of my mother quick though.

"Hey."

Aaron grinned at me, he bounced on his toes with excitement. I loved how excitable he was. His boundless energy was one trait that had always drawn me to him.

"Where is everyone?" he asked, looking around like he expected the rest of my family to materialize.

"So, you know how my family is all accepting about our dating and stuff?"

"Yeah?"

"They're all out for the evening. So I guess we have the house to ourselves."

"Oh, my god. I think my parents only sent me to stay with you because they hoped to avoid leaving us unsupervised in an empty house."
Aaron laughed. I shrugged, he was right. His parents were much stricter than mine.

"Mom bought us a bag of supplies. She was not subtle—at all."

"So, want to fool around?" Aaron suggested, his expression hopeful and his fingers tapping out a rhythm on his thigh.

"I thought we might eat first? Mom made her lasagna."

It was a delay tactic; nerves getting the better of me now that things were getting real. I was playing dirty too, Aaron loved Mom's lasagna.

"I'm not hungry yet," Aaron said. He seemed oblivious to my nerves, but I saw his excitement in the way he fidgeted.

"Okay. I guess we can go watch TV downstairs?"

Aaron led the way through the living room and down the stairs to my bedroom. We had a big screen television and all our video games in the finished basement. Aaron and I had spent countless hours playing down here over the years.

When I turned sixteen, my parents had agreed to let me move into the guest room in the basement. So Sofia and Luca didn't have to share a room upstairs anymore. Sofia was thrilled at the prospect of getting her own room, and I enjoyed the freedom of having a little distance.

Aaron ignored the couch and television. Instead, he strode straight into my bedroom. He tossed his bag onto my desk chair. For a moment I thought he might flop onto my bed or something, but he only gave the bed a longing glance. Then he turned back to face me.

"What show should we watch?" Aaron asked.

I trailed behind him as he wandered back out to the couch and flipped on the television.

"You pick," I told him, slumping onto the couch beside him. He curled into my side, snuggling into me, and I relaxed. Not that much different from how we always watched TV. Except instead of a gradual migration toward each other over the course of the night, Aaron draped himself all over me from the start. I liked that.

I didn't count on him slipping his hands under my shirt, but I liked his hands on me. For all that his nimble fingers always seemed to twiddle at something when he got worked up, his used a firm touch now. Sure of himself as he explored my chest.

I don't know where the night might have gone if events hadn't conspired against us. But before we got halfway through whatever show Aaron had picked he clung to my arm in a way I was certain had nothing to do with sex. His gaze darted around the room with a panicked expression.

"Jake, I can't see," he said, his voice shaking.

I stared at him for a moment, then shifted so I could take his face between my hands. I didn't see a problem with his eyes. His wide pupils flicked around unfocused as his grip tightened on my shoulders though.

"What do you mean?" I asked, trying to sound calm despite my rising anxiety.

"I can't see, everything is like fuzzy black squiggles and flashes. Oh my god, what if I'm blind?"

Aaron got worked up. If he hadn't feared letting go, I think he would have been flailing his arms. Which might have been comical if he didn't sound so scared.

"Okay, uh, try to relax. I'll call my mom, she'll know what to do," I said, even though I was freaking out inside too.

"I'm scared," Aaron whimpered. And he clutched at me when I disentangled myself to get my phone from my pocket. "Don't leave me alone."

"I'm just getting out my phone," I narrated my actions. "I'm not going anywhere."

"Okay," Aaron said, his voice small and scared. I noticed him shivering, and I wasn't sure whether to attribute it to nerves or another symptom of whatever strange condition overtook him. He climbed into my lap. His face buried in my neck while I did my best to accommodate him.

Mom didn't answer her cell phone the first time I called. Which meant she had already started her shift. I hated calling her at work, but this was an emergency, I was sure of it. Just not sure enough to dial 911. I needed her to talk me through it. So I dialed the extension for the nurses' station in the pediatric unit where she worked.

"Peds nursing, Steven speaking," someone answered the phone. I didn't recognize them, but I didn't know all the nurses in mom's department either.

"Hi, um, this is Jake Moretti, is my mom available real quick? She's a pediatric nurse."

"Antonia Moretti?"

"Yes, that's her."

"Hang on a second, I'll get her for you."

Hold music played over the phone.

"Hang on, Aaron. Everything will be fine." I said. Aaron's grip on me tightened.

"I'm dizzy," he said.

"Jake? Is everything all right?" Mom sounded concerned.

"No," I said, and hearing my mom's voice made me choke up. Like I didn't have to be strong for Aaron when I had my mom to be strong for both of us. But she wasn't here, and I needed to keep it together to figure out what we should do. "Momma, there's something wrong with Aaron."

"Tell me what happened," she said, and I recognized her soothing 'dealing with emotional patients' tone.

"We were watching TV one minute and the next he said he couldn't see, like everything turned to black squiggles and now he's dizzy, what do we do?"

"Okay, put me on speaker so I can talk to him," Mom instructed. I pressed the button and held the phone closer to Aaron.

"Hi, Aaron, *caro*. Has anything similar happened to you before?" Mom asked. Her voice sounded so calm, concerned and caring. Aaron relaxed against me a little.

"Um, not really. I don't think. I've been having dizzy spells sometimes."

"For how long?"

"Maybe a month?"

"Anything else unusual?"

"Headaches, and now my hands are tingling. Oh my god, am I having a stroke? Am I going to die?"

Aaron got himself all worked up again. The tension returned to his body, his fingers tapped against my back and fussed at my shirt.

"Oh, *caro*, no, I don't think you're having a stroke or dying. Do you have any psionically gifted relatives?"

"I don't think so," Aaron said, sounding puzzled at the question. For me, the question set off the first spark of mingled relief and fear. Relief the situation might not be as serious as my initial reaction implied. Fear that if he turned out to be a psion everything would change for us.

"Okay, Jacopo, *amore*, do you think you can stay calm enough to drive him here?" Mom asked me.

"Yeah, I can do that," I said, it took monumental effort not to betray my fear. One thing at a time, I could lose my composure after I got Aaron whatever help he needed.

"Okay, bring him in, park in the visitor lot and bring him right up to see me, all right?" Mom said.

"Yeah, we'll be there soon," I said.

"Do you need me to stay on the line with you?" Mom asked. She must have known how scared I was to even offer, but I understood how busy her work got most nights. Besides, I needed to focus on driving.

"That's okay, I'll call back if he gets worse," I said.

"All right, drive safe, Jacopo, hang in there, Aaron, I'll see you boys soon," Mom said.

The drive to the hospital appeared to drag into an eternity. I talked to keep Aaron calm. He clutched my hand like a lifeline. When we arrived, I considered dropping him off before I parked the car. But he clung even harder to my hand at the suggestion. He looked so scared that I ended up bypassing the drop off area and parking in the visitor garage so he wouldn't have to navigate the hospital alone.

As we stepped off the elevator on mom's floor, Aaron blinked a few times. He looked at me with such pure relief I could tell his condition must have improved.

"It stopped," he said, his voice held wonder and relief. He held his fingers up in front of his eyes, testing his vision.

"You can see again?"

Aaron nodded and then winced. "Okay, but moving my head makes the dizziness way worse. And now my whole arm is numb and tingling like it fell asleep."

"We are still getting you checked out."

"Yeah, that's probably a good idea."

I led him from the elevator to the children's unit where my mother worked. She met us at the doors, which worked out well since it was a secured area.

"Aaron, how are you, *caro*?" Mom asked as soon as we approached.

"Terrible, but whatever was going on with my eyes stopped at least."

"As luck would have it, Dr. Hobart, one of our specialists, came to check in on a patient after you called. She has agreed to take a look at you."

"Okay," Aaron said.

I trailed behind them as Mom swept Aaron into an unoccupied hospital room. The situation was out of my control. I felt helpless in the face of a potential serious medical condition. Something terrible happening to my Aaron was unbearable. But getting him here was the best I could do for him.

I loitered in the hallway, unsure if I would be welcome in the room with Aaron. Mom introduced him to a tall bronze-skinned doctor. I watched as Mom patted Aaron's hand and left him with the doctor. She joined me in the hallway.

"How are you holding up, Jacopo?"

"Is he going to be okay? For real, Mom, if it's something serious…" I trailed off, unsure how to articulate my fears.

"From what he said, it sounds like the early stages of PEPS. If that is the case then Dr. Hobart specializes in psion medicine, so she can help him. Mount Hope is top ranked for psion healthcare."

"PEPS? Is that like cancer?"

"Oh, Jacopo, no *amore*, PEPS is short for pre-emergence psionic syndrome. It encompasses a broad constellation of symptoms. Some of which are alarming, but it doesn't have permanent sequelae, and in most cases resolves after emergence. With proper care, he should be fine."

"Emergence?" I repeated. I felt numb. The implications of her earlier questions on the phone now clearer. "But that only happens to psions. Aaron isn't a psion."

"If it is PEPS he is a psion, Jacopo," Mom said.

"But isn't he too old?"

I was grasping at straws there. But I didn't want it to be true. Didn't want Aaron to suffer the stigma of being a psion. I didn't want it for us, because I knew even then, that it would change everything.

"Sixteen is the older end of the range, but not outside the norm."

"But, Mom, people die from emergence, he can't die. He can't," I said, on the verge of breaking down. Which she noticed. She let a little of her mom persona peak through her professional demeanor as she reassured me.

"Oh, *amore*, we will do everything in our power to make sure Aaron is fine. I promise you," and then it was back to business. "But if he is experiencing PEPS, then it will only intensify until his abilities emerge. Nobody can stop psionic emergence. If he is a psion, it will happen. What we can do is help him have as simple and painless an emergence experience as possible. And we can minimize the effects of the symptoms."

"I'm scared Momma," I sniffled. It was like flipping a switch. One minute she was a nurse explaining a medical condition and the next she was my mommy. And she was holding me while I tried not to cry. She was still whispering reassurances into my hair when the doctor joined us.

"Would you both join us?" Dr. Hobart requested.

I pulled away. We followed the doctor back into the room and went to stand next to Aaron. He reached tentatively for my hand. As if he wasn't sure if I would let him hold it. I gave him a gentle reassuring squeeze and then the doctor was talking to us.

"Aaron says he wants you to hear the plan too. My initial thoughts are that Aaron's symptoms fit a diagnosis of pre-emergence psionic syndrome, or PEPS. I want to run blood tests to confirm the diagnosis though. When we finish here, you will go down to the psion wing—right next to the ER —to get your blood drawn.

"Aaron, I could admit you overnight for observation. But since the onset is so new, it's unlikely that your emergence will happen in the next few days. So if you prefer to go home that's fine. We can discuss the test results at a follow-up appointment next week.

"The bottom line is you have time to decide. Assuming the results confirm PEPS we have two options. From our chat, it sounds like you would be a good candidate for Cereflux. It is an intracranial injection for the synthetic mediation of emergence.

"A specialist must administer Cereflux in the hospital. I am certified to do it. Emergence is safer under controlled conditions. Our team works with you to bring your abilities forth. Oscar, our anchor, is excellent at his job. He will keep your brainwaves stable throughout.

"They class it as a surgical procedure. There are risks involved. But for most young psions it is safer than organic emergence.

"Cereflux only received approval this year. So it is still a novel therapy, but Mount Hope was a test site during the clinical trials. So I have done the procedure numerous times and I assure you, it is both safe and effective.

"The other option is expectant management. We would monitor for other signs of PEPS. If you chose that plan, you would try to avoid the potential for dangerous situations. That means no driving, swimming, or activities that might pose a danger if you have another episode. Not until after your abilities manifest and the PEPS symptoms resolve. We wait and see.

"You can go with either option, but emergence can be traumatic and dangerous. In most cases, the hospital setting with access to a trained anchor is both safer and more comfortable.

"It is Aaron's choice, but I recommend the procedure," Dr. Hobart said, her delivery upbeat and almost conversational. I got the impression she would take good care of Aaron. Even if I didn't understand everything she said. But I was having a hard time processing. If the decisions were mine, I would have had about a million questions to clarify. Aaron only had one.

"Do I need to talk to my parents first?" he asked.

"You are old enough to give consent for the procedure without your parents. So from a technical legal standpoint, no. However, under ideal circumstances, you would discuss any major medical decisions with your loved ones. There are risks associated with either option, which we can discuss in depth after we have your test results," Dr. Hobart said.

"What about the cost?" Mom asked.

"Short answer, under PEEA—the Psionic Education and Equality Act—insurance covers most of the cost."

"Most, but not all?" Mom said.

"That is correct. PEEA mandates coverage of any costs associated with emergence for all health plans offered to minors. So they cover the procedure and associated hospital fees. Drug costs are the issue.

"It's an unfortunate loophole. Since Cereflux is new to the market, some insurers are not covering it yet. If cost is a problem, there are options we can discuss," Dr. Hobart offered. She even sounded like she regretted the cost.

"I want the procedure. I don't want to wait. Or experience more episodes like that. When can I have it?" Aaron asked.

I could almost convince myself that this was just his usual enthusiasm. He always jumped into new things with wholehearted abandon. But this time I could tell part of his eagerness was covering fear.

I suppressed the urge to question if he was sure. Demand he take the weekend to consider. Or at least learn the risks first. But it was his choice, and the doctor was already addressing him.

"It is a complex procedure. The soonest we could get you scheduled would be next week. Assuming the neurosurgery suite is available and our certified anchor is on the schedule to come in. Which I would need to check. Why don't we get your blood drawn for now?

"Antonia, can you get him scheduled for a follow-up appointment?"

"I can do that," Mom said.

"Perfect, book him with Oscar for Monday morning if possible," Dr. Hobart said.

"Will do."

"Great, so, Aaron, you can discuss any concerns you might have and learn more about the procedure on Monday. Oscar is the anchor certified for Cereflux and he can get you scheduled if the tests confirm the diagnosis. I will see you after your visit with him. We can talk about your results, if your bloodwork shows it isn't PEPS then I will be in touch about next steps, sound good?"

"Okay," Aaron said, but his shoulders drooped in defeat.

"I have work to finish up here. I'll be seeing you Monday though," Dr. Hobart said, already making her way over to the nurses' station.

"You want me to show you boys where to go?" Mom offered.

"Yes, please," Aaron said.

We didn't talk as we walked. I could tell Aaron's fear was still lurking just beneath the surface. Mom had to get back upstairs so she couldn't wait with us. She gave Aaron a big hug. They had a whispered conversation which I couldn't hear before she left. Some color returned to his pale cheeks after that, which let us both relax a little.

Aaron had a hard time waiting though. He kept chewing on his lip—which I knew he only did when he was nervous—while we waited for a phlebotomist.

"It will be all right," I said while we were sitting in a semi-private waiting area in the psion wing.

"I want to go home," Aaron sounded miserable. He swung his feet back and forth, restless.

"We will. After we know you'll be okay."

"I guess."

"Did you want to call your parents?" I suggested. In his position that would have been my first action. Aaron shook his head.

"There's no point. I'll just tell them when they get home. I don't want to disrupt Dad, he's trying to close a big deal."

"Yeah, but you're sick."

"There isn't anything they can do to help," Aaron shrugged. "The doctor said I should be stable for now, I'm getting the best medical care available. I know Dad won't mind paying for the medication if I need it. So I don't need to call them to know what they'll say."

That did not sit well with me. I had always known Aaron's parents weren't like mine. But it shocked me to learn he thought they wouldn't want to be there for him when he was sick and scared.

"Are you sure?"

"Yeah, I'm sure," Aaron gave me one of his fake smiles and squirmed in his seat. "I'm just glad you're here with me. If I'd been alone when this happened I don't know what I would have done."

"I'm glad I can be here for you, too," I paused and then added, "your parents suck."

Aaron chuckled weakly at that, "they aren't very sentimental."

"Are you worried about how they'll take you being a psion?"

"Nope. I doubt they'll care as long as it doesn't screw up my grades."

Aaron's defense of his parents notwithstanding, the hurt and bitterness in his voice made me wish I could fix this for him. I couldn't figure out the right response. So I only sat staring at the infomercial playing on mute on the television. Aaron said nothing for a while too. He was the one who broke the silence.

"You're pissed at them, aren't you? They aren't that bad. Just distant. Besides, I have your family. Why did you think I'm always at your place? It's all part of my plot to steal your family," he said. It made me laugh. Aaron was always good at that.

"Nothing to do with me?"

"Eh, I guess you're all right too."

"I see how it is," I feigned offense, "see if I let you sleep with me now."

"Oh my god," he moaned. "How did I forget that was the plan for tonight? Why the heck are we hanging around a waiting room when I could have you in bed?"

"Yeah, um, because we thought you were dying or something?"

After our medical emergency, I was not in any frame of mind to even consider sex tonight. I doubted he was still interested either.

"But I'm not, and they won't do anything about it until next week, anyway. I want you to hold me after the night we've had. And I regret not eating dinner earlier."

"I can tell. You get grouchy when you're hungry," I replied.

"I'm not grouchy. Much. Can we check how much longer they think it will be?"

Aaron was fidgeting again. I sighed and got up to go check at the nurses' station.

"You wait here and I'll see if I can find out," I said.

Just then a young woman in blue scrubs poked her head around the corner.

"Aaron Anderson?" she said.

Aaron popped up from his seat, "that's me."

She confirmed his date of birth and then invited him to follow her. I hesitated, but Aaron grabbed my hand and pulled me along in his wake.

While the phlebotomist got Aaron prepped, he refused to relinquish my hand. She seemed annoyed that I was in the way, working with his other arm and prodding at his elbow.

Aaron squeezed my hand like he was clinging for dear life while she drew his blood though. She took a few vials. Then she slapped a bandage over the puncture and told us we were free to leave. Aaron would get a call with the results on Monday at the earliest even though it was an in-house test, since it was the weekend.

"I guess I come here on Monday to see the anchor?" Aaron asked me as we followed the signs toward the exit.

It turned out I didn't need to respond. Dr. Hobart was leaning against the nurses' station chatting with the nurse on duty. She smiled at us as we approached.

"Aaron, just the patient I was looking for, I'm glad I caught you. I confirmed that we have you scheduled to see Oscar and I for the Cereflux consultation. Here at the hospital, on Monday morning at nine," Dr. Hobart handed Aaron a card with the appointment information written on it. "You can come in through the ER entrance and go to the psion reception area to wait. Be prepared to stay overnight," she handed him a brochure. "Here is information about PEPS and Cereflux. So you'll know what to expect."

"Thanks, Dr. Hobart," Aaron said. The doctor left, nodding at me in acknowledgment. Aaron bounced in place. He worried at the card until he forced himself to slip it into his pocket. He grabbed my hand again and gave me an expectant look.

"You all set?" I asked.

"Yeah, I guess," Aaron swung our joined hands.

"How do you feel about PEPS?"

Aaron shrugged, "it's better than going blind or having a stroke I guess. Can we go home? I want you to hold me."

"Yeah, let's go," I said.

Aaron released my hand for the walk to the car. Now that he wasn't afraid he was dying, he behaved more circumspect in public. I drove us home without saying much. Aaron fidgeted in his seat as he processed everything.

When we got home, we devoured the lasagna. Both of us were ravenous after everything that had happened. Neither of us brought up sex. We went straight to bed after we ate. Aaron clung to me in his sleep though. Under other circumstances I would have relished sharing the bed. As it was, I spent most of the night awake and worrying.

Chapter 4

Aaron

M y parents got back late on Sunday evening. They had picked up Chinese takeout on the way home, so once they had the car unloaded we all settled in around the kitchen table to eat a late dinner. I had eaten with Jake's family before returning home to await their arrival. But that had been a few hours prior, so I fixed a small plate and joined them.

"Everything go well with Jake this weekend?" Mom asked.

"Yeah, Jake is great," I said, "why?"

"We didn't expect you to be home when we got in," she said with a shrug.

"I wanted to see you guys," I said, stabbing at my noodles with my fork.

"Did something happen?" she asked, with obvious concern.

"Yeah," I said, "I had a scare on Friday."

"What type of scare?" Dad asked in his stern voice.

"A medical thing, my vision turned wonky. Jake took me to the hospital, and they ran tests, but I guess I have PEPS."

"That's a psion thing," Mom said. Her expression flat, betraying no hint of her true feelings on the matter.

"Yeah," I said, setting aside my utensils and lining them up on my place mat to give my hands something to do. "It is."

"But you aren't a psion," Dad said.

"Uh, surprise?" I made a weak attempt at jazz hands, which only deepened Dad's frown. I jiggled my leg under the table. The silence stretched until it became unbearable. So I added a lame joke. "So I bet you didn't think I could top coming out to you so soon, huh?"

"We don't care about that, Aaron," Mom chided. "We love you, no matter what."

"Yeah, I know, Mom," I brushed her off, feeling anything but loved by them at that moment. They exchanged a look I couldn't read. I stared at my hands wishing I could go back to Jake's house, surrounded by his family and their unconditional love.

Dad cleared his throat, pushing away his untouched dinner before he asked, "so they diagnosed you with PEPS, what does that mean?"

"I need a procedure, they said they might get me in this week. There are risks, but the doctor says it's safer than waiting for my abilities to come in on their own. The drug they use is expensive, but there are programs to help pay for it."

"We will pay for whatever you need, son, you know that," Dad waved away talk of cost.

"Yeah, Dad," I said with a sigh.

"Do you know what classification and grade of psion you are yet?" Mom asked, displaying more rudimentary knowledge of psions than I would have thought she possessed. Although, if she had much knowledge about psions, she should have known the answer to that question.

"No, not yet, Mom, they can't tell until after my abilities emerge. So, I guess we'll find out after the procedure."

"This will require adjustments. We will need to research the best programs for training your new abilities," Dad said. "I'll look into it tomorrow."

"All right," I said, "so, you guys are okay with me being a psion?"

"Yes, Aaron, you're still our son. Don't be ridiculous," Dad said in a tone that made it clear he thought I was overreacting. Then he pulled his plate closer and focused his full attention on his meal.

"Eat your dinner, dear, you must keep up your strength for your procedure. You're far too thin, you'll never be as strong as Jake and the other boys if you starve yourself," Mom changed the subject.

My body was another issue she had with me. I never could live up to her expectations of masculinity. I should be tall and muscular and I should walk, dress, and talk a certain way. If she could fathom how much effort I put into not being myself I wondered if she would care. Or at least acknowledge how hard I worked for her approval.

I was a runt, but I was okay with that. I was not okay with the comparison to Jake who was athletic by nature. And had been building on his broad, tall frame with a strict workout regimen since middle school. I was all for him working out because he looked darn good with bulging muscles.

In this context though, the reminder he was muscular when I couldn't seem to bulk up even if I tried was unwelcome. I was still waiting on the growth spurt that had sputtered out at the end of middle school leaving me well shy of six feet tall.

"I'm not hungry," I said, pushing away my plate. "Anyway, I ate at Jake's. My appointment tomorrow is early. So I should get to bed. Just wanted to tell you in person."

"Do you want me to accompany you to the appointment?" Mom offered. I perceived from her tone she would rather not.

"No, it's okay, it's at the hospital and Jake's mom will bring me, since she has to work anyway," I said.

"How will you get to school afterward?" Dad asked, interested in the conversation again at the hint I might miss class. I suppressed a sigh. Typical Dad.

"They might admit me. I guess I have to stay overnight before and after the procedure, if I need to get to school I'll take a bus," I said.

"If you're sure," Mom said.

"Yeah, I'm sure, but thanks for offering."

"No problem, dear. Let us know what they tell you," Mom said.

"Make sure you get a note from the doctor for your school, don't forget," Dad said.

"I will," I said, "and I'll tell you if I won't be home tomorrow night."

"We'll come to visit you at the hospital if you tell us when visiting hours are," Mom said.

"I'll let you know, Mom, anyway, I'm tired, good night," I said as I stood from the table.

"Good night, dear," Mom said, her voice warm.

"Good night, son," Dad said, having already lost interest in me again.

I cleared away my untouched plate. Duty to my parents discharged, I retreated to my bedroom and crawled under the covers with my phone to text Jake.

Aaron: I told them

Jake: how'd it go? U ok?

Aaron: about how I expected. I'm fine

Jake: U sure I can't come 2morrow?

Aaron: you shouldn't miss class. I promise to text when I have the plan.

Jake: <3 U

Aaron: me too. I'm going to bed.

Jake: C U 2morrow

Aaron: too tired for your text speak, night.

Jake: XO

I shoved my phone under my pillow and tried to fall asleep. I had been struggling with sleeping all weekend. When I looked at the paperwork from Dr. Hobart, I found insomnia on the list of possible symptoms. That only made me more anxious about it since the papers also said the faster I gained symptoms or the more I had, the worse emergence would be.

I had already experienced three more instances of the visual migraines that had terrified me on Friday night. At least Dr. Hobart had given me a name for them. And a potential cause.

Jake held me each time the visual disturbances struck. At least they ended as fast as they hit. Even knowing it wasn't something more serious or permanent, I still found the experience of my world going murky terrifying. Without Jake's comforting presence, I spent hours tossing and turning before dozing off around dawn.

An insistent knock on my door and Mom calling my name woke me way too soon, "Aaron, are you up yet?"

I made an incoherent sound in response and she opened my door enough to make eye contact.

"Mrs. Moretti is here to pick you up, Aaron," Mom said. She sounded disapproving as she added, "you'll make her late for work if you don't get moving."

"I'll be right out," I groaned as I rubbed the sleep from my eyes. After she shut the door, I rolled out of bed, pulled on the first clean clothes I got my hands on and stumbled down the hall. I made a quick stop in the bathroom to get ready, forgoing a shower in favor of expedience.

Mrs. Moretti was standing in the kitchen chatting with my mom over a cup of coffee when I got down the stairs. So I could have taken a quick shower.

They both looked up when I entered the room and stopped talking. Mrs. Moretti finished her coffee in one long gulp. They both stood, my mom grabbed their empty coffee cups and took them to the sink.

"Thanks for the chat and the coffee, Meredith. I'll check in on Aaron for you if they admit him this morning."

"I appreciate you taking care of him this weekend. Aaron, I made you some breakfast," Mom turned from placing the dirty mugs in the sink and handed me a warm breakfast sandwich wrapped in a paper towel.

"Thanks, Mom," I said.

Then I kissed her cheek because she looked like she needed reassurance I wasn't sure how to give her with words. I wondered what they might have been talking about. I figured it was about my appointment since Jake's mom knew more about what was going on with me than my mother.

"You ready to go?" Mrs. Moretti asked.

"Yeah," I said, hefting my school bag. "I even tossed clothes and stuff in my bag, just in case."

"Let's go then," she said. I followed her to the front door.

"Good luck today, Aaron," Mom called after me. I turned to smile at her, my cheery demeanor requiring far more effort than usual.

"Thanks, I'll let you know how it goes."

I jammed my feet into my shoes and followed Mrs. Moretti to her car, parked behind Jake's in their driveway. The drive passed in a blur. I was too nervous about everything to focus on what she said.

After a few attempts at conversation she gave up, patted my hand with sympathy, then cranked my favorite radio station for the rest of the ride. That helped to distract me from my racing thoughts about everything that could go wrong.

At the hospital, Mrs. Moretti dropped me off in front of the emergency department. She told me to go to the reception desk on the psion side where Dr. Hobart had her offices. She made me promise to text to let her know how my appointment went as soon as it ended.

The receptionist on duty at the desk took my name and insurance information, then told me to take a seat. I didn't have to wait long in the joint ER and psion waiting area.

Within a few minutes a tall guy with stylish bleached hair and dressed in rainbow printed scrubs poked his head through the swinging doors to the psion wing. He called my name, then glanced up from his clipboard to scan the waiting room with expectation. I stood and made my way over to him, receiving a warm smile as I drew close.

"Aaron Anderson?"

"That's me," I said. Then he confirmed my date of birth.

"Perfect. It looks like you're my patient this morning, Aaron," he smiled and pushed open the large door. He gestured for me to go through it as he said, "my name is Oscar Watkins and I am an anchor affiliated with Mount Hope. I am also certified to perform as support staff during Cereflux administration," Oscar said.

He directed me toward a room just inside the psion unit. The arrangement reminded me of the exam room at my regular doctor's office.

So that gave it a sense of familiarity amid all the uncharted territory I was dealing with at least.

"Take a seat," Oscar gestured to a chair.

He sat on a rolling stool which he wheeled close to a computer console. I sat and looked around at the walls while he logged into the computer system and pulled up my file.

The walls were interesting at least. Three of them sported bulletin boards. They plastered each board with informational fliers and diagrams. Images of the brain and nervous system vied for space with notices listing psion regulations. I even spotted an ad for a support group.

At the top of each board, someone had pinned a notice in all caps. Bright red letters reminded all psions that registration was mandatory under the Psion Education and Equality Act. The PEEA required hospitals to report psions to the psion registry.

Mount Hope submitted the name, demographics, grade, and classification of all psions upon emergence. A line at the bottom listed the penalties for failure to register. It was a felony. I shuddered at the reminder. Soon I would have to register too.

One poster caught my eye. It featured a large image of the iconic Uncle Sam army recruitment poster 'we want you'. Superimposed in one corner was the circular logo of a stylized tower and eye, the acronym SPIRE curving around the image in an arc. The fine print spelled out the acronym in bold letters—Special Psionic Integration Relations and Enforcement. The bottom of the page was a bulleted list of the benefits of a SPIRE training certification for all psions. It was on the tip of my tongue to ask Oscar more about it when he turned and asked me a question.

"All set, sorry about the delay, I have your test results from Friday here. Dr. Hobart notes they confirm her initial diagnosis. So why don't we start with establishing what you already know; what can you tell me about links?"

"Like cufflinks, sausage links, chain links?" I tried for a joke since I had only the barest understanding of what an anchor was. Or a link in this context.

Oscar chuckled, I noticed that it was a nice laugh, then he said, "psionic links. I am guessing you don't know much about psions?"

"Yeah, not much. We had a psi-ed course in middle school, but I thought it would have happened by now if it was going to?"

"Sixteen is a little on the older side, most of our emergence patients present closer to fourteen, but you are not the oldest we have had."

"That's good, I guess. I heard older age at emergence is a risk factor?" I swallowed hard, not wanting to contemplate what it was a risk factor for. My foot was bouncing with nerves and I had to concentrate not to chew on my lip.

"It is a risk factor. Morbidity and mortality are still associated with Emergence. But the risk from older age refers to adult brains. Studies show that teens—even older teens—still have the requisite neural plasticity to undergo emergence without harm. There are three key factors in positive outcomes—a safe environment, access to supportive care, and stable neural linking. With Cereflux, those factors are now under our control. My team and I will help you through this.

"My role as an anchor is to create a neural link with a psion to stabilize their expanded neural network after their abilities emerge. Psions can form links with people who are not anchors. Often links will form between loved ones or intimate partners. That style of link develops, given enough time. One of my recent patients compared it to girls periods syncing up over time," Oscar said with a wry smile.

"I wouldn't know anything about that," I said, wrinkling my nose at the disgusting analogy. I guess it made a weird sense, but still, not a mental image I appreciated. Oscar chuckled, amused at my dismay, but then he continued his explanation.

"An anchor is someone who can create a link bond without a deeper personal connection. It is easier to create, easier to break, and a trained anchor can use it to moderate the psion's abilities. The link stabilizes psionic brain waves.

"If it helps, you can think of it as training wheels. The peri-emergent period can leave a new psion off balance. The anchor helps make sure you don't tip too far one way or the other until you get used to balancing on your own. A link helps you to maintain control until you get used to your powers. A trained anchor can nudge you back on track if you lose control, make sense?"

"Yeah, I think so. Does that mean I'll need a link?"

"Long-term it's hard to say without knowing your classification and strength. For example, telekinetic classes are fine without a permanent link, unless they are grade A. Whereas even lower grade telepaths need link bonds to remain stable.

"If you still want to go forward with Cereflux, then the plan is for you and me to establish the basis for a link today. Dr. Hobart will perform the procedure tomorrow, and I will sever the link when you have stabilized following your emergence.

"If we determine you need a link bond after that point we can help put you in touch with services for that. Or facilitate link compatibility and anchor testing if you have a loved one willing to serve as your link."

"Okay," I said, taking a shaky breath.

It was information overload. Oscar kept talking about linking. All I could think about was Jake, and how I couldn't imagine being connected to anyone but him. It was too much to take. So I blurted.

"What do I have to do?"

"For the procedure?" Oscar clarified, he blinked at me a few times because my question had interrupted him in the middle of saying something about link relationships.

"For linking with you," I said, unable to hide my nerves. Oscar gave me a sympathetic look.

"You don't have to do anything. It is easier if we spend time together, I learn a little about my patients' interests. It can be easier to let our guards down around each other and relax if we first build a basis for trust."

"So, it's not a physical thing?"

"No. It is a psionic connection between our auras. How well it works will depend on how advanced your PEPS is. I can sometimes establish a solid link before the procedure. Since we caught it early, your aura might not be distinct enough for me to pick up on yet. If that is the case, then I will establish the link tomorrow once the injection kicks in and amplifies your aura," he said.

He must have noticed my eyes glazing over at the unfamiliar terminology because he added, "We refer to a person's psionic presence as their aura. Anchors can sense auras. An unstable aura develops appendages that reach out for a connection. A link happens when two people establish such a connection. A permanent link develops when the two auras in question become entangled. Temporary links are like two aura just touching. As for you, your file says your first noticeable PEPS symptoms started last week?"

"Yes, visual migraines, I sort of freaked a little."

"Sounds alarming. Not knowing what's happening can be upsetting."

"It was, yeah."

"Well, that being the case, I'm not surprised that your aura hasn't developed enough for me to establish a link yet. So what we will do is lay down groundwork to make it easier to link once the Cereflux helps your aura to develop. Sound good?"

"Yeah."

"What questions do you have about links?" Oscar asked, he regarded me with expectation. It was unnerving to have an adult giving me their full and undivided attention like that.

"There is a psion in my class, and she and her link are always touching, so I guess I thought it was a physical thing?" I said, it felt like I was babbling because I wasn't sure how to articulate my concern in the form of a question.

"Ah, yes. Well, touch enhances the connection," Oscar said. "We call it touch sensitivity. If a psion decompensates, it can become necessary to amplify the link through touch. Holding hands helps. Auras play a role too."

"How does that work?"

"Most psions find their link's presence soothing. Proximity to an individual with an incompatible aura grates. Your aura is your psionic presence. Everyone has one. Some will mesh well with yours, others won't. Sensing auras is a part of being a psion or an anchor. Telepath classes experience this phenomenon with more intensity. Good touches improve the link. A strong link helps with control. So there are often lots of touches among link-bonded pairs."

"So, when we're linked, will you touch me?"

Oscar grimaced, "okay, real talk? It is a possibility. If it becomes necessary, it will only be with your consent.. We are talking, hand holding, nothing that makes you uncomfortable, is that okay?"

"I think I can handle that," I agreed, with relief.

"It's also the standard protocol for you to meet with a social worker before we discharge you. They discuss psionic services and getting you connected with the local psion community. They can also connect you with resources if you are having problems at home, which is not uncommon with our patient population.

"If you aren't comfortable talking to the social worker, then part of the information they will give you will include a link to an anonymous reporting website. If you experience anything that makes you uncomfortable while you are here I urge you to report it. And if I do anything that crosses a line for you, please let me know.

"My primary aim is helping you through this difficult time," Oscar said. There was a sincerity about him that made me think I could trust him.

"Okay," I forced a smile.

I was sure he now thought my parents were abusive or something, but at least he didn't seem to be a threat. He put me at ease. I was still nervous, but I had the sense he would hold my hand through this process. And make it as painless as possible for me.

"All right, I have a list of standard questions before we get to the easier stuff. Some questions are uncomfortable if you don't want to answer that's all right. But the more information I have the better as far as being able to plan your care—is that okay?"

"Yeah, all right," I said.

Oscar wasn't lying when he said the questions were unpleasant. They were uncomfortable to think about. Not the first few, I wasn't depressed or suicidal and I didn't have much interest in drugs or alcohol.

Sure, Noah and some other kids at school picked on me sometimes. However, being friends with Jake—and by extension, the other jocks—kept it from going much further than the occasional shove or whispered insults.

The part where he asked if I was sexually active made my face turn bright red, but at least I could still say no, for now. So that ended that line of questioning. And no, making out with Jake and exchanging hand jobs with some of my theater buddies so did not count.

It was the part about my home life that made me want to squirm. Before the survey, I would have sworn up and down to him that no, my parents weren't abusive. They were normal parents who wanted the best for me and worked hard to give me the best possible start in life. But the words that flowed from my mouth told a different story.

"Would you say you have a supportive home environment?" Oscar asked, his voice neutral.

"Yes, my parents support me," I fidgeted because it wasn't quite the spirit of the question. My home was not a supportive environment, it was a place where I had to maintain a constant act. Playing the role of the perfect son and star student.

"Do your parents or guardians ever call you names or yell at you?" Oscar continued.

"They don't yell. Mom sometimes teases me by calling me scrawny or bag of bones," I attempted to make it a joke, but it fell flat. And I couldn't focus beyond a quick denial as he asked if I had experienced physical or sexual abuse. I gave a series of terse denials, needing the questions to stop. Then he finished with a doozy.

"Can you go to your parents or guardians with a problem?"

"No," I told him. I regretted my answer at once, so I babbled. "I mean, I have other people to talk to though. Jake and his parents, they are always there for me."

"Who is Jake?" Oscar raised an eyebrow. He had maintained a professional detachment accepting each of my answers without comment up to now.

"My boyfriend. We've been best friends forever and his parents have accepted that I'm their third son. Even before we got together. So it's not like I have no one I can go to," I said, sounding defensive.

"That's good. It is important to have people who you can depend on, Aaron," Oscar paused. He considered and then sighed, "the survey's purpose isn't to trip you up or make you anxious. I ask these questions in case there is an underlying issue we need to know of when you are undergoing the procedure.

"This is a vulnerable time, and if you have bad memories associated with certain things, then we want to avoid touching on them and making your emergence worse. I'm not here to judge you, or your family, okay?"

"Okay."

"Do you want to tell me anything else about your family situation?"

I shrugged, squirmed in my seat. Then avoiding eye contact I explained, "It's nothing. Only, I guess I figured it wasn't a big deal until I saw how people reacted? Like when my symptoms started my parents were out of town. Jake thought it was strange that I didn't call to tell them about it. And his parents agreed. But I waited to tell them when they got home. And they offered to pay for the Cereflux and told me to let them know how the procedure goes.

"They didn't ask about my symptoms. Or how I felt, they acted like it was no big deal as long as it didn't screw up my getting into a good university. It's like they don't care about anything I do, as long as I meet their expectations. And they never acknowledge how hard I try to please them."

"It sounds like you work hard for their approval," Oscar said.

"Yeah, I do. And it's like… I don't know, I wish they would see me for who I am, just once, you know?"

"It is normal to desire acceptance from your loved ones, Aaron. Everyone appreciates being seen for who they are. I can hear a lot of hurt in the way you talk about your relationship with your parents," Oscar said. I crossed my arms over my chest.

"Yeah, it's hard. I know they love me in their own way. Only…" I shrugged then added on a sigh, "I wish they were more like Jake's parents. When I thought it was something worse than PEPS, I wanted to see Mrs. Moretti more than my own mother. Is that weird?"

"Not at all, wanting to be around someone who makes you feel safe and accepted under stressful circumstances isn't strange. And it sounds like you have a good emotional support network, even if your parents are not as involved as you might like," Oscar said.

"I do," I said, and I felt better for having said it out loud.

Jake and I could talk about anything, but I hated complaining about my parents with him. I knew he already resented the way they treated me. So I didn't want to make it worse.

As a neutral party, it was easier to talk Oscar. He gave me the opportunity to get it off my chest. Processing it out loud put it in perspective for me. I might not have the most involved parents, but I had people who loved me and accepted me. It should be enough.

"Did you have anything else you wanted to talk about before we move on?" Oscar asked.

"No, I think you answered everything. Or, I guess, how do I make sure that Jake and his family can find out about my condition during the procedure? My parents won't be around, but I think Jake might come to support me. If that's okay?"

"I can put a note in your file you want us to inform them of where you are and your status after the procedure. If they are at the hospital for the procedure, then they can visit with you before you go to the prep area. You shouldn't be in the recovery room for long since Cereflux only uses a local anesthetic.

"They can meet you back in your hospital room afterward. There is a small family waiting room near the OR that has a screen with the status of all ongoing procedures based on your case number. The neurosurgery suite is in the same section of the hospital so your loved ones can see your status up in the waiting room. Does that work for you?"

"Yeah, that's perfect, thanks. And this is happening tomorrow?"

"If you still want to go ahead, then yes," Oscar confirmed, with a slight smile playing at the corner of his mouth. I gave him a full wattage smile, bouncing in my seat.

"Yeah, I want it. I keep waiting for my vision to go again and I hate it. So, the sooner the better."

"All right, I will go get Dr. Hobart to do a final consultation with you, go over the informed consent paperwork, and finalize the plan. Afterward, a nurse will be by to get you admitted. Once you're settled into your room I will be around to check on you. Let's meet for lunch in the cafeteria around noon to get better acquainted?" Oscar said as he stood.

"That sounds good."

"Great, I will see you in a few hours then, it was nice to meet you, Aaron," Oscar smiled at me.

"Nice to meet you too," I said with a tiny wave. When he left, I was more at ease about the whole situation. I only had to survive the procedure. Then life could return to normal. It was just a shot, like a vaccine, no big deal. Even if it was classified as brain surgery. Then everything would be fine. I would be fine.

Chapter 5

Jake

I drifted through Monday in a haze. When the final bell rang, I couldn't have said whether I had homework, let alone recalled anything from class. Even soccer practice did not take my mind off Aaron.

Most days once I stepped on the field, everything else in my life faded to background noise. My focus narrowed to the game. But everyone noticed my distraction and commented on how off my game was. I missed shots on goal, flubbed easy passes and tripped over my own feet.

Coach pulled me aside for a chat after practice. He didn't blink an eye at his team captain and star player having a boyfriend. His expression tightened when he asked why Aaron was in the hospital and I mentioned PEPS though. He still excused me from Tuesday practice. And told me he would waive the policy benching me for the next game after a missed practice.

After my meeting with the coach, I only had an hour before my shift at the restaurant. Not enough time to visit Aaron, but I texted him. He sounded upbeat about everything, but it was text. And if I knew anything about my boyfriend, it was that he was an expert at hiding his feelings behind a cheerful facade.

I stumbled through my shift in a haze. My job comprised bringing loads of dirty dishes to the kitchen and running hot food to tables to help the servers. Since it was Monday, we weren't busy, so I checked my phone for new messages as often as I could get away with it.

Busy or not, my mind was a million miles away and it showed. The expediter asked me to stop running food after I brought the wrong order to the wrong table for the third time in a row. It all came to a head when I dropped a stack of plates, smashing them on the floor in front of the industrial style dishwasher.

I lucked out because Alice was the manager working tonight. She was the nicer of my two bosses, Joan might have just fired me for my umpteenth screwup of the night. Alice stepped out of her office as the sounds of shattering ceramic and the sarcastic applause of my co-workers faded.

"Jake, my office when you have that taken care of please," Alice said. I hurried to sweep the broken shards and food scraps into the trash and then went to accept my fate.

"Sorry, Alice, I am having a rough day," I said as I joined her in the tiny manager's office off the kitchen.

"Everyone has an off night, Jake. Is something bothering you?" Alice asked with more understanding than I expected.

"Yeah, my boyfriend is sick. He's in the hospital tonight and having surgery in the morning. So I guess my head is somewhere else today."

"I'm so sorry to hear that; is this the boy you brought in last week?" Alice asked. It surprised me she remembered him. But then again she had comped his appetizer, so I guess that might have stood out in her mind.

"Yeah, it was all so sudden," I said. I resisted the urge to spill all the details. Once I got started, I thought I could talk for hours. Fret over everything that might go wrong. I didn't though. I wasn't sure about Alice's attitude toward psions, and I didn't want to find out tonight.

"It's a Monday night, things are slow. Take the rest of the night off. And I will call around to get coverage for your shifts for the rest of the week. I think you're scheduled for Wednesday and Thursday evening?"

"Yeah, that sounds right, and Saturday brunch."

"Okay, Sharon and Beth have been looking to pick up hours, I'll take care of the details. You don't worry about coming in until next week, sound good?"

"Yeah," I said, swallowing hard.

Under normal circumstances I would've needed to arrange coverage for my shifts. The task was tedious. But offering to handle it was typical of Alice. She always put her employee's interests first.

"Thank you, Alice," I said with heartfelt gratitude for her understanding.

"No problem, you worry about being there to support your boyfriend, all right?"

"Yeah, I will, thank you," I repeated my thanks, overwhelmed with gratitude and all the fear and worry I had been bottling up since Aaron first got sick.

"Now, get out of here before you break every dish in my restaurant," Alice said. Her tone was light, and she sat back in her chair with a smile to soften the words.

I left the office to my coworkers' teasing. I had to stop and reassure two servers who I was chummy with that I was fine, and that Alice hadn't fired me. Once I told them I was taking time off, they expressed sympathy. They sent me off with good-natured ribbing about my clumsiness tonight and well wishes for Aaron.

Since I got home early, my family sat gathered around the dinner table when I arrived. Sofia and Luca chattered about their day over their last few bites of meatloaf, mashed potatoes, and carrots. Mom and Dad exchanged a look when I entered the dining room.

"Why don't we clear the table and get started on homework?" Dad suggested, breaking into Sofia's retelling of a joke. He stacked his and mom's empty plates and stood. Sofia sulked at the interruption but she shoveled the last of her meal into her mouth and brought her plate to the kitchen without complaint.

Luca was more eager to leave. It looked like he hadn't touched his meatloaf other than to eat the part covered in sweet glaze, but that was nothing new; the kid was a picky eater. He scooped a final forkful of mashed potatoes into his mouth from the serving dish in the table's center before following Dad to the kitchen. I noticed Mom holding back a reprimand for his poor manners.

"At least he ate something," she said, "grab a plate and tell your mother what happened, Jacopo."

I took the unused place setting at my seat and fixed a plate on autopilot.

"Huh, I'm surprised they left any carrots for me."

"I saved a serving for you," Mom said. "Now, talk, *amore*."

"Is it that obvious?"

"Your schedule said your shift ended at nine tonight. It's now seven thirty—and you're frazzled."

"It was hard focusing today. I'm worried," I said, taking a bite of the sweet carrots. Not even that family favorite could overcome my lack of appetite. I set aside my fork.

"And work?" Mom asked.

I finished my bite and replied, "I got sent home early because I kept screwing everything up. So, I got this week off from work and soccer practice. Coach and Alice both understood when I explained about Aaron at least."

Mom regarded me with sympathy, "I'm glad they made allowances for the situation, *amore*. I visited Aaron before I left the hospital, he seemed in good spirits. He doesn't want you to worry."

"Like that's possible!" I said through another mouthful of carrots, I swallowed before saying the thing that kept me awake at night fretting. "He keeps saying it's a simple procedure, but it is brain surgery, Mom. I looked it up, the procedure could paralyze him. Or he might end up with permanent neurological symptoms, whatever that means. He might die."

"There are risks to any procedure, Jacopo," Mom said. "Those things might also happen with no intervention, psionic emergence has risks. Something may go wrong tomorrow. But the most probable outcome is the procedure goes well, and Aaron will recover fast. By this time tomorrow his PEPS symptoms should have resolved," Mom said in her nurse voice. I appreciated that she wanted to put the risks in perspective without dismissing my fears. But a part of me wanted my mom to assure me everything would be fine even if it might not be true.

"Yeah, I can't stop thinking about what if he's not," I poked at my food, all appetite gone.

"*Amore*, you know Dad and I care about Aaron too, right?"

"Yeah, I know," I said. I did, he had become part of our family over the years, well before he became my boyfriend.

"As a nurse and as someone who thinks of him as a third son, I think he is making the right decision about this," Mom said.

"I get that. But I need to support him. He shouldn't be alone," I let my frustration color my voice and Mom looked sympathetic.

"Visiting hours are over, *amore*. And as much as it hurts, you aren't his family to be staying with him tonight. You may visit him at the hospital tomorrow though."

"His parents won't stay with him tonight, will they?" I worded it as a question, but I knew the answer.

Mom's lips pursed, and she gave a sharp jerk of her head, "no, they're not."

"I hate them."

"Jacopo, this is no time for anger. Aaron needs your support right now."

"Yeah, okay," I stabbed at my meatloaf for a few minutes before shoving my still full plate away. "Will you call the school to excuse me for tomorrow? I need to be at the hospital."

Mom gave me an appraising look and nodded.

"I still need you to drop off Sofia and Luca in the morning, but yes. You can wait at the hospital. I doubt you could focus on classes anyway, huh?"

"Thanks, Mom," I said, relieved, "I think I'll try to sleep now if that's all right?"

"Go ahead," she said. I stood to bring my plate to the kitchen, but she stopped me. Mom cupped my cheek in her hand, studying my face for a moment. I hugged her, needing the comfort. She held me until I pulled away, then took my plate and tousled my hair with affection. "I'll take care of your dish. Good night, *amore mio*"

"Good night."

Once I was in my room I texted Aaron. He had sent me a series of cat memes over the hour since I'd last been able to check my phone. He only resorted to memes when he was trying to hide his nerves. My determination to be at the hospital with Aaron during his procedure only intensified when he asked if I got him notes from school. Because his parents were nagging him about not letting his grades slip.

It was a struggle not to tell him how much I hated his parents then. I couldn't stand them prioritizing his grades over his emotional wellbeing. And guilt ate at me because I had my parents' unconditional love and Aaron didn't.

I had always known Aaron's parents differed from mine. And I understood his family wasn't close like mine. It had seemed like a small difference before, the product of being part of a large loud Italian family with dozens of cousins, aunts and uncles. But this went beyond the difference between my boisterous family gatherings and his.

I knew there were reasons he ate more meals at my house than his own when he had the choice. But seeing Aaron sick and scared gave me a glimpse under the cheerful image he strove to present to the world, and what I saw worried me.

Aaron had spent most of the weekend huddled under my covers refusing to move. He got panicky anytime I left his sight, demanding to know where I was going. He seemed calmer when I sat with him. So I had rearranged some of my stuff to allow us to play old ROMs on my computer using an emulator. As long as I stayed close he stopped fidgeting and fretting.

Even with the distraction, he tensed anytime I shifted away from him. Like I would walk away and leave him alone. At one point I had joked that he could follow me to the bathroom if he wanted. He looked at me like I'd kicked him.

It took a minute for me to understand that he thought I was mocking his clinginess. Then I'd had to spend the next couple of minutes convincing him I had meant nothing by it. That I didn't think less of him for his insecurity.

Aaron's guard had been up for hours afterward though. All his nervous tells on display. His fingers ceaseless in their movements as he worried my blankets. The bed vibrated from his leg's constant jittering. He chewed his lip until I thought he might draw blood.

He even scooted away from me so we weren't touching. I hated that I'd hurt him, but I gave him space and he calmed down enough to lean into me again after a while.

The nights were worse; he seemed to gravitate toward me in his sleep, pulling my arms around him and thrashing closer if I shifted away in my sleep. It woke me up a few times. It was not at all how I had envisioned sharing a bed with him now we were dating. I struggled with guilt over how right it felt falling asleep with him in my arms, snuggled in close.

Over the years we had shared a bed countless times at sleepovers and on camping trips or vacations, but it had always been just as friends. And we had always maintained a careful distance between ourselves.

Before, it had meant nothing. Even if some of my soccer buddies thought it was weird. The subject of sharing a bed with another guy had come up on overnight trips for games. Smithy had delivered a diatribe on the topic, much to my annoyance.

It meant something now. I liked that I was the one he wanted when he needed someone. But I wished he had his family's support too.

I might have been a stupid jock, but I knew his insecurity had roots in the way his parents treated him. The fear I wouldn't want to be around him if he wasn't strong all the time was their legacy. Because they only paid attention to whether he met their expectations and not to him as a person. So I would have been at Mount Hope for him the next morning, regardless of having permission.

I was lucky my parents, coach and boss shared my concerns. So I didn't have to choose between my obligations and being there for Aaron. Not a difficult choice. Aaron was my top priority, he had been for a long time.

I was too worried to sleep, so I stayed up way too late. In part because I was reading articles about Cereflux and psions. Research comforted me, gave the illusion of control. I tried to stick to scientific articles after a psion forum scared me with stories of terrible complications or kids dying.

The other part of what kept me awake was texting Aaron to raise his spirits.

I figured if I was nervous, then he had to be that much more anxious about tomorrow. We didn't mention the procedure. We chatted about what he hoped his classification would be and whether it would be cooler to be a pyrokinetic or a telepath.

The benefits of controlling fire were obvious. But how cool would it be to talk in our classes with no one the wiser? I thought telepathy would come in handy for exams too.

Aaron was hoping for the ability to start fires with his mind. He said it would make him a real life superhero. We spent another hour coming up with superhero names and catch-phrases after that; he settled on Flamer for his name over my protests.

I visualized him shrugging with a big fake smile as he typed out the message he was reclaiming it. More like letting shitty things that the other kids at school said about him creep into his self-image. But it was after midnight by then, and he had already moved on to casting me as his sidekick, Sparky, so I let it go.

I slept through my alarm the next morning. Sofia woke me when she came and pounded on my door. She huffed a reminder she and Luca needed me to drop them off at school. Her delivery contained all the imperious disdain at my inconveniencing her that her tween-self could muster.

Sofia had waited until they were already running late to venture down to my bedroom. So I rolled out of bed and hit the ground running. I got my siblings to school on time.

Then I hit rush hour traffic between the elementary school and the hospital. So I arrived later than planned. At least I had a chance to text Aaron from the school. So he knew I was on my way, but running late. It meant that I missed seeing him before they transferred him to the OR prep area though.

When I arrived at Mount Hope, a receptionist at the front desk directed me to the claustrophobic waiting room outside the neurosurgery suite near the OR. There were a dozen chairs. Other anxious loved ones occupied a handful of seats when I arrived. I tried to be unobtrusive as I sat near the window. There was a color-coded screen on the wall reporting the status of each patient undergoing surgery.

Aaron's doctor's name and his case number were on the display along with six others. I watched as his status changed from a light blue highlight showing 'on time' to the green for 'in process'. His line read 'in process' for hours.

The table in the corner drew my eyes. It was covered in outdated magazines. A rack of brochures about common surgical procedures hung on the wall above the table. My attention drifted to the other wall mounted monitor where a muted local TV station with closed captioning played.

Around noon, a news report popped up. It only grabbed my attention because it mentioned psions. The camera panned in on a press conference. A banner at the bottom of the screen identified the old guy speaking as the Director of SPIRE, Norman Russell. The footage was his reply to a new budget that had increased funding for SPIRE recruitment and protests around the capital in response to the bill.

Russell delivered a prepared statement. He affirmed SPIRE's commitment to its mission—improving relations between psions and norms. Promised full integration of psions into public services around the country. His vision of psions working with local civil servants for the common good had merit. I got a bad vibe from Russell though. Like he had other motives.

Russell declared the new budget a victory for all Americans. It would further SPIRE's mission. And provide gainful employment opportunities. It was a means to harness the untapped potential of psions who wanted to serve their country.

Russell concluded his remarks. Then the news feed cut to a crowd. A barrier separated the pro-psion rights group from those on the pro-regulation side. The reporter mentioned local protestors organizing in Seattle and other major metropolitan areas as well. They said the protests were peaceful. I took heart at seeing more pro-psion slogans than slurs among the crowds.

The report ended by calling it a developing situation and promising to check back in for the next local news report. It made me think of Dad, he was a cameraman for a local news outlet. I wondered if he was part of the local crew on location filming the Seattle protests. It seemed like a work assignment he might enjoy.

I pushed it from my mind. Because around that time, Aaron's line on the status monitor turned from green to lavender for 'in recovery'. Lacking other information, I took it as a good sign that everything had gone well. It had to mean Aaron would be okay.

Aaron said he shouldn't be in recovery long. The procedure didn't use sedation, only a local anesthetic. He only needed to get his new abilities under control before being sent back to his room on the psion unit.

Sure enough, it only took around fifteen minutes for the status to change again from 'in recovery' to the yellow highlight showing 'complete'. Not long after that, his case number fell off the screen.

I dithered between heading right to his room or waiting to see if his parents might still show up in the OR waiting room and need directions. But I opted to seek Aaron out first. I followed the signs downstairs to the psion ward. I ran into Aaron's mom, Meredith, in the hallway outside of his room before they brought him back downstairs.

"Oh, I didn't expect to see you here, Jake," Meredith said and then she narrowed her eyes at me. "Shouldn't you be in class?"

"I got excused from classes for today, being here for Aaron was more important," I said. I tried to keep my hostility from showing. Conflict with his parents would only make things harder for Aaron so I needed to keep my mouth shut around them.

"Hm," she sounded doubtful. "It's not like he knew you were here. Is he done yet? His text said he should finish around noon and it's already almost twelve-thirty."

"Well, according to the status screen in the OR, they finished the procedure. So I think they'll bring Aaron back soon," I said. And it took monumental effort not to show how annoyed I was at her impatience with Aaron for being late after a surgical procedure he had no control over.

"I see. Well, I need a coffee while we're waiting, are you staying here?" she asked, oblivious to the fact I was grinding my teeth.

"Yeah, I'll tell him you're here if he gets back before you," I said, grateful that I would get to see Aaron first at least.

"Thanks," Meredith gave me a false smile.

It was disconcerting to see where Aaron had gotten his bright full wattage grin. He did a better job of making it look genuine though. She left me standing in the hall alone for a few minutes. Then a team of medical personnel in scrubs wheeled Aaron through the double doors. He was sitting up, looking alert and animated. When he saw me he smiled, his real smile, and I breathed easy again.

"You're here," he said, voice a little breathy, he sounded surprised and relieved.

"You're okay!" I said at the same time. And we both smiled. I stayed out of the way while the hospital staff got him installed in his room. Most of them filed out of the room leaving one guy in a scrub top covered in emoji faces chatting with Aaron. A nurse gestured for me to go in as she exited.

"Hey, Aaron," I said from the doorway. Aaron squirmed upright.

"I'm glad you're here, Jake," he said.

"Your mom is here too, she stepped out to grab a coffee."

"Oh, that's cool. I wasn't sure if she would make it," he said sounding surprised, but happy. Then he got more excited, bouncing as he so often did. Unable to contain his excitement. "So, guess what I am!"

"I'll guess telekinetic from how excited you are?" I said, glad to see him in good spirits, excited even.

"Oscar says I have TK, yep. I guess with TK it can take a few weeks to see if it's more specialized like pyro- or electro- or whatever."

"So you're a future superhero?"

"Yep. Oscar says he can help me with some basic exercises to see what I can do."

"Oscar?"

"Oh, right, I told you about the anchor thing, right?"

"You mentioned it, yeah, so you're like bonded to him or something?" I must not have done a believable job of hiding my discomfort about that. Aaron looked worried, twisting his hands in the sheets as he responded, avoiding eye contact.

"Linked, it's not a big deal, and it's only temporary, don't be mad at me?" he sounded small and scared again.

"I'm not mad at you, Aaron. I don't get the link thing I guess," I said, wishing to take back my words and the hurt they had caused.

"It's just to help with the emergence stuff," Aaron said.

I was an asshole. He shouldn't be the one reassuring me from his hospital bed. The guy with the smiley face scrubs must have picked up on the tension between us because he spoke into the silence before it became unbearable.

"Hello, I'm Oscar, you must be Jake?"

"Yeah, that's me," I said, giving him a quick once-over before dismissing him as competition for Aaron's affection. Oscar was attractive for all he was maybe five or six years older than us. But it was plain to see that even though he was amiable, he maintained a professional distance too. Approachable sure, but not over familiar.

"Aaron's told me a lot about you," Oscar offered me his hand. I shook it, he chuckled as we touched, "oh, well I can see why Aaron has such a calm aura. Are you aware you're an anchor, Jake?"

"A what now?" I asked, lost with the unfamiliar lingo.

"He is?" Aaron demanded. He almost bounced right off the bed upon hearing the news.

"An anchor, it means you are receptive to psions. It makes you an excellent candidate for linking with a psion. It feels like you two have already formed a fledgling link bond. That would explain why Aaron's aura was not as active as we expected once we got started today. And why we had an easy time getting him to stabilize for us after the Cereflux."

"So it's a good thing?" I asked, wary.

"It's perfect," Aaron piped up with his soft happy smile, not the big fake one he used most of the time. His reaction left me inclined to believe it was a fantastic thing.

"Being an anchor is part of you. Like having brown hair, or good hearing. It doesn't have to affect your life," Oscar put in, sounding like any other adult trying to moderate Aaron's expectations.

"It means we can link bond more easily," Aaron told me, his excitement overriding Oscar.

"I don't understand what that means," I said ruefully.

"Me neither, I mean, I have the textbook definition, but Oscar says it means our auras connect and you can help me control my abilities. I can sense you with my abilities and from what he said, it has something to do with how much calmer I am around you. And I want to feel you all the time, I want to link with you."

I forced my gaze away because I liked the sound of that more than I should. Aaron was thinking long-term, and that was overwhelming. He was on track to go to a big east coast school and I was working toward a soccer scholarship at a state school on the west coast. This situation, our relationship, would not follow the path he wanted. Even if I could be what he needed from a psionic standpoint.

Meredith saved me from having to respond in the worst way possible. She had chosen that moment to stroll into the room with her cup of coffee.

"You will under no circumstances form a link with anyone, Aaron," Meredith snapped. She shot me a poisonous look before fixing her attention on Oscar. Somehow it didn't improve my mood when she also gave Oscar a disdainful once-over before she asked with a sneer, "and who is this man?"

"I'm Oscar, I am a certified anchor with the hospital. I formed a temporary link with Aaron to help him through the procedure," Oscar said. He still gave off an amiable vibe, but it was more guarded now.

Meredith sneered at him, "I see. Well, my son seems fine now, so he shouldn't need you anymore, isn't that right?"

"He needs a link until we are sure he is stable. Emergent crisis characterized by prolonged and out-of-control hyper-gamma state brain waves is possible for the first few days after the procedure.

"Psion brain chemistry cannot sustain prolonged hyper-gamma. It can be fatal or result in brain damage and linking is the best preventative care. But I'll leave you with your son for now. I'm sure this is a stressful time for your family," Oscar said. His tone remained professional. Then he turned and gave Aaron a sympathetic look. "I will check back in with you later, Aaron. If you need anything before I return, press the call button and the nursing staff can get me sooner," Oscar said. He addressed the last to Aaron in a much warmer tone.

"Thanks, Oscar," Aaron sounded grateful and his eyes followed the man out of the room. His fingers twisted in the sheets and his lip was in danger of getting chewed off again. Meredith was scowling as she turned toward me.

"Would you excuse us please, Jake? I think this is a time for our family, you can visit with Aaron later."

Aaron looked ready to protest, but I spoke before he got himself in trouble, "Sure, Mrs. Anderson, I'll let you have time alone. Text me later, Aaron?"

"Yeah, I'll do that," Aaron gave me a half-hearted wave. His eyes seemed to plead with me not to leave him alone, but his mother had the power here. It would be better to cooperate with her than to fight her. I didn't need her getting security involved. Besides, knowing her, she wouldn't stay long, anyway.

I went over to give Aaron a brief hug. The height of the hospital bed made it awkward, but Aaron clung on hard enough to convey he didn't want me to go.

"Come back soon?" he whispered, too low for Meredith to overhear.

"Sure," I said, patting his back before stepping away.

"Bye, Jake," Aaron said.

"I'll see you later, Aaron," I said. And then I had to leave him alone with his mother. I couldn't shake the sense he took my departure as a betrayal.

Chapter 6

Aaron

The Cereflux procedure was not as bad as I built it up to be in my head. The worst part was the restraints on the exam table in the surgical suite. They strapped me into a big metal halo so I couldn't move my head, parts of it screwed into place. It was intimidating.

When they finished securing me, it immobilized my head, but the parts where it touched me weren't uncomfortable—only restrictive. The inability to move bothered me.

Oscar made it easier. He situated himself in front of me with the rest of the team arrayed behind me. He moved into my line of sight after they got the restraints in place and chatted with me throughout the process.

When Oscar noticed that I kept twitching at every sound he took pity on me. While the rest of the surgical team got everything prepped, he recounted what went on behind me. He also narrated his actions when they applied electromagnetic fields to make my brain more receptive to the Cereflux.

There had been a slight hiccough in the prep room when Oscar observed that my aura still appeared less agitated than usual for pre-emergent psions. That prompted an intense whispered consultation with Dr. Hobart. He claimed the situation made it harder for him to establish a link with me, but he had expressed confidence he could manage it once we began.

So I was on edge, hoping they wouldn't cancel the procedure at the last minute. I'd had a couple more of the visual migraines last night. In my unfamiliar hospital bed it had been harder to handle. Texting Jake with the text to speak feature on my phone took my mind off it, but I didn't want to spend another night like that. Scared and alone.

The electromagnetic fields must have done the trick. Oscar smiled and told me he had a link established not long after the first buzzing pulse crept along my skin. I responded with a shiver. Oscar grinned as he explained that a norm wouldn't have noticed anything. I sensed him after that. A general awareness of his calming presence. Like a lifeline. The increased receptivity to the link was an auspicious sign that my brain would be receptive to the treatment.

Dr. Hobart spoke after Oscar announced he had a link. She warned me before she administered the local anesthetic. There was a bite of stinging pain when she injected the first shot. I appreciated why they strapped me into place when I tried to jerk away from the sharp ache. Once the initial shot took effect there was no more pain, only pressure at the base of my skull.

It took a long time, but Dr. Hobart and Oscar explained everything they did. Dr. Hobart apologized for the prolonged injection time. Her spiel about Cereflux included too much medical jargon for me to follow. Something about fluid volume and infusion speed relating to headaches and side effects. The electrodes continued applying a weird buzzing sensation. It made my head fuzzy and numb. They had shaved my hair in the prep room to make it easier to apply the electrodes so I was cold too.

Oscar's grip on my hand soothed me in a way similar to my reaction to being around Jake. Settled me. I zoned out for chunks of the procedure, aware, but not concentrating on what happened around me. It was for the best since I found stillness for any length of time difficult when forced to focus.

When they released me from the halo brace, I couldn't resist the urge to shake my head around, to take advantage of my restored freedom of movement. Oscar chuckled, but he warned me to go easy; too much moving around might exacerbate the headache that was already brewing.

In the recovery room, I noticed the auras that Oscar had been telling me about. His was sort of mutable, almost like gentle waves along a shoreline.

Most of the other people in the room carried their auras close, like a second skin. I might touch their auras if I touched them, but not otherwise.

A shimmering thread connected Oscar's aura to my own. And it felt like the excess rough choppiness of my newly awakened senses could flow into that bond and dissipate. Become harmless.

At first, I thought that awareness might mark me as a telepath class. Since they were better at seeing auras from what Oscar had told me. But I guess it was a side effect of the Cereflux because I never did see auras that clearly again after my recovery from the procedure.

Oscar confirmed that my aura had shifted from a norm-like smoothness to the more pronounced edges of a psion. He also said it looked like I might have started to link before the procedure though he wasn't sure.

I observed the difference in him compared to the norm medical staff. Something drew me toward him. It wasn't a sensation I could have articulated though. I wanted him close, but that may have been a longing for a familiar face amid a scary new experience. Either way, I perceived him with a sense that hadn't been present before the procedure.

When I brought it up, Oscar told me that sensing auras was a non-norm thing, not a telepath specific phenomenon. Oscar said my brain wave patterns fit with a telekinetic classification. Which pleased me, and it delighted me when I saw Jake waiting for me downstairs.

I was fit to burst from excitement when Oscar confirmed what my nascent psionic senses told me. Jake was an anchor. My future link. I always knew our relationship was meant to be. My aura yearned to merge into his and I longed for that more than anything.

It peeved me when Mom strolled into my room and kicked out Jake. She had to take an interest now? But Jake abandoned me before I gave voice to my protests.

"What are you doing, Aaron?" Mom asked in an accusatory hiss as soon as the door shut behind Jake.

"Nothing, Mom. Just talking to Jake."

"You were talking about linking. I read, Aaron. I know what a link bond is," she said. The way she said it made it sound like a terrible dirty thing. Like public defecation or something.

"Huh?" it surprised me she knew anything about the term, but her opinion didn't mesh with my limited experience so far.

"If you think we will stand by and watch you throw away your life by bonding with that boy, then you have another thing coming, mister."

"But—" I protested. I focused on the wall behind her head to avoid having to make eye contact. I was receiving too much input. Something in me reached out, like I needed a release valve for all the pent up emotion her words tapped into. But she interrupted me before I so much as attempted to come up with a coherent rebuttal.

"You have your whole future ahead of you, Aaron. You will not be linking yourself to anyone right now. You're far too young to be making that kind of decision."

"But, Mom," I tried to get a word in but she didn't seem to want to hear it and I got even more worked up now. Everything around me seemed different somehow. Like I was experiencing reality in a way I hadn't before. A new awareness highlighting every object in the room, and the more frustrated and angry I got, the faster the little vibrations at their edges became. Until I swore I saw the whiteboard on the wall behind my mother twist from side to side.

"You're lucky that we let you date at all, do not make us regret that decision. Your top priority needs to be getting into a good school. That goes double now that you have being a psion to overcome."

The not so veiled insult to psions hurt. Her dismissal of my relationship rankled. I opened my mouth to protest, but nothing I said would make her listen. Or force her to see me. My growing frustration only made it all worse until the whiteboard went crashing to the ground with a clatter.

My temper drained away in the wake of my outburst and left me with the cold awareness I had done that. And that if I got angry enough, I might do something much worse than toss a whiteboard onto the ground.

"You see? Cut-rate work in the psion ward. You must work twice as hard now you're one of them. Am I making myself clear?" Mom demanded when I stared at her, realizing she hadn't connected the whiteboard falling with the fact I was a telekinetic now.

"Yeah, Mom," I said, sagging in defeat. Exhaustion swamped me in the wake of lashing out with my new abilities. It drained me. Like the meager display of power had taken everything I had. Or maybe the culprit was the knowledge of my mom's real attitude toward psions. Toward me.

"Good. Now, how are you doing, dear?" Mom asked, her tone back to the sugary-sweet concern she used when she didn't want to hear the truth. She acted as though she hadn't just crushed any hope I had that she cared about me as anything other than a status symbol. The perfect son to show off to Dad's colleagues. And I found the betrayal unsurprising.

"I'm fine. The procedure went well. I'm tired though," I said. I only managed to muster up a half-hearted effort at my usual false cheer. Still, performing the role of the dutiful son to her standards was second-nature, and it helped that it wasn't a total lie. It was early afternoon, but I was so weary. And I wanted her to leave.

"I'll let you rest, dear. Your father and I will be back to see you tonight during visiting hours," Mom patted my hand, and I flinched at her touch.

Despite everything she had said, it still hurt to realize that her aura irritated me. Her touch made my skin crawl. It left me prickling with nervous energy. I shifted around, restless, twisting up the sheets more with my hands.

"Okay."

I watched her turn on her heel to leave. I meant to text Jake as soon as she left, but I couldn't seem to unclench my fists enough to manage it. Lucky for me I didn't need to. Jake came back in before I gathered the energy to reach for my phone. He took in the room, then stared at me wide-eyed, looking at the whiteboard on the floor as he stepped around it with caution.

"Did you pull that off the wall?" he asked, incredulous. When I nodded he continued, "they bolt those into the cinder blocks you know."

"I think I did it. I got angry, and," I shrugged, "I don't know. It sort of happened."

"I meant to wait to come back until you texted me, but I felt something, do you think it's a link thing?" Jake asked.

"I don't know. I wish I didn't have to go home," I said. It was the first time I had admitted it to him in so many words, but I thought he might have already realized how much I hated home.

"What happened, Aaron?" Jake asked. His gentle kindness made me want to cry.

I shrugged, picking at my sheets. It took a titanic effort to gather the energy to brush off the statement. Pretend everything was fine, like I always did.

"Nothing, I'm just tired, ignore me."

"You sure, babe?"

Jake stepped closer, taking a seat in the chair at my bedside. My heart jumped at the endearment. He'd called me babe all weekend, but it still sent a thrill through me to hear the tenderness in his voice.

From the way Jake slouched into the chair, I knew he didn't plan to go anywhere soon. Perfect, Jake sat where I wanted him, as close as possible until they let me leave the hospital.

"You don't have to stay with me, I'll be boring since I'm planning on napping," I said. I offered him the out with obvious reluctance.

"I'll stay unless you want me to go, Aaron," Jake saw through me, he had practice at calling me on my bullshit.

We sat in silence for a while. Jake fiddled with his phone, and I was dozy when I blurted out what was bothering me.

"She called this a silly crush. Said our relationship won't last past high school. And she implied that she would try to stop me from seeing you if I let my grades slip."

Jake didn't respond for long enough I felt a creeping dread he might agree with her.

"And you think it's just a high school thing too," I said, feeling flat. Like I should have seen it coming.

"Aaron," Jake started, in that tone people often used with me that suggested I was overreacting. Jake never used that tone with me though.

I wanted to stop Jake. Whatever words he spoke next could only be things I didn't want to hear. I needed to make him see he was more my family than my parents. But I knew I couldn't force him to love me. So I sat in silence and listened to him try to let me down easy.

"You've got such a bright future ahead of you, love. You've been talking about the Ivy League, and you deserve that future. But that isn't for me.

"I will not be going with you, when you graduate. I'm going to a state school or community college, wherever I get recruited to play soccer. We've only got two more years. I will treasure our time together, but your mom is right. You can't plan your whole life around me. You deserve better than that."

"Don't I get to decide what I deserve?" I asked, and I dared a glance at him, but he wouldn't meet my eyes.

"You do," Jake said.

"Well then, I want you. I don't care about the other crap," I insisted.

"What if I can't live up to that, Aaron? Do you understand how much pressure you are putting on me with that?" Jake's voice shook. I took a grim satisfaction that at least he was hurting too. Like it might mean there was still a glimmer of hope I would change his mind. Convince him somehow that we were worth fighting for. But he had to want it too. It was impossible to force him to care about me. I knew better than to try.

"I don't want to be a burden, Jake. If that's how you see me, I guess I misjudged you," I said. Hope burned in my chest. Hope he would rise to the bait and change his mind about breaking up with me.

"You're not a burden. I don't want you to give up your future because of me though," Jake said with infuriating calm.

"It's my future!" I protested. "And all the fancy school stuff is what my parents want. No one bothered to ask what I wanted. I want you."

"I know you do, and I'm sorry, Aaron. It kills me to hurt you. But you're sixteen, I'm trying to be practical here. It's foolish to make a lifetime commitment to someone as a teenager. That's what you're asking for, right? Link bonds are serious aren't they?"

He stood, and he looked as upset as me. Small consolation there, it wasn't stopping him from throwing away whatever future we might have had together. And our present along with it. I watched everything I wanted slipping through my fingers, and I was powerless to stop it.

"You should leave, before we say something irrevocable," I said with a detached calm. Torn between wanting him to stay and wanting him gone. He hesitated, time stood still. Then he took a step closer. Hope flared he wouldn't leave me. Jake brushed his lips against my cheek in a glancing imitation of a kiss.

For that instant, as he touched me, everything felt like it might be okay. My aura settled. That part of me, everything that made me a psion, sang with the rightness of his touch. My psionic senses were no longer in turmoil. It reminded me of the glassy smoothness of a lake on a windless summer day. Then he left. And those same senses seemed muted without his presence. Dulled and deadened. It seemed more ominous than the loss of a new relationship when he walked away he took a part of me with him. I forgot how to breathe. It hurt.

I had no words to describe the loss. Like a songbird with no song. As though I had discovered some new color and then lost my sight. A cruel glimpse of a future which might have been, but had moved beyond my grasp.

I stared after him until my vision blurred. For a heart-stopping moment of sheer terror I was sure that the procedure hadn't worked. That something serious was wrong with me. I worried I was going blind for real. But then it registered that I was crying; it was just my tears making it hard to see.

I must have fallen asleep after Jake left because I startled awake when my parents knocked on the door to my room. It had gotten late enough that the streetlights were on in the parking area outside my window.

"How are you, son?" Dad asked as he and Mom came to stand over me.

I was numb. My head hurt, my heart ached, and I felt like I had just woken up after crying myself to sleep, but I only said, "okay."

"You're all blotchy, dear," Mom said. She wiped at my cheeks like she could brush away the evidence of my earlier tears. I thought with bitterness that I embarrassed her.

"Sorry," I pushed her hand away, it prickled along my new senses. Dad frowned at me.

"Your mother tells me you are telekinetic?"

"That's what they said," I said.

"Excellent, TK is much less intimidating, much more acceptable to society," Dad said.

"Yeah," I said.

I didn't have the energy to form an opinion on the matter. I wondered what he would have said if I was a telepath. It occurred to me, I would have known what they thought of me then. I shuddered at the thought. I didn't want to know. Their half-truths were miserable enough, let alone the words that remained unspoken.

"We spoke with your doctor. It sounds like she plans to discharge you by the end of the week. So you'll have a few days to pack and say goodbye to your friends," Dad said.

"Wait, what? Why would I say goodbye?" I asked, startled out of my comfortable numbness.

"If you paid attention, you would know I was explaining. I pulled a few strings to get you admitted at the Riverton Academy, effective next week. They are part of the national board of psionic youth preparatory schools," Dad said with impatience.

"What? But it's the middle of the school year," I said.

"It is the first month of classes, Riverton's term only started this week so you won't have much catching up to do. And it's a proper prep school, in Connecticut. They're a feeder school for Yale," Dad said.

"Yale?" I repeated.

"Yes, dear, everyone knows Yale is progressive on psion issues. It's the perfect choice for you. And Riverton is a premier boarding school with an excellent program for psions," Mom put in with her usual faux enthusiasm.

"Boarding school," I said, testing the words.

"They even have a drama club," Mom cajoled still in her concerned parent voice. The one that made me the bad guy if I didn't go along with whatever she said.

"You're sending me to Connecticut?" I asked when I could formulate an actual sentence.

"Yes," Dad said. "It's for the best, son."

"You're sending me away," I tried rephrasing it. As if that would change the meaning.

"Don't be dramatic. It's boarding school, it is a wonderful opportunity for you. You've no idea the strings I had to pull to get you in on short notice, don't be ungrateful," Dad's irritation was clear to hear and growing.

It would cost too much effort to make a fuss. I lacked the energy to protest. The arrangements were already final, knowing Dad. No amount of arguing on my part would change anything. And Jake didn't believe in us anyway, so what was the point of fighting?

A new beginning surrounded by other psions might be easier. And I wouldn't have to return home. So there was that. A fresh start instead of having to see Jake every day and knowing he didn't feel the same way I did.

"Okay," I said, "when are we leaving?"

"I booked you a flight for Saturday. That gives you Sunday to get settled into your room and get to know the campus before you start classes on Monday," Dad said, looking pleased with himself.

My parents not deigning to accompany me on my first trip across the country shouldn't have been a shock. Their lack of interest should have stopped disappointing me by now. It would be my first time living away from home. And they weren't coming to drop me off. A wave of longing for Jake hit me, but I quashed it fast. It was pointless wishing for what I would never have.

"All right," I said.

"You won't make a scene?" Mom asked with undue skepticism considering I always acquiesced to their demands in the past.

"No," I said.

Mom made a sound like she didn't believe me, but Dad patted my shoulder, his hand heavy, his touch unpleasant.

"I'm proud of you, son. Riverton will help you. You'll see."

"Yeah, Dad, sure," I said, then I faked a yawn, "I'm still tired from the procedure, sorry."

"We'll leave you to rest then. Your mother will pick you up once they discharge you, just call her," Dad said. He sounded eager to leave.

"Okay," I said. "Good night."

"Good night," Dad said. He turned to go.

"Good night, dear," Mom said, all happy and sweet again, she even leaned in to hug me. I let her, not returning it, but at least not pushing her away from me as I itched to do.

"Let's go, Meredith," Dad said, turning back in the doorway. She left without a backward glance.

I had never felt more alone than when I reached for my phone only to realize that I couldn't call Jake about it because we were fighting. Or something. He would tell me it was for the best. What a great opportunity. I would have cried again if I'd had any tears left.

I had to stay two more nights at the hospital before my aura stabilized. During that time, I learned not to make things go flying at the slightest provocation. Oscar coached me through some meditation exercises. Jake texted me dozens of times asking to talk and checking if I was okay. I ignored him, only responding to tell him I needed space, but I would be all right. My emotions were too raw to deal with our argument, so I evaded him online and he didn't come to visit me again.

Except for answering direct questions, I resolved to avoid talking to my parents. Even then, I stuck to monosyllables when possible. I wasn't sure if they even noticed though. I decided that it didn't matter. This was that last straw for me, sending me across the country without so much as consulting me about it. There were psion schools right here in Seattle, so it stood to reason they wanted me far away.

No more giving my parents the benefit of the doubt. No more pretending we were some stereotypical perfect family or trying to fit the role they pushed on me. It didn't matter if they loved me, I refused to keep trying to get affection from people who had none to give me. Soon I would be out from under their roof and it was an unmitigated relief.

After only one day back in public school, I realized that being a psion in public was hard. The teasing I got for being smaller than average and my lack of masculinity was nothing compared to how Noah and his cronies treated me after they learned I was a psion.

I had only gone to school on Thursday to return textbooks, say goodbye to my casual acquaintances and tell my close friends I was leaving in person. Not spending the day at home with my mom was a bonus. I ended up regretting the decision to attend classes though.

School was surreal. Some of my teachers treated me different. It was subtle with most. They were careful not to make eye contact. Some acted awkward with me, stumbling over their words. Careful not to get too close.

The worst was Mrs. Sullivan. She taught my AP history class. When I walked in, she backed away from me. And she insisted I move to the back of the room where she had a psion seating section because she feared psionic radiation. I couldn't see the point in attempting to explain psionic radiation didn't exist to an elderly woman with no interest in facts.

After Mrs. Sullivan's class, Noah and two of his friends followed me into the bathroom. Well, pushed me through the door, to be more accurate. They got a few punches in before Garrett—who was also in my history class—burst in and put a stop to it.

"Hey, buddy, it's a good thing I happened by and heard a strange sound, huh?" he asked. Garrett slung a protective arm around my shoulders and guided me toward my next class. In the past I didn't mind casual touches like that. And Jake's soccer buddies were loose with casual touches, for a bunch of jocks, so I was used to it. But now it grated against my psionic senses.

I shrugged out of Garrett's grip as soon as he would let me, already struggling with control of my abilities. Proximity to people who were unsettling to my aura only made my abilities more volatile.

The constant electric buzz just under my skin was unnerving. I had learned it preceded accidental uses of my power. Oscar taught me meditation techniques to get it under control. He had advised me if all else failed, a controlled use of my abilities might help channel those rampant impulses.

"Did Jake ask you to keep an eye on me?"

I was certain Garrett's arrival, at the exact moment I needed rescuing, wasn't a coincidence. In part, I was talking to distract from the fact that I was trying to float my pencil above the stack of books I was carrying. Garrett's only response was to wink at me.

My self-control pleased me, until my rescuer poked at the pencil. He knocked it out of the air, then gave me a wide-eyed looked as I scrambled to catch it without letting all my things tumble to the ground.

Garrett acted less warm toward me after that display. But he didn't let me out of his sight until he saw me installed in my seat for my next class, safe and sound. The escort seemed unnecessary. Noah wasn't going to attack me in the middle of a crowded hallway. I appreciated it though. If for no other reason then because it meant that whatever Jake's attitude toward me now, he must have kept our fight between us.

Or at least Jake hadn't told his buddies not to bother looking out for me anymore. In fact, judging from the roster of soccer guys shepherding me between classes for the rest of the day, it seemed like he had asked them to increase their vigilance. Maybe they were only doing it for Jake, but it was still nice not having to worry about getting punched again.

I appreciated the concern. My face and stomach hurt where Noah had hit me. The only thing that allowed me to maintain control of my abilities as the day wore on, was I knew his team had my back. How long would their protection last if they feared me though? For the first time, I considered that Riverton might be the best choice for me.

The worst part of the day was getting to the auditorium after school and finding out that the dynamic with my closest friends had also changed. Before emergence, my theater friends would have hugged me and fussed over my blackening eye. Everyone would have rallied around me and there would have been universal vitriol directed at Noah for hurting me.

Some of my friends did just that. But the hugs from my casual acquaintances were strange now, their auras uncomfortable as they scraped against mine to where I had to push them away. And some kids I thought of as close friends kept their distance.

I heard the murmured comments that Noah might have had it right about me all along. That hurt. And it hurt when I overheard a large group making a point of not inviting me along for burgers and shakes after rehearsal.

I had planned to attend school Thursday and Friday. After the disaster that was Thursday, I took the day off on Friday to pack everything I wanted to bring to Connecticut instead. I spent most of the morning purging my social media down to the few friends who had treated me like I was still the same person. And Jake. Because I couldn't bring myself to block him.

I ached to call Jake, to see him, but I didn't think I could handle goodbye. Besides, if I didn't call him, then we didn't have make our break up official. I wanted to have him for just a little longer, like Schrodinger's cat, our relationship wasn't dead until I looked in the box. So I did not look.

I dropped by his house Friday afternoon—when I knew he was traveling to a big soccer game—to say goodbye to his family. It was a coward move, dodging him, but I couldn't bear to see him. His mom knew

I was avoiding Jake, but she didn't call me on it. Instead, she wrapped me up in a hug I needed with desperation.

Unlike so many people now, her aura soothed me and I reveled in the embrace's comfort. She held me even when I had let the hug stretch for far too long by most social conventions. When I let go, she made sure I had her number and assured me I could use it anytime if I needed to talk to someone.

The situation was weird, but being in Jake's house and around his family settled my aura. It was the most settled I had been since Oscar broke our temporary link at the hospital when it was time for me to go home. My farewell was a nice reminder I had people who loved me.

On Saturday morning I got up before dawn. Dad brought me to the airport. We said our goodbyes in the car and then I was on my own. At least I had flown before so the airport and getting through security didn't intimidate me.

I guess someone told Jake about Riverton after I left. He must have blown up my phone while I was in the air somewhere over the middle of the country. When we landed, and I turned off airplane mode, my phone rattled and buzzed with a string of notifications that seemed endless.

Later, I learned that his mom had mentioned I was leaving. He was furious that I hadn't told him in person. His last text asked if I was breaking up with him. I deleted it without responding along with all the others.

I couldn't find the words to respond, and by the time I had the words, it was far too late. Between the imminent break up, Noah's new boldness in his harassment and my supposed friends turning their backs on me, Riverton didn't sound like such a bad idea. I needed a fresh start.

By the time my plane took flight, I had reconciled with never seeing Seattle again. The only connection I still wanted tying me there was Jake's family. And after the way I had handled our break up, I imagined they must not be my biggest fans either.

So besides my suitcases, I brought heaps of emotional baggage along with me. I had to begin at Riverton with a fading black eye courtesy of

Noah. And the knowledge that teachers who had liked me a week ago, and people I had been friends with since kindergarten, now only saw me as an object of fear and loathing.

Leaving meant that I had a blank slate. No expectations from people who had known me my whole life. No Jake to hide behind, or parents to mold me into their version of the perfect son. It was my first opportunity to be myself with no one telling me who I ought to be. To be honest, I wasn't sure who I wanted to be. But, it was liberating to know I got to decide for myself now.

I had expected to face fear, uncertainty, loneliness and anxiety with all the changes. And I experienced those, to an extent, but it also surprised me how welcome everyone made me when I arrived at my new school. It was a relief when I stepped out of the cab and onto the Riverton campus for the first time and found a place where I belonged.

PART TWO

4 Years Ago

Chapter 7

Aaron

Riverton Academy was a perfect fit for me. I did well with the structured environment and I thrived living with other psions. My academics improved under the structured environment. The school scheduled us straight from breakfast through to evening study sessions. The strict rules helped me to stay focused.

My roommate, Albert, became a fast friend and staunch ally when I needed one the most. It was serendipitous that he was an anchor. And maybe our link was inevitable, living in such close proximity as we were. But it soothed the ache of loss at leaving Jake—and everything else I cared about—behind. The incident that sparked our link happened not long after we met.

My first week away from home was the hardest. I missed Jake with a near physical pain. Between emergence, leaving home and losing my first link, my aura was unstable. Then I had an ill-advised indiscretion involving chocolate cake and coffee to fill the void. I learned first-hand why caffeine was not part of the approved diet for emergent psions.

Albert stepped in before I could go hyper-gamma, but it was close. Even a grade C could die from a prolonged hyper-gamma state during the peri-emergent period. Our abilities were prone to instability in the months following emergence. As an anchor, Albert's abilities allowed him to create a link out of our casual acquaintance. He stabilized me before I had a complete meltdown.

That cemented our friendship. And Albert was my link for the better part of the year. Until he linked with his girlfriend during our senior year.

Even with a stable link, I struggled with abilities training. Incidents occurred where my control went haywire.

It was bad enough that my instructor referred me to a SPIRE sponsored summer camp. And my parents agreed to let me stay in Connecticut over the summer to attend. The certificate I earned looked good on university applications so that didn't hurt my case.

By the time my first summer rolled around, I felt a cold dread at the prospect of returning to my parents' home—and their rules. A taste of freedom rendered returning untenable. So I made alternative arrangements. Summer camp lasted a month, and I lodged with a local friend who was a day student at the academy for the rest of the summer. My flimsy cover for not returning home was that I wished to take advantage of summer AP courses. No one questioned the excuse.

I learned more control in a month at summer camp than in a year of psion focused curriculum at Riverton Academy. Not that the academy skimped on our abilities training. Riverton required it for all students. Even the anchors learned to manage links and manipulate auras. But the SPIRE trainers at summer camp ran drills and had an assortment of tricks to teach us. The school wanted us in control. Capable of passing as norms in wider society. SPIRE's goal was different.

They designed their program to maximize our abilities. Their staff specialized in pushing our limits. Seeing if a strong grade C could strengthen their abilities enough to rank as a grade B. Or hone our personal skills to advantage. For instance, controlling inert objects came easier for me.

Some of us had better fine control whereas some of us could concentrate a strong short burst of power beyond our usual abilities. The cost of pushing the limits of our abilities included overuse symptoms. I got debilitating headaches. And a general malaise if I pushed too much. Like the prodrome of a cold that never quite manifested. It was worth the side effects to gain a solid understanding of my limits as a telekinetic though.

Summer camp let me hone my abilities from an average grade C strength to borderline grade B. Not enough to bump my grading up a category. But enough that SPIRE might give my application as a potential field agent serious consideration. Because I might achieve a grade B on a good day with a compatible anchor. Anchor boosting was an acknowledged possibility, even if it was not the norm.

And if it weren't for Eagle House, I might have enlisted with SPIRE. But Riverton required all students to complete service hours to be eligible to graduate. Along with some of my theater friends, I volunteered at Eagle House. It catered to psions whose families rejected them after their emergence. I loved working with the other youth.

Eagle House had two functional arms. The first operated alongside other area resources as a short-term shelter for homeless youth to find them permanent placements. I didn't have as much contact with the youth using the shelter services. They only stayed for short periods, weeks to months.

The second arm served as a group home that offered transitional housing to the youth who had telepathic abilities. While the shelter helped place any psion or anchor in need, permanent housing went to telepaths first. The Eagle House mission gave priority to telepaths. It was their niche. Since they were one of the few facilities that would accept telepaths.

When I started my service hours at Eagle House, our group offered tutoring. After a few sessions the need for abilities training for the residents became conspicuous. It was no surprise considering they had other things on their plates.

And public schools didn't offer psion specific courses like that. So we put together a program to fill the need. I enjoyed hanging out with the residents. Working around the center on weekends became a part of my routine, pitching in with chores and helping to prepare meals or whatever else they needed around the facility.

My involvement with Eagle House persisted over my two years at Riverton. After completing my school work and meeting my extracurricular commitments, I spent what little free time I had at the center. I made friends there. And I got to know the staff.

The shelter director was a middle-aged former social worker—Mrs. England. The way she helped the residents in her care inspired me. I wanted to be just like her, a fierce protector, loving mentor, and compassionate enforcer.

Mrs. England gave me my first inkling of what I wanted to do with my life. My observations of her engaged with the residents set me on the path to becoming a social worker. It was the first career I could see myself pursuing because it was what I wanted rather than what someone else expected. And I nurtured a growing desire to help other psions the same way she helped her residents.

In the summer after my junior year, the Pederson Youth Development Center network, or PYDC, acquired the housing arm of Eagle House. PYDC operated group home facilities around the country. It appeared to be the best thing that could have happened to Eagle House.

PYDC had better funding, they purchased a larger facility. It meant a move to a better school district and more available beds. Their operational budget was bigger. And SPIRE had a loose affiliation with PYDC. The details of that relationship remained murky.

I soon learned that it meant their kids got preference for SPIRE summer youth training camps, the same camp I had attended. And their job placement rates for the older teens were almost too amazing to believe. PYDC's close ties to SPIRE summer camps garnered them a contract to run similar camps for their residents and the wider psion community in areas where they operated. It meant the program expanded beyond the major hubs where SPIRE had facilities.

PYDC also maintained close ties with Riverton. They began a program to give PYDC residents access to our psionic abilities and history courses. Riverton offered a condensed form of both classes on Saturdays. Through the changes, I remained involved with the center, logging well over my required volunteer hours there.

Despite my other commitments, I worked hard to graduate near the top of my class. And I got into Yale along with several classmates. Dad had been right in that Riverton Academy arranged seats for their graduates with Yale's admissions department. For a psion, gaining admittance from a public school would have been next to impossible.

Graduation symbolized freedom for me. It meant working toward the life I wanted instead of the Ivy League goal my parents put in front of me for as long as I could remember. Albert and I planned to move from our Riverton dorm to an apartment near campus, which we shared with two of our classmates.

Mom and Dad flew out for the graduation. It was the first time I'd seen them in person since our Christmas holiday, skiing up north. They took the obligatory photo ops. Then treated me to a fancy steak dinner at a restaurant where even the wait staff wore suits and ties. The next morning they got on a plane home. I had expected to have strong feelings about the visit, but it was just nice.

Much as I resented my parents for their lack of involvement, sending me to Riverton opened doors for me. And I allowed myself a grudging gratitude for the favors Dad must have called in to give me the opportunity. I was trying to let go of my animosity toward them. Distance and time helped. Holding their inability to be what I needed against them was pointless. They had given me the best education money and influence could buy—whether or not I wanted it.

My life hadn't revolved around them in years now. So I could afford gratitude for a quality education without having to deal with bullies like Noah. Or figure out my abilities on my own. I didn't have to stumble through forming a link because I had dozens of examples of healthy links in my classmates.

Even though I held little illusion about my parents' involvement in my adult life, I still had a family I could turn to. Mr. Moretti, Sofia and Luca commented on my graduation pictures online. Mrs. Moretti called to tell me how proud she was of me and expressed regret that her family couldn't be there to celebrate with me. I thanked her and congratulated her on Jake's grad. Her call meant more than any steak dinner ever could.

I was excited to be starting at Yale in the fall, even if it wasn't quite what I would have chosen for myself. My whole future stretched ahead of me, full of promise. And with Albert by my side, it didn't resemble the leap into the unknown Riverton had been. And, of equal importance in my book, was the imminent start of my first real job.

I had applied for a job as a camp counselor. When Agent Jones, my counselor from the year before, got in touch to mention he was directing the camp and looking to hire young psions, I leapt at the opportunity. A little cajoling convinced Albert to apply too. After the amount the camp helped me, paying it forward was an easy call. And it thrilled me to learn that many of the residents from Eagle House were attending this year.

Albert and I got the job working together. Our assignment arrived the week of graduation and they set us up to work with a group of six psions with TK and two anchors, all aged fifteen to sixteen. I looked forward to the summer with eager anticipation, Albert went along with it, my ever patient companion.

Calling it summer camp made it sound like fun. It wasn't recreational though. SPIRE's summer training camp for psions was work. Hard work. I remembered just how hard we worked from last year.

Some aspects of the camp had changed now that PYDC took over running it. Some policies had changed. But the major details were the same. And SPIRE had stepped up in their sponsorship role. As evidenced by Agent Jones stepping in as co-director along with a representative from PYDC this year.

One aspect that hadn't changed was the basic camp structure. It was still residential and lasted a month. They still divided the campers into teams based on age and psionic classification. The anchors remained interspersed among the other teams for most sessions.

Counselors for each group still had the same class of ability as their charges. And the counselor assigned to the anchors pulled them aside for special one-on-one anchor only sessions on a rolling basis.

This year enrollment had skyrocketed with all the PYDC residents auto-enrolled in the camp. So the fifteen- and sixteen-year-old TK attendance was high enough that the directors divided them into three teams.

That didn't come as a shock since telekinesis was as common as dirt. Compared to other abilities at least. But telekinetic subclasses were rare. And much sought after. Psions with such an ability tended to be strong. They ranked as grade A or B. Pyrokinesis and electrokinesis were the two best known subclasses. But not the only ones.

SPIRE courted psions with PK for roles from liaising with fire departments to aiding the forestry service. A strong PK might aid in training firefighters, contain high casualty blazes, or work the front-lines of wildfires.

Electrokinesis had value too. EK could knock out a security system. Or allow remote access of electronics. A well trained electrokinetic combined the traits of a skeleton key and a smart device hub. SPIRE recruited psions with EK. Private businesses hired them off the books for corporate espionage. They were useful.

By contrast, I could fling all my school supplies across my dorm room and irritate my poor roommate—not that I was bitter or anything. While turning a textbook into a projectile had its practical uses, some days it seemed like TK was the most boring ability possible. And despite that I had struggled with control.

Even after Albert and I linked. The thing was, in the early days after emergence it felt like there was something tugging on my TK, like an elastic band stretched to its limits. And any attempts to use my abilities seemed to go awry. I got used to the sensation after a few months. But something about electronics still caused even simple manipulation to go astray.

Albert knew all about my lack of affinity for electronics from school. My first week at Riverton, we did an exercise with our cell phones and some quirk of my abilities made me lose control. The darn thing buzzed in my senses and it amped up my TK. Like it got when I overdid it on coffee. The best I managed was aiming the rogue device away from people before it flew off into a wall and smashed. I learned quick to avoid using my abilities on cell phones.

Much like I adjusted to caffeine over time, the weird added awareness of electronics lessened too. It was just a quirk of my TK. I noticed when an object wouldn't quite react the way I expected, but it didn't sear my senses as it did when I was still peri-emergent. Akin to a failing memory of a possible future. Missed potential.

At least it meant that my cell phone and chip card didn't have a blinding glow in my psionic senses like they did when I first started at Riverton. I didn't notice them anymore. They faded into the background these days. And I had enough control of my abilities to manage tasks with them if I put my mind to it.

The last vestiges of my electro-sensitivity translated into a propensity to frying any device I touched with my TK. Albert teased me about it often, though he was mindful not to undermine our camper's respect for me. I appreciated his restraint. Albert always could read a room.

The month flew by with the demands of our schedule. Our campers fell into their bunks, exhausted, after long days of training. The camp curriculum focused on abilities training and learning psion history.

Abilities training took most of the time. But we also had a schedule to follow with prompts for the daily lecture and discussion sessions.

We covered the divergence—the global development of psions as the result of mass exposure to a still unidentified mutagen. So called because it was where our kind—species according to some—diverged from norms.

Our lecture material covered the subsequent panic of psi-plague. In modern times we would classify it as a mass emergence event. And the quarantine camps that opened as a response. We also talked about how those events led to the existence of SPIRE, PEEA, the registry and other aspects of modern life as a psion.

I found the camp challenging as a camper. As a counselor, the challenge magnified, and I wasn't sure I could have handled the pressure without Albert at my side. But it was worth it to witness a skill clicking for one of our teens. Or the way Rita hugged me after I spent an hour helping her master a new trick in a one-on-one session. Or the blissful look on Marc's face when he linked with Louis to navigate the skills course using a lead ball he could barely budge on day one.

I remembered our first session with the obstacle course, when I demonstrated the obstacles to the teens. They seemed daunted at my ease with the exercises. Some obstacles took finesse. When I asked for a volunteer to go first, no one stepped forward.

At Albert's insistence, I showed the teens how hard working with electronics was for me. I fought my way through every obstacle to maintain control of my cell phone. Or even the electronic chip cards we used to access the dorms at Riverton. Albert and I made a good team.

Albert showed a knack for putting psions at ease, it turned out. He excelled at defusing stressful situations. And he made the deliberate decision to leave me floundering when he might have smoothed out my abilities' worst fluctuations with a touch on our first day with the campers. I couldn't resent him for it though since it had the desired effect.

My struggle must have eased their anxiety over the possibility of failure. A few of them volunteered to try next once I showed them screw ups were a part of learning. Albert's instincts proved correct.

After that, I had the bright idea of trying the course with various materials, to test affinity. Some campers found the course easier or harder with particular objects. It was interesting to see our team's affinities. One girl navigated the course using a coin with her eyes closed. But she struggled with the colorful plastic balls SPIRE provided. Another had the best luck with her favorite book. It was an interesting spin on the activity, and the campers loved it.

Their level of engagement fluctuated over the course of the camp, but they worked hard for us. And all our campers would receive a SPIRE certification. They had earned it.

It was hard to believe the month had already flown past. We finished skills testing the previous day and our entire team had passed. So today was about celebrating with them. The whole camp was abuzz with excitement over the certificate ceremony this afternoon and Albert and I got caught up in the high spirits.

The jovial mood might have contributed to Albert forgetting his phone charging in our cabin when we left to accompany our campers to breakfast this morning. I ran back to get it for him, using my TK to retrieve it from the doorway. And now it wasn't turning on. Albert fiddled with the phone as we walked. When we reached the mess hall, he sighed and gave up. He shoved the bricked phone into his pocket.

Albert and I grabbed decaf coffee and stood near our team. Not joining them, but available. As Albert finished his coffee, he turned to face me.

From his sly expression I knew this would be one of those times Albert channeled his frustration over my irritating him into a good-natured ribbing. I couldn't deny he had a right to feel upset about his phone, and I appreciated him not blowing up at me over it.

"You know, you're like the opposite of an electrokinetic. What would they call that?"

"I don't think that's a thing," I said.

"Sure it is, my phone worked before you got it for me. So, classification for someone who kills electronics with a touch? Electromancer maybe?"

"What?"

"You know, like a necromancer? But with fried circuitry instead of undead hosts?"

"Isn't it the necro part that has to do with death? So, wouldn't it be like, necro-electro-something?"

"Electromancer sounds better."

"Necrelectresis? Electronecrotic?"

"That just sounds gross, Aaron. Anyway, my point is, don't touch my phone with your TK."

"Wouldn't you love to have an undead cell phone though?"

"So like, the battery would never die? That would be wicked sweet. Except then I wouldn't have an excuse for not answering when my parents call."

"At least your parents call you."

"Yeah. I guess. So, could you actually make my cell phone undead?"

"No."

"Can you do anything besides fry it?"

"I can chuck its corpse across the room. Or make it float around you, like an avenging ghost."

"That's TK."

I shrugged, "I'm telekinetic."

"But it works different with electronics for you."

"Agent Jones says it's just interference," I said.

Agent Jones had grown into something of a mentor to us over the summer. He said it was like my brain waves were at a frequency that was extra susceptible to electromagnetic fields. Or I might have a semi-active recessive trait for EK or a mutation or something. He called it a latent ability. I figured he meant he didn't know for sure why my abilities had a defect. But the interference, if that was what it was, had faded since my emergence. And he said it might disappear entirely given long enough.

While there had been early speculation I might be an EK, nigh on two years as a TK made it clear I was only telekinetic. The weird interference from electromagnetic fields might mean I had a sensitivity to them, but it didn't give me EK. It only meant my abilities became erratic when any kind of electric charge got involved.

"So your TK around electronics is like a pacemaker beside a microwave?" Albert asked with a frown.

"Who knows? The bottom line is, even if I might have been an EK, it never happened. Like those stupid height predictions they do on toddlers? My pediatrician predicted I'd be tall. Never happened."

"You aren't *that* short."

"Tell that to, oh, everybody?"

Albert sighed, "You're too critical of yourself. Anyway, we should get the campers to their last session, you want to break it up between Marc and Louis or should I?"

Albert gestured to the table where our charges were finishing their breakfast. Two older teens on our team, Marc and Louis, were roughhousing. Everyone was in high spirits since it was the last day, but Albert was right, their altercation looked poised to cross the line into unacceptable territory.

The celebration this afternoon was the talk of the mess hall. But we still needed to get through our final sessions. I preferred not to end the month with a fist fight. I was sure our group would settle down once we got to the skills course.

Our team enjoyed the challenge of skills testing. The obstacle course was a major tool to improve elements of their abilities. Fine motor control, or speed, or even strength when we used the heavier weighted balls as the object of their TK. We also worked on linking skills. The evidence of how much our students had improved over the past month was gratifying.

And I was woolgathering when I should stop Louis from putting Marc in a headlock. The pair had clashed all month. Albert and I couldn't quite decide if they had a genuine dislike of each other or if they were flirting. The fun benefits of dealing with repressed youth.

As I waded in to break up the fight, I overheard Louis calling Marc a tick. Stupid move, Louis.

"Language," I admonished as I used my TK to help me pull the larger boy off Marc.

"Sorry, Aaron," Louis said.

"What are you two fighting about now?" I asked, trying not to show my exasperation.

"He said he'll be glad not to have a partial link with me anymore," Marc said, sullen. Louis was an anchor with our group. My understanding was that Louis's sibling was a psion, so his family sent him to the camp when they learned he was an anchor. Marc lived at a group home. He'd been placed there through Eagle House, so I knew him better. The two of them were an excellent match as far as it concerned their auras, according to Albert.

Anchors and telepaths perceived those things between other people. All I knew was how another person's aura felt to me. And no one ever held a candle to Jake. So I tried not to pay too much attention since I doubted I would ever find anything to compare to the bliss of being with my first love. But I needed to focus on Louis and Marc, not my stupid pining.

"And that upset you?" I asked.

"Yes."

"You're such a sensitive baby. This is why I don't like working with you," Louis said.

"That's not what you said before. You said you felt it too…" Marc looked like he might cry and I was so not prepared for drama if this was about Louis leading Marc on. Louis rolled his eyes.

"Okay, is this a conversation we should have in private?" I asked, far out of my depth.

"No," Louis said.

"Yes," Marc said, simultaneous.

"Let's go get this straightened out, meet me in the staff offices," I said. I pointed the two troublemakers toward the door. As we passed Albert, I drew him aside.

"Everything all right?" he asked.

"Not sure. Sounds like Louis was instigating things again. But Marc seems more upset than usual. I'll investigate if there is more going on between them than we thought. You want to get the others started on the obstacle course and we'll join you soon?"

"Sounds good. Good luck."

Albert slapped me on the back in encouragement. I squared my shoulders and tried to prepare for whatever issue Marc and Louis were having. From the sounds of it Marc had gotten attached. It was easy for a psion to fall hard and fast for a compatible aura. An unscrupulous anchor might take advantage. It made us vulnerable.

I hated thinking Louis was that kind of person. But it was always an unfortunate possibility. If he had misled Marc, there would be consequences. The bond between a psion and their link was sacrosanct. And the psion community was small enough that word would travel if Louis used Marc's desire to link with a compatible aura against him.

The law might not require anchors to register, but contact with the system would get their status noted. Attendance at a SPIRE affiliated training camp meant having a registry record. For anchors that included their name, anchor status and any long-term primary links. The public database didn't list anchors. But their certifications, links and status would come up in a background check.

Louis would earn a negative mark on his registry record for abusing the trust of a psion he linked. It would be a warning to anybody who wanted to employ a professional anchor he was one to avoid.

And none of that would do a damn thing to help Marc get over the betrayal of his trust. I hoped I misunderstood the gist of their argument. But somehow, I doubted it. Best not to leave the pair stewing for too long, I strode off after the teens.

Chapter 8

Jake

My first week at UDub was a bigger change than I expected. It was a process to learn my way around campus. At my high school the familiar faces of the kids I grew up with surrounded me. At university I knew no one. The syllabi I got on the first day made my coursework look intense and daunting. And the teachers were less approachable in a crowd with over a hundred other first-year students.

It was also weird adjusting to not having soccer anymore. After aggressive scouting early in my junior year, I had blown my chances when I blew out my knee during the championship game in my senior year at elites.

It was devastating. All of my plans for the future had centered on soccer. I spent every fall in youth development leagues since I was kid. Spring meant the school soccer season. Every summer I attended training camps. I had been captain of my high school varsity team for two years running, leading my team to back-to-back championships as a sophomore and again as a junior.

Then in the elite league championship senior year, I played the game of my life. And watched my dreams go up in smoke when I took a bad fall in the final minutes of play. We won the championship. But my injury benched me for good.

Missing the last year of my high school career had been bad enough. Multiple surgeries to correct the damage to my knee only added insult to injury. My surgeon had to put in pins and repair a torn ACL. And that was the end to my collegiate athletic aspirations. The only silver lining was that my insurance covered everything since we had a great policy through Mom's job.

If it hadn't been for Aaron's abrupt departure from my life, that last game would have been the worst day of my life. Before my injury, a few scouts approached me. Their interest came to an abrupt end once my doctor broke the news I couldn't play at a collegiate level. Not that I could blame them, but it still stung.

A year out from my injury, I could play for fun. I figured that I could join an intramural team, but it wasn't the same.

After the surgeries, getting back in shape was rough too. I wasn't there yet going into my freshman year of university. But the university gym was awesome, I made a point of coming in before my morning classes to take advantage of all the top of the line equipment.

Beyond missing the sport—and the physical setbacks—not being able to play was also hard on my social life. I had expected to count on my teammates forming the core of my social group. Other than Aaron, all my high school buddies had been on the soccer team with me, or at least on the junior varsity team. I missed that camaraderie now too.

Without the athletic scholarship I busted my ass to earn since I was a kid in youth development leagues, I had to take out loans for school. I needed to save money where I could. That meant living at home and commuting to school. Living off campus cut me off from even more of university social life.

My solution to my lack of social engagement was going to the activity fair to get involved. They held it near the start of the semester at the Hub. When I arrived, early in the day, attendance was sparse.

Most of the booths lacked any appeal. I signed up for an informal indoor soccer club that scheduled a few games a month. I chatted with the guys at the booth, and they were okay, but they seemed more into beer than soccer so I didn't stick around to socialize for long.

Not that I had a problem with the party scene, but it wasn't something I had ever gotten involved with. I had been an elite athlete before my injury ended that part of my life. So between my family's devotion to authentic fresh foods and my desire to stay in peak physical condition, my diet plan was a serious consideration; beer was not on the approved list for my weight training regimen.

I was getting ready to call the whole endeavor a bust when I walked past a booth draped in rainbow bunting. Two girls staffed it, their arms linked. A wiry guy with a preppy haircut and eyebrow piercing stood behind them.

I glanced at the name of the group they were representing, expecting it to be an LGBT campus group. Which I was at least willing to try. But instead, I read the word SaFE in bold green letters and then under that; it spelled out the acronym 'Society For Equality'.

"Hey, big guy, are you interested in psion rights?" the taller girl asked. She sported a shock of cotton candy pink hair swept forward off the top of her head. Her tattooed friend giggled at the overture.

The guy behind them made eye contact with me and a clipboard wiggled across the table toward me when he gestured toward me with his chin.

"Easy, Caleb, you'll scare the norm away," the tattooed one chided. The twink ignored her and leaned around the girls to give me a lingering look that left me thinking perhaps my first assessment of the booth had not been wrong; the guy was interested.

"You're not quite a norm, are you?" he said, licking his lips in a way that drew my attention to his tongue piercing.

"I'm an anchor," I said, then attempted to steer the conversation away from myself. "What does the Society for Equality do?"

"We fight for equal rights for psions," the girl with pink hair gave me a predatory grin.

"We want to abolish the psion registry," her friend said. "Also, we want workplace protections. If we add psionic status to anti-discrimination statutes, it would help. Simple changes to make life as a psion safer."

"We also propose disbanding SPIRE. Our stance is direct integration of psions into the civil services is a better option. It starts at the local level," Caleb said.

"State laws bar psions from police and fire departments in thirty states," the first girl added, she ticked off the points on her long fingers as she spoke. "And psions require a special waiver to receive teaching credentials in twenty states. In ten states, there is a ban on known anchors over the age of majority working with minors. And psions cannot serve in any of the norm branches of the uniformed services. Or work for other government agencies," she added.

"I knew some of that," I said. "I never heard of restrictions on anchors working with kids. How does that work with emergence?"

"Short answer? Kids die if they need an anchor and can't find one willing to break the law," Caleb shrugged. The gesture was not uncaring, just conveying it was a fact he had long since accepted. Thinking about that happening to Aaron when we were in high school made me shudder.

"How can that be a law?" I asked. But I knew how. Psions didn't have the same rights as norms. I'd paid more attention to the psions in my class after everything with Aaron. None of what they were saying was a surprise.

"Norms fear us," pink hair stated, "and plenty of them think anchors who want to work with kids are predators. Because they conflate the relationships between adult psions and their anchors with what the link is to us."

The tattooed girl draped her arms around her friend in a way I had become familiar with from watching other psions with their links. Psion-watching was something I had done far too much of after Aaron left, "like you two?" I asked.

"Jess and I are link bonded. For a few years now. So there is a primary link—or link bond—which is often like norm marriage. And then there are links, sometimes called partial links, which form with any relationship to a psion. Just because one relationship is sexual doesn't mean they all are. People don't talk about it as much, but familial and platonic links are important too. Most of us form partial links with the important people in our lives. From family to close friends. When I lived at home, I linked with my brother, it wasn't sexual. But it was still a primary link, he stabilized my aura. And Caleb, there," she pointed at Caleb, "linked with a platonic friend. Hell, Caleb and I have a partial link, because he's my friend."

"Yep, my primary link, Tess, and I are both in relationships with other people, but her aura fits with mine and we're good friends. I'm my boyfriend's primary link, so it's not always a reciprocal thing either. It works for us," Caleb said.

"I knew about temporary links, I guess I didn't realize you could have a long-term link that wasn't intimate."

"Oh, it is intimate, just not always sexual or romantic," Jess supplied, "so, I'm guessing you were close to a psion, if you got anchor testing?"

"I never got the official test, but yeah, my high school boyfriend was a psion."

"That's cool, so, you want to sign our petition?" Caleb asked. I smiled at the clumsy segue, but reached for the clipboard when he nudged it closer.

"Tell me about it?" I asked, glancing at the paper on the clipboard while Jess answered me.

"We're working to put an initiative before the legislature for Washington to withdraw from the psion registry. We were the first state to add psionic status as a protected class. Some companies have federal waivers to our anti-discrimination laws, so it's not perfect, but it is a start. We are planning a campaign to put an end to the waivers too, but that would require action on a national level. So we're starting with withdrawal from the registry. Or failing that, at least decriminalizing failure to register. That's the backup plan if they don't approve the first petition," Jess explained.

"Is that a big issue?" I asked, giving up the pretense of examining their form. I added my signature and filled out the other information the form asked for on a line three-quarters of the way down the page. There was a thick sheaf of completed pages under the one I was signing too. It looked like they excelled at collecting signatures, anyway.

"Em, you want to answer that?" Jess asked, taking the clipboard back from me when I offered it and the pen to her.

"Well, considering the latest data suggests only fifty percent of new psions receive medical care? Yes. It is a huge issue for those of us it impacts. The vast majority are minors when they reach emergence. Hospital staff are mandatory reporters of psionic emergence. So are public school employees. Curriculum requirements for public schools include psi-ed. But there is no standardized curriculum. Parents can opt out for their kids. And the rules exempt private schools from teaching psi-ed.

"Most psions charged with failure to register are minors at the time of the crime. Most kids don't know the legal code. Many were in no position to register. The grace period is laughably short after undergoing a medical crisis. Often without access to care. And then they are being punished over an often traumatic period in their lives. They already have enough obstacles to employment without a criminal record. Let alone these minors trying to afford the fines. It's not a reasonable burden for young psions," Em said.

"That sounds shady," I said, "how can I help get this to pass? And do you guys hold regular meetings?"

"We meet every other Thursday evening, not everyone comes to every meeting, but you're welcome to join us. We could use more anchors, our membership is often psion heavy," Em said with a pensive expression. "As to the petition, we are canvassing for signatures this weekend, if you're interested we can pass your details to Elliott, he is coordinating our signature drive. We have a few more months to get more signatures, we should have enough already, but we are aiming for a good margin over the requirements before we submit the paperwork. Just in case any are invalid."

"I'm free this weekend, and I want to help," I said. I thought of Aaron and what that kind of legislation could mean for him, and other kids like him. With soccer in my past, I needed a new purpose. Fighting for psion rights held more appeal the more I heard. And unlike the soccer bros earlier, I wanted to stick around and chat with Em, Jess and Caleb. Chat and perhaps flirt with the first cute boy who had shown an interest in me in ages.

"Have you ever linked with a psion?" Caleb asked, with a flirtatious grin. He leaned closer and I couldn't help noticing how attractive he was. He had freckles that reminded me of summers at the lake with Aaron. The way the sun brought out the little flecks of color on his pale skin. It was a fascinating contrast to my own swarthy complexion, courtesy of my Italian parentage.

"Um, almost?" I caught myself before I could get too far down memory lane and answered the question.

"Oh, that sounds like a story," Caleb leaned even further over the counter between us, "you want to share with the class?"

"It's not much of a story. Aaron, my boyfriend, turned out to be a psion. He got Cereflux injections because his PEPS symptoms scared the crap out of him and he wanted it to be over. After the procedure, his hospital anchor said I was an anchor, and that we had started to link already."

"Ah, that sounds sweet, you must've been close," Jess said, she was regarding Em with a lovey-dovey expression.

"I thought so. But then he moved across the country without even telling me. I found out from my mother because he was texting with her after he stopped answering my calls. Next thing I knew he had plastered his social media with pictures of him with his new link."

"Ouch, sounds rough," Caleb winced on my behalf.

"And yet you want to join the fight for psion rights?" Em joked, but she looked skeptical.

"Sure, just because things ended on a sour note doesn't mean I want him to suffer. And maybe if things weren't so shitty for psions he wouldn't have thought he needed to run away after his emergence," I reasoned. I believed that. Aaron might have up and disappeared on me, but I still cared about him.

"Cool. Care to stick around and get better acquainted?" Caleb asked. He eyed me up again, and it was not subtle.

"Elliott, Lynn and Tess should join us soon, so you could meet them if you stay," Em said.

"Em's our fearless leader," Caleb interjected.

"I got that impression," I chuckled. "Oh, I'm Jake, uh, Jake Moretti since I know all your names now."

"I saw that. When you signed," Caleb winked at me. "Caleb Gaetz," and he offered a hand to shake, which I knew was not standard greeting etiquette with psions, but he must have liked my aura enough to touch me. That was fine, I tried not to read too much into his lingering touch.

"I planned to check out the LGBT group next, I heard they were active? Are they around here somewhere?" I said. For all I enjoyed chatting, I knew the fair format stuck them in the booth. They were a captive audience, and I did not want to wear out my welcome. The three of them exchanged looks and a snort of laughter.

"Well, you're in luck, I'm the president of both organizations," Em threw up her hands in a tada jazz hands move, "surprise."

"So, I was not wrong in my first impressions about your booth?" I asked, amused.

"Not at all. UDub has both groups. But the overlap between campus psions and the LGBT community ended up being big enough we merged the two clubs for all intents and purposes. We focus on psion activism the first and third Thursday and LGBT issues the second and fourth. Fifth Thursday is a social hour. We split up our programming, to be inclusive of people in both groups who don't care to get involved with the other," Em said.

"That seems kind of weird," I said.

Em and Caleb laughed at my remark.

Jess smiled as she said, "you have not spent much time with psions, have you?"

"We tend not to fit in so well with societal norms," Caleb said. "Psions are more attracted to a compatible aura than any other single trait. So a lot of us identify as some stripe of bi, pan or otherwise queer. There are obvious exceptions though."

"Lots of trans folks and enbies too, the experts say it's because we put less emphasis on body stuff than norms. It's complicated," Em added.

"Makes sense. So, I guess it wouldn't be a bad idea to ask what you all's pronouns are?" I asked, self-conscious to be asking after already assigning pronouns to them all in my head, but better late than never.

Em gave me a Cheshire cat grin, "aren't you precious. I'm okay with she/her or they/them, I prefer the latter, but I don't have the energy to constantly correct casual acquaintances. Jess and I are monogamous. And I'm a telepath, grade C though, so no, I'm not reading your mind. I only get vague impressions without skin-to-skin contact."

"She/her," Jess added with a little salute, "and I'm an anchor too."

"He/him, pan, poly, I'm in a primary relationship with a guy. Elliott, so you two will meet if you're coming to canvas for signatures with us, but we are open, for dating or casual sex, if you're interested. Oh, and grade B TK."

I smiled back at Caleb, he was attractive, and he seemed like a nice guy. His confidence in putting himself out there was appealing too. I was open to casual. Finding a friend—or friends—with benefits on campus would create space from my family. As much as I loved them, I could use space.

"He/him, mostly into guys," I told them, "so, how politically active is this group?"

"We've got the petition which is our main focus right now. We've got a ton of canvassing to do and coordination with other like-minded groups," Em said.

"We also plan to do a voter registration drive. Which we will ramp up in the next few weeks to meet October deadlines for out-of-state students who want to vote absentee. And we organize rides to help people get to the polls for early voting and on election day," Jess said.

"And we do canvassing for other civil rights-related issues and candidates. SaFE also organizes protests. We have community outreach events planned, with norms and with youth to help them connect with psion resources. And Tess is working on setting up events for norms to interact with psions; if they have a face for the harm anti-psion legislation does, it can help to change hearts and minds," Caleb added.

"Is that a problem?" Em asked, arching a sculpted brow.

"Not at all. I'd like to get involved," I told her, or no—them—I had to take a second to correct myself. But I was committed to not misgendering them now that I knew their pronouns.

"We can always use active members," Caleb said. "And we aren't all work, we have fun too, right, Em?"

"The funnest fun," they agreed with a smirk, "tell him about your Halloween shindig two years ago, Caleb."

"One time. It happened once," Caleb moaned.

"What happened?" I asked, my interest piqued.

"I might have invited an empath to the party. And almost started an orgy?"

"How?"

"Empath. He didn't have an anchor. Even grade C empaths need an anchor to remain stable—Chase is grade B. So, anyway, we got carried away. I didn't realize that he was projecting until we finished."

"That's one way to put it," Jess said.

"In my defense, I was hosting the party, and we slipped away to my bedroom to do it. Also, if you're ever lucky enough to get with an empath, sex with them is the next level when they project at you, it's mind-blowing. Chase and I had fooled around before, so it didn't occur to me that the lack of warded walls inside the apartment would be a problem. Turns out, he had more range than I accounted for, so when he was getting off he was leaking lustful feelings all over the place. It was like a potent psionic aphrodisiac."

"Mm, like E, but better," Jess mused.

"It was nice," Em said.

"We tease Caleb about it," Jess said.

"That uh, sounds kind of… nonconsensual," I observed, shifting my feet with discomfort.

"Oh, no, uh, more it made everybody horny. Same as getting aroused organically. Empathic lust doesn't infringe on free choice. It was early enough that there wasn't a huge crowd yet. A few people left. And we got two anchors to go help Chase reign it in when we figured out what was going on," Jess said.

"I spent the rest of the party checking in with everyone who was there and making sure they were okay with it, it sucked. But yeah, it was all psions and they get what it's like to have your control slip, these things happen. If it's any consolation, almost everybody had the same reaction as Jess, that it was hot."

"It was worse when Chase and Caleb came back out to rejoin the party. Then Chase realized we'd all felt his orgasm. He almost swamped us all with his embarrassment about it. That was uncomfortable, poor guy. Everyone who noticed pitying him only made it worse, too much input for him to handle," Jess said.

"It's the psion equivalent of Chase getting loud during sex. That plus a misunderstanding about the thickness of the walls, and Caleb's nearest and dearest heard them doing it," Jess said. Her explanation framed it so I could better understand. I saw the humor in the situation. Not my sense of humor, but more benign than I had first assumed.

"I can't imagine why he lost my number after that," Caleb said, rueful.

"You should have known better," Em said with no sympathy.

"Sure, but I mean, can you blame me? Empaths are as hot as they are rare. And Chase is a good guy."

"Not arguing," Jess smiled. "It's a shame he didn't give you another shot."

"Hey, what are we talking about?" A new guy approached from behind the booth, coming up behind Caleb and leaning over his shoulder to give him a peck on the cheek.

"Caleb's Halloween surprise," Jess supplied.

The newcomer paled as he said, "oh that. Right. Poor Chase, it mortified him."

"Elliott, this is Jake, he's thinking about joining SaFE," Caleb said, gesturing at me. The two of them exchanged a look I couldn't read. Caleb squeezed Elliot's hand in a reassurance. Then Caleb said, "Jake, this is Elliott, my boyfriend. He's a telepath like Em."

"Not quite like Em, I get general impressions more than true telepathy. Em can read minds. I'd be a grade D if the grading went that low," Elliott said with a self-deprecating shake of his head. He stayed where he stood, arms wrapped around Caleb, possessive.

"Nice to meet you. I'm an anchor," I said, forgoing handshakes again. Psions didn't do unsolicited touch with strangers. I'd heard the phrase touch sensitivity thrown around as an explanation.

"I think we've got our hooks in him," Caleb said, "he even volunteered for canvassing duty."

"Sweet!" Elliott said. "I love it when I get a hot guy's number without even having to meet him first," he added with a saucy wink. Caleb laughed and Em snorted.

"Down, boy," Em said.

"So, I guess I should get going instead of monopolizing your time, huh?" I said.

"Or you could join us back here and we can keep chatting while we work the booth," Em said.

I hesitated, torn between taking advantage of the opportunity to solidify the tentative overture of friendship and not wanting to overstay my welcome. These people seemed close. I couldn't help feeling like a fifth wheel. But it was the most engaging conversation I had been a part of in ages.

"Or," Caleb drew out the word and gave Em a sidelong glance. "We could get out of here and leave the booth in Em and Jess's capable hands."

"Elliott just got here," Jess pointed out with good humor.

"Lynn and Tess are coming any minute," Caleb wheedled.

Em snorted, "or you and Elliott want to be. You realize this isn't a pick up fair, right?"

"Please, Em?" Caleb turned puppy dog eyes on them and I was sure he would be trouble.

"I'm not the one you need to convince," Em said. They gestured toward me, their meaning plain.

Elliott shared a look with Caleb, then turned to give me a thorough once-over.

"Did Caleb mention he is superb with that tongue ring?" Elliott said.

"He did not," I said, amused at the byplay. Their offer also intrigued me.

"Well, I'm sure he could give you a demonstration. If you're interested," Elliott said.

"And that's your cue to leave, guys. If you want to pick up tricks, then you can do it on your time," Em shooed them away.

"What do you say, Jake? Want to come with us?" Caleb raised an eyebrow in question.

"Both of you together?" I asked, though I suspected as much.

Caleb and Elliott exchanged another look and then chorused, "Heck yes."

"I've never done this," I said. But I was interested. The lack of interested partners had limited my experience with guys at my high school. I had fooled around since Aaron left, but my experience amounted to a discrete exchange of blow jobs. I lacked Caleb and Elliott's easy confidence in that area.

"We'll go easy on you, the first time anyway," Caleb's grin was lecherous.

"We'll take good care of you," Elliott said, his gaze lingering over my body now I had expressed an interest.

"It won't make working together with SaFE weird?" I asked, hedging.

"Not if you don't make it weird," Caleb said with a shrug. "No strings attached, just a good time between friends, no pressure though."

"We aren't suggesting a permanent triad right off the bat. We are offering sex, and friendship, maybe casual dating, that work for you?" Elliott said. "No expectations."

"Sounds good," I decided, and it did. Something about Caleb intrigued me. He was charismatic. If he and his boyfriend were into threesomes, then I could get on board. My main reservation was SaFE.

I hoped the club would be a good fit as a social outlet. If I didn't live up to their expectations in bed, I figured that could ruin a good thing. But I hadn't made a firm commitment to SaFE yet. So the risk seemed worth it. Especially since it seemed like this was nothing new to their friends. The logical conclusion was they had picked up a third before.

Em rolled their eyes, but they sounded more amused than annoyed when they said, "go on you guys. Jess and I can handle the booth until Lynn and Tess arrive. Jake, I hope to see more of you!"

"I plan to see more of him," Caleb said. "So much more."

"And soon too," Elliott added in a low undertone.

"You guys are ridiculous," I shook my head at their jokes. Caleb and Elliott came around the edge of the booth, each of them taking one of my hands. I let them lead me away from the activity fair.

Chapter 9

Jake

As we headed back to Caleb and Elliot's apartment we chatted. They informed me they were third-year students. It was surreal, going back to their apartment for sex after a few moments acquaintance, but I couldn't deny that Caleb's tongue ring intrigued me. We paused near the door to their building.

"So, before you come inside, in the interest of full disclosure," Caleb said, "I'm poz, that going to be a problem for you?"

I considered for a moment, blinking at him in surprise. He didn't look sick. I kicked myself for the thought—why would he?

"Um, no?" I said.

Elliott grinned and ruffled my hair, "good answer."

Caleb smiled as his swept open the door and gestured for Elliott and I to go ahead, "better than Elliott's reaction when I told him. I was sure he hated me."

"In my defense you sprung it on me," Elliott said.

"So, um, what information should I know? Or how does this work?" I asked as we entered an empty stairwell.

"Well, I'm undetectable and on medication. El is on PrEP, just in case. If this becomes a regular occurrence, then you should consider it too. As a precaution. As long as my viral load stays undetectable the virus is untransmissible."

"We still play it safe though. Condoms, even for oral, when we bring in a third," Elliott said.

"So, you guys have done this before?" I asked in the hallway outside their apartment.

"A few times. We haven't found the right fit for a more lasting arrangement yet," Caleb said.

"Caleb can be a little overprotective, and I'm picky," Elliott said as he unlocked their door.

"El," Caleb said in a tone that told me there was an unspoken subtext there. Conversation lulled as we all removed our shoes and Elliot and Caleb hung their keys on a hook beside the door.

"So, uh, what's the plan?" I asked, nervous when they both turned to face me. They exchanged a long look and Caleb licked his lips. Once again putting the shiny ball of his piercing on full display. What would it feel like pressed against my dick?

"That depends on your preferences," Caleb said, "you want to bottom for El? Or you can fuck me. Or we can start with blowjobs and let things progress?"

My mouth worked, but words deserted me. It was like the mental image of sex with these two had short-circuited my brain. I froze up at the prospect. This was the closest I'd been to having sex since the night Aaron got sick. Except for a handful of blowjobs on the down-low with a guy I knew from soccer camps. I wasn't sure I could go through with it.

I mean, my dick was fine with the idea. Already straining against my jeans. But I still felt hesitant.

Part of me resented the ache in my heart at the thought this would be an irrevocable admission that Aaron wasn't coming back. The first step toward getting over him. I wanted that. This. But another part wasn't quite ready. Couldn't let go of wanting more of a connection for my first time. Which was stupid. I was coming up on my twentieth birthday and I didn't want to be a virgin forever. Or mostly a virgin. Whatever. I opened my mouth to accept Caleb's offer, but words failed me.

Before I could tell Caleb I was open to whatever, Elliott took pity on me. Perhaps he was more of a telepath than he gave himself credit for, or I was just bad at hiding my angst and inner turmoil. Then again, it didn't take a mind reader to notice me staring at them like a deer in the headlights.

114

"Or we can all chill on the couch and watch a movie. If you're having second thoughts," Elliott said. Caleb gave a soft rueful chuckle.

"Or that," Caleb said, "didn't mean to come on too strong, big guy."

"Sorry, I'm not…"

"No need to apologize. Caleb can be a pushy bastard, but he won't pressure you for sex," Elliott said. He ran his hand down my upper arm as he walked past me into the kitchen, "you want a drink?"

"Water?"

"Sure, want ice in it?"

"Either way is fine."

"No ice then," Elliott said. Caleb brushed past me to plop onto the couch. He flicked on the television and pulled up a streaming service.

"Preferences?"

I flushed, reminded of the other preferences he had asked me about, "I'm not picky."

"Cartoons it is," Caleb hit play on an animated movie I hadn't seen. Something with sentient food and a raunchy sense of humor. Elliott returned, pressing a cool glass of water into my right hand and taking my left to lead me over to the couch.

"Don't be nervous," Elliott said in a gentle voice, "if you only want to watch television all afternoon, we can still be friends."

"And if you take me up on that blow job, then we can be friends with benefits," Caleb said. He directed a suggestive eyebrow waggle at me. But he scooted aside so there was plenty of room for me to sit between them on the couch without being too close to either of them. I couldn't help a nervous chuckle at the joke. Elliott reached across me to shove his boyfriend.

"You're incorrigible. Don't scare off my newest signature collector, Caleb. That would annoy me."

"Wouldn't want you pissed off," Caleb said.

"Damn right. So be quiet and let me hear the show."

They made comments throughout the movie. Both attempted to include me in their playful banter. Caleb ended up sprawled across both Elliott and I by the time the credits rolled.

"That was awful," Elliott commented.

"Sure, but the jokes—priceless," Caleb said.

"Were you watching the same movie as us?" I asked.

"What he said," Elliott said.

"Oh, come on, you can't go wrong with dick jokes."

"I think you just subjected us to a two hour demonstration to the contrary, now, up," Elliott shoved Caleb's feet off of his lap. "I need to pee."

Caleb stood and stretched. Elliott shuffled down the hall to the bathroom. With them both up, sitting on their couch became awkward.

"You want to join us for dinner?" Caleb offered.

"Um, wouldn't that be awkward?" I asked. But I wanted to accept. I was enjoying the camaraderie. It was easy to forget they were a couple, and I was the odd man out here.

"Nah, El likes you," Caleb said, "he let you touch him."

"Huh?"

"During the movie, he was leaning on you."

"So were you," I said.

Caleb waved away my comment, "sure, but I'm a giant slut, everyone says so. El is more particular. He likes you. So you're welcome to stay for dinner. As a friend. We said no strings or expectations and we meant it."

"I figured you were being polite."

"Nope. Let me clarify, the only expectation we have of you is honesty. I'll start—I invited you home because I am attracted to you. El agreed to join us because he likes your aura and has been hoping to find a regular third we both like. We invited you to stay after you got cold feet because we wanted to get to know you. And I invited you to stay for dinner because we are enjoying spending time with you. Your turn."

"I am enjoying getting to know you guys too. It's been a while since I had someone to watch a shitty movie with."

"Bad breakup with the ex?"

I shrugged.

"And you still love him? Is that why you changed your mind about sex?"

"No. I…"

"No pressure to share, but I'll listen if you want to talk about it."

"I haven't done this before."

"No?"

"Well, okay, I've tried oral."

"But not anal. Noted. Do you want to try or no?"

I shrugged.

"If you want to try it, we can. If not, we can do other things. Have dinner with us, I'm making pasta tonight, I have a sudden hankering for Italian," Caleb said, and he gave me an exaggerated wink.

Elliott guffawed as he rejoined us, "incorrigible," he said with a shake of his head.

"Pasta sounds good," I said, thankful that my summer tan hid most of my blush.

"And will you stay after?" Caleb asked.

"Don't pressure him," Elliott chided.

"Yeah, who am I to deny your cravings?" I said.

Caleb chuckled and slapped me on the back before ducking into the kitchen.

"Do you game?" Elliott asked gesturing to their extensive video game collection.

"Shouldn't we help him in the kitchen?"

"Not unless you want to annoy him. Caleb's particular about his kitchen." Elliot said.

"I heard that!" Caleb interjected, he waved a knife in emphasis. Elliott rolled his eyes, but his smile belied any real annoyance.

"Sounds like my Nonna," I said sotto voce. Elliott laughed and handed me a controller.

"So what do you want to play?"

"Do you have FIFA?"

Elliott groaned, "oh no, the muscles should have given it away, we've picked up a jock, haven't we? Do you play soccer?"

"I did until I busted my knee. Career ending injury and all that."

"Ouch," Elliott crossed to the shelf of games beside the television. He rummaged around for a minute before pulling out a dusty case, "you're in luck. We appear to have inherited a copy of an old version of FIFA from Tess. She unloaded a bunch of her old gaming gear on us a few months ago."

"Fun."

"Yeah, so, you have a favorite team or something?"

"I mean, for watching, Forza Italia, right? But for the game, Barcelona has the best stats…" I said. With my soccer buddies that would have started a debate and I could have gone on about the respective stats of my favorite teams and players. Elliott listened to my answer, but he looked like his eyes might glaze over if I launched into a spiel about player and team stats. So I changed tack, "Sorry, I have a thing for soccer."

"No problem," Elliott said, "but I've only played FIFA once."

"That's fine," I navigated the selection menus to start a game. I put Elliott on the same team as me so we could play against a computer since it was clear sports games were not his thing.

"So, I'm glad you're staying for dinner," Elliott commented while I was setting up our first match.

"Yeah?"

"Yeah. Caleb's been hoping to find someone with a compatible aura for a while now. Ever since I mentioned I wanted to try a third."

"And you like my aura?"

"It's nice," he said, "peaceful. A little melancholy? But nice. I think we could fit together, the three of us."

"And you want that?"

"Yes, we agreed to find a compatible third person because it's something we both want, okay? Caleb might have been the one making the offer, but it's coming from both of us. I thought you should know that. In case it matters to your decision."

"I appreciate that. Thanks. Caleb made his intentions clear, but I wasn't sure if you were just following his lead or what. It helps to know you want it too."

"Yeah, he's a force of nature," Elliott said with unmistakable admiration.

I chuckled, "He is. And you ground him, from what I've seen. I think you guys complement each other."

"And we both like you."

"The feeling is mutual," I said, and it was strange to let myself take more than a passing interest. But I had. Although we had just met, the two of them put me at ease. I wasn't sure I liked the sense of vulnerability the admission engendered in me, so I changed the subject. "Now, let's kick ass."

"Sure, tell me what to do," Elliott picked up his controller, and I hit start. He was hopeless at the game, but he was a good sport about it. He tried to follow my directions about what to do, and he laughed at how into it I got.

Elliott and I played a few rounds of virtual soccer until Caleb call us to the table for pasta primavera and salad. It was a meal my mom would have been proud to present to guests. Caleb's choice of menu surprised me with all the veggies and lack of meat. The meal didn't resemble what I expected from two college guys.

"This looks wonderful," I said when we sat.

"You mean it looks healthy," Caleb teased.

"No, great," I said, "unexpected, but good. I figured you meant spaghetti and jarred pasta sauce, maybe meatballs."

"Like I would feed a vegetarian meat and an Italian store bought sauce, do I look like I want to insult you both?"

"We try to eat healthy, and like he said, I'm a vegetarian," Elliott said.

"That's right, so, the only meat and balls to grace his pretty mouth are mine. And perhaps yours."

"Let's ignore the blatant solicitation of our guest," Elliott said, "this looks good. I didn't know you got more zucchini."

"Picked it up on the way home from class earlier."

"I think we might have some frozen garlic bread too?"

"Really, El? You are offering our hot date garlic?"

Elliott rolled his eyes.

"Um, no thanks, if the offer for after dinner activities is still on the table, I think I'd rather not have garlic breath," I said.

"It's not so bad if we all have garlic bread," Elliot said with a pout.

"You can have it, hun, I can't speak for Jake, but I'll still kiss you."

"That's true love right there," I teased. Elliot laughed.

"Yeah. He's a keeper," he said, "do you mind?"

"Nah, you can always brush your teeth if we will be kissing."

"I like kissing," Caleb said, "so, does that mean you're down for some oral action after dinner, big guy?"

"Yeah," I said.

"Great," Caleb said.

"I still want the garlic bread, if that isn't a deal-breaker?" Elliott said, he looked sheepish.

"It's fine," I said, unable to deny the guy when he gave me the puppy dog eyes.

Elliott stood, leaning down to kiss Caleb. He gave me an appraising look that made me think he was considering offering me a kiss too. But he settled for ruffling my hair on his way to the freezer to retrieve a slice of garlic bread, which he popped into the toaster. And that ended speculation over our plans for after we ate.

Dinner with Elliott and Caleb was pleasant. The food tasted delicious. Our conversation was light and peppered with banter. It reminded me of meals with my family. Caleb and Elliott's interactions reminded me of my parents, or Zio Gregorio and his husband. From the looks they exchanged to the way they seemed to anticipate each other's needs. Their mutual devotion was obvious.

They had a shared history and their affection spilled over into their words and casual touches. But unlike other couples I knew, they kept drawing me into their interactions too. Like when Caleb handed me the salt and pepper he let his fingers linger on mine the same way he did with Elliott over the butter dish. It was strange, but pleasant. And it made me think.

For all his flirting, Caleb had a clear passion for psion rights. And he seemed committed to Elliott. He wasn't just looking to score an easy lay, contrary to my initial thoughts.

As for Elliott, he came across as aloof, but I got the sense his demeanor masked hidden depths. A distant mask to protect a fragile heart. And their auras fit with mine.

I knew the sensation wasn't the same for anchors. That the tentative wisps of Elliott that reached out to me and then curled in tight felt different to him. Or that Caleb's aura, nosing at me like a brazen dog sniffing an interesting stranger told him something about me.

Their presence was reminiscent of the satisfaction found in fitting the last piece of a challenging puzzle into place. An acknowledgement that the piece fit. For psions it was something more. A sense of completion they craved. I'd heard psions compare finding a compatible aura to sex or a high. And it had the same effect on their brains from what I understood. Something to do with dopamine and oxytocin and emotional bonding.

So while I could learn about a person from the way their aura interacted with mine, it connoted about as much intrinsic excitement as noticing brown hair, or a pretty smile. For them, finding an aura they both liked was more intimate. And it showed in the way they kept drawing me closer.

I thought their enthusiasm might make it easy to fall into a relationship with them. And the idea held appeal. Only, I wasn't sure I was ready for the level of commitment inherent with an anchor bonding to a psion.

After we ate, I volunteered for cleanup duty. In part, buying time to consider. Elliott put away our leftovers and then excused himself. Caleb helped me put away the clean dishes, by the time we finished Elliott had returned. He stood close enough I could smell the fresh mint of his breath.

I didn't think twice when Caleb hugged me from behind and nuzzled my cheek.

"What do you want to do now, big guy?" he asked, dropping a kiss on the corner of my mouth. And what did I need to consider? They said no strings, so why shouldn't I allow myself some pleasure? I was certain Aaron hadn't been celibate, so why should I?

"More of that?" I offered, I turned my head to catch his mouth, but he pulled away to smirk at me. Elliot was watching us with interest, but he leaned against the counter, waiting for some cue.

"Just kissing?" Caleb asked.

I ground back against Caleb, and the hardness of his groin against my ass sent a jolt of pleasure through me. I liked having his arms wrapped around me too. He kissed me, then evaded my lips when I tried to pursue more.

"Nuh uh, tell us what you want first."

"I want to kiss you."

Caleb rewarded me with another brief kiss.

"That all? Elliott too, or just me?"

Caleb let me grind against him, but he held still and gave me a chance to answer.

"More than kissing. I want your mouth on me. Both of you."

Elliott stepped in close at my answer, he cupped a hand over my dick and stroked me, then stepped even closer when he noticed how hard I was. He pressed his thigh between my legs and kissed my neck.

"You can have us both, how do you want us?" Caleb asked, implacable even though I could feel how aroused he was too.

I shook my head, I couldn't think let alone speak while sandwiched between them. It took all my restraint not to hump Elliott's leg.

"I don't know."

"You want me to suck your dick?"

"Mhm," Elliott moaned into my skin and I shuddered. I rocked against him, helpless to stop myself. Elliott pushed into me, making a sound of encouragement.

"Please," I said.

"So good. Your aura meshes with ours, Jay. You feel it too, huh, El?" Caleb asked, he rolled his hips into me, pushing me against Elliott again and I liked it. I doubted I would last long between Elliott and Caleb.

"Mm," Elliott moaned.

"You with us, hun?" Caleb reached around me to stroke Elliott's face, encouraging eye contact. Elliott blinked and then nodded.

"Yeah, I'm okay. This is good," he said.

"You good too, Jay?" Caleb asked. I blinked at the nickname, but decided I liked it, liked all of this.

"Great. Kiss me again?"

"Bedroom first," Caleb said. He released me and gave me a gentle push into Elliott's arms. My back felt cold at the loss of his heat. Until Elliott kissed me and I almost got lost in it.

"Bedroom," Caleb repeated.

Elliott pulled back and made a face at Caleb, but he took my hand and led me down the hall. Caleb followed on our heels.

When we got to the bedroom Elliott pivoted and pulled me in for another kiss, pausing just before our lips touched so I had to close the distance. I did. His kisses were rougher, more assertive than in the kitchen.

Where Caleb let me guide things, Elliott pushed into my mouth and took what he wanted. His grip on my wrists conveyed a sense of restraint. I liked it. It turned out, I liked it a lot. I could imagine the mild-mannered Elliott—who was becoming a friend—manhandling me in the bedroom. It was a major turn-on. Who knew?

Then Caleb pressed up behind me and Elliott broke off our kiss and met Caleb's lips over my shoulder, I made an undignified noise of protest.

"We aren't forgetting about you," Caleb whispered near my ear when their lips parted. Elliott drew me to their bed, we stumbled with trying to kiss and move at the same time.

"Lose the pants? or no?" He asked. I nodded and then scrambled to shuck off my jeans and underwear. Elliott unzipped too. He made eye contact with Caleb and said, "you want to suck us, babe?"

Caleb smirked, "that what you both want?"

"Yeah," Elliott agreed, he seated himself on the edge of the bed and stroked his erection, "you, on your knees for us sounds perfect, right, Jake?"

"yeah," I said. My mouth turned dry at the prospect and my dick had never been harder. I felt grateful we were sitting, I wasn't certain I could stand just then. Caleb stood in front of us while he stripped. I heard a wooden drawer sliding and the crinkle of a condom wrapper. But it didn't register that Caleb was using his TK until two condoms and a bottle of lube floated past me. Elliott took them both and suited up, then he smoothed the second condom onto my dick while he distracted me with more kisses.

The heat of Caleb's mouth closing over the head of my cock was almost enough to make me come. Elliott's tongue invading my mouth, his fierce grip on my hair, holding me in place had me on edge. And the things Caleb did with his tongue had me moaning and bucking. Time seemed immaterial as I got lost in sensation. I could discern their auras. Something I didn't have much practice with, but with the close contact we couldn't avoid it. Their auras twined with mine, like a pair of feral cats marking their territory. Like a claiming. And I welcomed it. Embracing everything they had to give me.

I had my hands tangled in Caleb's hair, thrusting into his talented mouth. Elliott had pressed me into the bed, half on top of me as we kissed and his lover sucked my dick. Caleb knelt between my legs, one hand on himself and the other stroking Elliott.

It was all too much. I came way too soon. Caleb didn't pull away until I had recovered enough to get embarrassed at my lack of stamina. I unclenched my fist from his hair. He grinned at me as he dealt with the condom and tucked me back into my briefs, all efficiency.

"Good?" he asked.

"Mm," I made a sound instead of a proper response. Elliott was kissing and nipping at my neck, he seemed oblivious to the fact I had gotten off already.

"Good, stay in bed," Caleb directed me. Then he transferred his attentions to Elliott's erection, and I got to observe the full mastery of his technique when unfettered by my hands in his hair. Elliott clutched me tighter. His teeth scraped against my shoulder and he gave a muffled shout when he came. His whole body jerked and convulsed with the force of his release.

I was almost scared of his intensity, except with him plastered to my chest I could feel his aura. Without understanding how I knew it, I could perceive his deep sense of wellbeing. It was comfort and peace and completion. When it was over he nuzzled into my chest and fell asleep.

Caleb gave Elliott an indulgent smile when his soft snoring drifted to our ears. He crawled onto the bed to spoon Elliott from behind. I realized that Caleb still hadn't come, and I considered offering to help him out but before I could he gave a contented sigh and sought my hand.

"Want to stay the night?" Caleb asked.

"Mhm, don't know if my legs will work with how hard I came," I said, still muzzy.

Caleb snorted, "El too, he didn't break the skin did he?"

"Huh?" I touched my shoulder, over the spot where a forming bruise ached. Right where Elliott had bitten me during his climax. My fingers came away clean of any traces of blood. "Uh, nope, not bleeding."

"He has a thing for biting necks. I swear he was a vampire in a former life or something," Caleb said. He carded his fingers through Elliott's hair with affection as he spoke.

"Does he always zonk out after?" I asked. Caleb tensed.

I squirmed into a more comfortable position, on my back with Elliott's head cradled on my chest. He still had one of his legs thrown over my hips and his arms around me. Caleb readjusted too, so he remained wrapped around Elliott.

"No. Not usually," Caleb lapsed into silence for a long time. I had drifted close to sleep myself when he added, "he has nightmares after sex, sometimes."

"Oh," I said. His words sent a chill through me.

Caleb sighed, "if I thought it would be an issue I would have had him tell you before. He isn't one for cuddling after, the touch sensitivity, you know what that is?"

"Yeah, psion thing, like a stranger's touch hurts your aura or psion senses?"

"Close enough. Yeah. It's too much for him once the endorphins wear off, but I guess you're compatible with us. So. He has PTSD. It's not my place to share the details, but if he wakes up shouting, or acts disoriented or weird, that's why."

"What should I do if that happens?"

"Follow his lead. Don't restrain him. He has never gotten violent with me, sometimes he gets sick though. So, try not to get puked on? Or you can sneak away before he wakes up if it's more than you bargained for."

"I'm fine where I am, as long as you both don't mind me staying."

Caleb snorted, "I think El's made it clear he likes you right there too. Stay. Just, if we're doing this, try to be sure you can handle our baggage. I don't want him to get hurt if you change your mind. He's had too many people walk away already."

"Can we take it slow? I, uh, don't even know if we're talking about casual sex or dating or what this even is."

Caleb squeezed my hand, "today was a date. You can tell based of the movie and dinner before the sex. Another clue is the cuddling and sleeping over after even though it's not late and no one is drunk. You are spending the night?"

"Yeah."

"Good. And we can take it as slow as you like. Like we said, no pressure, no strings."

"Not sure how that works. Dating a couple I mean. Whatever will I put on social media?"

Caleb snorted, "It's complicated? Seriously though, there aren't rules. If you date or sleep with other people, it's between you and them. Elliott and I agreed to talk about sex with other people before it happens. And he lets me know how much detail he wants during the discussion. If this gets serious, then he might want a similar arrangement with you. I would feel more comfortable about sex if you went on PrEP too. Just in case. Accidents can happen. If my numbers change, I would hate to expose you. El thinks I'm paranoid, but I worry."

"Noted. Do you both date other people too?"

"I have a handful of other lovers. El and I have been seeking a third for a couple months, no one's been the right fit until you though. I know he isn't seeing anyone else one-on-one. Speaking of which, what are your thoughts on exclusivity? You get an opinion too."

I considered, "I always just assumed I'd be in an exclusive couple. Never considered the dynamics of a threesome before, or whatever you call this. But I enjoyed our date if that's what this was. I like you and Elliott. And if you have an arrangement that works, I can live with you seeing other people."

"A triad," Caleb said, "if we are talking a long-term relationship. El is my primary relationship, but I have others. El comes first. That's the way it has to be, I'm his family. El has no other entanglements, and he prefers it that way. I don't mind if you two want to have sex without me, but we will have to discuss logistics and expectations with Elliott when he wakes up. I'm open to anything from casual sex to a potential poly-fi arrangement. Elliott mentioned that his eventual goal is a polyfidelity situation.

"Okay, so poly-fi refers to polyfidelity?"

"Yes."

"And it means?"

"What it sounds like, a poly relationship where all parties expect fidelity or exclusivity within the group."

"So a traditional relationship, except with multiple people."

"Yep, and similar to monogamy, we wouldn't jump to exclusivity without getting to know each other better first. We will see if all our desires are compatible. Think it over and we can discuss with Elliott. Perhaps over brunch?"

"If you're cooking, I will be glad to stay for breakfast. Don't tell my Nonna, but your primavera rivals hers."

Caleb laughed, "I'm flattered."

"You should be. If Nonna Varone heard me say so she might never talk to me again. Cliche as it sounds, pasta is serious in my family."

"You're joking."

"Scout's honor. Nonna—that is my grandma on mom's side—didn't talk to Zia Allegra or my mom for a solid six months once. Over a compliment on Mom's cooking."

"Are you serious?"

"Nope, Zia complimented my mom's lasagna by saying 'it's the best I've ever tasted,' in front of Nonna. It was this whole ridiculous thing. And your primavera got me into bed, so don't underestimate the power of pasta."

"That is an impressive grudge to hold," Caleb chuckled, "but I think you would have slept with us regardless of my cooking skills."

"Maybe."

We lay in a silence punctuated by Elliott's soft snores for a while.

"You falling asleep on me big guy?"

"Mmph."

"Good night then," Caleb patted my hand.

I was on the brink of sleep when Caleb extricated himself from Elliott and me. I heard him rummaging around, felt the warmth of the blanket he tucked around us. Elliott burrowed closer against me. I felt his aura burrowing into mine. As though he sought a link that wasn't there yet.

He mumbled in his sleep, but nothing intelligible came out. Caleb brushed kisses to both our foreheads before slipping out of the room. I drifted off to the muted sounds of a video game on the television in the living room and Elliott's even breathing.

Chapter 10

Aaron

My first day of classes at Yale burst the happy psi-positive bubble that Riverton Academy had wrapped around me. Overall, I enjoyed my classes. I liked university and the part of New Haven I lived in was all right. My plans for the future came crashing down because of a class I had dismissed as pointless.

A silly intro to the university course, more a retention program than an actual class. Required freshman education. Nothing that boarding school veterans like my roommates and I needed. Or that was what my friends all agreed when discussing our schedules. I thought it would be redundant since Riverton had accustomed me to taking responsibility for myself. I'd lived on my own for years now.

There were two reasons I didn't skip it. The first was that it was convenient since it was in the same building as my previous class. Second, I thought the small group setting might be nice. An easy way to form new friendships on campus. The first matter of business was introducing ourselves, we all shared a little about ourselves. When it was my turn, I gave a casual greeting.

"Hi, I'm Aaron Anderson. I'm from Seattle, but I've been living in Connecticut for two years now. Out in Woodhaven. I am a grade C telekinetic, and I am majoring in psychology, with a minor in business. My plan is to pursue a career as a social worker."

"Nice to meet you, Aaron," the facilitator said with a frown. "You and I should have a quick chat after introductions."

"Okay," I agreed, I fidgeted in my chair, unsure why he singled me out, but suspecting it related to my psionic status. I had been a psion long enough to half expect it anytime I wasn't in a pro-psion space, like Riverton or Eagle House.

My school records contained that information since I was on the registry. There was no point in trying to hide my TK. The summons to a private chat had me distracted and irritable for the rest of the introductions so I only paid minimal attention to them. Or the instructions for the icebreaker game that came next.

The facilitator passed out bingo sheets with typical icebreaker questions printed in each box. I was thankful he granted me a reprieve from playing the silly twenty questions game when he gestured me over to his desk. I stood and approached him.

"What's the matter?" I asked. His clear discomfort over our conversation only bolstered my confidence I knew what was coming.

"Aaron, are you aware of Connecticut regulations regarding social workers?"

"I mean, I'll need a master's degree, and I have to work my butt off, and take an exam to get licensed. It's years down the road, I know that," I said.

I looked into the requirements. I'd even looked at the bachelor's degree social work programs offered at other schools. My ultimate decision was to complete my undergrad at Yale. Then I would consider a master's programs.

My motivation was to avoid the inevitable disowning had I declined my admission at Yale. And Mrs. England had agreed with my logic. She assured me the extra life experience and educational background would only help me be a better social worker.

The facilitator drew my attention with a heavy sigh.

"I could be mistaken, but I think social workers are among the many professions for which psions and registered anchors are ineligible for licensure in Connecticut. In fact, only a handful of states license psions. And since you won't be able to get licensed, most programs won't admit a registered psion. Not even in places you can apply for a license."

So it wasn't what I had feared. It was much worse.

"Wait, you mean I can't work with kids and other vulnerable populations because I'm a psion? Why the hell not?"

"I didn't make the rules," he held up his hands in a placating gesture, and then continued in a more sympathetic tone. "But I thought you should be aware before you got too far down the path. The only reason I know about it is that my brother is a psion. He only discovered he couldn't get a teaching certification when he applied for it. No one bothered to tell him that his degree would only be useful in a few states or at a private psion institution.

"The whole ordeal got him interested in what other regulations are in place and if I recall, he mentioned social work is one area that does not allow psions to practice."

"But psions, and psion youth in particular, are among those most in need of social workers. How can they justify not allowing the people in the best position to understand our needs to help? It makes no sense," I protested.

"I agree with you, but the laws do not. The PEEA established the states' rights to regulate psions outside of those rights explicitly delineated under the act."

"How did I not know this?"

It was a rhetorical question though. Driven by the knowledge I had received a better education than most regarding psion legislation. Because Riverton was a psion specific school. We had entire courses on psion history, including a section on the PEEA. I should have learned this.

"It's not common knowledge, the laws passed as a later amendment, under the guise of protecting children from unsavory influences," he said. He looked like he might want to pat my hand or some other gesture of comfort, but he refrained. "For what it's worth, I'm sorry to have to tell you about it. But my brother wished he found out sooner. So I thought better your hear it now than after four plus years of school."

"Yeah, thanks."

"My brother got involved with the Society for Equality after he found out about these laws. Have you heard of SaFE? They fight for reform.

There is a student branch of the organization on campus. I can give you their information if you have an interest in joining."

"Thanks, I might check it out. I appreciate the heads up," I thanked him despite my vexation at the news.

"No problem, and again, I'm sorry to be the bearer of bad news," he said, his sympathy sounding genuine.

"Not your fault," I pasted on my biggest fake smile.

With a pang, it hit me I hadn't experienced the need to play at happiness in ages. It was a bittersweet revelation. Realizing I hadn't needed to pretend at Riverton. But it still sucked to be only a day outside of my high school experiences and already struck square with anti-psion sentiment.

I went through the motions of the icebreaker bingo game. But I didn't have my heart in it. Anyone who knew me well would have seen straight through me. But my new classmates were none the wiser as I smiled and joked my way through the remainder of the class.

I cranked up the happy-go-lucky persona that attracted casual friends with ease while also keeping them at arm's length. And I was thankful it was the last class of my day so I could go back to the apartment and crash with my phone.

Once ensconced in my room, I felt safe to let the bad news sink in. I returned a text from Mrs. Moretti to tell her that my first day had gone all right. I sent her a goofy selfie I had taken in front of one of the elegant old buildings on campus earlier in the day. It was from before everything turned to shit, so my playful expression was genuine.

Then I looked up the laws my facilitator mentioned. And he was right. I might get a job in the social work field—with connections and luck—but licensing was out of my grasp in Connecticut. And my immediate follow up thought was if the laws needed to change then I should be a lawyer.

At first glance, it seemed feasible. But a few hours of painstaking research proved otherwise. I had to dig into message boards for aspiring lawyers to reveal the problem. The bar in most states functioned on a 'psions need not apply' basis. So I had stumbled upon yet another instance of psions excluded from a profession.

It was not outright illegal for psions to practice law, but it was a battle I didn't have the energy to engage. Perhaps if I felt passionate about it, the hassle might have been worthwhile. But my motivation was I hated all the restrictions on what I could do because I woke up one day with a terrifying medical condition.

I only wanted to help teens like the ones at Eagle House. Because I could so easily have been one of them.

Mrs. Moretti texted me back a few hours later. When I didn't reply to her texts to her satisfaction, my phone rang. I picked up with a sigh.

"*Ciao, bello,*" she said.

"Hi, Mom," I said, aiming for a light tone, trying not to let my anger and frustration come through in my voice.

"Don't you 'hi, Mom' me, what's wrong, *caro mio?*" she chastised. I envisioned the concern on her face from hearing her voice alone. A longing to see her struck me, powerful enough to bring the burn of unshed tears to my eyes. Today had sucked.

"Did you know psions can't work with children in most states and that we're barred from many professions?" I asked. I teetered on the verge of a breakdown. My leg jittered, out of my conscious control as I talked. So I got up to pace off the restless energy.

"I was not aware, no, does that include social work?"

"Yeah," I held back the emotion, "it does."

"Does that list of states include Washington?"

"I'm not sure," I admitted. It never occurred to me to check.

"Why don't you look into it. It's okay if you need to come home, all right? We've missed you," she said.

"My parents…" I trailed off, the protest sounded weak even to my own ears.

"Carlo and I still consider you like one of our own, Aaron. You have family here who will help you get on your feet if you decide that Connecticut isn't for you anymore," she said, earnest.

"What about Jake?" And that protest was more legitimate since I hadn't reached out to him in the past two years. This despite staying in touch with his parents and even chatting with Sofia and Luca sometimes.

"What about him? Neither of you talks about it, but whatever bad blood exists between the two of you is between the two of you. Jacopo knows we still talk, he gave his blessing when I asked how he felt about it. He understands that we've all known you most of your life too. You babysat Luca and Sofia. You ate at my dinner table for over ten years, came on family vacations with us, that means something. We miss you, and we care about you," she sounded genuine. It made my heart ache to know I had people who cared about me back in Seattle.

"I can't take advantage of your kindness, Mrs. Moretti. I appreciate the sentiment though."

"Well, the offer stands. If you change your mind. And the University of Washington has an excellent social work program," she said, sounding resigned.

"How would you know that?" I asked, awed by the implications inherent in her statement.

"Hmm, why would I know that? When my adoptive son wants to be a social worker and I want him to come back home?" she said. The amusement and affection were clear in her voice.

"You checked for me?" I did not hide my surprise.

"Just in case, it's always good to have a backup plan, right, *caro*?"

"I might need it," I said letting the sense of defeat from my earlier research color my voice.

"Oh, *caro*, I wish you were closer so I could be there for you. This setback hurts, *giusto*?"

"Yeah, it does. I guess I can reach out to UW and see if they accept psions into their social work program. I might apply there after I finish up my undergrad here."

"*Va benissimo*. I'm proud of you no matter what you do, you remember that, all right?"

"Thanks, Mrs. Moretti," I said.

"I'll let you get back to your evening, but don't you forget to stay in touch."

"I won't, thanks for cheering me up, Mom."

"It's in the mom job description," she said in a teasing tone. "I won't keep you. It's getting late there, *ciao bello*."

"Good night, tell everyone I miss them."

We said our goodbyes, and the line went dead. I pulled up the contact for Jake, wanting to text him. But after resisting the urge for two years, I wasn't giving in to the impulse tonight.

I backed out of the text window and pulled up social media instead. It was an unhealthy preoccupation, stalking his pages to torture myself over whether the pictures of him with his new friends were, in reality, pictures of him with a new boyfriend.

Had he slept with the cute twink making a silly face while he posed with his hand encircling Jake's beefy biceps in his most recent selfie? The one—I realized with a twinge of regret—who looked like me to a suspicious degree. I needed a better hobby. This was not helping my mood. I closed the app and swiped over to a hookup app.

I needed to blow off steam. The clock only read ten. On a Monday. Plenty of time to make arrangements. I opened the app, and a few swipes later found a potential Mr. Right Now. I arranged a hook up at a local gay-friendly bar.

My friends and I had been intentional in picking an apartment in an LGBT neighborhood. The local storefronts displayed rainbow flags, and of equal importance for us, the little green gold and purple emblems showing support of psion rights.

So I felt confident it was a safe enough area to walk around with a guy after dark. Not that I was defenseless with my TK, but no need to invite trouble through carelessness. In the few months I'd lived here over the summer, I'd seen no cause to change that initial assessment.

I had time to grab a quick shower and get myself ready for my night.

Mr. Right Now introduced himself as Jason. He was cute in person even if he was not my usual type. As ripped as the torso shot on his profile promised though. What more could I ask for in a quick hookup?

I gave brief consideration to going for the classic bathroom blow job, get off and go home. While I was considering, he bought me a drink. We got to chatting, and I relaxed into the easy small talk.

Jason's aura was not too grating when his hand brushed against mine, I could live with it. He invited me back to his place before I suggested getting down to business here.

"Why not, you live far?" I agreed with a shrug. Nervous excitement had me fidgeting on the bar stool. I wanted this.

"A few blocks, we can walk or take a cab."

"Let's walk, it's a nice night," I suggested. Then I finished my beer in a single swallow and offered him a smile, bouncing in my seat.

"You ready?" he asked. His stare just the wrong side of too intense, it made me shiver.

"Yeah, you?"

"Yep, let's get out of here."

Jason stood and stretched before gesturing in a sweeping after you move. I walked out ahead of him, glancing back I caught him watching my ass. That was fine. I didn't mind him checking out the goods since we were on our way to his place for sex. Since I had an appreciative audience, I put more of a sway in my step.

When he caught up with me outside he gave my ass a surreptitious squeeze, but his hands didn't linger where anybody on the street might see us. He walked close but not touching me again while he led the way to his place. And that was fine too. As a psion I didn't care for gratuitous touches from a one-night-stand.

Everything was going well until we got inside his apartment. As soon as we stepped through the door, Jason pushed me up against the wall of his entryway, kicking the door closed behind us. That wasn't the problem. He was a decent kisser, and he tasted like the yeasty beer we had just drunk. I was down with that.

I liked the way his hands drifted down my back to my ass. Jason could touch me all he wanted. I kind of liked his aura now that I was in the mood, the way it prickled against mine a tingling in my awareness. My ability to tolerate him in the long-term was negligible. But as a one-off the incompatibility lent an edge of excitement to the experience. And then he came up for air and ruined everything by talking.

"You good with bottoming?" he asked into the skin of my neck before kissing me there, he had to lean at an awkward angle to manage it, what with our height difference. His hand slipped inside the back of my waistband to explore. He acted as if the question was just a formality, and he didn't question whether I would go along with the change of plans.

"Um, no, it says right on my profile. And I told you when we agreed to meet up—I don't bottom," I said, pushing him away to create space. He let me step away from him at least. Not trying to pin me or keep feeling me up. So he wasn't a complete asshole. I was acutely aware of how much bigger than me he was in that moment though.

"Sure, sure, just, you know…" he trailed off, with a vague gesture in my direction.

"I know what?" I arched a brow in an unspoken challenge.

"You look like a bottom."

"Oh my god. Are you even serious right now? Why are you wasting my fucking time if you can't bother to read my profile?"

I was talking louder than I should have, and my arms flailing in emphasis only made it worse. Behaving overwrought, Mom called it when I couldn't maintain the calm demeanor she thought befit a gentleman. She wasn't the only one to look down on me for it either. And sure enough, I got a big eye roll from Jason.

"Sorry, man, no need to overreact. Calm down," Jason made a keep it down gesture. It made my blood boil even more that he was acting like I was the unreasonable one here.

"God, whatever. Are you down for blow jobs instead?" I offered, frustrated, but still horny.

He had the audacity to sound disappointed, "I was in the mood to fuck."

"Well, so was I you absolute fucker, but I'm not the one who couldn't be arsed to say what I wanted. Your profile says vers," I said. At that point I decided that I didn't care if he sent me home with no action. But to my surprise, he seemed into it again instead of continuing to act like I had been the asshole in this scenario.

"Sure, but that was before we met. It's hard to tell from your pic, you know? But, it's all good, you are hot when you're all ragey like this," he commented. Then he reached out to touch me again. The motion tentative, giving me the chance to bat him away or tell him no. When I didn't stop him, he cupped my face. I winced at the crackle of his aura without the kisses to counterbalance the unpleasantness. He dropped his hand.

"It was hard to tell what I told you about my preferences?" I said in a flat tone. He considered me for a moment, running a hand through his hair like he was thinking hard, I braced for him to stick his foot back in his mouth.

"That you're—" he cut himself off, and for a second I was sure he would call me a name. I watched the wheels turning as his brain caught up to whatever insult he planned to voice, then thought better. In a visible act of restraint he instead gave a vague gesture encompassing my person and shrugged.

I waited.

"Whatever you are—do you want to fuck me or not?" he said.

"Sure, if you're offering."

Easier to let it go. It didn't matter why he expected me to bottom. If it was because I was smaller than him, or because he perceived my clothes and mannerisms as femme, or for some other reason. I was sick of hearing shit about who I should be. But he had dropped it and backed down on his assumptions. I didn't want to fight or try to educate an asshole, my only goal here was to get off.

"Yeah, just, you know… maybe keep acting all pissed off at me?" he asked. I almost felt bad for him at the vulnerability in those words. Or I would have if he weren't a jerk.

I smirked at him though because I could get into roleplay even if it didn't require much acting after his behavior.

"Sure thing, dude, you like being called names too?"

"Uh, yeah," Jason swallowed, licking his lips. "That works for me."

The husky note to his voice and the lust in his eyes made it clear it would do more than work. I fixed him with a hard stare, thinking perhaps the night might still be salvageable. I had just gone into this expecting to get off, and now I also got to unleash some of my pent up frustration at an eager target. It wasn't my usual turn on, but I enjoyed acting so it was no hardship to work with his preferences.

"All right, asshole, why don't you quit wasting my time and go get the condoms and lube?" I said. He scrambled to obey, and his renewed excitement over being bossed around helped me get back into the mood. This could be fun.

Chapter 11

Jake

My first morning with Caleb and Elliott was strange in that it felt natural. I woke up when Elliott disentangled himself from me.

"Morning," he mumbled, turning shy once we were no longer snuggling.

"Morning, do I smell coffee?"

"Decaf, Caleb can't handle regular."

"Don't suppose there's bacon with that?"

"Maybe? Caleb sometimes gets the turkey kind. Should be bagels though."

"Oh. Right, no meat. You do eggs?"

"Sometimes. You still want to come collect signatures today?"

"Yeah, if that still works."

"Sure, do you need to run home and change beforehand?"

"I should, but no rush."

"All right, so that gives us a chance to hash out 'the dreaded talk' over our hash browns," Elliott said with a shy smile.

"The talk, huh?"

"Sure, it isn't every day we meet a person who meshes well with us both. Are we coming on too strong?"

I considered, it seemed excessive for just having met them. But I yesterday was one of the most pleasant afternoons I could remember, so if they wanted to make sure we were on the same page, I could respect that.

"No. Only different from what I'm used to."

"Okay," he sounded relieved that he wasn't scaring me away.

Elliott looked adorable, all tousled from sleep and sex, his brow furrowed with concern. I kissed his cheek as I slid out of bed. Elliott's expression softened as he caressed my arm in response.

Then he crossed to the dresser and pulled on some sweatpants. He tossed me a spare pair. With the drawstring loosened they accommodated me well enough. I was bulkier than him, but Elliott was as tall as me. And Caleb was only a few inches shorter. He was stockier than Elliott's lithe build too. I took time to appreciate Elliott's graceful movements as we got ready.

Dressed, we joined Caleb in the kitchen. As Elliott had guessed, there was a carafe of decaf. Along with a full spread of breakfast foods. Bagels and their fixings, turkey bacon, and fresh fruit on the table. Caleb presided over the stove with a pan, flipping an egg.

"Oh perfect, you're up! I was about to come ask how you wanted your eggs."

"None for me today," Elliott said.

"Jake?"

"However you're making yours is fine. I'm not picky."

"It's no hassle, what do you prefer?"

Elliott groaned, "just tell him what you want, big guy," he clapped me on the shoulders before sauntering closer to his boyfriend. "Trust me, you don't want to get Caleb started on the vital importance of communicating your preferences to avoid resentment."

"Hey, it's important!"

"Sure, but not everyone cares that much about their eggs, Caleb. Sometimes breakfast food isn't a metaphor for the state of our relationship, sometimes it's just food."

Elliott softened the words with a kiss and Caleb got distracted enough not to offer a rebuttal. But he turned to face me after Elliott stepped away. He wagged his spatula at me in a mock threat.

"Don't think you're off the hook, what would your platonic ideal of eggs be?"

"Um, scrambled?"

"Oh, great elder gods preserve us, now you've done it," Elliott made a theatrical gesture as though warding off Caleb's response to my request. Caleb looked unimpressed, hands on his hips as he addressed us.

"Don't be dramatic, El. Excuse him, he's on a Lovecraft kick at the moment. So, how do you like your scrambled eggs, Jake?"

"Um, scrambled? Is it too late to change my answer to over easy?"

"Yes," Caleb and Elliott chorused. Elliott leaned against the counter and crossed his arms as he observed, a smile twitching at the corner of his mouth.

"Runny or dry? Large curds or small? How fluffy? Cooked in butter or oil? Do you like pepper? How many? Any other add-ons like cheese or onions?"

"Two is fine. Fluffy I guess. No pepper. Curds sounds gross, what even is that? Not runny, but not rubbery either. I never put much thought into eggs. Mom always makes enough for the whole family, so no individual alterations. I think she puts sour cream in them toward the end?"

"And you like it with the sour cream?" Caleb asked. His tone reminiscent of an adult wheedling information from an uncooperative toddler. Or at least, it was how I sounded when I was babysitting my young cousins. Elliott snorted with suppressed laughter.

"Yes."

"For future reference, the curd size refers to the texture—nevermind. I've got this," Caleb said, cutting himself off at my glazed look in response to his explanation. Elliott snickered.

Caleb seemed exasperated, but he plated his eggs before cracking two more into a small bowl, humming to himself as he cooked.

"So, FYI, this is a perfect preview of how our 'ground rules for the relationship' conversation went. It's not too late for you to remember you had other plans," Elliott said.

"I mean, isn't it premature to have the big relationship talk?" I asked. Because it made me uncomfortable. Relationships made me uncomfortable after the disaster that had been my first one.

Elliott choked back a laugh and shook his head at me.

"It's never too soon to establish good communication," Caleb said. "If we are all clear about what we want and expect from each other, it will save us trouble further along."

"Fair point."

"So, no time like the present," Caleb said as he slid my scrambled eggs onto a plate and then handed it over, "let's discuss this at the table."

We all took our seats. I got a brief respite as we filled our plates and Caleb made sure we had everything we needed for the meal.

Once we had made a start on our food, Caleb began the conversation.

"So, we can start simple. Elliott and I are together. I have a few lovers. He doesn't at the moment. That arrangement has worked for us. But Elliott approached me about bringing in a third person to our relationship a few months ago so that's where you come in. Are you open to dating us?"

"I mean, I told you I was last night."

"When you were still high on endorphins from mind-blowing sex. And El was zonked out. Does it still sound appealing in the light of day?" Caleb asked.

"I still want to try. Yesterday was fun. I mean, the stuff in bed, but everything else too."

"Okay, great. So, if we proceed…"

After an in depth conversation, we agreed to date. Boyfriends, because it was an easy way to characterize things. Caleb made a point of the fact that his relationship with Elliott was primary, but that didn't mean I was a second-class citizen. I had a hard time wrapping my brain around the distinction. But I adopted a philosophy of taking it one day, or date, at a time.

Part of what we talked about was arranging times for the three of us to spend together and one-on-one dates. They had an online calendar which they added me to so scheduling would be easier. We also laid out a few rules.

Elliott had reservations about me and Caleb being intimate without him so anything beyond kissing was off the table. Caleb didn't mind if Elliott and I had one-on-one encounters.

For now, we were sticking with an open arrangement. Caleb slept with other people. I was free to do the same. They didn't expect me to keep them apprised of my sex life outside of our relationship. That eased my trepidation over how fast things seemed to be moving.

This wasn't a singular big commitment talk. Or Caleb laying down the law. This was figuring out the logistics of dating multiple people. That key aspect made everything more complex. And I found I appreciated the candid discussion on the mechanics of our fledgling relationship. So it differed from my preconceptions. But in a positive way.

We agreed to reevaluate at regular intervals. Rather than dreading the relationship talk, I came around to agreeing with Caleb's assertion it was only a matter of clear communication. It made me less uncertain about where I stood with them. Not a one-night-stand. We had the potential for something special.

I still found it strange to consider this a relationship after one night. But my only real dating experience was with Aaron. So it wasn't like I was an expert on the matter. We weren't exclusive, I didn't owe them anything beyond our agreed upon dates. We were just dating, getting acquainted. And the opportunity to explore sex with two people I liked only sweetened the deal.

After breakfast and our talk, I headed home to change for signature collecting. Mom was there, but she didn't question why I was coming home in the same clothes I wore to class on Friday. She gave me a knowing look. It could have been awkward, but Mom respected my privacy. Still, living at home had definite drawbacks. I was glad to have an excuse to head back out soon after arriving home.

Collecting signatures with Elliott and Caleb was a blast. We goofed around in the car between stops, snapping selfies and joking. Caleb drew us into a convoluted debate on which psionic abilities his favorite video game characters would have if they were real. We also chatted more about SaFE. And Psion rights.

It was easy to agree to spend the night again. And this time Elliott and I got to give the blowjobs, paying Caleb back for his attentions the previous night. I liked it more than I expected, enough to cream my pants before Caleb even finished. Elliott jerked himself off afterward, Caleb's hand wrapped around his length alongside his own.

The sight of them together, Elliott splayed over Caleb, got me half-hard again. But I felt content to curl up with them after we got cleaned up. I lay between them. They both looked sated and content. Their auras coiled around mine even as they wrapped me in a tangle of limbs. It made me aware of what it meant to be an anchor, and the aptness of the term. Like I grounded them, gave them a haven to let go of their control. And being there for them made me feel lighter. We fit together, the three of us.

My first one-on-one date with Elliott occurred a week after I first slept with Caleb and him. He took me to a club to dance. Caleb smirked and wished us well at the door to their apartment. He had standing arrangements with his friend, Tess. Elliott jumped at the chance to have a date for dancing. One the loud music and strobing lights wouldn't bother.

We made the plans after a casual comment from Caleb on Sunday before I had to head home.

"Hey, I have a game with Tess and Lynn on Friday. Why not invite our new boyfriend out dancing, El? Isn't Vibe having a youth night?"

Elliott perked up, "yep, college night on Friday. Do you dance, Jake? Caleb hates it, he pretends not to so I can have company, but I know he does."

"I don't hate it. The crowds, music and lights bother me, but I like watching you dance," Caleb said.

Elliott rolled his eyes.

"I've never been to a dance club or anything," I said.

It was surreal hearing Caleb toss the boyfriend word into casual conversation, but we had agreed to try it. I was enjoying our arrangement.

After a weekend of fantastic sex and companionship, I liked it even more. And we hadn't even progressed beyond blowjobs in bed yet.

An evening spent clubbing was a new experience. A night catering to the under-twenty-one crowd didn't assuage my discomfort at feeling out of place. Elliott looked different in his clubbing clothes. They were tight, form fitting, and he applied eye make-up too. Something dark and glittery. It was a sharp contrast to his usual baggy sweatshirts.

I felt underdressed when I showed up in faded old jeans and a tee. But Elliott assured me I was fine. At the club the bouncer greeted Elliott with warmth. He introduced me as a new friend and got us in without having to pay the cover charge.

The gorgeous gogo dancers all seemed to know him too. They greeted him like an old friend. One hopped down off his little stage when we approached, calling out he was taking his break so he could chat with Elliott.

Their reunion didn't last long since it was hard to hear over the music, and the other guy had to get back to work. El got us soft drinks and then maneuvered us to a spot near the dance floor before I could realize just how out of my depth I was.

If I had known Elliott was a real dancer, I would have spent the week researching dance moves and how not to make a fool of myself instead of reading articles about polyamory. As it was, I resisted when he pulled me onto the floor, protesting that I had two left feet.

"You're an athlete, you can learn," Elliott said, "just move with me, like sex."

"Oh god," I said as he spun me around so my back was to him. Then his hands were on my hips and he pressed in close, his breath warm on my neck as he murmured encouragements.

I couldn't dance, and his body pressed against me made my clumsiness worse. But he didn't seem to mind as he ground against me, moving us both to the beat. I was self-conscious at first, but as one song faded into another and Elliott seemed to revel in the experience, I relaxed and enjoyed the ride.

After a few hours, I felt fantastic. Despite youth night meaning there was no alcohol to help my buzz along. Amped on the energy of the club. And horny. And Elliott kept giving me teasing kisses and lingering touches. He broke off one of them and said we should go home.

My dick and I were on board that plan. I wanted to keep touching Elliott in the cab on the way back to his place. But something in his posture made me forbear.

Caleb was playing video games on the couch when we stumbled in.

"You guys have fun?" He asked.

"Yeah, El has the moves."

"Did he tell you he used to work at Vibe?"

"No."

"Yeah, he was one of the pretty boys shaking his ass on a pedestal, huh, El?"

"I'm still pretty," Elliott said, but his tone was off. Caleb paused his game to watch us.

"You okay, El?"

"You are so pretty," I agreed, I reached for his face, wanting to touch the sparkling eye makeup he was wearing. In my lust-fueled state it seemed like a great idea.

"Easy, big guy," Caleb warned, standing.

Elliott pushed my hand away, his touch gentle but firm, "not tonight. Sorry."

I gave him a puzzled look, but nodded, "did I do something wrong?"

"No, I had fun. Goodnight, Jake, I should get to bed. It's late," Elliott said.

He forced a brief smile, too tight and pinched to pass as genuine. His arms crossed over his chest, and his breathing hitched, but he strode to his bedroom before I could ask for further reassurances to his wellbeing. Caleb sighed as we both watched Elliott flee.

"It's late, you can stay in the guest room," Caleb said.

"Is he all right?"

"He will be," Caleb ran a hand through his hair, "I'll check on him, did anything happen at the club?"

"We danced. He spoke with some friends. He's gorgeous when he's dancing. We kissed, and I thought he wanted… well, I guess I misread what he wanted."

"He's the only reason I tolerate going to a club," Caleb agreed, "too much touching for most psions. It overwhelms him, he'll be all right. Like I said, you are welcome to stay the night."

I considered going home, but I didn't want to wake my family and I didn't want to leave, not really. So I stayed.

And I was there when Elliott woke up from nightmares. I couldn't help listening to his shouts through the thin walls. And the soft soothing sounds Caleb made in response.

It seemed like my fault and I considered slipping out to go home. Pretend it never happened. I didn't though. Instead, I stayed up tossing and turning.

Elliott wouldn't meet my eyes the next morning at breakfast. Not until Caleb whispered something low and intense in his ear. Then his gaze snapped up, and he focused on me. He appeared to be nerving himself up to say something.

"I'm sorry if I made things worse last night," I said to break the tension when no words were forthcoming.

"You didn't. I love dancing. But I don't always handle crowds well. I should have warned you I might get like that."

"So, was I imagining you wanted me last night?"

Elliott winced, "no. But it wasn't all coming from me."

When I looked puzzled Caleb jumped in to clarify.

"He's a telepath, big guy."

"Not that you aren't hot, I liked dancing with you," Elliott said.

"But we were touching, and I was feeding all kinds of lust filled thoughts into your psionic senses, huh?" I asked, understanding dawning, "I'm sorry, Elliott."

"Not just you, the entire atmosphere. And it's not your fault. but it was too intense for a first-ish date. I should have known better."

"So, are you an empath subclass then?"

"No, my abilities are just weak. I get vague impressions. The gist of a person's thoughts, so if a club full of people are all thinking about sex… it's a lot of input. Touching you was a mistake, but I wanted you. And you wanted me too, so that was a whole feedback loop. I can't project well most of the time. Just receive, but you're an anchor, so you might have picked up some of what I was reading. I'm sorry if I gave you like, a contact high or whatever you want to call it."

"It gave you nightmares."

"I'd hoped you slept through that," Elliott said, rueful. "It happens. Not as often as it used to. PTSD is a bitch. I panicked last night, I didn't mean to lead you on, or anything. Right now I'm just embarrassed."

"You didn't. We had a good time dancing, right? I didn't realize it got to be too much. I hope I didn't make it worse for you."

"You didn't. Make it worse, I mean. Not on purpose at least. And I had fun too. Thanks for getting me home safe. And letting it go when I asked you to stop."

"Of course. So I guess our next date should be something more low key, huh? Maybe you could teach me some of your moves so it's not as overwhelming?"

"You want to go out again?"

"Yeah. Why wouldn't I?"

"Because I teased you? I got you riled up, then freaked and turned you down?" Elliott said. Caleb bit back a reply, allowing me to field that one. I sighed.

"I'm not an expert, but I don't think kissing equals consent, right?"

"No, it doesn't," Elliott allowed.

"I'm in over my head here, Elliott. I am trying to follow you and Caleb's cues, okay? You guys didn't push me when I got cold feet the first day you invited me over. I hope you don't think I'd pressure you over sex?"

"No. Not really."

"There you go then, don't worry about it, okay?"

"Yeah. All right. Sorry…" Elliott dropped his gaze to his breakfast.

"You apologize a lot," I observed. My intention was to lighten the mood with a gentle tease.

Elliott winced. I'd said the wrong thing again. I learned later that Elliott made constant apologies when he got insecure. And his anxiety magnified all his insecurities when he had a night like last night. Being called on the habit only made it worse. I hated the way he always seemed braced for rejection. But I learned the best way to help him was to let it go.

The morning after our first date, I was in the dark. All I could do was follow Caleb's lead when he suggested we all cuddle on the couch and watch something.

"So, how about a movie day today?" Caleb changed the subject.

"I'd like that," Elliott said, then he added, "you're not obligated to stay, Jake."

"Do you want me to stay?"

"If you want to."

Elliott was evasive when he wanted something but wasn't secure enough to ask for it. I learned that too. Caleb nodded from the other side of the table, confirming the invitation was genuine.

So I stayed and over the course of the day Elliott relaxed back into his usual demeanor. No longer hunching in on himself and avoiding eye contact or offering excessive apologies. He even leaned his head on my shoulder during the last movie of the night. His aura coiled around me again as it had on our other encounters. It allayed my guilt.

I left before dinner because my mom was cooking and it seemed like all of us needed time to sort out our feelings about the date. Caleb demanded a kiss goodbye. Elliott watched us with hungry eyes. But when it was time for us to say our farewells, he bussed a rushed peck on my cheek instead of a proper kiss. I didn't push, just told him I'd see him soon.

That night Elliott texted me while I was delving into the internet to understand PTSD. He opened with a joke from a movie earlier in the day.

That led into a conversation that stretched over the next few weeks. Where he got comfortable with me. We talked about school, hopes for the future. Experiences in the past. Getting to know you stuff.

Then he told me about some of his history. How his family abandoned him after his emergence. Never quite fitting into any of his foster homes, facing homelessness. Abuse. And those vague accounts, coupled with my research put the way our date had ended into a framework that made sense.

It also filled me with a nebulous sense of outrage on his behalf alongside being on top of the world at earning his trust. Because the quietly funny Elliott that peeked through when he let his guard down was someone I admired and wanted intimacy with. And as much as I wished our first date ended on a much different note, I was glad he was letting me into his life on a deeper level than just sex.

My first date with Caleb was less eventful. We planned an evening in with video games and pizza on a night when Elliott had a late class. It was fun. I sucked at the survival horror games he preferred and he was hopeless, not to mention bored, with FIFA. We ended up booting up a racing game instead and having a blast.

The pizza tasted good too. Although Caleb's reaction to it was the best part for me. The guy acted like he hadn't had pizza in ages. Turned out he saved it for special occasions. He moaned over the meat lover's special we'd ordered like it was better than sex. I couldn't bring myself to tell him I preferred plain cheese, not with the open longing in his expression as we discussed toppings.

"I love El, but I miss pepperoni sometimes."

"You can still eat pepperoni."

"Well yeah, but then I feel bad kissing him. And El's kisses are worth avoiding pepperoni. But this tastes so incredible."

I couldn't argue with that. Elliott was fun to kiss. He got so into it. He gave the impression the rest of the world could go screw for all he cared. Caleb wasn't bad in that department either.

"Well, you can kiss me with pepperoni breath," I said. Caleb smirked at me.

"Is that so?"

"Yeah."

Caleb finished his last bite and slid into my lap, "if you're good with keeping it to only kisses until El gets home we can do that."

"When should he be here?"

Caleb glanced over to check the time.

"Another hour."

I groaned as Caleb ground against me; I was already hard from just having him astride me. No way I could last an hour with him touching me.

Caleb chuckled, "too much?"

"Sorry. Don't think I can hold out for an hour."

"Okay, but consider how amazing your orgasm will be if you do though," Caleb kissed me, a gentle deliberate kiss, then he pulled back, "you ever tried edging, Jake?"

"Um, no?"

"Want to?"

"What is it?"

"I would bring you right to the brink. Over and over until you beg me for it."

"Mm," it sounded amazing. And like torture. And no way did I want to risk breaking Elliott's trust. Caleb picked up on how aroused kissing had me though. He eased back and gave me an out.

"Or we can try another game," he said.

"What kind of game?"

"Something with short rounds. And the loser of each mini game owes the winner a kiss. Overall winner gets a blowjob later."

"So we kiss after every round?"

"I mean, is that a problem? We could raise the stakes…"

I snorted, "no, you're just…"

"I'm what?"

"Fun. You're fun."

Caleb ruffled my hair, then he gave me another quick kiss and slid off my lap to change the game.

"So, if we were raising the stakes, what would it entail?"

"Winner chooses who bottoms for El when he gets home. But I don't want to push you into something you aren't ready for over a silly bet."

"We can stick with blowjobs for now. I like taking this slow with you guys, and I made an ass of myself last week, with El."

"You got all wound up at a club which was Elliott's intention, you did nothing wrong."

"I gave Elliott a nightmare."

"No, you didn't. El gets those. Nothing to do with you. You didn't force him into anything he didn't want. He loved dancing with you."

"I wanted more than dancing."

"And he didn't. So you didn't."

"True. I'm nervous I might ruin this though."

"You're doing fine. We like you, okay?"

"Yeah, I can tell," I said with a grin. It was the truth. We had a group text going where we chatted throughout the day. And I carried on individual conversations with each of them too. Caleb liked to message me with crude jokes or in depth debate over which fictional character would win in a fight. Where Elliott's conversations ranged from the mundane details of his day to the philosophical. I was enjoying getting to know them.

My mom suspected I was dating. Not just because of my overnight stays, but also because of the goofy grin on my face when my phone pinged with a notification one of them had messaged me. She didn't press me for details though. And I wasn't ready to share with my family. This was new, and I wanted it to remain private. Just between us for now.

We played for another hour, Caleb stealing kisses until I had all but forgotten the game and was just enjoying the sensations. Caleb glanced up with a toothy grin a moment before the scrape of a key heralded Elliott's return. I took a second to realize he sensed Elliott's aura through the door. I wasn't familiar enough with them yet to perceive it. But their link attuned Caleb to his partner.

It was strange to realize that I wanted that. With them. A link was something I had only ever given serious consideration to for Aaron.

Elliott joined us in the living room, he took in the pizza boxes and shook his head.

"You guys got pepperoni, didn't you?"

"Yes," Caleb said. He looked sheepish. Elliott heaved a long-suffering sigh.

"Come on, big guy, time to hit the mouthwash if you want El to join us," Caleb nudged my leg.

"I mean, fair's fair, you have the same rules about garlic bread," Elliott said.

I chuckled as Caleb hauled me down the hallway, stealing one more kiss before we got freshened up. The knowledge Elliott was waiting for us in the bedroom leant an urgency to erasing all traces of pepperoni breath.

PART THREE

Present Day

Chapter 12

Jake

"Tell me again, why are we protesting a youth center?" I asked Em. I was driving the fifteen passenger van that SaFE had borrowed from the university to our latest demonstration. They were sitting in the passenger seat. Behind us, the van was full of the chatter of our friends as they spoke among themselves.

"I got a tip from a friend of the cause," Em said. "And because SaFE is protesting PYDC and SPIRE summer camps nationwide."

"What sort of tip?" I asked.

Em leveled an assessing look at me and said, "you can't say anything until we get confirmation."

"Confirmation of what?"

"That PYDC has an affiliation with SPIRE."

"Yeah, I know that. It's right on their website," I said, suppressing the urge to roll my eyes. I needed to focus on the road.

"Did you know their connection goes through SPIRE's recruitment arm? And that they place over eighty percent of their program graduates with SPIRE? And that number is over ninety-five percent of grade A and B psions? The list of PYDC graduates with records for felony failure to register corresponds almost one-to-one with youth who refuse placement with SPIRE."

Em arched a brow at me in challenge. I got lost under the barrage of statistics, but I knew Em well enough after four years working with them to understand they thought there was a connection.

"That sounds like a shady coincidence," I acknowledged. "But maybe SPIRE doesn't allow felons to join? Isn't that a rule with government agencies?"

Em rolled their eyes, "you can be so naïve sometimes, Jake. It's not a coincidence. It's how they control the kids dependent on them for care. Did you know PYDC owns a huge share of all psion youth shelters nationwide? And that they have worked the system so they get government funding to help with their operational budget?"

"I did not."

"And that after they received their government grants, the rates of higher grade and unusual classifications of psions at their facilities increased?"

"You're implying what? That they somehow got those kids removed from their homes to force them into working for SPIRE?" I tried to follow their logic.

"I am just saying, the statistics do not support those numbers happening by random chance," Em stated.

"You're the math whiz," I said, because they were. Em was working on a doctoral degree in biostatistics. They were smart.

If Em said the numbers looked suspicious, I had no basis to say otherwise. But Em also had a tendency to buy into any theory that supported their distrust of SPIRE in particular—and any government dealing with psions in general. The vague theory that PYDC was procuring strong psions for SPIRE without giving them a choice sounded far-fetched. Even if Em's data might be suggestive.

"So what are we protesting?" I asked again. The optics of protesting a kid's summer camp made me hesitant. Since I was our PR guy, our image was my concern. At the least I needed a clear message for my contacts in the media.

"SPIRE's recruitment practices," Em said, succinct. "Even without the rest, you must admit the situation smells fishy, right? They run summer camps for homeless kids to force them to enlist with a paramilitary organization. The situation is egregious. Tell me you see that?"

"Their PR does a good job of making it appear charitable. But I see your point."

"And that's why we are picketing their camp. We want to get attention on the organization and get the public thinking about it. How would the average suburban parent feel about their kids being sent to army recruitment events and being targeted by coercive messaging to join?"

"Not great," I acknowledged.

"So that's why we are going, to change public perception. Or at least put the issue in the national dialog. And we will keep picketing until my contacts get more concrete proof. If the protests go to plan, we'll have planted the seed of doubt in the public consciousness for when we go public with what's happening."

"You are diabolical Em," I told them and they grinned at me like it was the best compliment they had ever received.

"Why thank you, Jake, you are good for my ego," they cooed, "I knew there was a reason we kept you around."

"So who else knows about the big picture?" I asked. I had a good idea it was the rest of the leadership team though. Em shrugged.

"Jess. And Caleb and Elliott. The core group," they said. Which meant the five of us who were club officers and showed up to every meeting and event without fail.

"And I'm the last to hear? I'm hurt," I played it off as a joke, but being the last to find out stung. Em rolled their eyes again.

"Of course I told Jess first. And Elliott put two and two together as soon as I announced we were protesting PYDC. He lived at one of their facilities as a teen, but he aged out around the time Pederson Youth Development Center bought the facility and enacted these policies.

"It was part of a wave of acquisitions of small local group homes and transitional housing. It all happened around the same time that PYDC went public and got grant funding for summer training programs. Around five years ago," Em said.

"I see," I said. This sounded more and more like a conspiracy, which Em loved, but Elliott wasn't prone to buying into such a narrative. If he thought there was something to Em's conjecture after living at a PYDC facility, it inclined me to believe him.

"And El told Caleb what PYDC was like so I guess he figured it out for himself too, huh?"

"Yes," they confirmed.

I sighed, whether there was anything to Em's suspicions or not, being the last to know struck at the heart of my insecurities. I understood that Em would tell Jess first. But Caleb and Elliott should have clued me in sooner. It wasn't fair to blame them for their closeness, but I still felt left out.

Elliott almost never talked about his life before UDub though. Caleb was the only person familiar with all the details. In part, because he knew Elliott when he lived at the group home. While Elliott was my lover too, that didn't entitle me to the details of his past. He had shared enough for me to fill in the blanks, and I knew that took a lot of trust.

My lack of emotional availability complicated our relationship these days too. I slept with them, well, I had until last week anyway. Now I was staying in our guest room. But we had shared an apartment for the past three years.

I understood my recent distance was putting a strain on us all. The sex with them was great, it always had been. Early on, it had happened with startling regularity. Well, it startled me at least, since it was my first sexual relationship of any significant duration. We didn't have a problem in the bedroom. Or hadn't until about a week ago when my aura started bothering Elliott.

We had settled into a steady pattern once the honeymoon phase wore off. There was no expectation of exclusivity with them, emotional or sexual. But they expected honesty and open communication.

It had worked for us for the better part of four years. I loved them, but a part of me couldn't let go of the past. I wasn't over Aaron and I wasn't sure if I ever would be.

Caleb and Elliott loved me anyway. Unlike my other disastrous attempts at relationships over the years. They accepted that I could continue to love Aaron and still love them too. They only expressed concern I was pining over someone who, to all appearances, did not return my feelings. They never made me feel less loved for it. But something was missing.

My aura had always felt the slightest bit off kilter, ever since I learned how to sense it. But linking with Elliott and Caleb had helped. Centered me.

Over my last semester at UDub I'd been pulling away though. Preparing myself for the great unknown of entering the world of a nine to five job. The sense of disconnect was worse now I had graduated.

I was caught up in figuring out what to do with my shiny new degree. Sometimes it seemed like I was leaving the safe bubble of academia and the second family I had created for myself there. Like graduation obliged me to leave them before I could start this next chapter because they were both pursuing advanced degrees.

I worried they might not have room in their lives for me once I found an adult job. If I found an adult job. My lack of clear job prospects was not helping me to feel like I had much to offer them.

I was uncertain what it would mean for our relationship. And something had changed in the last week. The distant ache of a missing piece had become a sharp tug, never far from my mind. Sometimes that longing was hard to deal with. Sometimes, I thought I was too demanding of their time and affection to be what they needed.

Elliott drew back from me when I got too tangled up in the past. He didn't like touching me then, said my aura burned in his senses when I was brooding. Like it was reaching for someone and it wasn't him. He found my presence soothing under usual circumstances.

Of late there had been more nights when I slept alone in our guest room because my aura irritated him though. And then last week he had asked me to stay there for the time being. I hated that. Not the sleeping alone, the pushing him away.

I had too much time to ponder these things, alone in our guest bed. To compare what the three of us had to the all consuming passion of my first love. It hurt. Especially with the looks Caleb and El shared sometimes, like the rest of the world ceased to exist.

Watching the two of them interact these days made me feel left out. Like they were already moving past me and I couldn't stop it. I missed our easy communication. I missed them. And I missed Aaron. Even after six years of carrying a torch for him, I couldn't seem to shake his hold on my heart.

As a result, I sometimes thought I was the fifth wheel on our leadership team or the third wheel in our relationship. The kicker was, I knew if I told them how I felt, they would work overtime to prove otherwise. But I said nothing. I wasn't ready to talk about it yet.

Even when I pulled back though, I still loved them. We could work through this funk. I had to believe that.

"You all good?" Em asked. I glanced over and saw they were watching me. They ruffled the close-cropped hair on the top of my head. Em read my silence for the brooding it was.

"Everything alright with Caleb and Elliott? Or are you thinking of someone else with all that angst?" They must have picked up on the direction of my thoughts through the touch. Telepaths.

"We're good. I'm happy with Caleb and El."

"If you say so. Caleb worries about you. Says you're withdrawn, and he thinks you plan to leave them. And you have Elliott convinced he's pushing you away."

"I'm not planning on leaving them. And I'm not seeing anyone else, no one else has caught my interest in ages. I love them. I'm just struggling with figuring out what comes after UDub and how our relationship fits in with whatever is next for me."

"You should tell them that," Em said.

"Yeah, I… don't know how."

"Well, you should figure it out soon. Caleb says you've been distant since the party celebrating the registry initiative. Are you planning to talk to them about whatever's got you down?"

I shrugged, reluctant to think about it. I remembered the party well enough. It had been the last time I'd hooked up with a random. I got swept up in the celebratory atmosphere. We had just learned the second iteration of our registry initiative passed—albeit in an almost unrecognizable form —on the statewide ballot.

Em's gaze bore into me, but I was lost in thought again and they didn't comment further. Come to think of it, the last few months had been so hectic, my chat with Caleb after that hookup might have been the last time I had a real honest and open conversation with him.

I'd had a busy spring term with finishing my degree. Elliott had been immersed in his master's thesis, since he'd graduated this spring too. Spending long hours at Mount Hope with the anchor who was helping him conduct research about Cereflux.

Caleb was patient with the two of us having busy schedules. His own coursework kept him busy too, although he had opted to finish his master's degree in the fall rather than cram a capstone into his spring semester.

My love life was depressing, I could sense Caleb and Elliott slipping through my fingers and I didn't have the courage to stop it. And the ballot initiative that had kicked off my activism was not much better. So the reminder was not a welcome change of subject. Still, now that I had gone there, I couldn't help thinking about it.

Our initial petition to withdraw from the registry had almost been approved. But the state legislature balked at enacting it. Then a challenge in the court system alleging the state lacked the authority to legislate enforcement of the registry had derailed things further.

The courts determined that Washington had the right to legislate how it handled offenses at the state level, but could not withdraw from the registry. So we started the whole process over with a new petition. The process took years.

We set out to decriminalize failure to register. That was what our second petition demanded. The legislature came back with a plan to reduce the penalties to a misdemeanor charge rather than a felony. They asked for the maximum penalties allowable for a misdemeanor. A maximum sentence of 364 days in jail and up to five thousand dollars in fines. Both versions appeared on the state ballot for the people to decide.

The misdemeanor option was the one that passed. It was still a step in the right direction, but considering how hard that step had been I couldn't help the sense of defeat. Four years of work to take a tiny step forward. At least it was the law now, codified in early March.

"You ever wonder what's the point to fighting back?" I asked, thinking about the registry initiative.

"Nope," Em said, popping the p. "We might not win every battle we fight, but we lose every single one we choose not to fight. And don't dodge the question. Are you doing all right?"

"I've been busy with graduation," I said. It sounded defensive.

Em tsked, "psions need touch, Jake."

"I'm not a psion," I pointed out. "Just an anchor. And I don't need sex to get the touch I need. Not with this crew," I forced levity into my tone and they cracked a smile.

"That's true enough. Turn here," they directed me to the exit from the highway. I took the turn, our conversation over for the time being as they navigated me out to the campground PYDC had rented for their summer camp.

I pulled into a parking spot in the camp's large gravel parking lot, Em stretched and waved to Jess as she pulled up in another van beside us.

"Good turnout considering it's the summer session," they said. And it was. Our meetings had anywhere from fifteen to fifty students present during the school term. We didn't have regular meetings in the summer.

Our official membership rolls were closer to a hundred but getting everyone to show up at once was a lost cause. Despite that fact, between club members and their contacts, we had somehow drummed up thirty people for this protest.

Em swiveled around to address the people in the van's passenger seats, they whistled to get everyone's attention and then when the chatter ceased they spoke.

"All right, we're here. This action is to protest the affiliation between SPIRE and PYDC. The plan is a peaceful protest. We are calling into question their association. We are not alleging specific wrongdoing.

"Most of you have been with us at other protests, but just to reiterate, we do not break the law, we remain peaceful no matter the provocation. If there is media attention stick to the talking points as we have discussed. Our goal as an organization is a re-examination or end to SPIRE as a divisive influence between psions and norms.

"If you aren't sure how to answer a question, refer it to one of the governing members. Jake, Jess, Caleb, Elliott and I are here to help if you have any issues or questions. You have your posters and you know the drill, so let's do this!"

There was a ragged cheer and then someone flung open the doors to the van with a grating rattle and everyone tumbled out. Controlled chaos reigned as both vans unloaded and everyone got organized and figured out who should take which signs.

They held the camp at a state-owned facility so it was on public land. We had permits to protest outside of the actual facility. Em had all the paperwork organized on their clipboard. They confirmed who was present to make sure we had a record of who we had brought. So we could take responsibility for their actions and their safety. Or bailing them out should it become necessary.

We had discussed that potential should arrests occur. It was always a possibility at a large action against a well-connected group like PYDC. Em and I exchanged a feral smile.

"It's showtime! You notified the local news?" they asked.

"Yes," I said.

I had been liaising with the local news network since I joined. It had been a natural role for me since I had connections through my dad's work. Our chapter of SaFE had cultivated a strong working relationship with the media over the years. I was capitalizing on it now. My contacts assured me we could expect coverage.

I had already scheduled an interview before the event for the local print newspaper since we had established a good relationship with one of their journalists. If the protest picked up steam, then I would be in touch with morning drive DJs to drum up local interest.

"Let's go," Em clapped my shoulder, and we exited the van to join the chaos. They found Jess, who had coordinated with other chapters of SaFE. She must have information from her contacts to share as we got set up.

Some east coast chapters would have been picketing for hours already. I hefted my sign and went to stake out an area close to the facility's entrance. Somewhere I would be visible to anybody in our group who needed to find me at the front of the crowd. Caleb joined me before too long, Elliott not far behind him. I rubbed absently at the sore spot in my chest.

"Good turnout," Caleb said. He sounded chipper.

"Better than I expected," I agreed. "We were lucky the second van was still available."

"Good thing it is the summer session," Caleb said, "although we might have gotten better turnout during the term."

"This way everyone in attendance is more engaged," I said.

"True. Don't look now, but we have company," Caleb said over the noise of the other protesters gathering around us.

I looked, which was Caleb's intention anyway, and saw a commercial bus pulling into the far end of the parking lot. Along with the local news van bringing their camera crew.

"Do not interfere with or touch the facility staff or the campers," I said. I raised my voice to remind the people around me as the bus disgorged a group of young adults in SPIRE branded athletic wear in a variety of colors.

The adults all had 'STAFF' printed across the back of their shirts in large capital letters. They lined up and waited for the campers to exit the bus, each of the teens also wore SPIRE branded clothing in an assortment of colors. They gathered around the adult in the matching color in a babble of noise and activity.

The adults consulted clipboards, taking attendance. Once they accounted for everyone, the group filed past us and in through the entrance to the main building.

While the camp staff and students were getting organized, the local reporter and her cameraman had gotten out of their van. They scrambled to get the best vantage point as the group from the bus went by us.

We didn't want to give them anything to turn public opinion against us. The optics of a group of protesters harassing children at a summer camp were not great. However, that those children were all branded with the SPIRE logo and most of them were older teens played into our narrative. So we held the line, leaving enough space that the video footage would not substantiate any allegations of interference.

We raised our signs and chanted our slogans. It was an exercise I was familiar with after four years with SaFE. The newscaster approached our group to get sound bites as the last of the staff escorted clusters of teens inside the nearest building.

I planned to be the one she spoke with. But something happened as the last camp counselor filed past.

He was not much taller than his young charges, but he still stood out in a lime green t-shirt. The uniform was anything but flattering to his already pale complexion. The color brought out brassy orange tones in his red hair.

He followed the same resolute path as the other camp counselors, none of them glanced over at us, staring straight ahead. As if someone had coached them. They led their charges past our group pretending we weren't there.

I felt the pull of his aura on mine before I got a good look at him. It was an electric buzzing of that sense that made me an anchor. The one I had honed after so long spent socializing with psions. And living with two.

This was different though. It was like that missing piece of myself that I had ached to find was right in front of me. The painful yearning intensified, sharpy and insistent, until my chest felt like it might burst from longing.

I wanted to get closer, to touch, and be touched. I needed to be closer to him.

And he must have perceived it too because he stumbled as he pulled even with me. His head turned toward me in an almost involuntary action. My world seemed to move in slow motion because I recognized the face that turned to stare at me with a stricken expression.

I had once kissed the lips that silently shaped my name, his disbelief clear even at a distance. Even all grown up and sporting a tidy beard, he was still recognizable as my Aaron.

"Aaron?" I breathed.

The shock of seeing him again—here of all places—made me stop mid-chant to just stare at him. My hands with the sign held aloft dropped to my sides. But then Aaron's expression hardened, and hid my sweet happy Aaron behind a cold mask. He recovered his footing and his composure.

Aaron marched into the large building with his young campers trailing in his wake. And I stared, slack-jawed, at his back. My sign hung from limp fingers as he disappeared. I was only aware of Caleb beside me when he nudged my shoulder and gave me a concerned look.

"You okay, big guy?" Caleb asked.

"No, not really," I told him, swallowing back my emotions and forcing myself to lift the sign back into the air.

"Want me to take the interview?" Caleb offered.

"Please," I said, with heartfelt appreciation.

"Go with El," he gave me a gentle push toward our lover. Elliott must have caught the odd nonverbal exchange between Aaron and me because he met me halfway. I stumbled into his arms.

Elliott wrapped me in a tight hug, somehow enfolding my larger frame despite his wiry build and whispered near my ear, "you look like you saw a ghost."

I nodded against his shoulder.

"Come on then, big guy, you're taking a little break in the van," he said.

He took my sign from my hands and guided me away from our group and back to the van. He got me a bottle of water from the stash in the back and settled me on one of the bench seats.

"That was Aaron," I said, trying to test how I felt about it. I was unprepared to see him again.

"Your ex?" Elliott asked, hovering over me with a concerned expression.

"Yeah."

"So, why do you look like he returned from the dead, Jay?"

"It's worse than that, he came back from the east coast," I said, but the joke fell flat. "He didn't reach out to say he was coming back."

"I didn't think you were in touch with him."

"I'm not. But I can still sense the link between us. It hurts," I rubbed at my chest. Elliott grimaced. The dull pull I sometimes felt in my aura had blossomed into the ache of a long atrophied muscle pressed back into sudden service. The sudden intensity made me think that maybe he'd been back in Seattle for a while. It might explain the recent changes to my aura.

"I didn't know."

"Huh?"

"You never severed it?"

"I didn't know how back then. And I didn't realize it was still there, it's how my aura has felt ever since I learned how to feel it. I thought inactive links faded away over time?"

"A temporary link will," Elliott shrugged. He smiled at me with a sympathy bordering on pity, smoothing my hair. "You still love him, huh?"

"I don't even know who he is anymore," I protested even though we both knew he was right.

"So?"

"You should get back to the others," I attempted to change the subject.

"I'm not going anywhere while you're still upset, Jay."

"I'm fine."

"You're not," Elliott sighed. "The link explains things at least. If you had a link with him all along, it makes sense why you don't always connect with us. Why it took so long to form a proper link between lovers, anyway. Why your aura sometimes seems like it's searching for something it can't find. Like you're settling with us."

The sadness in his voice jerked me out of my thoughts. "No. It isn't settling. Never that. I love you, Elliott. You and Caleb both. Don't you call what we have settling."

"Fine, not settling, but you still wanted him too. Don't bother denying it, I've read you."

"I'm sorry. Em told me you and Caleb are worried. I didn't…"

"Don't apologize for how you feel, Jay. We only worry because we care."

"So, now I know about it, I can sever the link to him. Maybe then it won't seem like I'm missing a part of myself. This is why my aura hurts you sometimes, right? Why it's been worse the past week? I can fix it."

"Perhaps, is that what you want?"

"I want you and Caleb."

"And Aaron? Because you can have both. You can love all of us. Caleb and I only want you to be happy."

"I don't know. I mean, about Aaron. He cut me out of his life. He ran away and put a continent between us. Aaron would want me to sever our link."

"You can't know without talking to him first."

"You didn't see the way he looked at me."

"He's working. For the organization we are protesting. Not the best circumstances for a warm reunion."

"I don't know what to do."

"Think it through. You've held this link for—what, six years now? A few more days shouldn't matter."

"Yeah."

"If you need room to explore whether there is something worth saving between you and Aaron, you know we'll give you as much time and space as you need."

"I know."

"Good, and we will talk about what's been bothering you when we get home, all right? Caleb thought we should give you space, but I think you needed reassurance more, huh?"

"Maybe. I'm sorry."

"I'm sorry too. We'll figure it out, all right?"

Elliott hugged me and I clung to him for a few minutes while I regained my composure. If Aaron could pretend we had nothing between us, then so could I. And once I broke our connection, I could commit to the relationship I had built over the past four years in full. I pulled away when I had my emotions under control.

"I'm okay now," I said.

Elliott considered, then said, "you're sure you're okay?"

"Yeah, I need a minute to process and I'll be back."

"Okay, big guy, take your time," Elliott brushed a kiss against my temple and then left me to watch my friends protest without me.

I drained the bottle of water and that helped steady me. The cold water numbed the almost physical ache of having Aaron so close after so long. I itched to check up on him, to go to the social media pages where I had unfollowed him years ago to avoid temptation.

Aaron should have graduated from Yale, according to Mom. He should be building a fantastic future for himself. He should not be in Washington, or involved with SPIRE.

It turned out sitting in the van with nothing but my thoughts and my phone was the last thing I needed. I wanted to talk to Aaron, but we hadn't spoken since the hospital. There had been a few unreturned texts. A message—passed through my mom—apologizing for leaving without seeing me. And then nothing but bitter regrets about how it ended.

So I couldn't just contact him out of the blue. And I couldn't walk onto the grounds to talk to him. That would only end in my arrest since our right to peaceful protest did not include barging into the facilities his camp had rented. At the least it wouldn't reflect well on SaFE and as much as Em was a close friend, they would not appreciate me screwing up our action today.

I looked across the parking lot and saw the camp staff were unloading the bus. My heart stuttered when I glimpsed lime green in amongst the staff shirts. He was right there. I resolved to go rejoin my friends. If I stood with the others, it might take my mind off Aaron. I needed Elliott and Caleb. Their presence could soothe the ache of longing.

Or if I was honest, I hoped to catch another glimpse of him up close. That was the closest involvement with him I could hope for now. It might even ease the sense of loss. A few more minutes in Aaron's presence before I cut off any lingering connection to him.

Chapter 13

Aaron

My aura surged as I walked by the protesters leading my team of campers. I didn't think much of it, my aura and my abilities had both been acting up since I returned to Seattle a week ago, after graduation. I had been chalking it up to a combination of stress and jet lag. I had bigger concerns than a recalcitrant aura anyway—I had teenagers to mentor.

Team lime comprised the fourteen-year-old and under TK group. Which meant most of them had undergone their emergence in the recent past. That raised the stakes even higher for providing them with a good role model. And part of that meant walking past the protesters with our heads held high.

All of my good intentions crumbled when my aura gave a disconcerting pulse at someone in the crowd. My footsteps faltered at the shock.

My aura reached out for someone. An anchor, I understood on an instinctual level. Not shocking, anchors were a given with all the psions present.

I didn't expect to identify the particular individual in the tight press of the throng though. Except that when I turned to look, it was Jake. He had grown even taller and broader than he had been in high school. No surprise there.

Jake's arms bulged with muscle. He appeared even more cut in person than in his online pictures. But I had forced myself to stop creeping his profile over a year ago, so it made sense he had changed.

We made eye contact for a second that seemed to stretch to an eternity. He appeared as shocked as me, but I pulled myself together faster. I had a responsibility for the teens in my care. So I needed to act like it.

My first priority had to be getting my teens out of sight of the protesters and news crew as soon as possible. So I hurried the young campers into the large building that would serve as a mess hall and gathering place over the next month.

As the door shut behind our group, one of my kids spoke up. Sam, I recalled the name from the picture with their file, asked in a small scared voice.

"Why are they protesting us?"

"They're like us, why do they hate us?" another, Elle, asked. Her question justified since it would have been obvious to all the young psions that the protesters also had psionic abilities. And a loud buzz of other young voices asked similar questions all around us. I raised my voice for my whole team to hear me.

"Hey, lime team, gather round," I gestured for the eight youth on my team to move in close. Once they quieted down and clustered close enough so I didn't have to yell, I addressed them. "That was unexpected, huh?"

They nodded and one boy—I thought his name was Tim—said, "their signs said they want to abolish SPIRE."

"Some of them had shirts with SaFE written on them," another of the teens piped up. And her voicing a specific concern gave me something to work with.

"Well, the good news is that SaFE is a pro-rights group. So I don't think they are here to hurt anyone. We will have to see what the camp director says, but it looks like they aren't protesting against us per se, their problem is with SPIRE."

"But why? If they are for psion rights why would they protest against SPIRE?" Sam asked.

"I'm sure they have their reasons. They might have misinformation about SPIRE or our camp. Let's not worry about that though. We are here to work on your control of your abilities, so let the adults worry about the protesters, and you focus on what we are here for, okay?"

"Okay," the kids agreed with varying degrees of enthusiasm.

"Okay, well, let's take a seat. You can chat while I go check out the anchor situation," I said.

I waited until my team sat around a table alongside the other six teams. Then I joined the gathered camp counselors at the front of the room.

"What is the commotion about?" another staff member asked as I approached. Our boss, the camp director Joe Armstrong, scowled at his clipboard as though it contained all the answers.

"So far we know that it is organized by the Society For Equality, a radical psion rights group. They want to repeal all psion related legislation and abolish SPIRE and the department for psion relations.

"This appears to be part of a coordinated effort, with small protests at several youth camps run by the Pederson Youth Development Center network. I heard we might attract protesters, but I didn't want to upset anybody if it turned out to be nothing."

"Is there a credible threat to the children's safety?"

Joe shook his head, "nothing solid. SaFE has no record of violence or even property destruction. Their ideas may be radical, but their methods have remained peaceful," Joe sounded pained at the admission.

"So what is the plan?" another counselor asked.

"We will proceed with all camp activities as planned. The protesters may gather in the parking lot, but they may not enter the actual grounds since we have rented the entire facility for the month. You all have your cabin assignments?"

We all nodded, and Joe continued.

"Good, we will unload the students' bags from the bus and bring them to the correct cabins rather than have the campers go through the protesters again. There are reports of counter-protesters at some sites so we will keep the campers away from both sides in case of any clashes.

"The situation is being monitored, and SPIRE's local headquarters dispatched some agents for additional security as a precaution. They should arrive soon. I will keep you all apprised as the situation develops.

"That being said, we will carry on as normal for now, silver team, are you ready?"

The counselor in the gray shirt stepped forward.

"I think so," he said. "I'm Harold, for those I haven't met yet. This year we have nine anchors making up the silver team, so I will assign them among the groups. The three most experienced ones will work with the telepath teams and we will distribute the others two to each telekinetic team."

"All right. Harold, why don't you assign the anchors to their teams. Harold and I will stay with the kids while the rest of you counselors get the bus unloaded. I want the unloading done before we have to deal with counter-protesters adding fuel to whatever is going on at our gates," Joe said.

We dispersed to follow orders. At least they had given the campers color-coded tags to put on their bags so it was easy to figure out where to bring each bag. It still took over an hour for the eight of us to lug everything for all forty-five students. Plus the ten adults.

The irritated commercial bus driver did a final check to make sure we had everything off of his bus before driving away. The protesters were still going strong, chanting as we filed past them. To minimize the number of trips necessary, we tried to carry as much as we could manage.

I resisted the urge to search for Jake with each pass. But I didn't sense him in the crowd anymore. I wondered if he had left, but the telltale pull on my aura persisted, so I suspected he remained close.

I used my TK to lighten my third and final load, but it took effort and I needed to pace myself. If I wanted to be any good to my students for the first day's sessions, then saving energy was imperative. So I ended up straggling behind the others with my last three bags.

That was how I ended up cornered by a news reporter. She stuck a microphone in my face with an assertive air that bordered on aggressive. She asked for a comment from PYDC or SPIRE.

I froze, losing my concentration and dropping the bags I was carrying in a heap. A heavy suitcase bounced off my toes. I held back a string of curses even though I wanted to hop around and erupt like an enraged cartoon character.

"I don't have a comment, and I don't speak for either PYDC or SPIRE," I said, reaching over to correct the largest overturned suitcase.

She thrust the microphone toward me and asked if I had a comment, anyway.

"No, I'm only here to teach underserved youth," I snapped at the reporter. I shouldn't have said anything because I didn't speak for either organization. They wouldn't appreciate my talking on their behalf even if I had tried to clarify my intentions.

"Can you comment on allegations that this is a recruitment event targeting children as young as eleven?"

"It is a summer camp to teach these youth life skills," I fumed, hands on my hips, and then thought better. "I mean, no comment."

I scrambled after the other two suitcases, making a belated attempt at ignoring the reporter.

She gave me an almost sympathetic look. Sympathetic or not, she still opened her mouth with another question at the same moment when Joe came barging outside. He must have wondered what was keeping me. Everyone else was back inside already. He looked livid when he saw me talking to the press.

"Anderson, what are you doing?" Joe bellowed from the doorway.

"I'm getting ambushed by a reporter," I said. I tugged the last bag back onto its roller wheels.

"Well, get in here with those bags," he snapped, and two of the bags jolted toward him. Joe was a telekinetic too. Grade B, much stronger than me. The two bags slid across the intervening distance to Joe's side. I picked up the remaining bag and rushed toward him. Drawing on my abilities to hoist the bag as though it didn't weigh fifty pounds. God, what were the kids packing, bricks?

"What the hell did you say to her?" Joe snarled up close to my face. He met me halfway across the open space, angling us to hide our confrontation from the cameras.

"I told her I don't speak for SPIRE or PYDC."

"I told you to keep your mouth shut," Joe looped his arm over my shoulders to guide me back inside. His touch crawled along my skin like spiders. "I'll deal with it, see if they will agree not to air anything you said, otherwise we might have to let you go. If the media plans to use your words to misrepresent the camp or its sponsors."

"But I did nothing wrong," I protested, resisting his efforts to shove me back inside.

"Someone has to take the fall, kid, try not to worry about it yet. I'll see what we can work out," he gave me a more gentle push toward the building, but I stayed rooted to the spot.

I watched as Joe put on as much charm as he could muster to approach the reporter. From her defensive stance and Joe's decline in composure, it didn't seem like their conversation was going my way.

Well, there went my summer plans. What was I supposed to do without the camp to keep me occupied? And would it affect my future prospects at SPIRE? Grade C telekinetics were a dime a dozen. My only real value to SPIRE was my involvement with their youth training camps since I was seventeen.

SPIRE was one of the few employers who regarded being a psion as a plus on a job application. It was possible they were the only large employer where it was a requirement. I was planning to start my master's program at UDub in the fall, but SPIRE was my backup plan in case things fell apart on me again.

Joe turned back toward me, looking livid. And then the tug of the atrophied link twisted, pulling and intensifying, and I lurched to a halt. Jake. Without a doubt, I could pick Jake out of the crowd at Joe's back with my eyes closed.

Jake had returned, there was no longer a mass of people—and by extension their competing auras—between us. He was at the front or the crowd, close enough to talk or step into touching distance. And my aura wanted to tangle together with his. I closed my eyes and tried to focus, but his influence did something to my abilities.

It was like a jolt of caffeine amping me up. I had to focus hard not to launch the suitcase I was carrying. Instead, I dropped the darn thing and tried to lock down my abilities. My control slipped in a way it hadn't since I'd been a raw kid, fresh off my emergence.

I clenched my fists and something in me reached for the cameras the same way I had reached for things when I was first learning. On an instinctual level and without real intent. I tried to pull back; I didn't need to add property damage to my list of sins. Even if Joe might appreciate the footage not airing. And it was if the thought had given shape to the amorphous tendrils of my abilities.

I reached out, with a surreal sense of experiencing it as an observer, not to smash or destroy as I had when I was first learning. No, this was a zap of power through the camera's circuitry. Almost like a static discharge in the machine's guts. Or an electric pulse.

The camera guy fussed with his equipment. His movements became more frantic until he lowered the camera to prop it on his hip and yelled, "hey, what did you do to my camera?"

"I did nothing," Joe snapped, taking an aggressive step toward him.

"Well, it was working a second ago, and now it's fried. No telling if we still have the footage," the camera guy blustered.

"Seems awful convenient when you were just demanding we turn over the raw footage," the reporter said.

"None of my students or staff is electrokinetic, you can check the registry," Joe barked back.

I pitched forward then, god; I felt weak. And did Joe just say electrokinetic? Because EK existed, a subclass of TK.

A subclass I had never displayed more than the barest signs of before. So the thought looping through my brain was crazy—right? Only it didn't seem so crazy as the ground rushed up to meet me and a classic overuse headache pounded through my skull. Did I do that?

I groaned and rolled onto my side, overusing my abilities hurt—I knew that. So I was always careful. I recognized my limits, and I avoided pushing them too far. Because I was a wimp about pain. And now I was rolling around on the ground in front of a bunch of semi-hostile strangers and my boss who was not my biggest fan at the moment.

"What the hell, Anderson?" Joe was bellowing at me. I grabbed at my ears trying to block out his angry yelling. I hoped the pressure would help counter the way my psionic abilities seemed to want to push out through my skull. My aura wouldn't settle. And I had a buzzing awareness of my surroundings. It was like when the Cereflux had first kick-started my abilities.

Details I hadn't realized were out of focus snapped into clarity, everything had a crisp sharpness, better definition. I gained a sudden new awareness of the world around me.

Only, instead of an awareness of neighboring objects, I sensed the pulse of every electronic device around me. The buried power lines running underground, and the ones strung up along the roadside overhead. The jumbled interference I used to get around electronics had morphed into glorious detail. A second, more specialized, psionic sense. It was strange. I blinked to clear away the afterimages, but my eyelids didn't block the sense, it wasn't sight, even if I often described it that way.

It was overwhelming. And, oh god, it was too much. I needed an anchor; I had tipped too far off balance to correct it on my own. Except, I didn't have a link here. I hadn't needed one since high school when I had learned to control my limited abilities.

There it came again, the insistent tug of an unsettled link. Everything tilted back onto the correct axis in a dizzying lurch that made me glad I was already on the ground. The world's new buzzing undercurrent dimmed. I still sensed every cell phone resting in every pocket. But something muted it to a bearable level.

The aura that had been pulling at me since we arrived here was meshing with mine at last. Closer, closer, oh please closer. Right next to me. Close enough to touch. My aura reached for it, twisted around it. It reminded me of a dog rolling onto its back in the mud, wallowing.

"You're all right, Aaron," Jake's voice, deeper and rougher than I remembered, but unmistakable as his.

I shivered at his hands touching me. He pulled me up off the hard dusty ground. It would be so easy to forget the years between us. I was desperate to snuggle into him like I was still a besotted teenager.

The rest of the world faded to insignificance when I looked into his familiar face. Only inches between us. My hand lifted to touch his face without my volition, cupping his cheek. I caressed his stubble with my thumb.

"Jake," I sighed, content. In my anchor's presence, I could let go as last. Jake would make everything all right.

"I've got you, Aaron," Jake said. He pressed me against his chest as he stood. I wanted him to hold me, but this wasn't the time for a teary reunion.

I sensed our link strengthening, my aura settling back into a stable state, his nudging it toward equilibrium. The jagged pieces that never seemed capable of settling clicked into place. That rogue element of my abilities made sense now and—instead of the relentless pull toward some unknown destination—it thrummed with contentment. Like my aura was saying here, home. Mine.

"That's better," I mumbled into his shoulder, reluctant to release him. I never wanted to surrender my claim on him again. But clinging to him was a luxury I didn't have. I pulled back far enough to take in his familiar face.

"Who the hell are you, and why are you touching my employee?" Joe snapped.

Joe's approach jolted me out of the pleasant haze of being anchored. He was in a snit. He was also standing far too close. I took a step back even though it forced me to step out of Jake's embrace. The distance amped up the intensity of my headache and my new perceptions—I faltered, but Jake reached out to steady me.

"He's my link," I said, not thinking of the potential repercussions until the words were out of my mouth.

"Your link was here with the protesters?" Joe looked even angrier.

"Estranged, his estranged link," Jake said.

"Your application said you didn't have a link," Joe said. His eyes narrowed.

"Because we parted ways, and I didn't realize that he hadn't severed it. It was almost six years ago," I said, defensive.

Jake still stood close, his arm brushing against mine with each move I made. The touches eased something in me.

"Did you fry the camera?" Joe demanded with quiet intensity, the heat draining from his voice as he changed topics.

"Maybe?" I said. I couldn't say for sure, but my suspicions grew that I had done it. "Not on purpose. I've never had electrokinesis before."

As I talked, my body swayed. I liked it when I brushed against Jake's hard body. He made no move to discourage the touches, so I didn't try to hold still.

"Your registration lists you as a grade C telekinetic," Joe said, accusatory.

"That's what I am," I said, and then amended my statement. "Or what I thought I was."

"You two are coming with me until we get this sorted out," Joe said.

"I'm not going anywhere with you, and neither is Aaron until he has a moment to recover. He was just on the verge of going hyper-gamma," Jake crossed his arms, widening his feet in a defensive stance.

The shift in his weight placed him in my personal space. I pressed against him again, his aura was irresistible. At least the mob of protesters behind him were all psions. They wouldn't find my need to touch him inappropriate like a norm audience might.

Not that I cared enough to stop myself; not when the low rumble of his deep voice thrummed through my body as he talked. It echoed the electricity I now controlled.

Jake leveled a defiant glare at Joe. I had to remind myself this was real. Jake was here, standing up for me as he always had when we were kids. Like nothing had changed.

God, I loved Jake. I couldn't afford to dwell on that thought. Our love had gone out the window a long time ago. And I had doubts as to whether we could move past the things he said, or the things I hadn't said. But for this moment I allowed him to hold me together while I adjusted to power I was not ready to handle.

I longed to snuggle close and pretend nothing else existed in the world. It wasn't an option though. And as nice as it was to have Jake fight for me, I needed him to acknowledge my ability to stand up for myself now. I wasn't the same kid he had protected from bullies. So I turned to face Joe, albeit with reluctance.

"We need a minute," I said, and then I took Jake's hand.

Joe's expression turned thunderous. He didn't appreciate being ignored. But since Joe had already threatened my position with the camp, I figured that didn't leave him many other avenues for retaliation. And I would choose Jake over a job any day.

I didn't have a specific plan, per se, but there was so much unsaid between Jake and I and we needed to talk. I hoped that we could carve out five minutes of privacy.

The unmarked black SUV pulling into the lot put paid to any hope of getting a moment alone. Two SPIRE agents in tactical gear emerged from the car as soon as they had parked.

"About time they got here!" Joe huffed. "Stay here, Anderson, we'll deal with you in a moment."

Joe moved to intercept the SPIRE agents.

"You all right?" Jake steadied me, and I nodded.

"I am as long as you're close, overuse is a pain in the ass."

"Your abilities?"

"Yeah," I said, "hold me?"

Jake wrapped me in his arms and I melted into his embrace, letting it mute the worst of my overuse reaction and the awakened electrokinetic senses I shouldn't have.

Three protesters broke off from the others and approached us. I didn't spare much thought for them, at the moment clinging to consciousness was about the extent of my abilities. I only noticed them because of the way their auras melded with Jake's.

Jake was close to the approaching psions. Had links to them, two of those links took precedence over the stunted, atrophied connection between us. Buzzed with the vibrancy of a permanent link bond. That hurt.

But then it meant Jake had the practice with anchoring necessary to ease my out-of-control abilities.

"Hey, Jay, everything all right here?" one stranger asked.

"Hey, Em. We're good now," Jake said, still letting me snuggle into him as he greeted his friends.

He laced our fingers together and pulled me closer, almost a possessive gesture. I peered under his arm to get my first good look at Jake's friends. I only had a clear view of the one who had spoken. The other two hung back behind her, though their features had a vague familiarity.

By focusing on every detail of the interloper's appearance I could keep my mind off whatever upheaval my new abilities were about to unleash upon me. Tall and willowy, most of the hair on their head shaved away leaving a long section on top dyed bubblegum pink and swept forward in a manner that defied gravity.

Small silver hoop earrings glinted along the entire outer edge of their ears. Dark eyeliner and lipstick. Their aesthetic was something out of an old punk rock music video. Pins, patches and badges cluttered their distressed denim jacket proclaimed their support for a variety of causes.

The patches included the psion flag, a rainbow patch, and a rectangle with yellow, white, purple and black stripes. That one took me a second to place, but I had attended an all psion school. So I had a more than a passing familiarity with the non-binary pride flag.

"So, this is the famous Aaron?" Em drawled.

"This is him," Jake nodded, "Aaron, this is my friend Em, they're a telepath."

"Nice to meet you," I said with a smile, noting his slight emphasis on the word they.

Trust Jake to clue me in on his friend's pronouns without making a big deal. Another reason to love him. Which okay, we had only reconciled less than five minutes ago, so it might be too soon to jump to love. And reconcile was maybe too strong a word for him saving me from myself. Reunited then.

A big part of our downfall had been my moving too fast. Still, I could work with like. I bounced up on my toes to kiss his cheek, a quick peck because I was giddy with being close to him.

Em chuckled, and it was a lovely low sound.

"You weren't kidding about him," one guy behind Em said.

"What do you mean?" I demanded, on my guard.

"Nothing bad," Em said, "the big guy just said you reminded him of a puppy when you get excited."

"Did he?" I said, not appreciating the comparison. But I didn't have the energy to get too riled up over it.

Em cleared their throat.

"That pair of SPIRE agents are headed your way. I think they're almost done with the guy who screamed at you about the reporter. Jake, I take it you're going with Aaron?"

"I'm his link. And he was just on the verge of hyper-gamma. If they arrest us, I will get in touch when I am able."

"We'll be there to bail you out," Em put a reassuring hand on Jake's shoulder.

Jake sounded apologetic about wanting to stay with me. But at least he wanted to stay. I would take my victories as they came.

I gave him a lingering once over. God, he was even hotter now. All grown up. I spared a moment to wish we had nothing more pressing to deal with than getting to press our naked bodies together at last. It had been months since I bothered to hookup. If our auras were any sign of our chemistry, then sex with Jake would be way hotter than a one and done with an internet stranger.

We were compatible, which made a huge difference in how his touch felt on my skin. God, even leaving sex out, it had been a long time since anyone's touch had settled me the way Jake's did. Since Albert and I severed our link. I glossed over the mention of arrests, SPIRE wouldn't arrest me. On what grounds?

"I am not a puppy," I said. To get Jake's attention back on me where it belonged.

"I know," Jake said, ruffling my hair, and I scowled at him patting my head after the dog comments.

"Jake, a word in private?" his friend asked, from behind Em. He sounded anxious. His aura made me bristle, the way it slid between mine and Jake's made me want to claim Jake. Chase away the competition. Stupid psionic senses, making me act like an idiot over a guy. I thought I'd outgrown that tendency. Perhaps it was tied to Jake.

Jake gave me an apologetic glance, "will you be all right for a moment?" he asked.

"Go ahead, I'll see what they want. I'm not a helpless kid anymore, Jake. Don't worry. I can handle it," I said, waving him off with a feral grin.

"I can see that. Just don't overdo it, overuse is serious if you're displaying grade A strength."

"Time is ticking," his friend pointed out. "Come on," he took Jake's hand and pulled him aside for an intense whispered conversation.

I didn't catch the rest of their conversation. Distracted when the two agents in tactical gear with the SPIRE logo stenciled over their chests strode past the protesters. I figured that they were coming for me, so I squared my shoulders and stepped further away from Jake. It took an enormous effort of will. But I didn't want them to perceive me as weak. And I needed to brave this on my own.

Choking down on my abilities to keep them from overwhelming me, I braced for a confrontation. It was a pleasant surprise to feel Jake's aura propping me up even as he held a whispered conference with his friends. I spared him a final longing glance.

"Are you Aaron Anderson?" the big burly agent asked.

"That's me," I said, "who are you?"

"Senior Special Agent Merchant and this is my partner, Assistant Special Agent in Charge Davis," The agent said, gesturing at himself and his partner as he talked.

Merchant was a big swarthy guy, tall, but not as broad or as dark as Jake. His partner was about my height, and she'd swept her blonde hair up into a tight bun. He was an anchor, and she was some stripe of psion. I couldn't tell her classification from her aura the way an anchor could.

"We are investigating allegations you submitted false or misleading information to the registry," Davis said.

Her expression was cold. I suspected she had already decided on my guilt. So, Joe informed them of the camera incident. And that it should have been beyond my capabilities.

"I didn't lie," I protested, "I am a grade C telekinetic. That's what the registry says, that is what every assessment has confirmed from my emergence until today."

I flailed my arms in emphasis, despite my resolve not to overreact. And I bit my tongue at that last part because Davis picked up on the wording. Her eyes narrowed as she crossed her arms over her chest. Her partner spoke up before she pounced though.

"You aren't being charged with a crime yet. For now, we are just asking you to come back to our local headquarters to answer a few questions. With any luck, we can clear up this misunderstanding before the situation escalates," Merchant said, gesturing with his hands in a calm down motion.

"Sure, you're just accusing me of a felony. No reason to worry," I said. And antagonizing him was stupid too. It wouldn't help my situation if I turned the guy who seemed open to listening to my side of the story against me.

"Are you going to cooperate with us, or must we force the issue?" Davis asked. It may have been paranoia, but I got the distinct impression she might prefer it if I made a fuss.

"I will assist with your investigation in any way I can," I fell in line, trying to convey the sense I had nothing to hide.

"Happy to hear it, Mr. Anderson," Merchant said. "Now, would you be able to point us toward Jake Moretti?"

"What do you want with Jake?" I hedged. Their interest in Jake renewed my wariness. Nothing good could come of this. I felt Jake at my back, still conversing with his friends. The men he shared a link with.

"The report names him as a key witness. I understand that he is your anchor?"

"Yes, he is my link," I said. I had already admitted as much to Joe, so I didn't see much point in denying it now.

"How would you characterize your relationship with Mr. Moretti?" Davis demanded. As though her job granted her the right to pry into my personal life.

I blinked at Davis, "I don't see how that is relevant."

"We will decide what is relevant, you answer the questions," Davis said.

"I think I want a lawyer present for your questions," I said. Her condescending tone irritated me. I crossed my arms and set my jaw. The last thing I wanted was Jake getting caught up in my trouble.

"You may involve third parties, but that might force us to bring this through official channels. I thought we were in agreement that this was a simple misunderstanding best resolved through an honest conversation," Merchant said, his tone regretful. He gave me the distinct impression I was being manipulated.

I suppressed a derisive snort. Merchant made it sound like they wanted to avoid pressing charges. But they wanted me to believe they would. So, it was a threat. Or not a threat, blackmail. As though I hadn't cut my eyeteeth on emotional manipulation.

But if my assumptions were correct, it meant I had something they wanted. And it didn't take a large leap of logic to see my only value to them was my alleged electrokinesis. I didn't have a choice here though, I either went along with the agent's cordial requests or I would be subject to their forceful demands.

Chapter 14

Jake

Merchant and Davis did not speak to us on the drive from the summer camp back into the city. Aaron's thigh bumping against mine with the frenetic bouncing of his foot made the tense drive bearable. He was stressed and clingy. Reminiscent of our last weekend together, and the memory ached in my chest.

Aaron took the middle seat to stay close. The tacit evidence he still took comfort in my presence eased my guilt at how things had ended. His proximity made the downtown traffic snarls easier to tolerate.

I had forgotten the sense of rightness I got from being near him. He kept fidgeting, tapping his fingers, until I grabbed the hand closest to me, then he settled a little. In a clear effort of will he tucked his other fist under his leg to prevent himself from fiddling. He squeezed my palm before glancing over at me.

The look in Aaron's eyes was full of so much adoration it floored me. I jostled him to break the mood. If he kept looking at me that way, it would be too easy to forget our situation and lean in to kiss him.

His bemused smile said he understood my motivation. He bounced our entwined hands on his knee a few times, then leaned his head on my shoulder for the rest of the drive. He might have dozed off, but I wasn't sure. His display of EK at the camp must have left him exhausted though.

We drove into the parking garage under a residential skyscraper in downtown Seattle. It had no distinguishing features, other than a small placard with the SPIRE logo emblazoned on its side. Our escorts called it 'the tower'. As far as I could tell, it was nothing special.

The two agents led us to an elevator. Davis tapped the security pad before pressing the button for the second floor. We all avoided eye contact for the brief ride. When the doors opened, we followed Merchant to a cramped room at the end of a lengthy corridor.

"Go right in and make yourselves comfortable. Someone will be here to speak with you soon," Merchant said, sweeping the door open and gesturing for us to go through it.

Aaron and I entered. Merchant shut the door behind us and I heard the lock engaging. I could also sense the vibration of psionic warding around us.

Aaron drooped with exhaustion in one of the hard plastic chairs in a loose arrangement around a flimsy table. At least his aura had stabilized since that awful moment when he had collapsed at the summer camp.

I stood near the doorway for a long moment, watching Aaron. I let the fact he was here sink in. Back in my life. A chance to patch things with Aaron almost made being held by SPIRE worthwhile. Almost.

Aaron looked pensive, his lips pursed. The expression reminded me of how he used to chew his bottom lip when he was nervous as a kid. Absorbed in thought, Aaron ignored me at first, then shook his head.

"They aren't recording us," he said, sounding puzzled.

"Are you sure?" I asked, moving to lean against the table at his side. Aaron's brow furrowed even more.

I felt the pulse and roll of his abilities. Instinct made me reach out to steady him with my aura and my hand. I gripped the nape of his neck. When I gave him a gentle squeeze, he leaned into the touch with longing.

"Hmm, that's nice," he said. "I don't know if it's the wards. Or if they skimped on the electronics in their interrogation chambers. Well, except the lights, the locks and the outlets. But I don't sense a camera. Does that make sense?"

I considered him. He fidgeted in his seat, looking all around the room. Like he thought the plain white walls and industrial gray carpet might have sprouted something of interest since the agents escorted us inside.

"It makes as much sense as it can, without being a psion," I said. Years among my friends from SaFE had accustomed me to being around psions by now, so descriptions of senses I lacked were easier to accept.

"I can feel the lock, but they embedded it in the wards, I don't think I can touch it? Perhaps with training. If they were watching us, it would have to be by psionic means, I think. They set the wards in the walls," he frowned, brow furrowed in deep thought as he reasoned. "I don't think a telepath could peak through the wards. A strong grade A might get a vague impression?"

"So, you can sense electronics now?" I asked, still not understanding how he could have developed electrokinesis without warning, even though it was becoming ever more plain he had.

"I think so," Aaron admitted. "But I swear that I couldn't before. It's like… okay. So, when norms inevitably ask, I tell people that being a grade C—for me at least—is like being in an old school point and click video game. And my psionic senses highlight the things I can influence. Like objects you can interact with in those old games, you know? And after frying the camera, it was like unlocking a new ability. Now the old stuff is still present, but with a whole additional layer I can interact with?"

"That sounds like a big change," I said, getting the gist of the explanation.

"You have no idea," Aaron rubbed at his eyes, "my head hurts."

"Can I help to mute it somehow?"

Aaron flashed me a grin, "touching me helps. Not the headache, but the electrokinetic senses. And the warded room is nice. Less stimulus, the drive here got intense between the car, the agents' gadgets and all the stuff we were driving past. Like bright strobe lights, or pressing your ear to a speaker at a metal concert. Almost made me glad they took our phones," he forced a chuckle. "It's nice not to have so many stimuli."

"I noticed you were twitchy in the car. I still want my phone back though."

"Yeah," Aaron said. I let a comfortable silence stretch then because it seemed like he might need a minute to process.

"Jake?"

"Yeah, Aaron?"

"Are we okay?"

I took a moment to consider my response. We needed to discuss everything that had happened between us. No use pretending the last six years never happened. But I could tell nerves and adrenaline were all that kept Aaron upright.

I reached for him, placing my hands on his shoulders. Offering comfort and verifying that it was truly him. Whatever else this was, Aaron and I were facing it together. I smiled at him. My touch eased the tension in his muscles. His gaze on me said he still felt something. There was a tenderness there that I remembered with fondness. Hope bloomed that we might work out our problems.

"I've spent six years without a word from you. What do you expect from me?" I said, my emotions under tight control.

"I'm sorry," Aaron said "I didn't know what to say, or how to say it."

"You could have told me to my face. Or at least break up with me."

I had meant to keep my tone mild, but the words came with more force than I had intended. The pain behind my grievances took Aaron aback. I sensed the dissonance in his aura though. The way things ended hurt us both.

"I realize I didn't handle it well," he said, his eyes watery with unshed tears. "But I was so overwhelmed, Jake. It killed me to lose you on top of everything else when I had just gotten you. I convinced myself if we never said the words to end it, then it might not have to be over."

"It hurt to lose my boyfriend," I said, "but you know what was worse than that?"

"What?" he asked, bracing himself against my answer, but giving me the room to speak. As though he felt he owed it to me to listen.

"The worst part was having my best friend throw me away like I was nothing to him," I said, refusing to pull my punches. His abrupt departure upended my life. My relationship with Caleb and Elliott still suffered from the fallout damage.

I didn't quite trust them not to leave me behind too. The realization, struck me like a physical blow. It seemed so obvious now that I'd seen the connection. But this conversation was about me and Aaron, so I needed to focus.

Aaron flinched at the accusation; people turning their back was something he was familiar with. I understood that, but it was what he had done intentional or not. And I found I had more to say. I pressed on, my voice filled with a quiet intensity that bordered on fury without quite tipping over the line. Because I wasn't angry at Aaron, not anymore. But the old wounds still hurt.

"You cut me out of your life, Aaron. I had to find out you were on a plane to Connecticut from my mom. I learned from my teammates that Noah punched you that last day. All our friends kept asking me how you were doing with the move. Or if I'd heard from you. And I had to pretend everything was okay when my heart was breaking. Because I didn't want to alter their opinion of you.

"And it was worse not knowing if you were okay. The constant worrying you weren't. Do you know what that was like? God, Aaron, I was so envious of my mom because you fucking talked to her, and I was also grateful because at least you were talking to someone."

"I'm sorry, Jake," he said. I shook my head, not denying forgiveness, but forestalling it. This was like lancing a boil, we needed to get it all out in the open where it couldn't fester. No sweeping it away with a simple I'm sorry.

"Tell me why?"

"Why what?" Aaron blinked at me in confusion.

"Why did you cut off communication?" I asked, my voice almost broke.

His arms twitched, like he longed to touch me. Try to erase the hurt between us. And it took everything I had not to let him brush the rest of the conversation aside and wrap him in a warm embrace. But I wasn't the only one hurting. And the problem had started with him keeping all of his hurt to himself when he should have come to me. Let me be his best friend. So I waited for him to tell me why.

"Why? Because you learned all that stuff secondhand, but I had to live it.

"I survived the most hellish weekend of my life because I had you at my side. I had brain surgery, and you all but broke up with me almost as soon as I was out of recovery. You called me crazy for wanting to be with you, for loving you.

"I told you I loved you, and you threw it in my face. And maybe I was naïve to think a highschool crush could last forever. But I wanted the chance to love you.

"And then my Dad came in and announced he was sending me to boarding school across the country with no discussion.

"My last day at our school, Mrs. Sullivan—the sweet old lady who always said I was one of her favorite students—made me sit in the back row. As far away from her as possible. She wouldn't even look me in the eye.

"Noah and his buddies beat me up in the bathroom after *her* class. She was standing in the hallway a few feet away when it happened. You think she didn't hear it happening? They called me a tick and psi-scum right in front of her, she watched them pushing me through the door.

"I had to depend on one of your soccer minions to save my ass, and I hated it. I didn't want you to know it happened, and I knew Garrett would report back to you. Tell you I couldn't protect myself.

"And I was the one who found out that half of my friends hated me. Because I gained the ability to move small objects short distances with my mind. Even though my abilities were weak they still turned my whole life upside down.

"I'm the one who had to register and have people call me a freak. I'm the one who wasn't sure if my best friend still wanted anything to do with me. And the stuff you said at the hospital hurt, Jake.

"I typed hundreds of messages to you. But I deleted every one, because as much as losing you hurt, knowing for sure you didn't want me would have hurt so much more.

"I was forced to navigate becoming a psion while I was going through my first breakup and moving away from home. Not to mention changing schools and getting cut off from all my friends and family.

"My parents called once a month if that. Otherwise I only heard from them when my grades slipped or if I screwed up. I could not take hearing you didn't love me on top of all of that, okay?"

"I didn't realize," I felt as close to tears as he looked.

"Yeah," he said, swallowing hard. "But that's all over, okay? Can we try to just start over?"

"I don't think that's possible, Aaron," I said. Aaron dropped his eyes as his tears flowed, not wanting me to see him fall apart. My heart wrenched with guilt as I realized he had misinterpreted my answer, I hated seeing him upset.

"Okay, I understand," he choked out, his voice quavering.

"Oh, no, Aaron, sweetheart, I didn't mean it like that. I mean, I don't want to throw away all the good times we had just because we both fucked up. And for what it's worth, I am sorry that I made you think you couldn't reach out to me."

I kept my touch on his chin light as I tipped his face up toward mine. I brushed away a tear with my thumb.

"It's not your fault," he hiccoughed. "I want my friend back, can we be friends again, Jake?"

"Yeah, Aaron. We can be friends. I never wanted to stop being your friend."

"And you'll be my link?" he asked, sounding less sure of my agreement on that point. For all he knew, I was in a happy and committed relationship or link-bonded to someone else.

"Yeah, I guess I never stopped being your link," I said, my tone rueful. I pulled him into a tight hug.

"Good, because your aura is like the psion equivalent of catnip for me," Aaron leaned in close and nuzzled into my neck.

I was thankful for my time with El and Caleb. For my understanding of psion behavior with their links. So I didn't overreact to the strange intimacy of the gesture or push him away when he needed comfort. I tightened my arms around him and held him close.

I nudged his aura into a more settled pattern. Years of practice with El and my other friends serving me in good stead. I knew how to be an anchor. I could be that for Aaron.

We would address the boyfriend issue later. He needed to know about Elliott and Caleb before we committed to anything beyond a link between psion and anchor. For now, having him agree to renew our friendship was enough. I didn't have the courage to broach that topic.

"Mm, so good," Aaron sighed with contentment against my skin. With the air cleared between us, we both relaxed.

"Get your fix now," I said with a slight chuckle. I sobered, the reality of our circumstances hitting home. "I think we will have questions to answer soon."

"Huh?" Aaron asked, struggling to focus.

Now that our conversation no longer placed immediate demands on his attention, he seemed to struggle to focus. He fidgeted at my side. The rapid manner our link solidified in was disconcerting.

Our reunion caused the ethereal thread of connection, which had persisted unnoticed between us, to expand. It bonded us. The way he had longed for from his hospital bed years ago. The rough, reaching, edges of my aura made whole for the first time since Aaron and I shattered any trust between us.

"Correct me if I'm wrong but, you weren't electrokinetic before today?" I asked, puzzled. Psionic abilities didn't work like that. Subclasses of TK manifested within weeks to months after emergence, not years.

"Yeah," he said, "well, mostly? My psionic abilities teacher thought I might develop that way, but it never happened."

"So, how is that possible? People don't wake up a different grade or classification. If you are a grade C TK during emergence, then that's what you are. I mean, barring people who have a borderline level of strength being able to shift between grades."

Aaron shrugged, "I don't know. But I sensed you right before it happened. When my aura touched yours it kind of amplified? I was losing control. Then Joe mentioned deleting the videos. And it was like my abilities thought 'hey, that's a great idea, let's do that.' Then the ground rushed up at me."

I tightened my hold on him, but I couldn't help the hint of amusement coloring my voice when I said, "you are still the same, Aaron, huh?"

He pushed back to regard me with suspicion, "what's that supposed to mean?"

"Nothing, just the way you talk. And your energy, nothing bad. I like it," I smiled at him, the lazy grin which was only for him.

Aaron threw caution to the wind and dove in for a quick kiss, the barest brush of his lips over mine. There and gone again before I allowed myself to get carried away by his taste and the soft scrape of his beard against my lips.

"You better like it," he teased, searching my eyes for any objections.

Aaron would not find any. I wanted him as much as he wanted me. And Elliott and Caleb gave their blessing to any direction my reunion with Aaron took. It was one topic we had discussed in our brief chat before the SPIRE agents took Aaron and I into custody. I needed to tell Aaron about them though. And we were still waiting in a psionically warded interrogation room. We shouldn't get carried away.

But I couldn't help kissing him back. He made this sound in his chest, almost like a physical impact and then his hands were in my hair. He kissed me. Like his life depended on it, all teeth and tongue and need. I clutched at him, giving as good as I got.

I pulled back when Aaron moved to climb into my lap though. Resting my forehead against his and smiling to forestall any fear of rejection. His pupils blown and his bright red curls tousled under my fingers. My cheeks flushed and I must look at least as wrecked as he did.

"We can't do this here."

"They're not watching," Aaron said, lip jutting out with his usual stubbornness. "I want you."

"Me too. But they might return at any moment."

"I guess. At least touch me?"

I stood, moving behind his chair to give myself access to rub his shoulders and he melted into my touch. We lapsed into silence for a time. Aaron fidgeting in his seat. He craned around to look at me, teeth worrying at his lips in the old anxious habit I remembered so well.

"It's a felony," Aaron blurted.

"What is?"

"Falsifying registry records and failure to register. The two things they accused me of doing. I didn't do it. Not on purpose."

"I know," I said, resuming my shoulder rub. He leaned into my touch. Aaron swallowed hard.

"If I'm a felon, I can't be a social worker. Not as a psion. Or work with kids at all. I mean, not even in the few places that allow psions," he said, sounding scared and small.

"Is that what you want to do?"

He had piqued my curiosity because the Aaron I had known never showed an interest in working with children. Although he had always liked helping me babysit so perhaps I shouldn't have been so surprised by that revelation.

He nodded, "yeah, you know why I work at that camp?"

"No," I told him.

"At Riverton, I had to have volunteer hours. I got involved with the local psion youth shelter. PYDC bought the facility while I was volunteering there. So I've been part of their summer training camp out east since high school. This will be my fifth year as a counselor. Sixth year with them if you count attending after eleventh grade.

"And you know the shit I told you about, with my one day of being a psion at a public school? Those kids have it worse than I ever did. I only wanted to help them, you know? Try to give them even a fraction of the opportunity my parents gave me by sending me to Riverton."

"Oh," I had no words. Because Aaron's reason for supporting SPIRE was why I took a stand against the organization—we both wanted to improve the situation of psions.

"I don't get it. Why were you there, Jake? I keep thinking about it, and I can't understand why?"

"Well, I joined SaFE in my first year at UDub, this is a coordinated action across SaFE chapters nationwide."

"Okay, sure, but why is SaFE protesting a camp that gives young psions a chance to learn about their abilities and provides them with mentoring relationships? A place that gives them training certifications that can help them get jobs? Isn't your group supposed to be fighting for our rights? How does it help psions to attack one of the few organizations that values us?"

I sighed, Em was better at answering those kinds of questions. I had been listening to them talk about these issues for that past four years though. Long enough, I figured I had to attempt an answer.

"Because SPIRE exploits psions. They don't care about you, they want to use you. If there weren't laws to keep psions out of civil service jobs, then you wouldn't need SPIRE to serve your communities. SPIRE is just another iteration of separate but equal. Without the pretense of equality," I said.

"Okay, I can see your perspective on SPIRE, not that I agree, but I can accept the reasoning. But why target the summer camp? The youth I am supposed to be mentoring are all under fourteen, your friends scared them. Don't you think they experience enough hatred in the real world?"

"It's circumstantial evidence, but we believe there is something shady going down with PYDC. They are the targets of the protests, not the kids. PYDC and the precise nature of their association with SPIRE."

"You say that, but I was with the campers after they got past your picket line. One of my girls asked why you hated us even though you were psions too. How am I supposed to answer that?"

"I'm sorry that we scared the kids. I am. But PYDC is not their friend, Aaron."

"PYDC facilities have the highest successful job placement rates of any psion youth program in the nation. They have more available beds than any other shelter in every major city. They help psions. Do you understand how difficult finding work and housing are when you are on the registry?"

"I know. Eighty-two percent of program graduates find job placements or get into institutions of higher learning. And if you only look at the numbers for grade A psions it's even higher. While other similar programs have placement rates in the sixty to seventy percent range. Did you stop to wonder why?"

"No. I didn't question it. Just appreciated that people like me—my friends—weren't ending up on the streets. Or forced to accept any job they could get. No matter how dangerous or illegal their work conditions turned out to be, because their employers knew they needed a paycheck," Aaron snapped.

That hurt, not just because what he described sounded awful, but also because it was a reminder that Aaron had a whole life apart from me now. And that the facts and figures that had motivated me to get involved in SaFE were names and faces and real people he cared about for him.

"Em is a statistician," I said. "From what they say, the reason for the high placement rates is that PYDC is forcing their charges to enlist with SPIRE. The three percent of grade A psions that aren't getting jobs? Yeah, almost every one of them has a felony charge on their record for failure to register. And out of the other grade A's, do you care to guess how many find jobs outside of SPIRE?"

"A few?"

I snorted, "Em says less than two percent. Don't you find that suspicious?"

"That sounds like conspiracy talk. The government is not putting together a secret superpowered special ops force of psions. It is ridiculous to think they could."

"No? Then why have they made it so that the only major employer who will hire a powerful grade A psion is their own paramilitary organization? Why do they have ties to the largest network of psion shelters in the nation? Why are those kids being put through a training program modeled after the SPIRE equivalent of boot camp? At a minimum your camp is grooming those kids."

"SPIRE isn't like that. To an outsider, it might look sort of like that, but the camp is about helping teens, not exploiting them."

"I don't see it that way. As far-fetched as it sounds, Em knows what they're talking about. And I trust them."

"Well, I trust what I've seen. I have friends who work for SPIRE. If it were doing something that shady I would know about it," Aaron set his jaw and crossed his arms over his chest.

I sighed, I doubted arguing about it would convince him. Aaron could be stubborn when he decided about something. Maybe seeing SPIRE in action would change his views. Or it might change my mind. I could at least try to assuage his fears. And, if possible, improve his opinion of SaFE too.

"Agree to disagree. For what it's worth, SaFE has been working against failure to register laws. I don't know how that will work for you since you have been living out of the state, but earlier this year Washington reduced it to a misdemeanor offense. At the federal level it's still a felony, but with a sympathetic prosecutor they can charge it at the state level and then it's a misdemeanor."

Aaron forced a smile for me, but it was a small brittle thing, "I heard about that. You worked on it?"

"Yep," I said, proud of my efforts.

"I doubt it will help me, I haven't lived in Washington for six years, almost the entire time I was 'failing to register'."

"It might give you grounds to fight. If they bring charges?"

"Maybe," Aaron sounded doubtful.

I sank into the chair next to him. I was reluctant to relinquish contact with him, but I wanted to get more comfortable. For all I knew, they might leave us cooling our heels for a while. I bumped my knee against his to convey that I was there for him. He forced a tight smile for me, and I watched him do that thing where he slid into his happy-go-lucky persona without a worry to his name. I first noticed it around the same time I realized his home life was worse than he let on it was. His 'everything is fine' act was one thing about him that hadn't changed.

"I'm sure it will all work out," Aaron said.

I wanted to call him on the obvious lie, but I held my tongue. Instead, I scooted my chair closer and bumped his knee. We settled in to wait.

They didn't leave Aaron and I waiting as long as I feared they might. Without my phone, I had no way of saying how long it took, but it couldn't have exceeded a few hours. The door's lock disengaged putting an end to our relative privacy. We swung around to see who entered.

When the door opened, it revealed a tall woman in a dark pantsuit flanked by the two agents from earlier, still wearing their tactical gear.

"Good afternoon, gentlemen. I am Special Agent in Charge Smythe," the woman said, giving us a brisk assessment.

Smythe skirted around the table to take a seat across from us. Davis went with her, staying between us and Smythe. Davis took up an at rest stance at Smythe's side. Her posture mirrored Merchant's. The big burly agent stood posted in front of the door, sending the clear message that there would be no escape from this conversation.

Aaron and I turned our chairs to face Smythe. The change in position afforded me the opportunity to squeeze his knee in reassurance. He gave me a tight smile. Smythe had brought a folder in with her. She paged through its contents with a bored expression until Aaron was fidgeting and squirming in his chair beside me.

"I understand your registration lists you as a grade C telekinetic, is that correct, Mr. Anderson?" she asked, keeping her focus on the file until she addressed him, then her gaze bored into him.

"That's what all measures of my abilities have showed since my emergence," Aaron said. His voice shook a little, and I offered my hand in comfort. His hand found mine, and he squeezed my fingers with a painful force under the woman's disdainful regard.

"I see. This incident report, filed by Joe Armstrong, alleges that you displayed grade A strength electrokinesis this morning. Do you have a comment?"

"This morning is the first full manifestation of electrokinetic abilities I've ever displayed," Aaron said.

"That's impossible," Smythe said.

"I've been through the SPIRE training certification program. A SPIRE agent ran the camp I attended. I graduated from Riverton Academy. Where I received lessons on using my abilities. And I got Cereflux injections at Mount Hope Hospital during my emergence. An entire medical team supervised the procedure. My hospital stay included a link with a professional anchor. All the staff at those venues had a mandate to report psionic abilities. Don't you think someone would have alerted the registry, if I had displayed any signs of such a rare ability? Or do you think they all conspired to hide my EK?"

"I'm sure they would have reported it, had they known," the woman said, her tone cool.

I resented the implication that Aaron had hidden his abilities when he was too inexperienced to make that feasible. Even if it occurred to him, he would never have thought he had reason to hide.

I scowled at them all, but I kept my mouth shut—for now. My focus needed to be on offering my silent support. I had to trust Aaron to stand up for himself. That was what he wanted. He'd told me as much.

"This morning was the first time I had electrokinetic abilities," Aaron insisted, "you will not find any evidence to the contrary, because it does not exist."

"Mr. Anderson, please," Smythe looked irritated. "You seem to be under the mistaken impression I do not understand how psionic abilities work. I assure you—as the top ranking SPIRE official in the state of Washington—I know how emergence works. Psions do not develop new abilities outside the peri-emergent period. Your story makes no sense."

"Well, I don't know what you expect from me. All I can do is tell you what happened from my perspective," Aaron said, his face set in a stubborn mask.

"Go ahead," Smythe said, with an edge to her voice.

"This morning I was a grade C telekinetic," Aaron said. "I strained the limits of my abilities by using them to carry three fifty-pound suitcases. I had a brief altercation with my boss. He took exception to a statement I made to a news crew. The situation escalated. Then I felt the proximity of my link boosting my abilities. At which point I lost control and the alleged electrokinetic incident occurred. Without volitional control on my part.

"I am not clear on the details of what happened next. I experienced overuse symptoms. Jake said I entered the early stages of hyper-gamma destabilization. That seems like an accurate assessment of my experience. My anchor stabilized my brain waves. Since the incident, I gained electrokinetic senses that were not present before," Aaron told his story by rote. Like he had been rehearsing it in his head. I suspected he had done just that.

"Mr. Anderson," Smythe sighed, and repeated her earlier assertion. "You and I both know spontaneous changes in classification simply do not occur. I want to help you, but I can't do that if you aren't honest with me."

"I am telling the truth!"

"How do you propose this occurred then?"

"I don't know how it happened," Aaron said. "There is only one other factor that changed today. Jake and I reunited around the time of the incident. We had formed a nascent link years ago. That link formed over the course of my bout with PEPS before my emergence. I guess thinking back, there were early indications I might develop EK, but it never came to fruition.

"The most plausible explanation I can think of is that separation from my anchor caused it. Perhaps being three thousand miles away from my primary link during emergence masked my EK. Or stunted its development. Or when the link between us reactivated it caused exaggerated link boosting. That's the best I can figure. I'm not an expert, maybe a psion specialist could tell us what happened."

"Boosting, hmm?" Smythe mused.

"As the head of SPIRE in the state, I'm sure you've heard of boosting," Aaron threw her words back at her. "It's a well documented, albeit rare, phenomenon in high compatibility anchor matches."

"Hmm," Smythe flipped open her folder again looking contemplative before fixing her attention on me over the top of the papers. "You are the anchor in question," she glanced down as if to check my name, "Mr. Moretti?"

"Yes?" I straightened my posture.

"And you have established a long-standing link with Mr. Anderson?" she asked, like she was fishing for more details. I had no intention of giving her any more information than she demanded though.

"Yes," I agreed.

"And do you corroborate Mr. Anderson's account of events?"

"Yes."

"Can you be more specific?" Smythe sounded exasperated. I changed tactics rather than pushing her when she had the power here.

"Yes, I'm his link. Yes, we lost touch almost six years ago, during his peri-emergent period. And yes, we started to form a link bond back then. I was unaware of how to sever a link when it happened. By the time I learned about that aspect of being an anchor I assumed that our link would have faded away.

"Based on today's events, it had not. When I noticed Aaron at the campgrounds this morning, I felt our link reawaken. When I got closer to him, it intensified to where it was strong enough to allow me to stabilize him when his brain waves entered a hyper-gamma state. As he told you."

"None of that is objective evidence," she said. She looked contemplative now though. "From an unbiased perspective, this seems to be a clear-cut case of falsifying registry records, if not a full-blown failure to register. Those are serious offenses."

"Washington state classifies them as misdemeanors," I pointed out, a little smug.

"Yes, that is true. But Mr. Anderson's abilities had not received their final classification and grading during his hospital stay at Mount Hope. He submitted his full registration two weeks after his emergence. Within the grace period, but while he was living in Connecticut. Where the statutes are stricter."

"That's not fair, he was a Washington resident at the time of his emergence and the incident in question occurred in Washington," I objected.

"And he lived in Connecticut under a false registration for six years, which is illegal in every state."

"But I *was* a grade C. I couldn't do anything with electricity and my abilities were never strong," Aaron objected.

"We only have your word for that. I'm sure you can see the position that puts us in? We can't have strong psions going around flaunting the laws. That behavior damages public perception, which hurts all psions. You must understand our position?" Smythe appealed.

The condescending words didn't match her tone. Her calm delivery made her sound eminently reasonable. As though she were a paragon of patient understanding. Aaron looked venomous. This was the exact wrong approach for her to take with him. It was too reminiscent of the emotional manipulation Aaron's mother favored to keep him in line as a child. He saw right through it. That was a relief, considering how eager he was to give SPIRE the benefit of the doubt when we spoke earlier.

"No, I don't understand at all," he said in a much milder tone than I expected. His aura and posture betrayed his tension. I put my concentration into smoothing out the rough edges of his aura and it pressed against mine in response.

"Look, Mr. Anderson, I am inclined to believe there was no ill intent. SPIRE, as a practice, prefers not to prosecute when another alternative is available."

"What alternative?" I asked. My eyes narrowed, I saw where this conversation would end.

"Our goal is to help psions by letting them help their communities. Prosecuting an honest mistake serves no one. Here is what we can offer you," she tried to mollify him and Aaron's expression softened a little. "If you place yourself under our jurisdiction, we can absolve you of the consequences of this little incident. Understand?"

"No, I can't say I do," Aaron said putting on a perplexed look, then added with a tentative softening in his rigid posture, "are you offering to help me?"

"SPIRE remains committed to helping psions serve their communities," she said, latching onto the hope in Aaron's voice and feeding it.

I recognized Aaron's fake smile as he trained it on her, "that's what I want to do. Help people. What do I have to do?"

"Enlist with SPIRE. I saw that your records indicate that you already got our youth program certification, so we can offer you an accelerated track for our training program. From your records, you would make an excellent candidate to be a field agent."

"That's it?"

"Yes. That's all," Smythe said. "Once you are an agent, the incident report goes away. We will amend your records to reflect your new classification and grading. The changes will be retroactive to your original registration date. Clerical errors happen.

"As an agent, we can keep an eye on you. Make sure this incident isn't part of a pattern of behavior. We can chalk this up to nothing more than an honest youthful error in judgment. Being a grade A can seem daunting to young psions. We try to make allowances where possible for the pressures of a higher grade's greater power."

Aaron was silent for a long moment. The bald manner in which she laid out the proposal floored me. This whole conversations exposed the exact suspect recruitment tactic that Em had accused SPIRE and PYDC of using on their young charges.

It chilled me to learn how blatant they were. But if this was routine practice how had it stayed hidden? Someone they had blackmailed into joining had to realize how wrong this was. Why had no one come forward?

I wished they hadn't taken our phones so I could have recorded the conversation. Now I understood the lack of recording equipment in the room. They wouldn't want records of their shady dealings that could leak to the public.

Aaron licked his lips, his eyes darted around the room and he vibrated with nerves. I laid a hand on his back and tried to soothe him. His aura curled around mine at the touch and he calmed, "okay, yes, I'll do it. I'll join SPIRE."

"Wonderful. You are making the right decision. It would be such a shame for your considerable potential to go to waste over something I'm sure you didn't intend to do," Smythe said. She pulled a few pages out of her folder. "We will also need Mr. Moretti to agree, if your abilities are because of link boosting then logic dictates you will need your anchor at your side in the field."

My mouth went dry. I should have seen that coming, but somehow I hadn't. Aaron gave me a pleading look. I couldn't let him down. I knew what Em would think of me joining the enemy, but I didn't have much choice. Em would forgive me, I hoped, but if I didn't go along with this, then Aaron might not. And I didn't want to discover Smythe's response if I refused.

"Okay, whatever Aaron needs," I said.

"You're making the right choice," Smythe affirmed with an encouraging smile. She pushed a second set of paperwork toward me.

"Where do we sign?" Aaron asked, returning her smile with a tentative one of his own. I didn't smile, but I signed the papers they put in front of me.

Chapter 15

Aaron

S AC Smythe left with the completed contracts as soon as Jake and I had both signed and initialed the paperwork she put in front of us. Davis fell in behind her. I forced myself to play the role of the willing recruit. Grateful and relieved that we came to an agreement.

I knew how close I had come to ruin, so dodging charges was a welcome respite. But the fact I could tell Jake was not happy about the outcome tempered my relief. I wanted to talk to him alone, to have privacy to see where we stood, but Merchant stayed in the room with us. So I flashed a cheeky grin at Jake, hoping he would accept our situation.

It wasn't as though joining SPIRE was my first career choice either. But I was coping. I hoped Jake would too. And SPIRE wasn't all bad. Even if these three agents undermined my faith in the Seattle office. Corruption happened, that didn't mean it had to be widespread as Jake seemed to think.

"So, since they didn't tell us how this will go down, I am guessing you drew the short straw, huh, Merchant? Escort duty?" I aimed for a comical suggestive tone. I stood and turned to face him. Jake stayed at my side, his solid presence reassuring. Merchant lingered near the door, looking bemused.

"You might as well call me Roy, since we will work together."

"Roy, huh? Not Agent Roy?"

"SPIRE isn't a huge organization, at least not at the local level. Besides, you know what interacting with a group of psions is like."

"I have no idea. Why don't you tell me about working with psions, Roy?" I asked, voice sticky sweet.

I batted my lashes. Irritated at him for acting as though he understood what it was like to be a psion. Not to mention perpetuating stereotypes even if they were accurate. He might be an anchor, and that made him a part of our larger community, but it wasn't the same for them. To start, anchors didn't need to register.

Jake reacted to my tone of voice. Out of the corner of my eye I caught his lips twitching into a bemused smirk, but he put a hand on my shoulder. A tangible reminder to rein in my temper. He always had excelled at reading me. Merchant shifted, betraying his unease. He must have picked up on my annoyance.

"Sorry, that was a bad choice of words. I only meant we are on the same team now. So we should try to be friends. Anna, my partner, is a grade A telepath. There aren't that many grade A psions assigned to Seattle. So, we'll be seeing a lot of each other. I know we didn't meet under the best circumstances," he gave every sign of being genuine in his apology. So I offered grudging acceptance to his overture of friendship.

"We're good. So, are you sticking around to assuage a guilty conscience, or are you here for a reason?" I asked.

"Why would I feel guilty? I volunteered to give you a quick and dirty orientation if you agreed to enlist," Roy said. There was a twinkle in his eye as he spoke. Through our link I noticed Jake seemed tense, so I dialed back my attitude. Merchant was not the one who had threatened us. He was just there as the backup. I didn't appreciate his involvement. But he had been decent to us at least.

"How dirty are we talking?" I teased with a playful leer. Jake drifted closer, and I bumped our arms together, just to touch him. Roy looked amused.

"Aaron," Jake sounded aggrieved, "tone it down a notch?"

"Sorry," I glanced at him. I flashed Jake a small genuine smile because with the way he was looking at me, how could I not? Roy didn't appear to mind the flirting. Nor did he seem to think I was serious, so I figured it was okay as long as Jake knew it was harmless. Roy cleared his throat to draw our attention back to himself.

"Let's stick with quick," he said.

"I love a good quickie," I couldn't resist the quip, and the comment surprised a laugh out of Roy. Jake's hand landed on my nape again—possessive. Like staking a claim. Not in a gesture of control, more like he needed a physical connection. It imparted the sense he needed to touch me in the same way I desired his touch. It steadied me.

"Focus, Aaron," Jake said.

"Right, so, orientation?" I asked.

I bit my lip against a comment along the lines of divulging my orientation. Then I shot Jake a look, trying to convey to him with my eyebrows that he should be proud of my restraint. He only rolled his eyes with exasperated affection so I must not have developed telepathy along with my electrokinesis.

God, I had missed him. The stolid way he accepted me. It was as though something rooted him firm enough to take all the boundless enthusiasm that sometimes wanted to bubble out of me and just absorb it. He grounded me and let me be myself. It would be easy to let myself need him.

"We use a scheduling app. So you'll be able to access your training schedule through your phone. Once your training program starts. That reminds me, here, you can have these back now," Roy interrupted my musing. I swayed into Jake's personal space. Roy pulled out our cell phones and returned them to us. We slid them into our pockets without comment. But I had to reach into my pocket and turn mine off because I couldn't stand the way it buzzed so close to my skin.

I only caught parts of Roy's explanation of how SPIRE worked. Doubtless, I should have paid more attention to what he said, but I was crashing hard after the events of the morning. The adrenaline of thinking Joe's allegations would derail my life was wearing off too.

I mean, my plans for the future had changed when I signed Smythe's contract, but that was life. Since I had enlisted, it seemed safe to let my guard down with Roy. He posed no further threat to my future. Well, the future SPIRE had compelled me to accept.

My dreams of getting hired as a social worker was always a long shot, anyway. And it would have gotten much longer as a grade A with a criminal record. I might have found a position as an aide somewhere, but working for SPIRE would be easier. And SPIRE helped psions. My work would still further the interests of young psions. It wasn't all bad, SPIRE had always been my second choice.

Still, I slumped at the full realization that this put the final nail in the coffin for my career aspirations. I couldn't help a sense of defeat. I leaned into Jake's side as Roy continued his spiel.

"Anyway, we are delaying getting you into training by a month. Joe Armstrong, from the summer camp, was insistent that he didn't have time to replace you for this session. SPIRE and PYDC are partners in providing these summer camps, as you know. He requested that we provide an agent to work with him. So, you have clearance to serve as a camp counselor as scheduled. SPIRE sends unpaired anchors to help run the camps anyway, but no one is available on short notice, so it falls to the pair of you.

"The plan, as it stands, is for Joe to work with your group today. To let you settle in here. Then in the morning, you will return to the camp until this session ends. At which point we expect you to return to the tower for your training requirements."

"When you say 'settle in', what are you implying?" Jake asked.

"You may have noticed this is a residential building? SPIRE provides housing to everyone in our training programs. Since housing policies can otherwise make it hard for psions to find suitable living arrangements in many areas where SPIRE operates.

"We offer courses for psions who require a certification for job placements outside of SPIRE besides training our field agents. New agent training is a five month process. The accelerated track SAC Smythe mentioned takes two months. For the duration of your training, living in the tower is mandatory.

"They assign link bonded pairs to the same quarters to promote bonding. Once you become a field agent if you want an apartment, then they are a part of the compensation package. One of the many benefits of working for SPIRE. If you opt not to live in the tower that is your prerogative.

"SPIRE encourages partners to maintain proximity in their living arrangements. It helps hone the link. But it is no longer mandatory once you complete your training.

"So, I meant you can get settled into your assigned housing after I give you a brief tour of the public areas."

"Tell me more about these benefits, they sound fascinating," I waggled my brows, Roy snorted but didn't laugh.

"You are trouble. Regarding the apartments, they're small, but you each get a room. Fully furnished down to your toiletries during the training period. If there is an issue with housing, we have strict harassment policies in place. We enforce those policies. Psions might live up to the stereotypes of needing good touches, but we take harassment seriously here, okay?"

"Sorry," I dropped my gaze, worried that I made him uncomfortable with my teasing.

"No worries, I'll tell you if you are bothering me," Roy said. "So, do you have questions before we get started?"

"You mentioned compensation, what else does SPIRE include?" I asked, just to show I could be a responsible adult. I didn't even put any emphasis on the word package, so points for me. And negative points for tuning out Roy's response.

My brain remained hung up on getting to live with Jake. I had no problem with that. I hoped that Jake wanted it too. If I hadn't cohabited with psions for six years it might seem like too much, too fast.

Jake and I were apart for ages, we might as well be strangers in some regards. But link bonding meant that I wanted him close. Relationships between a psion and their primary link often developed fast by norm standards. Even between relative strangers. And I had known Jake almost my entire life. I wanted the excuse to live together. Even if whatever was between us never progressed beyond the link bond.

"The details are in the paperwork I'll get for you when we go by the main office downstairs."

"Will we see the whole tower?" I asked, daunted at the prospect of walking as far as the elevator, much less going on an actual tour of the huge building.

"Not the entire building, only the public floors. We can start with the main office and the offices for building management and maintenance. Those are in the lobby. Our fitness center, laundry facilities, a mailroom, a 24-hour cafe, and a lounge area are also located on the ground floor.

"The first floor comprises conference rooms and smaller meeting rooms we use for educational presentations. The mezzanine level houses a small library. It contains an extensive collection of psi-lit. This floor is the warded psionic training rooms. As you may have observed, we can also use them as holding cells for powerful psions.

"A few floors above this one are offices for the higher-ups and our tech folks. We have desk jobs. That won't be you, your abilities are too useful in the field to hide you behind a computer."

"I am down with that," I said.

I was bad with sitting still. The academic part of school was all right, but being stuck at a desk always made me antsy and distractible. I used to drive Albert, batty during study hour. He complained my pacing and tapping with my assigned reading made it difficult for him to concentrate.

"We will grab the paperwork to kick things off. I'll give you my number so you can ask if you have questions as you read through everything since we are trying to get you squared away fast.

"Oh, I should mention, we have a housekeeping staff. SPIRE provides all the amenities in the short stay rooms. If you live here long-term the upper floors are more traditional housing, no housekeeping services.

"Since SPIRE requires all agents to meet fitness standards, they try to encourage active use of the fitness center. So stashing workout clothes in your closet is their not-so-subtle reminder to hit the gym. There are more details on everything from dress code to security clearances in the policy manual you will receive."

"Makes sense," I said.

I was not keen on gym time, but I figured Jake would appreciate the convenience. Although, I might like the gym better with a nice view of Jake all sweaty and pumping iron.

"Right, so, ready for the grand tour?" Roy offered, rubbing his hands together.

"Sure thing," I agreed.

In reality, the only sight I had any interest in seeing was the inside of my apartment. Alone with Jake if I got my druthers. And naked. I sighed, well maybe not naked. My whole body ached so the naked could wait, or we might restrict it to nude cuddling while we slept. Sleep sounded amazing.

I longed for today to be over. But Roy was right, we were now co-workers. So it made sense to meet his efforts at friendship halfway. I only hoped the tour would be quick. I pasted on a smile to cover the exhaustion and moved to follow Roy. Jake caught my elbow when I swayed off kilter.

"I think we can wait on the tour, Roy, if you don't mind showing us to our assigned housing? Aaron's already pushed himself to his limits, and he's too stubborn to say so, but he needs to rest," Jake said in a reasonable tone.

Jake directed the last part of his comment at me in his fond but firm voice. I wanted to muster irritation at Jake for talking for me as if I were a child or incapable of standing up for myself. But my relief at avoiding a tour made up for it. And if I was honest, I liked the way he always looked out for me.

Jake was right. I was dead on my feet. Far too tired to convince everyone around me I enjoyed being here. And after our meeting with Smythe, it seemed prudent to put on an act. At least until I was more secure about my position here.

"Of course," Roy said, "sorry, I should have considered, going hyper-gamma takes it out of you, huh?"

"Yeah," I said through a yawn. It was like the acknowledgment that the morning's events justified my exhaustion gave me tacit permission to stop pretending otherwise.

"Let's get you to bed then," Roy said.

"Mm," I said, but couldn't resist adding a sleepy, "I'm not gonna object to two big strong men getting me into bed."

"I think that must have sounded much less creepy in your head, babe," Jake said. He slid an arm around my waist to steady me and steered me toward the door.

"Yeah, I agree with Jake on that one, you're falling asleep on your feet, Aaron."

With another shrug, I yawned again, turning sheepish. I must have been even more tired than I thought because I went where Jake directed me, docile as a lamb. When Roy opened the door and all the electronics outside the warded room flashed back into my awareness, I winced.

The hallway wasn't so bad, not compared to the drive downtown. But it still surpassed my current processing capacity. I leaned into Jake and his aura wrapped around mine in response, blunting my new senses. Like sunglasses cutting through the glare on a bright day.

"You good?" Jake asked, concerned.

"Yeah," I said, leaning into him for the short walk to the elevator. The panels inside buzzed with electricity. But I ignored it. Roy escorted us as promised, showing Jake the key fob he used to get it to work. He explained that we only had access to the lobby without the fob.

I sensed the tiny electric pulse in the little blob of plastic. I had a distant awareness I could replicate that little spark between the fob and the security pad. But I had no interest in trying it just then.

Roy unlocked the door to our assigned room by punching in a numeric code, "your key fobs will work on the door too, once you get them. I will deliver them along with the papers explaining benefits, health, and dental, and policy manuals. It should cover the basics, the training program covers the rest. Contact me with any issues that arise, all right?"

"Sure, thanks, Roy," I mumbled, drained. I would have agreed to anything short of 'and this is where we do the ritual sacrifices of baby animals to initiate new agents. Pick a knife and a puppy!'

I walked into the entryway, kicking off my shoes and looking around. It was nice enough. Better than my student housing had been, anyway. Everything appeared bright and clean, the furniture was sleek and modern like everything else I'd seen so far in the tower. But I couldn't take in the details underneath the buzzing along my electrokinetic senses. The omnipresent pulsing along my senses overwhelmed me—a glowing overlay to the room.

The wards I sensed in the walls had the added benefit of muting the wiring. But the kitchenette was lit up to my new senses. The fridge, the digital clocks on the stove, coffee maker, and microwave. An expectant glow of potential in the power cords on everything from the toaster to the coffee maker to the stove.

I glossed over the rest without closer inspection. The living room featured an entertainment center. It pulsed with the power of the television and cable box. Lighting fixtures dangling over the small kitchen table buzzed, lamps on the side tables glowed.

The sensation intensified when I moved away from Jake. I stood frozen in the entryway, leaning against the bathroom door jamb. It proved to be a mistake since the bathroom held another whole set of electronics.

I stumbled further into the apartment as Jake and Roy finished talking and Roy left. The door shut. Jake came up behind me and wrapped me in a hug and everything dulled back to bearable intensity.

If electrokinesis was anything like my TK, then I knew I would adjust to the new sensations over the next few days. But for now, it burned too bright for me to process. I twisted around in Jake's arms to hug him.

"I need a shower," I mumbled into his chest after a long moment of just drinking in the feel of him pressed against me.

"You're dead on your feet, take a nap first," Jake suggested.

"Stay with me?" I asked, plaintive.

"I'm not going anywhere," Jake said. Then he maneuvered me around to face the bedrooms. His hands rested on my shoulders as he guided me to one of two matching doors. The room was small, but well appointed. The bed dominated the space.

I flopped down on top of the covers. Jake stepped away, and I made a wordless protest, but he shushed me. Then he nudged me over until there was enough room for him to join me.

I snuggled in close, pulling his arms around me. Sleep dragged me under before I cataloged all the perfect details of his body. Jake was correct, there would be time to shower later. And perhaps other—more exciting—things too.

Chapter 16

Jake

I woke from our nap to Aaron staring at me from scant inches away. His mouth pulled into the soft, genuine smile he used to reserve for me. His fingers ghosted over my face like he wanted to memorize it.

"Morning," Aaron mumbled, voice heavy with sleep. I smiled and captured the hand on my face to kiss his fingers. Aaron responded with a soft moan, and I had to kiss him. Aaron met my lips with eagerness.

The kiss led to us grinding against each other. Aaron rolled on top of me, writhing to find a position that let us continue kissing while our groins lined up, not the easiest task with the difference in our height. His fingers were working at the button on my jeans when my cell phone chiming interrupted us.

By unspoken agreement, we tried to ignore it. The phone stopped, but then the ringtone sounded again, insistent. I stole a final kiss and nudged Aaron's face away. He sat up, straddling me.

"I should get that," I told him, rueful.

Aaron groaned a protest when I prodded him, but he rolled off of me and flopped onto the bed in a dramatic fit of pique. The incessant ringing forced me to retrieve my phone with a raging hard-on making my jeans tight. By the time I reached it, the call had ended. The screen displayed several missed calls and text message notifications.

"My friends must wonder if I'm locked in a dark ops prison or something," I joked.

"You left with SPIRE, not a shady secret police force," Aaron rolled his eyes at me.

"Same thing in Em's book," I informed him. Aaron looked like he wanted to protest, but I saw the moment he capitulated, he shrugged me off with his lips pursed against further protest.

"Whatever, I'm hitting the shower, call your friends and tell them you aren't in lock up somewhere. Or getting tortured or whatever other wild conspiracy they've concocted involving SPIRE," Aaron said, dismissive of my friend's concerns.

He gave me a peck on the cheek before sauntering into the bathroom. I wanted to follow him. But he was correct, I needed to call my friends.

So I slumped on the couch with blue balls, trying to reassure my friends I was fine. And no, SPIRE wasn't interrogating or imprisoning me. Meanwhile, Aaron was naked in the shower with nothing but an unlocked door and this conversation to keep us from finishing what we had started.

I hit the notification for the video chat app Em had installed on my phone. It was the latest app that Em insisted on using for SaFE communications. The app encrypted transmissions and kept no records of messages sent on the platform. It was all very secure they assured me. I had something like twenty missed message notifications from Em and a few each from Caleb and Elliot across multiple platforms.

I sent a text to Caleb and Elliott with a summary of events. In my message to them I mentioned Aaron wanted to link, and we had signed on to work for SPIRE. And I informed them I would be in touch tomorrow with more details.

I sent a similar message to Em, leaving out the details about joining SPIRE. That news would go over better in person, so they wouldn't stew over it. A moment after I sent the message my phone buzzed and jangled its ringtone for an incoming call.

I picked up on the first ring.

"You're all right?" Caleb said without preamble, his relief clear.

"How do we know you're not under duress?" Elliott added.

"I'm fine, guys," I said, "honest. I can explain the details about SPIRE in person. I'll be at the summer camp tomorrow morning so you can see for yourselves that I'm safe, but I didn't want you to worry."

"We appreciate that," Caleb said.

"So, what we talked about, you wanting to reconnect with Aaron? Does he want the same thing?" Elliott asked. I knew him well enough to hear the insecurity in his voice. His underlying fear of never being enough.

"I think so," I said, I didn't want to hurt Elliott, but I couldn't lie to him either.

"Have you slept with him?" Caleb asked.

"No, but I think I might."

There was a beat of charged silence.

"El?" I asked, because I knew Caleb didn't mind. But Elliott was sensitive to feeling inadequate.

"I told you it was all right."

"I know you did, hun, but you don't have to say that if it's not true."

"It's fine. I want you to be happy."

"Elliott, my wanting him is in no way a reflection on how I feel about you. I love you."

"I know. I just, can't do this right now. You can sleep with him, but I don't want to hear about it."

"Fair enough. Are you holding up okay?"

"Yeah. Just, seeing Armstrong brought up some bad memories. I'm glad you called to let us know you're safe, see you tomorrow, Jay."

The phone speaker picked up the sound of footsteps retreating and the dull thud of a shutting door. Caleb sighed and said, "El needs a moment to process. Can you tell me what all this means for us?"

"I don't know. Aaron and I haven't talked, not about a relationship or sex. He might be fine with what you and El and I have."

"And if he isn't?"

"I don't know. I love you, but I love him too. Even if it's been a dog's age. I don't know what I'll do if he makes me choose, but I'm hoping he won't."

"We want you to be happy. Even if that means our relationship changes. But don't cut us out of your life, Jake. Please? It would crush Elliott."

"I wouldn't do that. I can't promise nothing will change. But you and Elliott are my family. Nothing will change that—not even Aaron. I wouldn't hurt you like that."

"I hope you're right. And the situation with Aaron works out. I understand how you feel about him."

"I'm his primary link. Still. After six years apart. That says something, right?"

"Yeah, big guy, that says a lot. I'm thrilled you get another chance with him."

"Me too. And I'll see you and Elliott tomorrow."

"Yep. Anyway, I should go check on Elliott. SaFE crossing paths with PYDC is rough for him, brings up bad memories."

"Okay. Remind him I still love him and I'm thinking of him?"

"Will do, love you, Jay."

"Love you, Caleb."

I disconnected the call in time to receive a video chat request from Em. I wanted nothing more than to talk to Aaron. And touch him, hold him, fuck him. I scrubbed at my face in frustration, but answered. Em was persistent. Better to get this conversation over with.

"There you are!" Em exclaimed as soon as the call connected. I felt bad to have worried them. Their voice revealed a mixture of relief, irritation, and concern. I glimpsed Jess with them in the corner of the frame.

"Hey, sorry I worried you. I'm fine, but to make a long story short, I joined SPIRE," I confessed. Em looked as murderous as I expected. I hoped we cleared the air expeditiously. Not only did I hate Em thinking of me as a traitor to the cause, but the sound of the shower running was a constant reminder of Aaron's proximity.

"You joined SPIRE?" Em's voice was flat. That was ominous.

"They didn't leave me much choice."

"There is always a choice," Em said, their voice sharp, "so while we worried about your safety, you were off joining the enemy. Damn it, big guy!"

"Let him explain, love," Jess soothed, leaning over Em's shoulder to make herself more visible. "What happened, Jay?"

And all right, I needed to focus. Remember there was more at stake than whether I got laid. I glanced up to be sure Aaron was still in the shower before telling them, "remember what we were discussing earlier? About recruitment?"

"I remember," Em said, their tone implying that I should get on with it.

"They threatened to charge him with felony failure to register if we didn't both enlist."

"That's not legal," Jess said. Then added with burgeoning excitement, "this is the proof we need, right?"

"Sure, but it's our word against theirs, isn't it?" I said.

"Please tell me you got a recording," Em said, but their tone implied that they knew I would have led with that if I had.

"They took our phones before the interview. And Aaron said they had no recording equipment in the room, I guess he can sense electronics now."

"So, he is electrokinetic, huh?" Jess mused.

"Focus, Jess," Em chided. "We might not have proof, but now we know for sure that this is happening. So there must be concrete proof somewhere. If we can get recordings of the youth being offered similar deals that would clinch it. There is no way they can deny they do it if we get video footage in the public eye."

"Sure, but how do we get footage?" Jess asked, pensive. "Unless your boy would turn whistleblower?"

"I don't know, but I get the impression he would be reluctant to risk it without solid evidence. His fear of what a charge would mean for him seemed genuine. I don't think he would risk losing the deal he struck if he isn't sure it will change anything."

"If we get a video?" Em pressed.

"Maybe? But it's his sincere belief that SPIRE helps psions."

"Okay, well, we will have to get solid proof. But hey, now we have a mole in SPIRE," Em said.

Em smiled at me, and I knew they forgave me. Even if they would have selected a different path. They hadn't seen how scared Aaron was. While I admired their conviction, I believed there was room to be practical too.

Regardless, signing the contract was the only reasonable option under the circumstances. And as Em had pointed out, now I was better positioned to get the concrete proof we needed.

Guilt afflicted me over using my position to snoop under Aaron's nose. But I figured he would forgive me if it meant protecting the kids he was so committed to helping build a better life.

"Just like my secret spy fantasy," I joked, trying to cover my ambivalence with swagger.

"You're totally a secret agent, big guy," Em teased, but I thought they saw through me.

The bathroom door swung open and a very naked Aaron emerged in a cloud of steam. I swallowed hard, speech becoming difficult as my throat tightened with desire.

Aaron looked good, his body well toned. The freckles I admired in our youth had faded, and his pale skin held a red flush from the shower. My gaze drifted down to the trimmed red curls around his erect dick.

"Um, Aaron's back, I need to let you go," I choked out.

"I'll be in touch," Em said over the sound of Jess giggling at my slack-jawed expression, but I was already thumbing the end call button and tossing my phone aside.

Chapter 17

Aaron

"See something you like?" I asked, jutting out my hip to strike an indolent pose for Jake's benefit.

"Yeah," he agreed, voice husky.

His eyes roved over my body before he picked his chin up off the ground and looked back up at my face. His smile was dazzling, and I returned it. Jake stood, moving toward me. I met him halfway, crashing into him.

I pulled Jake down into a hungry kiss, his fingers scrubbing through my short curls. He held me close while our tongues tangled. My mouth tingled with the taste of mint from the toothpaste I'd discovered in the medicine cabinet, but Jake tasted like himself and his presence hit me on a metaphysical level.

Jake felt better than anyone I'd ever been with. Like he was a missing piece of myself. I noticed the hard bulge of his dick between us, rubbing against my hip.

Our kisses grew more heated as his hands strayed down my back. He squeezed and caressed first my shoulders, then my hips. And I did the same, reaching under his shirt to touch his back, and then pawing at the waistband of his jeans, trying to gain access.

I wanted to feel his skin against mine. To have my aura join with his, the way only sex allowed. I grabbed his ass, keeping him pressed against me, grinding against his thigh. He pulled back from the kiss to smile at me.

"Take off your clothes?" I asked, voice breathy with desire.

I had waited ages for this moment, for him. Jake all but tripped over his own feet in his rush to comply. I observed him, my gaze intent.

While he shucked off his shirt, I stroked myself but it wasn't the same as being pressed against Jake. I shivered at the inadequacy of my hand. Jake got hung up with the legs of his jeans and his stumble surprised a chuckle out of me.

His olive skin flushed with embarrassment. But I couldn't shake the mental image of him if he fell. Trussed up by the tangled pant legs around his ankles. I swallowed hard against the thought and reached out to steady him.

"Don't you dare kill yourself before we finally get to do this," I admonished. He laughed.

"Sorry, I'll try not to fall on my face."

The flush faded from his cheeks, and he leaned on me as he kicked off the entangling clothing. I leaned in for another kiss. I dialed back from the aggressive tongue fucking we had been doing, kept it gentle and brief. Then I pulled away, tracing my thumb along his jawline. He regarded me through hooded eyes.

"We should discuss what we're doing here," Jake sounded reluctant.

"I'm thinking we're about to fuck," I said, with equal parts amusement and frustrated impatience.

"Sure, but I don't have a condom on me, do you?" he asked.

"No," I admitted, and I stepped back to get room to cool my head for a talk.

We stood a few feet apart, and I wanted nothing more than to throw caution to the wind. I wanted the conversation over fast.

"So, I'm on PrEP," I blurted, "so I mean, we could do it without? Most of the time I use a condom, because psion," I shuddered. The one time I'd foregone that precaution had been intense. Too intense.

It occurred to me, rather belatedly, that he had no reason to understand touch sensitivity. How it grated to be skin-to-skin with someone whose aura didn't mesh well with mine. In true fashion, the words tumbled out of my mouth. A babble to mask nerves while I swayed from side to side, my dick a bobbing distraction from the motion.

"But your aura feels so good and I don't think I would need one with you," I said, "not for aura incompatibility, anyway. And I get regular testing, and it all came back negative since my last hook up, so it should be okay?"

"Stop, Aaron. I'm on PrEP too. And I have recent negative test results. But I need to tell you something. Well, I guess two things. One of my partners is poz, he's a psion too, so we used condoms for touch sensitivity at first. And he is undetectable, but if it bothers you, I would rather you know before we do anything."

"No, that's fine, good, fine. Um okay. Wait, one of your partners? Are you involved with someone? I should have asked before we were both naked, huh?" I wilted, I knew he noticed my distress as I shifted from one foot to the other. It was awkward.

"I'm not in an exclusive relationship," Jake said. He stepped closer, kissing my temple. I sighed, it felt so good just to touch him again. But his words prickled at my brain, because he had not said that he was single. My mind flashed to the two psions he was linked to at the camp.

"So you are seeing someone?"

"I am in a committed open relationship with two other people," Jake said. "And I told them about you, so they know I want to sleep with you."

"Okay. Are you going to keep sleeping with them?" I asked. I didn't know how to feel about this conversation. On some level I had realized Jake had fucked other people. Hell, I'd slept with other people. But it was always casual. Hook-ups. But Jake was talking about a relationship.

Partner he'd said. And used to use condoms. Committed. So it sounded serious. Was I prepared to accept that?

It wasn't like this was the first time I'd fucked someone in an open relationship. But there was a difference between fucking someone and loving him. And I loved Jake. Never stopped.

"Do you want me to stop?" Jake asked. He braced himself for my answer. I had the power to hurt him, I realized. A few words and I could take my revenge for him daring to care about someone else. A psion, or psions, since he's said two. Psions who meshed well enough to avoid touch sensitivity. If I asked him to give that up, would he? Did I want him to?

If I was honest, I wanted Jake, however he would let me have him. In my heart, I wanted to pick up where we were before I left Seattle. Before my emergence. But there was no going back. And I didn't think I could be cruel enough to make him choose between people he loved. And a part of me feared that it wouldn't be me he chose.

So I had no choice but to accept him, including his love of these other nameless psions. If sex and a link bond was all he could offer me, then I would take it. But I hoped for more.

Jake was staring at me, waiting for an answer. And he looked so worried, like it caused him physical pain to offer me the choice. I bit my lip, then shook my head. I couldn't do it.

"No? I don't think. Can we talk about what this means relationship-wise when I'm not so horny? I want you wicked bad. For now, I only need to know you aren't cheating."

"No, not cheating," Jake agreed. "And I want you too."

"Good. We can talk about exclusivity and labels and open and whatever else when we aren't three seconds away from fucking, okay?"

"Yeah, that sounds good."

"Fantastic."

"Top or bottom?" Jake asked.

"Top," I said. I braced myself for Jake's response. Because I was used to at least a derisive snort when I made my position clear.

"Okay, that's good for me," Jake said, "I like it either way. Roy mentioned they stock the bedrooms with supplies. Why don't you go look for the condoms and lube."

"That sounds good, real good," I said, though I scowled at the reminder of the practical side of sex and sighed. Jake leaned in to kiss me again.

From the light brush of his lips and the awkward angle of his body leaning over me, he intended it to be brief. I grabbed his face and deepened the kiss, drawing it out. It brought me right back to the brink of throwing out all thought to practical realities. With reluctance, I allowed him to draw back, but I chased his mouth for one last peck before releasing his neck.

I let out a plaintive whine that turned into a half-sob half-laugh, and led the way toward the bedroom we'd taken our nap in earlier. Maybe it was a little overdramatic. But I didn't care, I wanted Jake. He took his time following me, his eyes on my ass as I crossed the room.

"You're killing me," I said. "Come here."

I found what we needed in the bedside table drawer and got everything laid out in easy reach. Jake paused in the doorway. With a gesture toward the bedside table I brought Jake's attention to the condom and lube I'd found.

"They think of everything. Come here, I want you in the bed," I said.

Jake obeyed without comment, sitting on the edge of the mattress. I plucked up the lube and kissed him while pushing him back onto the mattress.

"I want you like this. On your back so I can see you," I demanded, leaning over him to claim another kiss before issuing my next order. I let my voice drop to a deeper register, rougher and more commanding. "Now scoot back, the bed is the wrong height for me to get a good angle if I try to stand."

Jake shivered under me, I hoped he experienced the same thrill of anticipation I did. He scooted further onto the bed and I followed, positioning myself over him. I paused, taking a moment to peruse the gorgeous planes of muscle laid bare before me with open longing. Impress this moment into my memories.

I allowed my eyes to devour every detail before tracing my hands along the same path. Touches tracking from his shoulders, over his pecs, along his abs down to skirt around his cock.

I considered ignoring Jake's erection for now, but it proved too tempting. Still, I kept my grip light and teasing at first while I explored. I made eye contact as I played with him. One hand stroking and teasing the other caressing over his balls and back to his ass. "This is gonna be mine," I breathed. "You want to be mine?"

"Yes, make me yours, please, Aaron?" he begged. Neither of us caring if we sounded like the script from a bad porno. I smiled and pressed a kiss against his inner thigh.

"Soon, babe," I soothed. My grasp on his cock firmed as I traced an experimental path around his rim.

"You gonna let me get you all ready for my dick?" I let my tone convey my desire as I fingered him.

"Uh huh, please, Aaron, I need you now, please?" Jake pled. My heart swelled at the display of vulnerability.

"Hush, I'll take care of you," I shushed him. Then I reached for the lube so I could get him ready. When he was writhing and begging I took my hands from his body. He arched up with a low moan, trying to maintain the contact. I chuckled at his reaction. The needy sounds he made went right to my balls though.

"Aaron," Jake entreated.

"Shh, getting myself ready, babe, touch yourself for me."

"Hurry it up already."

"Bossy. Get your hand on your dick and show me how you like it."

Jake wrapped his hand around his dick, obedient to my command. God that was heady. The sense of controlling his pleasure. I wondered if his own touch seemed as woefully inadequate as mine had earlier while I waited out his phone calls in the shower. I wasted no time getting the condom on and slicking myself up, but I held off on touching him.

Savoring the beautiful tableau, Jake spread before me, his face caught between pleasure and need. And it was all for me.

A veritable feast for my senses. Especially for my aura, I could glut myself on his touch and never get enough. I wanted my hands on him, to savor every moment.

When I gave in to the need to touch Jake again, it was to get him positioned. I lifted his hips and shoved a pillow under his lower back to create a better angle. Jake bucked against me, impatience clear.

I had other plans though—I reached for him again. Instead of getting right to the main event, I knelt between Jake's splayed legs as I stroked along the arches of his feet. The hairy curves of his calves. So good.

The way his aura matched mine, like being wrapped in a warm blanket on a frigid day. I craved his warmth. Needed to wrap myself in it, and every touch seemed to loop another coil of his soothing presence around me, binding us together irrevocable.

I trailed my fingers up to his knees, rubbing the sensitive spot behind Jake's knee that wrung a gasp out of him. Delicious. So right.

I shuddered at the pleasure. In need of a moment to pull myself together, absorb the physical sensations along with the psionic pull of Jake's presence. I paused at the long pale scar bisecting his knee. Had he mentioned an injury? Didn't matter right now.

I frowned and shook my head, dismissing thoughts of the scars with one last quizzical glance. I pulled Jake's legs up onto my shoulders as I worked my way up his body. My hands moved to his thighs, stroking along the line where his legs rested against my chest with wonder. It was almost too much—I had to close my eyes, block out the sight of him naked under me. Jake's aura wrapped tighter around me with every scrap of contact.

The exploration was sweet torture; it emphasized all the untouched parts aching for contact.

"Please, Aaron?" Jake begged, using the leverage of my shoulders to lift his ass toward me. Oh, god, he felt it too—the needy, desperate desire. I took it in stride, but I couldn't stop my hand's slow inexorable trek up the length of his body.

"Soon," I crooned, my voice sounded dreamy to my own ears. He kept making beseeching little noises and panting my name. He sounded wrecked.

I listened, I couldn't deny him anything, no matter how much I wanted to explore everywhere our skin touched. At last I allowed myself to knead Jake's ass cheeks, I couldn't get enough of touching him. His skin was like a drug. Giddy exultation bubbling up inside me at the contact. And I wasn't even inside him yet.

A distant part of me wondered if he understood. If his other lovers lost themselves in him like I was. If he understood what it was for a psion to be with his link.

The natural consequence of all our skin touching, our auras enmeshed. The link burgeoning with every touch. So intense. Almost too much to stand.

I could get off on these tender touches alone. Something in Jake's expression shifted, and he stilled his efforts to buck against me, watching me with wonder and desire. Everything about him drew me into him further.

I regarded my newly complacent lover through hooded eyes as I continued to smooth my hands over his body. Seeking all the places our skin touched where his legs rested against my torso. Jake bit his lip, in a clear effort not to beg for more. He allowed me to get my fill of him, however I wanted him. It did something to my heart. That utter submission.

Jake craved more though. And I needed to give it to him. To kiss him, to fuck him, claim him before I came apart from just touching.

I reached for the lube, not trusting my TK to behave at the moment, before fingering him again. I wanted this to be as good for him as it already was for me. He made a low, frustrated sound in his throat as he thrust against my fingers. Made it clear it wasn't my fingers he wanted; he wanted my dick.

I flashed him a smirk, attempting to focus on the physical instead of the sense of completion he filled my psionic senses with.

"I've wanted your ass for so long, you ready for me, Jake?"

"So fucking ready, please, Aaron?"

"So impatient."

But I withdrew my finger and before Jake protested the loss, I pushed the blunt head of my dick against his hole. Jake bucked up against me. I swatted his ass. "Just a second," I chided.

My voice tight with strain as I pushed in and, oh, yes, that was what he wanted. His expression going from desperate and needy, tightening for a moment at the stretch and burn, then fading to bliss as I shifted to get the angle just right. I wanted him to enjoy this. Needed it to be perfect for him. And from his expression as I slid into his body, I succeeded.

At first I kept my thrusts slow and measured, but it was still overwhelming. Too much. I couldn't spend after two thrusts though. No way. I stopped and shifted my weight, leaning over Jake, folding him in half to plaster myself against him, chest to chest. The position trapped his dick between us, his legs bracketing my upper body. I shuddered against him. So perfect.

Jake attempted to ride me, but with me leaning over him, he only managed the shallowest of thrusts. I made a soft sobbing sound because I couldn't handle anymore sensation. So much pent up pleasure it seemed like I might explode. And it was Jake. My love. He stilled under me.

"Are you okay?" Jake asked, frozen with fear that something was wrong.

"So, so good," I moaned, rubbing my face against his chest. I teetered on the brink, close to coming undone.

Jake gave up on getting me to move and wrapped me in his arms, holding me against his body. I gasped and let out a long shuddering breath. Jake waited until I got myself under control. It was the sweetest torment. The longer I rested there, the more Jake tensed. I couldn't seem to think through the haze of pleasure though.

"I'm in you," I breathed at last. The wonder in my voice failed to convey the extent of my joy at being here—with him—at last. I raised my head and looked into Jake's face.

"Aaron, baby, please, you've got to move," Jake begged.

"Gonna come," I said, apologetic. "I can't, too good. Can't hold off. I'm sorry."

"It's okay," Jake said, pawing at my hair, turning my face to look at him. I nodded and reared back up to kneeling again.

I gripped Jake's hips, fingers splayed over his ass, digging into him and held him where I wanted him. And then I moved, fucking into Jake hard.

Rough, making up for my current lack of stamina or finesse with enthusiasm.

I panted with exertion, my grunts of effort mixing with the sounds of flesh on flesh. Jake reached between us to stroke himself, no longer able to stand the lack of friction on his dick. Each thrust drove me closer to my climax. Leaving me transfixed at the knowledge it was Jake under me. My Jake.

Jake met my gaze, and he was gorgeous when he was losing control. So close. I usually hated the vulnerability of those moments surrounding my climax. But with Jake it was different. He made it seem safe to let go as he bucked up to meet my thrusts.

"Aaron."

My name fell from his lips. A chant and a plea, repeating until it lost meaning and our rhythm faltered. I pushed in hard, a few final savage thrusts, curling over Jake, every muscle in my body trembled with the effort of holding myself back from my orgasm. I fumbled to join my hand with Jake's around his cock, needing to bring him over the edge with me.

"Please," I groaned, hips stuttering as I thrust in deep. "Jake, please."

Jake came over our joined hands, clenching around my cock. I moaned, his hips stuttering in their movements.

"Come for me, Aaron," Jake gasped out. "Want to feel it."

"Oh, god," I moaned. I pressed my face into his chest as my body tightened and shuddered with my release. I ground against Jake's ass, trying to get as close as possible through my orgasm.

The vulnerability of the moment made me want to wrap myself back in his body, to block out everything except our auras meshing. Try to extend the transcendent rapture for as long as possible.

Afterward, I collapsed onto Jake's chest and held him there for a long moment as our ragged breathing steadied. We lay there in a heap until the cold overcame post orgasmic lassitude. I was suffused with a languorous sense of completion. The link that had lain dormant for so long a bright spark in my chest. Jake craned up off the bed to kiss my temple where my face still pressed against his chest.

"We need to get cleaned up," he said, with reluctance.

I made a disgruntled sound, but forced myself up away from Jake. Jake grimaced at the sticky mess between us from his orgasm, then hastened to roll out of the bed. He wrinkled his nose as he took in the wet smear on the pillowcase.

"That was incredible. I meant, it was so fucking good," I dealt with the used condom, then flailed my arms in emphasis.

"So, you liked it too, right? I could have just laid there, and found it fantastic. Stupid psion shit, my aura has never been that in tune with another person. I can't even imagine how much more intense it would be without the condom. But it didn't suck for you?"

"It was good, Aaron. You're smoking hot in bed, and I'm sure on plenty of other surfaces too."

"Hm, we'll have to put that hypothesis to the test. Soon."

Jake grinned, "will we?"

"For sure. You know, I could have come from being inside you alone. Touching you. I kind of almost did, in case you didn't notice. It would have been super embarrassing."

"I noticed," he said. "It would have been hot watching you get off on touching me, maybe another time though."

"We should try that. I want to try everything with you, to be honest."

"I can get behind that plan."

"Cool, I am all about your behind," I teased, then looked at Jake and laughed, "oh my god, you're a mess, we should shower."

"Yeah," Jake said, playing it up a limping gait for my benefit as he shuffled toward the bathroom. I laughed as I trailed behind him.

It was a perfect vantage for admiring his ass, the reddish impressions of my fingers branding him. Turned out, I had a thing for leaving my mark on him. I let Jake get as far as stepping under the hot spray of the shower before I initiated round two by blurting out I wanted to blow him.

Chapter 18

Jake

After we got cleaned up, we found a spare pillow in the closet to replace the one we'd ruined. I could get used to how SPIRE anticipated the needs of its residents. An unused condom from earlier caught my eye, and I smiled at the thought of putting it to use later.

"What?" Aaron asked, craning around to follow my line of sight. When he saw where I was looking he laughed, "thinking about round three, babe?"

"Do I get to fuck you for round three?" I asked, meaning it as a gentle tease.

Aaron stopped laughing. I had a heart-stopping moment of fear someone had hurt him and my unthinking comment had brought up past traumas, but he cuddled into my side.

"I can see you panicking," he observed, "I don't like bottoming. Nothing bad happened to me, but it doesn't do much for me," he shrugged, "is that going to be a problem?"

"No, of course not," I rushed to reassure him. The wariness in the question made me think it had been a problem for his partners in the past. And the next words out of his mouth confirmed that suspicion.

"We can compromise and do intercrural?" Aaron offered. He brightened at his own suggestion, bouncing with his characteristic ebullience. "Hm, thinking about it, can we do that next? It might be super hot with you."

I smiled and squeezed him in a tight hug. "You never have to compromise on doing things you don't like in bed with me, Aaron. But if you want to try it, then that sounds good."

"I want to be touching you. All the time, all over. And having you behind me, leaning over me, your aura encompassing me," he shuddered with anticipatory pleasure. "Yeah, I want that."

I laughed at his enthusiasm. "Then we'll try it, but not yet. I am ravenous. We missed lunch, and it's getting late."

Aaron pouted, "spoilsport," he accused. "Fine, we can eat first," he said over his shoulder as he flounced into the living room. I followed him as he made his way toward the couch and flopped down on it.

"Insatiable," I countered, moving to sit beside him.

"Can you blame me for taking advantage of our private time? We've got six years lost time to make up."

"We do. Speaking of lost time, how have you been these days? And what brought you home?"

Aaron worried his lip and sighed.

"Think we can order a pizza? That way we can catch up while we eat," he suggested.

"Pizza works."

"Cool, you can look up a place that will deliver on your phone."

"We can both look," I said. Aaron wrinkled his nose with disgust.

"Looking at the phone hurts my eyes right now. Well, that's not quite right, more focusing on electronics pulses in my senses? That's not quite right either, but it is unpleasant."

I didn't push it since I noticed that his new perceptions were bothering him without sex as a distraction. He kept jerking around like something was moving in his peripheral vision, and he seemed to need to be touching me at all times. Although that may have been nothing. Aaron had always liked being close. So I let it drop and read him the list of specials instead of squabbling over who had to do the googling.

"Okay, none of that sounds great, how about we each pick a topping?"

"I still like plain cheese," I said with a shrug.

"Does that mean I can get anything I want, since you can eat around it?"

"No, the cheese gets funky flavor divots that way, and it's a mess. And if the whole cheese layer comes off with the toppings, it isn't plain cheese pizza, it's soggy bread with essence of tomato."

"Flavor divots?" Aaron raised a brow.

"It's a thing."

"Fine, how about half and half then, or two pizzas, sound okay?"

We compromised by ordering two pizzas, one abomination pizza with pineapples, anchovies, and olives for Aaron and one plain cheese for me. The negotiation seemed strange. I was used to meals with El and Caleb. Where it was a given that the menu would adhere to Caleb's nutritionist approved meal plan. And consider Elliott's aversion to meat.

Aaron's blase approach to mealtime presented an odd contrast. The comparison made me miss my other lovers. I shook it off by teasing Aaron over his pizza preferences.

"Well, somehow your taste in pizza got even worse out east," I commented after we had placed the order.

"Hey! I don't mock you for liking the missionary position of pizzas," Aaron objected with a roll of his eyes.

"Pretty sure you liked missionary not an hour ago," I pointed out, "and I have the bruises on my ass to prove it."

"Well, yes, I think I'd like most anything with you though," he said, sounding wistful. He broke into a massive grin at the reminder though. Then added with a mischievous grin, "and remind me to check later. About the bruises—for science."

"Science, huh?"

"Definitely," Aaron nodded, and kissed my cheek. "I like being able to do that."

"Me too, but maybe we should wait on the kissing until the pizza gets here?"

"Sure, spoil my fun," Aaron pouted and then he bounced up off the couch to pace in front of me. "Okay. I can restrain myself. You wondered why I came back to Washington, right? I missed home. And Mom, I mean your mom, told me UDub has the master's program I wanted. Plus,

Washington is one of the few states where I can get a social worker's license without jumping through a ton of extra hoops. So I came back."

"Mom mentioned you were at Yale," I said, tentative, almost making it a question.

"They take a lot of Riverton grads," Aaron brushed off the accomplishment.

"You still had to work hard for it, I'm proud of you. You know?"

"Thanks," Aaron said dismissing the praise, and changed the subject. "So, you still a soccer star?"

"Um, no. Mom didn't tell you?" I thought she would have mentioned it to him since the medical appointments had consumed a huge chunk of my senior year of high school.

He frowned and cut his eyes to my knee. "The scars? You got hurt?"

"Screwed up my knee during the elite championship game senior year. Had to have surgery to fix it. I missed so much school I almost had to repeat the year. It sucked. I was getting scouted before that," I shrugged to show it was okay now. "But it worked out, UDub was a good fit for me. I was looking at smaller schools further from home if the soccer thing had panned out, which I'm not sure I would have liked. I'm a little surprised Mom didn't mention it, I know she still talks to you."

Aaron fidgeted, "she said you got hurt. And I saw online that something happened, but I didn't hear the details. I didn't realize it was that serious."

"Online?" I cracked a slow smile. "Did you stalked me online?"

"Yeah. You didn't?" he replied, his arms crossed over his chest.

"I had to unfollow you when you posted pictures of you and the little blond guy."

Aaron favored me with a blank stare for a minute and then he let out a bark of laughter.

"Oh my god, do you mean Albert?"

"I didn't bother learning his name," I scowled. "I only knew seeing you two together hurt. I couldn't deal with it."

"Albert was my roommate. We were never a couple, it would have been weird," Aaron said, sounding amused.

"Oh, well, that's nice I guess," I tried to play it cool. It was a relief to learn the blond kid who I had thought of as my replacement was not his boyfriend though.

"You jealous?" Aaron asked, seeing straight through me. He came back over to the couch and sank down beside me again, jostling my leg with his knee.

"I was," I admitted, there was no point in lying to him. We lapsed into a brief contemplative silence.

"I slept with other people," Aaron said sounding guarded.

"I figured. So have I. It was more the idea you had moved on within weeks when I was still raw about it?"

"Yeah. I get that. I had to stop looking at your pictures with your soccer buddies, I was so jealous that they got to touch you and I couldn't."

That amused me, "you should know me well enough to know I wouldn't have risked team dynamics by sleeping with a teammate."

"I guess. So, the guys you mentioned earlier, your partners, do I get to meet them?" Aaron asked, his fingers tapping against his palms in a nervous fidget.

"If you want. You saw them at the campgrounds. Caleb was standing beside me when I first saw you at the camp. And Elliott was behind us. And they were with Em before Roy and Davis took us into custody."

"I only noticed you," Aaron admitted, "you have a picture?"

"Sure."

I swiped to wake my phone and scrolled to a decent picture of Caleb and Elliott. It was one I had snapped a few months ago when the three of us had spent a warm spring afternoon hiking. Aaron blinked at the phone trying to focus for a long minute when I handed it to him. He brought it closer and then further like it was fuzzy, squinting his eyes almost shut.

"Trippy," Aaron commented, "it's weird looking at the screen, give me your hand?" I complied, and he smiled as his eyes opened a little more, "that's better, ok, I see the appeal. Which one is Caleb?"

"The blond."

"He looks like me," Aaron pointed out. He grinned at me, and gibed, "do you have a type?"

"*You're* my type."

"Elliott doesn't though, look like me I mean. I'd bang him."

"I don't know if he'd go for that."

"If he did, how would that make you feel?" Aaron peered at me with open curiosity.

I shrugged, "depends, are we having a four-way with them or just you and El?"

"Either way."

I considered, it made a pretty picture—Aaron sweaty and tangled up with Elliot. "I would be ok with that, so long as Elliott and Caleb were cool with it too. And I get to watch."

Aaron laughed and handed my phone back. "Okay, so voyeurism is one of your kinks?"

"I think I might like anything, if you're involved."

"You romantic. Okay, so I guess we should discuss that. You and them and how I fit into your life. You mentioned that you're in a relationship with them both, so you sleep with them both, together, right?"

"And separate," I said. This conversation had the potential to destroy any chance of a relationship with Aaron, or it might ruin what I had with Elliott and Caleb. Neither of those possibilities were acceptable. If Aaron wanted me to choose, I wasn't sure I could.

"So, I guess, the obvious question is, do you love them?"

"Yes," I said with no hesitation.

"But you aren't exclusive?" Aaron cocked his head, not quite puzzled, but as though he was trying to understand.

"No. And they both know I still love you."

"You do?" Aaron asked after a brief silence, he sounded shocked.

"Of course I do. I think I've loved you since I was five years old and you came up and demanded that I play with you."

"I was a demanding little shit," Aaron acknowledged with a snort.

"Were?" I gave him a playful poke in the ribs. He squirmed around and settled against my side.

"Hey, you liked it in bed," he defended himself.

"Well, I liked it when we were kids too."

"I know we parted on bad terms. And I know you thought it was ridiculous to plan our lives around each other, but I never stopped loving you either."

"I'm sorry I pushed you away. Everything spiraled out of control and I got spooked."

"We already talked about that," Aaron said, "no need to keep apologizing. I have a question for you though, do you still want to sleep with them?"

"Not at the moment," I answered. I aimed for lighthearted to mask my roiling anxiety at the possibility of him not understanding. Aaron fixed me with a stern look so I answered the question. "They're important to me too, so yes."

Aaron considered, then said "you can. I mean, not that you need my permission. I want you in my bed too though. And I want your heart. But if anyone has a big enough heart to love more than one person, it's you, Jake."

"Thank you for understanding," I said, choking up with overwhelming relief.

"It's not what I expected. But I would rather share you with them than lose you. And I don't want to make you choose. Not if you love them. But only them, I can handle you wanting to be intimate with people you love, but I don't want to share with strangers. As long as you continue to be open and honest with me about it, then I'm on board. I know we need to get reacquainted. And it might not work out, we've both changed. But I want to try. We don't have to be exclusive, but I want you to be my primary link. A permanent link-bond. Does that work for you?"

"Are you sure, Aaron? I need you to be sure. Because I don't know if I'm capable of choosing between you and them. If we try this and you change your mind…"

I was surprised my voice didn't break with emotion. My heart might survive ending things now, but if we gave this relationship another chance I didn't know if I could let him walk away again, not without breaking.

"I'm sure. I wouldn't do that to you," Aaron said. His confidence was enough to convince me he meant it.

"Thank you," I said, I didn't have time to elaborate because he tackled me into a warm bear hug.

"I love you, Jake," Aaron soothed, "I can't promise we won't break up over something else, but your relationship with them won't be the reason. We can figure out the details as we go. Maybe talk with Caleb and Elliott about it? Since it involves them. I'd like to be friends with them—it's obvious they are important to you."

"I'd like that too."

Aaron grinned, "good. We should be on the same page. No misunderstandings, you know?"

"Agreed. I'll talk to Caleb and Elliott about arranging for all of us to hang out. I want this to work between us," I said.

"That works. And now I wish we had time for round three before dinner."

"I am not risking having the pizza guy interrupt us. That isn't even hot in porn."

"I don't mind pizza guy porn," Aaron shrugged. "But I guess I can agree that it might be less hot in real life. Where is that pizza?"

"The app says it should be here any minute," I said as I checked the time on the app.

"Well, I want it to be here now," he groused.

"Patience."

Just then my phone rang with a call from the delivery driver to say he was in the lobby with our food.

"Speak of the devil," Aaron said.

"I'll go grab the pizza and our welcome packets from the lobby, you see if SPIRE's attention to detail includes napkins in the kitchen," I said.

Roy had mentioned that I could retrieve my key fob in the manager's office. So I planned to take care of that while I was in the lobby. I grabbed my phone, checking that I had added Roy's contact information in case I ran into an issue getting back upstairs. I shot Aaron an 'I told you so' look before I went to go get the pizza from the lobby. He beamed at me before going to explore the kitchenette.

Chapter 19

Aaron

Waking up beside Jake had always been a highlight for me. Even when we were kids, and it was a platonic sleepover. When I got to spend the night at Jake's place, it meant being with my favorite person in the world. And a homemade breakfast crowded together with a family who had love to spare.

I had always treasured waking up to Jake's presence. It was even better to find the adult version of my best friend snoring a few inches away from me. Our limbs in a loose tangle of sheets, one of my legs thrown across his thighs, his arm tucked around me. And because he was also my link, my morning got off to a fantastic start.

Had it only been yesterday they had hauled me in under suspicion of a serious crime? It didn't seem possible. Everything starting with waking up from my nap in Jake's arms to falling back asleep curled around him last night seemed almost dreamlike.

As though it existed in a perfect bubble outside of time. I let myself laze beside him for a while, taking in the even rise and fall of his chest. I rested my head just there, over his heart, so I could listen to its rhythmic thumping. Its steady strength.

I could almost imagine the steady beat of his pulse. With a startled blink I realized that it wasn't my imagination, I sensed something.

When I snuggled into my anchor, our auras wound tight together, all the other electronic inputs in the room reduced to static. I focused my concentration on Jake alone. And when I did that, my electrokinesis just picked out the little buzzing impulses that fizzed inside his skin.

The thought terrified me; I had no interest in dwelling on its implications. Lucky that Jake afforded me the perfect distraction when he stirred. He seemed to be more asleep than awake still, but he rolled his hips up a little. His morning wood pressed against the thigh I had draped over his groin.

My half hard dick appreciated the added pressure against his hip. I was sure it would feel even better if I rolled on top of him. My thoughts strayed to how glad I was that we had taken the time to get cleaned up before bed last night.

Even though I had been grumpy when Jake left the warm bed to grab a washcloth. While I was still limp and languid with the afterglow. I had learned two new facts about myself last night. One was that I adored it when Jake came from fucking my thighs, and the second thing was that I got clingy afterward.

I never needed the reassurances I had craved last night. The vulnerability of the act had gotten under my skin though. Perhaps it was trusting him to only take what I was offering when all the skin-on-skin contact left me utterly wrecked and begging him to fuck me.

Whatever the reason, when he left my sight, anxiety bubbled up in my chest. Still, not waking up crusty was worth a few moments of acting like a codependent mess. And Jake hadn't called me on my behavior, just held me close until I calmed.

Jake was squirming around more now, still bleary with sleep, but seeking more of the friction I was giving him. I was pondering whether we had time for sex when a loud rap at the apartment door interrupted us.

Jake startled awake, looking confused. His confusion morphed into pleasure as his arms snaked around my back and pulled me the rest of the way on top of him.

"Morning, Aaron," he rasped, his voice gravelly and deep from just waking up.

"Morning," I replied, grinding our dicks together because they were hard and lined up at a perfect angle in this position. He seemed amenable.

The knocking repeated, more insistent. Jake made a disgruntled sound of protest.

"I guess we don't have time," I sighed, only then glancing at the alarm clock beside the bed to confirm the early hour, just after five.

"Guess not."

Jake pushed me off of him, gentle in his actions, and rolled out of the bed to answer the door. I lounged on my side, palming myself with idle pleasure while I enjoyed the view of his sweatpants riding low on his hips. And the way the muscles of his naked back shifted as he walked out of my field of view. I listened as Jake yanked the door open, using more force than necessary. With him gone I gave up on my morning wood and rolled out of bed to follow him.

"Rise and shine," Roy said in a cheery voice as he breezed inside past Jake. Roy raised an eyebrow at me. "Well, I see you are taking the rising part literally anyway, huh, Aaron?"

I sulked as I adjusted my erection in my loose boxers, I should have put on pants before leaving the bedroom. "I was going to before you got here. Way to cock-block us."

"I'm sure you two rose to the occasion just fine yesterday," Roy commented, dry as dust, his voice containing no sympathy. "Are you ready to head out? The camp sessions start in just under two hours and it's an hour drive even without factoring in morning traffic."

"I need a shower," I grumbled as I slipped past them and into the bathroom to perform my morning ablutions.

Roy granted us minimal time to shower and dress before he hustled us to the cafe in the lobby for coffee.

As soon as the barista handed my drink over I dumped in a generous helping of milk. I added enough to cool the coffee to a drinkable temperature then downed about half the cup in a few gulps. I paused when I noticed Roy's dubious expression.

"What?" I asked, perplexed.

"Nothing—isn't the EK a new development?" Roy said. I tried to detect any hint of suspicion in his tone, but he only sounded amused.

"It is," I said, wondering where he was going with the observation.

"So, if it's new, why are you mainlining caffeine like it's going out of style?" Roy asked, arching an eyebrow at me.

"Oh my god," I groaned as understanding dawned. "Why didn't you say something sooner? Now I'll be ramped up for hours!"

"What's the issue?" Jake asked, looking between us for answers. I observed that for all that his lovers were also psions, Jake must not have spent much time with peri-emergent psions if he didn't know about emergence dietary restrictions. They were a running gag among my high school buddies.

"Caffeine boosts psionic abilities, not a ton, but it seems to have a more pronounced effect around emergence. Most psions have to cut it out of their diets for the peri-emergent period," Roy explained, and there was no question he laughed at my pain.

"Oh my god, way to make it sound all clinical and like it's no big deal," I groused. "You do not understand! I snuck coffee back when I was on emergence restrictions at school. Because I was having the worst week ever, and there was a three layer chocolate cake at dinner and I deserved cake damn it.

"Pro tip: chocolate cake is on the restricted list of the emergence diet for a reason. Chocolate and sugar and the fact that everyone knows you have to have a nice warm beverage like coffee with your chocolate cake. It was miserable. That was when my roommate linked with me. I was lying in the middle of our floor dying and he rescued me."

"Dramatic much?" Roy said. Meanwhile, Jake's concern only deepened. His scowl impressed me. Though I was unsure if it was for my past self or a warm up to rain down righteous indignation on poor Albert for somehow taking advantage of me.

"That was Albert, right? Did you agree to the link?" Jake asked.

Trust him to worry about whether I consented to a link. I had after the fact, but still, it was akin to asking if I had consented to the Heimlich maneuver.

Albert had done what was necessary to stabilize me when he found me collapsed in our room with random objects flying around overhead. I had a distinct memory of a vicious attack from a particular textbook that had swooped off the shelf over Albert's desk.

It had been all the more memorable for being the most impressive display of my abilities I had ever manifested. Until yesterday anyway. In retrospect, maybe the chocolate cake incident had something to do with my link to Jake still being fresh and giving my TK a boost. Or it might be unrelated.

"Yes, it was Albert. And I wasn't in any position to do anything but thank him for saving my life. But afterward he offered to sever it and we agreed not to."

All true, we had linked for the rest of the year. As to the insistence he had saved my life, it was doubtless only a slight exaggeration. I had been close to a hyper-gamma state when he found me.

Not that caffeine alone would cause that. But I had been nowhere near stable. My grade C status ameliorated the danger. Albert's skills might not have been up to the challenge of stabilizing a grade A psion. A strong anchor could save a psion's life in hyper-gamma crisis, if they established a link in time.

Jake didn't need to know that. And it appeared Roy was familiar enough with psions to know that caffeine alone would not pose a life-threatening danger for a grade C with TK. I might owe the guy an apology for thinking he wasn't part of our community. He understood psions at any rate.

Roy rolled his eyes, "I doubt you were on the brink of hyper-gamma crisis from a cup of coffee and some cake."

"Sorry, I can't hear you because I am about to die," I amped up the hysterics to get a rise out of Roy. Jake looked concerned, but he cut a look to Roy instead of taking my word for it.

"He won't be ill or anything, will he?" Jake asked Roy.

"No, of course not. We wouldn't serve coffee in the tower if it were that dangerous," Roy said. "Caffeine can overstimulate psions, like a toddler on a sugar high, a new psion who overdoes it with caffeine will get a little out of control and then they crash."

"A little out of control?" I barked because now I sensed the intensifying buzz of my EK. And no, my tone was not hysterical. My concern was proportional to the egregious belittling of a terrible life choice. "It's more like the psionic equivalent of getting a bout of diarrhea. And responding by devouring a box of laxative. Because how much worse could it be? And then you get hit with the world's worst hangover once you come to in a puddle of your own shit."

"That is a spectacularly disgusting analogy, Aaron," Jake said, "so I guess, good job?"

"Thanks, so, on that note… here," I thrust my half finished coffee into his hands. Before it tempted me with its siren song to take just another small sip because I had already inflicted the damage on myself. May as well enjoy my morning brew, right? Jake took it without resistance, our hands brushing as he did so. I shivered at the cool soothing touch, it helped with the heightened senses.

"Will you be okay?" Jake asked. He displayed more patience than I could have mustered.

"Do you need a psionic toilet for all your spewage?" Roy teased.

"Yes," I moaned, laying on the dramatics. And that answer worked for them both so I left it at that and reached for Jake. "You still want to fuck me even if I talk about liquid shit pouring out of me, right?"

"Um, no, not at all right now, it turns out," Jake said, but he let me wrap his arm around my waist so I decided that I could be magnanimous.

"You're welcome then," I told him, nuzzling into his neck and yes, that helped to dull the intensifying blazing glow of potential EK all around us.

It did nothing to tamp down the lingering arousal I still felt from our abortive attempt at morning sex.

"At least one of us doesn't have to spend the day with blue balls."

"If that was your goal, mission accomplished," Jake assured me, voice wry, and then he asked in a softer tone. "Are you okay?"

"Yeah, just, don't let go?" I asked, with a plaintive sigh.

"Not going anywhere," Jake said.

True to his word, he kept me snugged against his side as he pivoted to dump my coffee in the trash. He stroked his free hand down my back and it felt fantastic. I longed to go back to our apartment and wrap myself up in him. To have his aura mesh with mine until the dull throb of my senses returned to a more bearable level.

"We are all going somewhere, in case you forgot. You have obligations, Aaron," Roy reminded us.

"It's too bright," I objected.

Roy frowned, "what is?"

"Everything, do you realize how many electronics are in this room alone?"

"You can sense all of them?" Roy asked, sounding intrigued. "What's your range?"

"I think so? With everything boosted its kind of one big pulsing blur, I can't tell how far it extends. There's too much noise, you know?"

Roy gave a thoughtful nod. "We will have to test you when you're not hopped up on caffeine and running late."

I only moaned in response and pressed my face into Jake's side. He kept patting me and I drank in the touches.

"I don't think he's up to talking about it yet," Jake said.

"No, I can see that. You must have a caffeine sensitivity. It never affected Anna that bad," Roy said. He sounded almost apologetic.

"I'm not Anna," I pointed out, groaning at the way energy seemed to skitter and slide across every surface when I dared a glance up at Roy.

"I can see that. Can you drag yourself to the elevator so we can get you in the car?" Roy asked.

"Uh huh, sure," I agreed. "As long as Jake doesn't stop muting it for me."

It was awkward to move without giving up my grip on Jake, but we shuffled to the elevator. In the garage, Roy let us wait by the elevator while he went to get a sleek black sedan. He pulled up in front of us and Jake slid into the back first, pulling me along the bench seat after him.

I might have crawled into Jake's lap because the coffee was hitting me hard now. But he buckled us both into our own seatbelts. That limited the amount of contact between us, leaving me disgruntled until he touched me again.

The drive to the camp was trippy. When I first woke up at the tower, it seemed like I was settling into my new perceptions with the constant low buzz of electronics pressing at my awareness. But this outing was proving otherwise.

Whether it was the effects of the caffeine or the increased quantity of stimuli, it was rough. Even the car itself was a constant whir of changing electric impulses. Not to mention the tiny pulses of the people and their possessions both inside with me and those that we passed along the way.

Those pulses seemed odd though. Oh right. My freaky half understood discovery from this morning reasserted itself. Despite my best efforts to suppress the thought, and the horrifying implications thereof. I was not prepared for this.

My new awareness extended to the bioelectric impulses in people. Without my hot boyfriend distracting me with his nakedness, I could no longer avoid it though. The revelation left me reeling. If I could sense it, I could control it. Maybe.

Getting a handle on the sheer overwhelming pervasiveness of my new abilities was out of my reach at the moment. So trying to zero in on the tiny fluttering heartbeats would not happen. But I had felt it earlier, I was sure of it now. The shock of noticing those pulses in another person unnerved me.

The sensation was faint, something I wasn't sure I could manipulate, but there was an awareness. It was sobering to think someone less scrupulous than me might find some awful use for that barely there buzz.

The sensation was minor in relation to other inputs. But the potential significance made it stand out in stark relief. Even against the backdrop of the bustling downtown core where the sheer ubiquitousness of electronics washed everything beyond a few feet into a haze. The area past the sidewalks was a flashing pulsing blur. But Jake's body pressed against my side appeared highlighted to my EK senses. How strange.

I could just pick out his heartbeat, the flickering along his muscles when he moved, the mercurial flashes buried under layers of matter in his brain. Humans were weird. I wondered if an android would look much different from a human to my EK.

I figured the robot would be more steady. There was an ethereal quality to all the little flickers and pulses of the bioelectric charges in his body. And I was freaking myself out by thinking of Jake as something that my EK could influence so I shut that line of thought down again.

I didn't have a handle on it yet and the only thing keeping me together was Jake's arm around my shoulders. Contact with him helped me to mute the new inputs, and he was my ideal anchor because he got that, staying close. Roy volunteering to drive us made the prospect of getting in the car bearable.

When I found out I wouldn't have to put up a fuss about Jake staying with me, it mitigated my anxiety too. As a grade C, I hadn't needed links or anchors; they were just nice to have available. Even after less than a day I understood why grade A ranked psions almost always had an anchor or, failing that, a strong primary link. I needed Jake around to remain stable right now.

I was sure that my original emergence had been just as overwhelming despite my much less powerful abilities. Or my sudden reliance on Jake might have alarmed me more. Jake seemed to take my clinginess in stride, enjoying it even.

That thought brought me back to last night and all the wonderful touches we had engaged in until it had doubtless been far later than we should have stayed awake. I sighed against his shoulder and Jake dropped a light kiss on my temple in response.

"Are you all right?"

"I will be," I said. "It might take a few hours for me to even come close to using my abilities though, too volatile when I'm like this. You've linked with other people, right?"

"I have."

"Can you help to mute it without touching me? I shouldn't be pawing my boyfriend when I'm supposed to be mentoring a bunch of thirteen- and fourteen-year-olds."

Jake carded his fingers through my hair and I noticed the shift in his aura as he brought it to bear helping to dampen the EK inputs. I sighed at the reprieve.

"Better?" Jake asked.

"Much," I said, craning my neck to smile up at him.

"Good. So, I'm your boyfriend am I?" Jake asked.

"Um, shit. Yes? If you want to be? This was not how I planned to broach that subject."

"I want to, Aaron, I want us to be together, whatever we call it."

"Ok, good."

"But I draw the line at laxative jokes if you want to get laid, deal?"

"But I can't help it. They just flow out of me," I protested with an eyebrow waggle so he would understand it was a clever joke.

Roy guffawed from the front seat, but he stifled it quick. I glanced up and made brief eye contact with him in the rearview mirror, his eyes sparkled with humor and I smiled back at him. It was nice having a potential friend who got my sense of humor. Even if he had played a role in strong-arming me into joining SPIRE.

Jake face-palmed and groaned, "that was terrible. You have a problem, babe."

"I thought it was funny," Roy said with a shrug.

"See, I'm funny!" I said. I injected false good humor into the words.

At least as we hit the highway and left the downtown behind, I could sit up in my seat without being altogether overwhelmed by my EK. Although a part of me would have been content to spend the whole drive plastered to Jake's side.

I needed the distance. Needed to return to the correct headspace to be a good mentor for my team. Instead of dwelling on my hot new boyfriend and all the things I still wanted to try with him in private.

It was comforting to arrive at the camp. The site was in a forested area. While there were power lines, and the buildings were all wired, there weren't many fancy gadgets.

The rules didn't allow the campers to bring electronic devices. So the little blinking bursts of phones were absent once we got past the knot of protesters picketing in the parking lot. The protest maintained a sizable presence even if there were fewer of them this morning compared to the day before.

Jake waved to them as we went past, following his gaze I saw the cute twink and his boyfriend. Jake's other boyfriends. I expected to feel jealous of them, but more so, I was glad that Jake had close friends. Lovers even. That he hadn't been alone.

Roy escorted us into the main building where the campers were all gathered around the tables eating breakfast in their assigned groups. Joe was sitting with my kids in their lime green t-shirts.

I had worn one of the generic gray SPIRE shirts from the drawers in the little apartment at the tower. It was oversized on me, so I would need to get my bag from wherever it had ended up yesterday and change before long. My first order of business was getting to know my campers though. Jump back into the swing of things.

"Hey, team lime, did you miss me?" I greeted the teens as I approached the table.

"You're late," Joe snapped, he stood though and gestured for me to take his seat.

The kids mumbled greetings, most of them still half asleep, even if it wasn't all that early anymore. I couldn't blame them for their lack of enthusiasm.

The camp maintained an intense training schedule. And we had only spent a few hours together before I had my incident with the camera yesterday so it wasn't like we had time to bond much. Not at all with the two kids in gray shirts, marking them as anchors, who were sitting with my group.

I took my place at the table and set about trying to draw the teens out of their shells with varying degrees of success. I tried to ignore Roy going off with Joe, the two of them engaged in an intense whispered conversation.

Jake pulled over a free chair to sit impassive nearby while I chatted with my team. My attempts at drawing them out met some initial resistance. I was up for the challenge though, and soon had a few of them warming to my presence.

This was familiar, I liked working with teens; I had years of experience with the camp and putting on the happy-go-lucky act was second nature. It didn't matter if I already had the beginnings of an overuse headache just from trying to block out my new electrokinetic perceptions. Or that my amped up senses were still doing a number on me. I had a role to perform here, and I intended to live up to it to the best of my abilities.

Chapter 20

Jake

I meant to bring up the recruitment problem with Aaron back at the apartment. But somehow the opportunity never arose. I knew the fact I didn't want to broach the subject stood in the way. But I enjoyed being with Aaron again, rekindling our friendship.

I'd wanted Aaron since we were both horny inexperienced teenagers. Neither of us wished to pass up the opportunity to live out our youthful fantasies. And the reality surpassed my imaginings. Our link only added to the intimacy of the connection. I could feel how much stronger it was even after our one night together.

A link almost strong enough to rival my connection to Caleb and Elliott. It was strange. For all the times I had thought of Aaron while I was with them, they were present in my heart and mind during my time with Aaron. It seemed like the height of privilege to have all three men in my life.

So I dropped recruitment conspiracies when Aaron got cagey. I brought up the threats leveled against him earlier in the day over dinner. He summarily dismissed my concerns. And I left it at that.

Aaron believed in SPIRE. He acknowledged that there may be a few unscrupulous agents. But he thought the purported good SPIRE did in the community outweighed the bad. He blamed it on a few bad actors. So my quest to find solid evidence of systematic abuses inside the camp remained a solo mission.

I felt exposed sitting in the mess hall. Watching Aaron joke around with the kids on his team was a welcome distraction from my agenda here. He looked so relaxed as he gently teased one of the older boys about his professed skills with TK. It didn't take long before he had the kid offering to help his less skilled peers during the morning training session.

Not long after, the cafeteria erupted into controlled chaos as the allotted time for breakfast ended. Everyone got up at once to clear their trays and get to their next assigned tasks.

I fell into my role as Aaron's anchor with ease. It was almost frightening how I anticipated his needs. I hadn't expected the intensity of the first session.

Roy's nonchalance aside, Aaron hadn't exaggerated the way coffee affected him much. Even with me muting his EK senses, it cost him when he had to tap into his abilities.

He didn't let it hinder him though. Despite the difficulty, he showed each task to the campers. I had to work hard to stabilize him after each exertion.

After a few hours of offering silent support, I pulled him aside because he worried me. Even the campers were looking a little concerned at how strained he seemed by a simple demonstration where he moved a ball through a course.

"A word, Aaron?" I asked when he settled the ball at the end of the course.

"Yeah, just a second," Aaron said with a fake smile. "Okay campers, please divide up into two teams of four TKs and one anchor. You've earned a fun activity. When we finish with some preliminary practice exercises, we'll do a relay race to see which team can clear all the obstacles fastest."

The teens perked up at the mention of a competition. Aaron waited until their excited murmuring died down. Then he outlined the activity.

"For our first exercise, each of you will get to try the course," Aaron said. "Those not controlling a ball should observe to make sure everyone completes each task along the way. If your teammate gets stuck you can talk them through it but no helping out with your TK. The anchors can help with boosting or stabilizing, make sense?"

The teens chorused their agreement. Then erupted in a babble of young voices talking over each other as they sorted themselves into two groups. Aaron kept an eye on them as he stepped aside to confer with me.

"What's up, Jake?" he asked without turning away from overseeing the teens. They chose their teams and stood clustered in two groups near the start of the course.

"Are you all right?"

"Can we start?" Elle demanded.

"Ready? Set? Go!" Aaron called to the two teens looking at him in expectation. Their colored balls, set on top of the start line, jerked into the air as they began the exercise. Then Aaron spoke in an undertone.

"It's the EK, it's taking it out of me right now. I need to adjust and it will be fine. But with all this amped up energy it's a constant battle to keep it from trying to lash out," Aaron said. He flashed me a quick grin and then called out to the teens, "way to go, Elle! Very precise maneuvering. Tim, you're doing great, try to pace yourself though, no need to wear yourself out trying to be fancy."

The girl beamed at the praise and the boy scowled, but the ball he was controlling dropped out of a fancy flourish to the same height as the girl's ball. It also stopped wobbling around and took a much smoother and more direct path through the course.

"So, you're all right, for sure?"

"Yeah, it will take time to adjust. I'm okay though, for real."

"This morning is the first time I've seen you use your TK, you know?" I said. Turned out, I enjoyed watching him in action.

"How do I stack up?"

Aaron flashed me a cocky grin, and I resisted the urge to pull him close and ruffle his hair or kiss him. Fooling around had to wait until we weren't in front of the teens he was mentoring.

"You are great with them, very engaging," I said instead of kissing him. "Your control rivals any of the psions I know, you may be better. I'm not sure how your strength compares. Caleb is grade B. I don't know how that would translate to EK plus TK?"

Aaron snorted in reply.

"Good handoff, Tim," he called as the boy finished the course and turned over control of the ball to his teammate mid-air. Elle had set her ball down before her teammate picked it back up to wove it through the obstacles.

"Great work, both of you. Elle, your control is adept already we can build on that and push the limits of your strength more. Tim, you did great once you focused on the task at hand. You're strong but we should work to harness that strength and fine tune your control," Aaron said.

Then he gave me a wry grin.

"Way to rub in that your other boyfriend is stronger than me," he said, dropping his voice. Just for me, he sounded amused rather than upset at the comparison.

"Yeah, not the best thing to mention. He doesn't have EK though. So you're my strongest boyfriend now," I offered as I rubbed at my neck, feeling self-conscious. His acceptance of my relationship with Caleb and Elliott meant more than I could put into words, but it still felt tentative, fragile almost. Aaron just snickered and muttered something under his breath though.

"Is there something I should do?" I asked. It was a blatant attempt to steer the topic away from our personal life and any further comparisons.

"You're doing it," Aaron told me leaning into my space. He closed his eyes for a second, like he was savoring my presence.

I gave in to the urge to touch him then, patting his back. I lifted my hand to rest on his nape. He pressed into the touch. I lapsed into silence and watched him offer tips and praise to his team.

Most of the teens breezed through the drill with minimal correction. Sam, the youngest, struggled to even get the ball into the air. When they managed it, their control was spotty. The ball careened above the course, zinging first one way and then another. The first task was maneuvering the ball through a hoop.

Sam struggled because they made sharp over-corrections for every little wobble. The ball's trajectory fluctuated with each effort. After their third off-kilter approach failed, Aaron shrugged out of my grip and went to join them. They put their heads together for a hushed chat.

Sam looked near tears at their inability to manage the simple task. Aaron waved over one of the young anchors, he placed anchor's hand on the young psion's shoulder and spoke to them both.

Sam sniffled, wiped at their eyes, hunching like they were self-conscious, and then tried again. While it wasn't perfect, with the anchor's help and Aaron's murmured advice Sam painstakingly cleared the course. Aaron cheered and celebrated with the kid as the ball dropped into the basket at the finish line, clapping and high-fiving like it was the world's greatest accomplishment.

The other teens were good sports. The competition that had been brewing between the two teams momentarily forgotten. It was nice to watch.

The sense of camaraderie reminded me of working with the younger players on my soccer team back when I was team captain. I liked mentoring. And developing young talent was an integral part of building the best team in the state.

Watching Aaron cast in a mentoring role gave me all kinds of warm fuzzy feelings. They only intensified when he glanced over at me with a triumphant grin. He ruffled Sam's hair with affection while the teen looked up at him in open adoration.

"All right. Let's do another run through of the obstacle course," Aaron said. "This time let's work on building trust with your anchor and working with a partial link."

"How are we going to do that?" Tim asked.

"I'm glad you asked. Psions, you will turn so you can't see the course and your anchor will direct you. Anchors, I want you to establish a partial link. Use verbal communication and the link to get the ball through the course. You may require skin-to-skin contact to make it work. So psions, pair up with the anchor you feel most compatible with for this exercise.

"Is that plan agreeable? I do not expect anyone to form a closer link than they are comfortable with. And to be clear, by skin-to-skin I mean holding hands, let's keep everything PG, is that clear?"

The teens voiced their understanding and divided up into teams again. Sam and Elle went first. To my surprise, Sam struggled less with their back turned on the ball and their fingers entwined with the young anchor with whom they were working.

Elle struggled this time. Her precise control floundered in the face of being reliant on another person's perceptions. The worse she did, the jerkier the ball's movements got until she ended up flinging it straight into the air in frustration.

I had an abstract interest in the training exercises, but watching the particulars got dull after a while. Watching Aaron held endless fascination though. He gave the teens different goals each time.

Each task focused their talents or compensated for their weaknesses. By the final runthrough, he had found a way of using the course that allowed each of the kids to work on their weaknesses and showcase their strengths.

Aaron gave each teen an opportunity to shine. It was remarkable. As he laughed and offered gentle suggestions, calm corrections and celebrated even minor successes, it was easy to see why he wanted to work with teens. How passionate he was about helping youth.

There was not much for me to do other than keep his aura from spiking when he exerted himself. I stood to the side and observed. And brooded. Because these teens were the potential victims of what we suspected SPIRE of doing. If Em was right, then SPIRE was preying on these vulnerable youth; and it was clear they were vulnerable.

The way Sam had latched onto Aaron after he helped them with the first exercise was adorable. They hung on Aaron's every word after that, eyes as big as saucers, their expression almost worshipful. But it made me wonder how little support they had if a little praise could earn undying loyalty. The other teens also appeared to be falling for his charm, but not to the same extent.

Still, by the time the blue team came to use the obstacle course, the lime team all looked to Aaron with respect. He gathered his team around to let them watch the older group practice with the course for a few minutes.

The blue team comprised the fifteen- and sixteen-year-olds with TK. Their counselor had them start out by executing a team-building exercise. They worked in pairs of two psions, passing control back and forth after each obstacle.

The display enraptured the younger teens. Elle demanded to try something similar next time. Aaron favored her with an indulgent smile and agreed that they could try it tomorrow. When the demonstration ended, Aaron thanked the blue team.

"That was a great demo, blue team," he enthused. "Thanks for letting us watch, we appreciate it, don't we team lime?"

The campers took the prompting and thanked the older teens. Then they fell into line to follow Aaron away from the obstacle course. I followed in their wake.

"All right, our next session is fun," Aaron said. "We are learning about psion history. So quick vote, we can go into the mess hall and sit at the tables to chat, or we can find a nice spot outside. What do you all think?"

The teens all clamored to voice their opinions at once until Aaron had to resort to doing a quick vote by a show of hands. The teens favored sitting outside by a wide margin. Elle sulked at losing, but she seemed to get over it when we found outdoor seating around a fire pit near the cabins where the campers were staying.

Aaron waited until everyone settled, either on the ground or one of the rough log benches around the empty fire pit, before starting.

"I think there is a pyrokinetic in the violet group, wouldn't it be neat to have a campfire you guys? We should roast marshmallows tonight, before lights out," Aaron said, his excitement contagious, he caught my eye.

"I like marshmallows," Georgie said.

"Finn, the pyrokinetic, is my sibling," Tim boasted, "I can ask them about a campfire."

"Did anybody bring campfire stuff?" Elle asked. She sounded dubious.

"We have marshmallows with the provisions," Aaron said. "I saw them when we were unloading the bus. I love roasting marshmallows," he added with a dreamy look, and he caught my eye. Something about the way he said it and his expression made me think he was talking just to me, reminding me of our disastrous first date.

"They're okay," Elle allowed. "S'mores are better. Are there ingredients for those too?"

"We can raid the supplies and find out," Georgie said, giving Elle a playful shove.

The possibility pleased the teens. They broke into pockets of excited chatter. Sam pulled on Aaron's sleeve to get his attention while talk of a campfire distracted the others.

"I've never had a campfire before. What's a s'more?" Sam asked in a small voice intended for Aaron's ears only. I overheard since Aaron sat pressed close to my side, the short benches giving us an excuse for close contact. Sam was sitting on his other side. And it shouldn't have been a surprising question—coming from a city kid—but it hurt to hear this sweet kid had never been camping. Opportunities to leave the city were something I took for granted.

Visits to our lakeside camp had been the highlight of my childhood summers. Aaron explained s'mores to Sam while I considered the many nights we had spent around a campfire on the edge of the lake with my family, happy and laughing. Or the times we had gone out there when we were older—just Aaron and me.

We had so many firsts out there. From our first sleepover as little kids to our first taste of beer. When my dad forgot a six pack in the fridge not long after I got my driver's license. To our first date. Aaron met my eyes, and I knew his thoughts were on those memories too.

"All right, team. Enough chatting. We have a lesson plan to get through," Aaron interrupted after giving them enough time to get the initial excitement out of their systems. "Tim, you and I can approach Finn at the lunch break about the fire, and maybe a little PK demo if your sibling is amenable. Let's get started with the history lesson for today. Who knows about the psionic divergence?"

"You mean how we became freaks?" Elle asked.

"Oh goody, our collective superhero origin story," Georgie added.

"Something like that," Aaron said. "I remember learning this stuff when I was seventeen, at school. But I attended a psi-only boarding school. Jake and I had psi-ed in middle school through the public school system and they glossed over the divergence."

"We learned that it was a major crisis," Tim said. "When it first happened they thought emergence was an engineered viral neurologic infection."

"That's correct. It caused a panic. Young teens had the best survival rates. People much older than twenty had a high mortality. And the survivors developed psionic abilities.

"The exact mechanism is still unelucidated. We now know psions result from epigenetic changes. In simple terms, those changes turn gene expression on and off. They occur in a set of genes which regulate neural signaling pathways.

"Global exposure to an unknown mutagen set off the divergence. It turned psion genes on en masse. Many older people had the psion trait, but in an inactive form until exposed. They lacked the neural plasticity to survive emergence. People dubbed it psi-plague, though we now understand it is not an illness.

"The altered genes are heritable. So now those born with the psion trait undergo emergence when the genes become active around puberty. No further trigger needed.

"How does that work? No one in my family was a psion before me," one teen asked, brow wrinkled in confusion.

"Well, genetics are more complex than the punnet squares you learn in school. It takes a specific set of genes—including the epigenetic factors—all being active to make a psion.

"Many genes that code for psion traits are also recessive. So it is a matter of having the psion trait without the dominant non-psion genes. That means it can take a few generations before introducing a psion gene results in a child with psionic abilities.

"Psions are rare. Efforts to map the exact genes involved bring up ethical concerns. And many of us refuse to take part in any voluntary mapping efforts after what happened with the quarantine camps.

"And that brings us back to the history lesson. Civil unrest ensued once the divergence started. It scared people. Speculation ran rampant. First, they called it an attack. Then, once the global spread of the phenomenon made it clear that psi-plague spanned geopolitical borders, the situation became even more chaotic.

"Some policies put the priority on eradicating a potential contagion, at all costs. Others worked to contain the spread. For a brief period euthanizing those with what we would now call late stage PEPS symptoms was an accepted practice in some countries. The US, and other places, implemented a quarantine. The chosen sites drew attacks from fringe groups. Those camps lasted for almost a decade. Society took time to adjust to our presence.

"We discovered neural linking between emergent psions because of close quarters in the camps. We learned that link bonding stabilizes psions. It saved many who would not have survived otherwise.

"Within the camps there were health professionals and scientists who volunteered to help. Or worked for the public health service to provide care to psions. Those individuals braved their fears to work with psions in the early days of the plague. Their work ruled out a viral or prion etiology —which many had suspected of being the cause. These scientists were among the early predecessors of SPIRE.

"The challenges facing psions at that time are hard to overstate. When the public learned that the condition was genetic, it eased some of the tensions. Panic subsided. The UN passed the International Psion Rights Charter.

"The charter forbids depriving anyone of their human rights based on their psionic status. It placed a global ban on martial use of psionic abilities. And requires that any experiments conducted on psions must conform to human test subject guidelines. And it puts limits on laws to protect norms from psions. They attempted to balance psion rights with norm fears.

"The US signed the charter. Then they started the process of integrating those held in the camps back into society. Congress established PIR—Psionic Integration and Relations—as a branch of the public health service. PIR splintered off and merged with PAL—the Psionic Action League—which was an FBI task force created to handle psionic crimes.

"PIR and PAL only existed for a short time. When the president established the Department of Psion Relations, PIR and PAL merged to form SPIRE. The Department of Psion Relations still oversees SPIRE. It is the arm through which the federal government handles psion affairs. SPIRE is the most well-known branch of the department. It is the number one employer of psions in the nation.

"The other major development in response to the charter was the passage of PEEA. We will discuss the intricacies of psion legislation another day, but I want to point out that lawmakers created the registry to fulfill PEEA requirements. Let's take time for questions before we break for lunch," Aaron wrapped up his lecture.

I wanted to jump in and dispute his characterization of SPIRE. And the way he had just skipped the horrors of the quarantine camps and cast them as almost a necessary evil.

"My grandmother was in a quarantine camp as a kid," Elle said. Georgie put a comforting arm around her friend's shoulder as she talked, "they did experiments on her. The scientists, they weren't benevolent volunteers. Not all of them anyway. She didn't talk about it much, but she was a twin and my great aunt Helen told me some of it before she died."

"I don't deny the camps were a terrible period in our history," Aaron said. "If you want to share stories from your grandmother, I'm sure we would love to hear about her experiences. But it will have to wait until tomorrow's session, all right?"

"Okay. But SPIRE wasn't in the camps to help us. If they wanted to help us, they wouldn't have experimented on us. They wouldn't have watched us die when they knew about links and how they could save us," Elle bristled.

"I'm sure some bad apples took advantage of the situation. But SPIRE didn't exist until years after they decommissioned the camps," Aaron said. His reasonable tone made me cringe on Elle's behalf.

It seemed callous for him to dismiss Elle's concerns—concerns with which I agreed. But I knew him well enough to understand that he was oblivious to how bad it had been, not denying it out of willful ignorance. He was always one to see the silver lining.

"The same people who ran the camps established SPIRE," Elle said. I had to give her credit for persistence.

"We should remember this was sixty years ago. It was a different time. Psi-plague scared people. They didn't understand what was happening. Not to argue that the camps weren't an atrocity. Or that rampant fear justified crimes against psions.

"But tribunals held those responsible for illegal experiments accountable. And SPIRE didn't even exist yet. The man who later became the first director of SPIRE helped to dismantle the camps."

Aaron's frustration came across loud and clear. He balanced toeing the company line about SPIRE and coming across as a quarantine apologist. He skirted around dismissing Elle's concerns outright. It made me uncomfortable to hear him spouting rhetoric used against psions to this day. I had to remind myself that he believed in SPIRE.

"You don't get it, there is no excuse for what those doctors did to my gran," Elle gritted out.

"I'm sorry to hear that was done to your family, Elle," I broke in before Aaron could make things worse. "We are lucky to have you here with us to pass on her experiences. We can all stand to be more aware of our past as a community. Remembering helps us to avoid similar things happening again."

My comment gave Aaron a moment to gather himself and come up with a more diplomatic approach. It shouldn't have surprised me as much as it did. He was always keen to keep the peace.

"Your gran sounds like quite the person, Elle. I'm sure no one here would defend the quarantine. This summer camp is affiliated with SPIRE though. I can understand why you are skeptical of their motives. But can we all agree that the opportunity to learn and grow as a psion is valuable to our community?" Aaron asked.

Elle gave us a long considering look and nodded. "Aunt Helen always said it was important to remember what happened. I guess if SPIRE owns up to their origins in the divergence, then that's not a bad thing."

"I know sentiment about SPIRE is mixed among psions. I've only seen them offer opportunities to psions which would not otherwise be available to them. But as you said Elle, terrible things happened during the quarantine. And awareness is the best prevention," Aaron said.

"Awareness and standing up against any efforts to infringe on civil rights," I added with a small smile.

Aaron shot me a warning look. His reaction confirmed he understood I was alluding to the protest my friends were staging in the parking lot. Elle flashed me a bright smile though. At least she felt one of us was on her side. Since Aaron had alienated himself from her with his naïve faith in SPIRE.

"And on that note, it's time for you scamps to get your lunch before we start our afternoon sessions," Aaron dismissed the teens. "I need a word with my anchor, but we will join you in the mess hall soon. Tim, we can talk to Finn when I get there."

"Sounds good," Tim said.

Most of the campers stood, finding their friends and chattering as they walked away. Sam stretched and hesitated before leaving our proximity.

The anchor they had been working with earlier took their hand and struck up a conversation. And the pair trailed behind the older teens.

Elle hung back after the others had gone.

"Sorry, I didn't mean to pick a fight in front of everyone," she said.

"Nothing to apologize for," Aaron said. "My perspective might be different if I grew up with loved ones who experienced the camps. While I don't believe SPIRE is to blame for the atrocities. Thank you for sharing your unique viewpoint with the group."

"Most of us who have elderly psion relatives, from the time of the divergence, have similar stories, Mr. Anderson. You get that, right?" a hint of Elle's earlier defiance still shone through, but she seemed resigned to Aaron's stubborn optimism at this point.

"I do. I understand why even a tangential association with the camps might seem so terrible. But SPIRE didn't even exist during the quarantine."

"SPIRE allowed the people who wanted the camps to hide in plain sight. So they could continue to exploit us," Elle said, matter-of-fact. "It was about using us, and now they can't do it in the open they do it undercover through SPIRE. No one invests in homeless psion kids out of the goodness of their hearts, not on the scale that PYDC does. There has to be money in it. Where do you suppose that money originates?"

And the little imp had summarized my worst suspicions. Elle was one to watch out for. I wondered how she had ended up with PYDC since she came from a multigenerational psionic family.

The chances a psion family would kick her out at emergence seemed remote. Unlike most of the other teens here, her family sounded supportive. It wasn't just PYDC youth the camp served, though. The PYDC youth had priority for admission, but other teens could still apply to attend. Whatever her background, I was thankful that Elle was only fourteen. The odds of her being recruited so young were lower.

I hoped we brought the scandal to light before she had to choose. I couldn't see her responding well to threats of prosecution if SPIRE tried to do to her what they had done to Aaron. Aaron was too loyal to view it as anything beyond a misunderstanding or an anomaly. He could be naïve in the extreme.

"There is grant funding for youth camps," Aaron said. It was clear he remained set in his thinking, but he tried to go for a light approach to end the uncomfortable conversation. "Funding, which is paying for the delicious lunch you are missing as we speak. Go on, Elle. I don't expect to change your mind about SPIRE, but we don't have to agree to respect each other's views, okay?"

"Okay," Elle sounded unimpressed, but she turned toward the mess hall and left Aaron and me alone by the cabins.

"So, you learned about psion history after I left?" Aaron asked, turning to face me with a small frown.

"I learned everything I could about psions," I said. "And Em is big on education, so they put on lectures at our SaFE meetings. We've even had quarantine survivors come in and do a panel."

"You agree with Elle."

"Yes. I know you think SPIRE is there to help psions, and maybe it does, but at what cost, Aaron?"

"I've seen SPIRE help homeless kids, Jake. How do I make that fit with an evil exploitative organization?"

"I don't know, I only know what I've seen. And what I saw yesterday does not reconcile with a group out to help psions due to any benevolent impulse."

"What do you mean?"

"Aaron, they threatened you. They coerced you into putting your now considerable abilities at their disposal. Who do you think pushes the laws that left you without alternatives? You've got to see what's happening."

"You're wrong," Aaron said with a frown, he shook his head. "But if you feel that way, why did you agree to join SPIRE?"

"You needed me," I said. And it was the truth—but it wasn't the entire truth. He was too familiar with me to allow me to get away with the deception. His eyes narrowed.

"I could have found another anchor. You could have worked something out. Stayed long enough for me to locate a new partner. Agreed to link but not work together. Why did you agree to join SPIRE with me if you hate it so much?"

"I don't hate SPIRE, but I don't trust it either. Why do you think I agreed to this, Aaron?" I asked with a sinking feeling.

Because I loved him and I had agreed to it for him. But I was also using him and his connection to this place. I didn't think I could keep that from him. Sure enough, his mouth worked and when he found his words they came out harsh and angry.

"Fuck you, Jake. You talk about using people? Did you plan this all along? Using me to get inside access?"

"Of course not, Aaron. I was unaware you had returned to Seattle until yesterday. And I had nothing to do with the EK thing unless it was something to do with our latent link suppressing your abilities."

"How am I supposed to believe you? I don't even know you anymore. For all I know, you knew the link lay dormant between us. You might have planned this all along. And I can't link with someone who would use me like that. I can't. I'm sorry, Jake, but I think you should leave."

"You need an anchor, Aaron," I said. The constant need to dampen his senses was fading, but he was still hyped up and jittery.

"I'll talk to Joe about getting a temporary replacement. The silver team leader is an anchor, so it shouldn't be a problem. Just go, and please don't make a scene?"

"If that's what you want, then I'll go."

"It is."

"You have my number if you change your mind," I said, reluctant to leave him when he had been so dependent on me all morning.

His aura was still pulsing and surging and his anger was not helping his control. I did my best to use the link to smooth the sharpest edges before he sent me away. Much as I wanted to help him, I couldn't force him to keep our link nor would I want to do that. I had to trust him to take care of himself.

"I won't," he said. He set his jaw and crossed his arms. There was no arguing with him in his current mood.

"I love you, Aaron. And for what it's worth I agreed to enlist so I could be your link. The other part came after."

It took an enormous effort to restrain myself from babbling excuses, begging forgiveness, or reaching out to touch him. To stroke his cheek as I would have done before this conversation. I shut down my emotional response for the time being, I needed to get through this and then I could fall apart once I was certain he would be cared for. My dishonesty had brought this on myself, Aaron was the injured party here, not me.

"The other part, huh? Be more specific, Jake, do you mean the part where you decided to use me?" Aaron snapped. And yes he sounded angry, but he was also sad and hurt and I was just making it worse at this point. "You don't use people you love. I need you to go. Please?"

"I'll go, I'm sorry," I said. I wanted more than anything to take the hands he held clenched across his chest like he was trying to hold himself together.

This hurt him. I'd hurt him. But my only recourse was not making it any worse. I turned and walked away, stopping in the mess hall to send the guy in the silver STAFF shirt out to find Aaron.

He would need a link to be stable as a grade A. The emotional turmoil of our fight and the lingering effects of his morning coffee exacerbated the need for a link. And the strength of his EK left me with no doubt he was a grade A now, even without a formal ranking.

I couldn't bring myself to sever our link outright just yet, I still held out hope he might forgive me given time to cool down. But I muted it to almost nothing as I walked away.

At least my closest friends were right there to help me through losing him this time. Aaron had no one. That thought almost made me turn around and beg his forgiveness.

Give up the mission and just commit to him. But then I thought of passionate perfectionist Elle and shy sweet-natured Sam and I couldn't do it. Not if it meant turning my back on them—and the thousands of kids just like them—whom SPIRE might even now be coercing into joining their ranks.

So I squared my shoulders and walked away. It hurt. The prospect of losing Aaron for good after just getting him back was a physical ache. It was even worse to lose the dream of a future with him. But this was bigger than my desires.

I couldn't further abuse his trust by trying to worm my way back into his good graces though. Even if it would make our task of bringing down the conspiracy easier. A lie of omission was bad enough, I wouldn't compound it by lying to his face. We would find another way to gather the evidence we needed. We would have to.

Chapter 21

Aaron

I coasted through my afternoon sessions on autopilot. In a fortunate turn for me, Harold, the silver team counselor, agreed to work with me after I explained that my anchor had left on short notice. It didn't hurt that the silver team comprised entirely of anchors. So they spent most of the camp dispersed amongst the other teams anyway.

That left Harold free to offer help where needed. And I depended on the temporary link he set up with me. The last thing I needed was losing Jake, on top of my new abilities kicking into overdrive. A part of me wondered if I had overreacted, but I didn't have time to dwell on it. My schedule was packed.

My distraction led to a small mishap putting away the training gear toward the end of the last afternoon session. I sliced my hand. And while it was a shallow cut, dealing with blood-borne pathogen precautions meant I had to disinfect the item in question. And get my hand bandaged. I left my team in Harold's care while I went to the camp offices to get the supplies I needed.

Only to find the office door locked. The electronic lock flared in my senses, and the room itself glowed to my EK with a variety of devices. Joe sat at his desk, typing away on his laptop. He let me in when I knocked, and gave me a first aid kit along with a snide lecture on my many failings as a counselor.

He helped me doctor my cut though. I fled the office to find the cleaning supplies elsewhere. By dinner, I put the incident out of my mind.

As the sunlight faded, my team clamored for their promised campfire activities. At least the lingering effects of my morning coffee had faded away. I'd leaned on Harold's help too much. It made me feel pathetic.

The prohibition on personal electronic devices among the campers had my undying gratitude. The lack of other inputs left the bioelectric impulses to shine though. It made them even more obvious to my psionic senses, much to my chagrin. I didn't want to see it.

Once things settled, I hoped I would require less help from an anchor. I refused to rely on Harold all summer. We weren't a good match even though I liked him well enough. His touch soothed my EK, helping to bank it to controllable levels, but it did nothing for my agitated aura. Funny, how that worked, the inextricable connection between the two things, yet their reactions could be so different.

My aura had no way of knowing Jake had betrayed me though. It only knew he fit with me. And that part of me wanted him back where he belonged. Touching me. At least Harold hadn't pressed the issue when I told him I had no desire to talk about why Jake had left early.

Elle had picked up on our conversation earlier being related to why he had gone, though. She acted subdued all afternoon. Just before dinner, she asked if Jake and I fought. And if it related to what she said before lunch. She sounded guilty about it. So I reassured her it was nothing to do with her.

It was the truth. The fight was about us whether we could still trust each other at its heart.

The fire seemed like a brilliant plan with Jake by my side. Now it only served as a reminder of his absence. All the happy memories tied up with campfires when we were kids turned to bittersweet ash. There wouldn't be more campfires for Jake and me. No more sitting side by side, the area aglow with flickering firelight.

The aroma of wood smoke served as a forcible reminder of nights with the Moretti clan. My first inkling of family. The fond teasing, the tender touches, the unselfconscious laughter and the easy conversation. The way they gave me unconditional love.

Then in later years, there was the yeasty bitter grapefruit taste of my first beer, the warmth of huddling together against the fall chill. And our last night before everything fell apart. That one perfect night, straddling Jake's lap. The sweet chocolate flavored kisses from our first date.

"Hey, Mr. Anderson?" Sam's soft voice interrupted my reverie. I blinked the afterimages of the dancing flames out of my vision.

"Uh, sorry, something distracted me," I apologized and focused on my youngest charge.

"You said you would show me how to make a s'more, remember?" they asked. The innocent, hopeful expression on their face reminded me of Luca, just before I left Washington. Sam wasn't much older than Luca had been.

"I remember, here, first we have to roast a marshmallow," I told them, grabbing a stick from the bundle the older teens had gathered. While I browned the marshmallow, I directed Sam to get the graham cracker and chocolate ready.

I focused on making sure Sam enjoyed the activity. They provided a welcome distraction from thoughts of Jake. Their raucous laughter as they burnt their marshmallows and blew out the flames, copying the older teens soothed me.

Tim's older sibling put on a small pyrotechnic display once the teens had cleaned out the bag of marshmallows. Their control of their PK was remarkable and the colored balls and flares of flame they manipulated fascinated my team. I was also impressed by the demo.

Finn leaned on Tim afterward, in a way suggestive of a close link bond. That wasn't surprising though, siblings often linked as teens. I didn't think much of it.

My team stayed up past their curfew to let the fire burn down to embers. I didn't object since they were having such a good time bonding. Even Elle warmed back up to me. So that was worth some minor sleep deprivation and a walk down memory lane.

Still, it was late when I got the campers to their assigned cabin. Once they settled, I fell into my bed in the separate room at the front of the divided bunkhouse.

I didn't bother powering on my phone to check for messages since I didn't want to know if Jake had tried to get in touch. Or hear what he had to say. Besides, I wanted to preserve the battery.

I woke up the next morning to the sounds of the teens stomping and banging around as they got ready for the day. I gave them enough time to get dressed and head to breakfast.

Before checking on the campers, I waited until I figured most of them were already on their way to breakfast. I used the gradual reduction in noise to judge when most had departed. I knocked on the door and announced that I was entering their area to be sure I wouldn't catch any stragglers unaware.

The fourteen and under kids all shared this cabin. The counselor for the telepaths, pink team, also had a small separate room at the other end of the building. But she had already left when I did my check of the cabin.

I confirmed no one lingered behind before I headed along the path between the other cabins toward the mess hall. I was running late, so I didn't encounter anyone else along the path.

That must be why I noticed Finn having a heated conversation with Joe Armstrong in the narrow space between two cabins. Everyone should have been at breakfast already. The spot they were in was far enough away from the main path I only saw them by chance.

That was odd, as far as I was aware, Joe had no reason to be talking with Finn. While I didn't buy into a narrative that cast SPIRE as some great villain, I didn't trust Joe either. Something about the way he talked to Finn put my hackles up.

I hesitated, wanting to see what happened. With how they were standing, Joe would have to turn around to see me and Finn's focus on Joe prevented them from noticing much else. Joe wasn't touching Finn, but his hands were on the wall to either side of the lanky teen's head, and Joe was in their personal space.

Joe's voice was too low and intense for me to catch what he said. I saw the fear and defiance in Finn's expression though. I wasn't sure which emotion would win out, but I felt the coiled psionic energy of Finn's abilities burning close to the surface.

Threatening a grade A psion was not a smart move. Finn might have only been seventeen, but they were also pyrokinetic. And judging from their demo last night, they had an admirable control for someone so young and with such a strong ability.

Young as they were, Finn was not defenseless. By their nature, they couldn't be. The potential consequences of using their abilities constrained them though. Using pyrokinesis against another person carried strict mandatory minimum sentencing—even in cases of self-defense. Finn would be in trouble if they lashed out with PK.

That might constitute a motive on Joe's part. But it wouldn't undo whatever damage Finn might cause if they lost control of their PK. Which begged the question why would Joe threaten them? What did he stand to gain? Would Finn be able to keep control of their abilities or would they lash out?

Finn was uncomfortable with what was happening, their body language broadcast that loud and clear. But I wasn't sure why. Or even whether it was an innocent conversation which I had misinterpreted or something more sinister. Though I suspected the latter.

I debated getting closer. But without knowing what I was walking in on, I was uncertain whether that would be the best course of action. I was not in Joe's good graces already.

My options seemed limited. I could walk away, sneak closer to gather more information or confront Joe. If Finn was being threatened, as seemed to be the case, then disrupting them might only delay Joe's endgame.

If I had better control of my EK, then I might use that somehow. Finn didn't have a cell phone, but Joe has his phone in his pocket. The telltale glow was like a beacon to my senses in contrast to the lack of electronics out here in nature.

I thought, with enough practice, I might finagle a way to manipulate his phone into transmitting audio to my phone. Maybe. But there was no way I would develop that skill level instantaneously.

I needed a clear idea of what was happening to prepare for the inevitable next encounter. That decided me to gather more information and then determine my next step once I knew what was happening. I left the main walkway and tried to get closer without drawing their attention.

With the vague idea of capturing a video of the confrontation, I pulled out my phone only to remember that it was powered off. I debated whether the startup music would give away my presence. I rejected the plan, Joe might notice, not worth the risk.

If I had the skills, I might block the impulse that created the sound, but I lacked enough familiarity with my EK to feel up to the task. I resolved to make honing my abilities a priority. I wanted my EK to be an actual usable skill instead of just a perceptual nightmare. This conflict would not be the only one between Joe and Finn unless I missed my guess. Not unless someone stopped whatever was going on between them.

I still wasn't close enough to make out what they were saying when Finn glanced up, making eye contact with me. I had done nothing to draw their attention. The look in their eyes almost froze me though, Finn looked terrified.

I wished that I understood Joe's intentions. I didn't hear what Joe said next, but he leaned in close and I heard Finn's sharp, angry reply.

"Don't threaten Tim."

Whatever Joe's response, it caused Finn to wilt. Their next reply was too quiet for me to make out words. They dropped their gaze to their feet. The two of them spoke more, Finn raising their face to make defiant eye contact with the camp director as the conversation continued.

Joe's voice remained quiet and intense, but the high note of fear in Finn's responses increased. Until Joe shifted closer to the teen and stroked Finn's cheek. Finn flinched away from the touch, eyes squeezed shut.

I couldn't watch anymore. There was no walking away now. And standing there while Joe terrorized the vulnerable teenager was a line I wouldn't cross. Consequences be damned, I jogged a step toward them as Finn shrank back against the wall.

Something about their aura brushing against mine as I approached warned me what was coming next. It reminded me of the previous morning when I had destroyed the news camera. No time to consider or analyze options and outcomes.

If Finn got anymore worked up, they would lash out with their PK. It would only end in disaster. And it would only be worse if they hurt someone. Come to that, property damage wouldn't look good for them either. Pyrokinetics were among the most feared of all the telekinetic classes. Finn would be in serious trouble if they lost control, no matter the provocation.

"Hey, Finn!" I called as I closed the remaining distance between us at a jog.

Joe took a hurried step back and Finn's eyes locked on me, still scared but mixed with wary hope now. I approached Finn waving and laying on the oblivious vibes thick.

"Tim was wondering where you were at breakfast, so I offered to check on you. I'm his counselor. We met yesterday, remember me?" I asked in a cheery tone.

"Uh, yeah, Aaron, right?" Finn replied, shaking off the fear and looking a little less like a cornered animal.

"Yep," I nodded and then I looked between the two. "Is everything all right here?"

"Yeah, Mr. Armstrong just had a question for me," Finn wouldn't meet my eyes, but their body trembled, betraying their fear.

I wanted to offer help and support. A quick temporary link perhaps, but they didn't know me and it might do more harm than good if we weren't compatible. And I feared making things worse. Finn seemed to have their PK under control now even if they looked agitated.

They impressed me, it must have taken excellent control to refrain from frying Joe Armstrong up extra crispy. From what I had seen, Armstrong had provoked them intentionally. Finn took a deep steadying breath, pulling themself back from the brink.

After another beat, they pushed off the cabin wall and hastened between Joe and me, back to the main path. They spoke over their shoulder, in a calmer register before leaving.

"I promised to eat breakfast with Tim, so I should get going," Finn said. They seemed more in control with each step as they fled. Joe and I both watched them go.

"Please tell me I didn't just catch you propositioning a minor, Joe," I demanded without looking at him. I didn't trust myself with Joe right now. And I wanted to see Finn make it to the mess hall where they would be safer.

"Of course not!" Joe said in a tone that implied the question was ridiculous. "I was asking if Finn had plans for the future. Pyrokinetics are in high demand. I'm sure with SPIRE's connections they would find a good position consulting with local fire departments, for example. I was offering to help them find a job since they graduated from high school this spring."

"That didn't look like an amicable conversation," I said, eyes narrowed.

"Well, it was. I know Finn, they've been to this camp three years running now. Finn wants to get guardianship of Tim. I only offered to help."

"I see."

"So this isn't a problem," Joe insisted, and he gave me a flat stare. "I provided Finn guidance and mentorship. That is the point of this camp, isn't it? If you have concerns about the campers' wellbeing, then I suggest you make sure that the ones in your care are where they should be. If you continue to cause trouble, it may force me to make a closer inspection to the radical activist you brought here as your anchor. So I suggest that you forget whatever you think you saw," Joe said. His tone by turns indignant and then condescending.

"All I saw was the camp director having a private conversation with one of the youth," I agreed.

Though it made my stomach roil to go along with his version of events. I realized I didn't know what he might have become accustomed to getting away with here. If he would intimidate Finn—who had pyrokinesis—out in the open, then what else might he be doing?

If he had provoked Finn into hurting him with PK, then it wouldn't have mattered what the circumstances were. The 'out of control dangerous pyrokinetic' would be the one on trial. Not the skeezy camp director who had threatened and scared them.

"Good," Joe clapped me on the back. "Keep being a team player, Anderson."

I took the dismissal and fled to the mess hall as quick as I dared to walk. I hoped that I had allayed Joe's suspicions for now, because everything Jake had said about PYDC and SPIRE took on a new light. It didn't seem like a ridiculous conspiracy theory any more.

I fumbled with my phone to turn it on; I needed to talk to Jake. He deserved an apology. I didn't have much time since I shouldn't be on my phone while supervising my campers. So I settled for sending a quick text to let him know I was reconsidering his concerns.

Lucky for me, Finn was sitting with their brother. They looked more relaxed, mussing Tim's hair and engaged in animated conversation. But they sat pressed as close to their brother as the cheap plastic seats would allow. I had a vague sense of the link between them helping Finn keep it under control.

Since Finn was sitting with my team, I had the perfect excuse to seek them out. I rushed to grab a tray with orange juice and oatmeal more for appearances' sake than any hunger on my part.

"Hey, Finn, you okay?" I asked as I slid into the seat across from them.

"Uh, yeah," Finn said. They weren't though. Up close I saw their hands shook as they stabbed at their food without eating it.

"How close were we to having BBQ out there, kiddo?" I asked, trying to interject humor without making it worse.

"I wouldn't have hurt him," Finn vowed, voice trembling, they placed their spoon down on their tray and with an emphatic gesture added, "I've never hurt anyone. Not even when it was new. I swear it."

"They haven't," Tim verified and drew himself up, he sounded defensive, like he'd heard the accusation before. Interesting.

Tim put a protective arm around his sibling, which Finn melted into. Yeah, those two had a strong link. It was what Finn needed, so I wasn't about to make a fuss. Not even when Tim added in a tone that told me there was much more to the story, "the fire was an accident. It wasn't Finn's fault."

"I believe you. But I also saw how close you were to losing control, Finn."

"I've got it under control. If he…" Finn swallowed hard, cut their gaze to their brother, then finished. "If anything happened, I was just going to scare him. Why were you even there?"

"I was running late and I happened to see you there. Was he threatening you? Because that's what it looked like. I know people who can help you."

"He wanted me to join SPIRE. I told him yesterday I was thinking about university or finding a job training program. He said I could do more good working with SPIRE. They want me to liaise with fire departments, they always need more PK for that. They've been trying to recruit me since Tim and I ended up at PYDC."

"Is that the first time he resorted to threatening you?"

"Mr. Armstrong? Yeah, at this point the only way I would enlist is if they forced me," Finn said, in a bleak tone. They picked their spoon back up and shoved more food around on their plate.

"We won't let anyone force you to do anything you don't want," I said.

"Sure, okay," Finn did not sound at all convinced.

"If he corners you again do you think you could record it?"

"Maybe, if I had my phone. No personal electronics, remember? Anyway, I should get back to my group before he comes in and sees us talking. Stick close to Aaron today, Timmy," Finn dropped a kiss on their brother's temple as they stood to go back to the table with the rest of team violet.

"What happened?" Tim asked in a small scared voice. He looked more upset now that Finn wasn't there to see it. At least the rest of team lime was chattering around us; if they noticed the drama, then they had the courtesy to pretend otherwise.

"I'm not sure, and I don't think it's my place to share details. If Finn wants you to know, then they will tell you about it," I said.

"It was Armstrong though, right?" Tim pried.

To avoid answering, I took a bite of my oatmeal even though eating was the last thing on my mind. Tim sighed.

"Armstrong bothered them last year at camp too, kept misgendering them. I think the only reason they signed up for it this year is me. To spend time together before they age out," Tim confessed.

I winced at that. I was familiar with the PYDC model where the teens got kicked out of the facility at eighteen.

"We can't accuse Director Armstrong of anything without proof, Tim," I admonished. Then to soften the chastisement, I said, "once we have undeniable proof, we can stop him from pressuring Finn. So, when is Finn's birthday?"

"End of July. They'll be eighteen. I don't know what they'll do then. SPIRE wants to recruit them, but they only want Finn for fire stuff. The problem is that Finn is afraid of huge fires. Our parents died in a house fire. They would hate working with it for a living."

"I see."

"Finn had nothing to do with it," Tim rushed to assure me. "They weren't even home when it started. But everyone who hears assumes it was them and my aunt thought Finn should have at least been able to stop it. I think working with big fires scares them. They would never join SPIRE if they knew it meant working with fire departments."

"And have they talked to SPIRE recruitment about that problem?"

"SPIRE needs their PK. What good is a PK who can't work with fire to them? If they got away from PK stereotypes, Finn might tolerate it. Maybe. But that isn't how it works."

The words poured out of Tim like he had been waiting for a safe person to say them to. I didn't have an adequate response, so I chewed on my oatmeal to buy time. Tim looked contemplative, his own breakfast untouched before him.

"I think they were considering doing it for me. So they could be my guardian. But that was before PYDC pressured them about enlisting with SPIRE," he said. After a long silence, this time in a scared small voice he added, "I'm their link. I don't know what Finn plans to do when they have to leave. Finn is a grade A. They have PK, so they can't just not have a link, you know? They need me."

"Yeah, I know. I'm not sure how, but I want to help you both. I can put in a good word with SPIRE, explain the situation to my bosses there. Did I tell you I work for SPIRE? I can look into resources for Finn. Even if we have to find them a temporary link."

"You would go out of your way to help us?" Tim sounded skeptical.

"Yeah, Tim, in a heartbeat. I signed up to be a counselor to help kids like you and Finn. It wouldn't be much help if I didn't at least try to help you figure this stuff out."

"I'm sure no one will let a pyrokinetic adopt me. Even if that wasn't an issue, Finn isn't the stereotypical nurturer. I don't expect everything to work out how we want in the legal system. But Finn's all I've got," Tim said, plaintive.

"I hear you, Tim, I'll do everything in my power to help, all right?" I promised. "Try to eat, we have a busy day ahead of us. And remember, if we want to get proof about Armstrong, then we need to act like we don't suspect him, you understand?"

"Yeah, but I don't have to like it. I haven't seen Finn that worked up or close to losing control in a long time," Tim said, dropping his gaze to his breakfast again.

"Just try your best, and remember you two aren't alone, all right?"

Tim nodded and went back to poking his food. I shoveled the rest of my oatmeal into my mouth, movements mechanical. To be honest, I felt awful too, I was having a crisis of conscious.

I couldn't shake the terror in Finn's eyes as they made a silent plea for help. And I kept second guessing whether I should have intervened sooner. So what if I was on Joe's radar? He already didn't like me after the reporter incident, what was one more reason? Finn appeared calmer now, but it might be an act.

I also had no earthly idea how to help Finn and Tim with their housing situation. Finn couldn't stay at PYDC after they turned eighteen and Tim was a ward of the facility if he was living there. So Finn aging out would separate them.

If Finn worked for SPIRE, then they would have access to housing or a housing stipend. With a stable job, SPIRE's backing, and a good home they should be able to show they could provide for Tim. I had little understanding of custody laws though. Mrs. English might offer guidance on that front.

My one certainty was that my intervention had stopped something from happening this morning. Whether it was Finn suppressing their abilities and being assaulted, or losing control and lighting something on fire was the only factor in question. The result would have been the same. Finn would be the one living with the consequences.

No one would hold Joe accountable. He would be free to continue intimidating the teens in his care. I refused to be a party to that. But I was in over my head.

There was only one thing for it, talking to Finn confirmed my suspicions. I had to swallow my pride and apologize to Jake. Perhaps with his help I could determine the extent and magnitude of what PYDC—and SPIRE—intended here.

When I looked up from my breakfast Elle was sitting beside Tim, offering him comfort and looking at me with open speculation.

Not long after, it was time to clear the tables. Tim bolted up to catch Finn in the chaos. Elle had already taken care of her tray before joining Tim. After he left, she leaned across the table and fixed me with a knowing gaze.

"You still think SPIRE is looking out for us?" she asked, the challenge clear in her voice.

"What do you know about it?"

"Finn's a grade A," Elle rolled her eyes, all teenage superiority. "They came in here shaking and ready to go hyper-gamma, doesn't take a rocket scientist to put that together. Something happened to them."

"How did you guess at SPIRE's involvement?"

"You look like someone who discovered his hero has a thing for torturing small animals. So unless you were a lot friendlier than I thought with Armstrong, you didn't know about SPIRE and PYDC pressuring us before, and now you do," she shrugged.

"You're kind of scary smart," I said, impressed by her powers of deduction. Elle shrugged off the praise.

"Or it's just obvious," she said, she twirled a lock of hair around her finger in contemplation. "What are you going to do?"

"I'll put a stop to it," I promised. Elle gave me an assessing look then gave an expansive shrug.

"Good luck with that," she said as she stood and added over her shoulder, "you should hurry. Don't want to be late for our morning session."

Elle sauntered over to join the rest of the lime team where they had gathered near the door. I scrambled to catch up with my campers on their way to the obstacle course. And I was wrong-footed all day. Distracted and dwelling on what I'd interrupted between Finn and Joe.

Chapter 22

Aaron

What little focus I mustered between supervising obstacle course runs, I bent toward manipulating my EK. I tried to get a feel for it and translate the finer points of my TK technique to the new avenue for my abilities.

I made good progress, I figured out how to power my phone off and on, how to mute and unmute the sound as it booted, and how to give the battery a boost. That last trick left me drained, and I had to rest for a while afterward.

I kept catching myself looking for Armstrong and Finn in every shadow. I wanted to reassure myself that nothing else would happen between them while I was busy. It was just as well that Elle had volunteered to tell stories from her grandmother and great aunt for our history session. I couldn't have kept my train of thought through a lecture in that state of mind.

Even distracted as I was, Elle's stories about her grandmother were heartbreaking. I understood why she hated SPIRE so much. If I believed the organization was complicit in those kinds of atrocities, then I would have hated it too.

I was itching to call Jake. Work through the new information with him. It didn't fit with the organization that helped psions, which I had seen up to that point.

The first chance I got to carve out free time to make a call was after finishing my dinner. All my campers gathered around the ice cream sundae bar that the counselors set up as a fun dessert option for tonight.

I made sure Finn was around too. They were helping Tim pile ice cream into his bowl. Joe sat with two other counselors, not perpetrating nefarious acts at the moment.

Without giving myself time to chicken out, I stepped outside to make the phone call. Jake picked up on the first ring. I was glad he didn't leave me in suspense as to whether he would accept my call after what I had accused him of the previous day.

"Hey," I said, when he connected the call.

"Aaron?" Jake asked. I couldn't parse his tone of voice.

"Yeah. I'm sorry I didn't listen to you... did you get my message this morning?"

"Yeah, I got it. I don't suppose you can elaborate on what happened?"

Before responding, I looked around to confirm no one lurked close enough to overhear me. I needed to talk this through, but I knew enough to keep the details vague. The last thing I wanted was to alert anyone who might overhear us to my concerns about Joe and the camp. I didn't need to make myself more suspicious. I walked further into the trees, to be on the safe side. Then I spoke into the phone, my voice hushed.

"I saw Joe corner and threaten a camper. He terrified the kid. I wanted to record it, but my phone was off this morning," I said, bitterness tinging my words. I should have been able to do something with my new EK, but it had proved useless.

"Is the teen he threatened all right?" Jake asked. I loved that his first thought was for Finn's wellbeing.

"Yeah, Finn is okay, for now. I need to talk to Roy or someone about what we can do to help them out, but that's a different issue."

"Do you know what they discussed?"

"They didn't want to talk about it much. But the implication was that it was part of a coordinated effort to get them to enlist with SPIRE after they age out of PYDC. He said something that the teen took as a threat against their younger brother."

"I see. Did it seem like Finn would report what happened?"

"I doubt it, not unless there was more evidence than just their word against the organization. PYDC controls whether they have any contact. That would be bad enough, but the little brother is also their link."

"Sounds like they have Finn between a rock and a hard place. I'm sorry that you had to find out about SPIRE and PYDC this way, Aaron. For what it's worth I wish we had been wrong about what's going on there."

"Not your fault," I said, rueful. I shuddered, god, when I closed my eyes I could still see the way Joe had leaned in and touched Finn at the end there. It was stomach turning to be honest, and I had to talk about it to process it. "I think he planned to hurt Finn at the end. They're a pyrokinetic, so he might've just been trying to provoke an attack, but that was genuine fear I saw."

"Well, getting Finn to break the law by attacking with PK would provide Armstrong with more leverage. Watch that kid like a hawk, Aaron. And be careful. We don't know how deep this goes or how far they're willing to go to hide it."

"Do you think if I reported this, that it would help?" I asked, but I knew the answer already.

There wasn't enough evidence. Just my word, and Finn was just as likely to deny anything I said to protect their brother as they were to corroborate my report.

"That all sounds bad, but it's not an ironclad case, by any means. Did you hear anything incriminating at least? In an ideal world, we need Armstrong spelling out the whole thing. On tape if possible. 'Enlist or I will charge you with a felony.' The implication the felony charge is bogus or manipulated would make a better case."

"I know."

"We only have a witness and hearsay that Armstrong exhibited inappropriate behavior toward a teen at the camp. If we tip our hand too soon, it might just remove you from the equation, which leaves no one looking out for Finn. Or gathering hard evidence," Jake laid out the details, confirming my suspicions.

"We need evidence then. Joe has a laptop. I might get something off it?"

"Try not to take unnecessary risks, Aaron," Jake cautioned.

"I'll be careful, and I'll keep an eye on the kids. Um, I'm sorry we fought. I might have overreacted. It looks like, you might have been right," I said.

I was unsure how to fix things between us, but I had to try. An apology over the phone was less than ideal. But it was my only option right now.

"It's water under the bridge, how are you hanging in there?" Jake asked with his characteristic concern.

"Okay, the EK is easier to control the more I get used to it, and the lack of personal electronics out here helps some, less stimulus."

"I'm glad to hear it."

"Um, I keep thinking I should have stepped in sooner, not waited to see what Joe did or try to figure out a way to get it on tape. I feel like I was using Finn. And then I feel like shit for accusing you of using me when I was willing to use something like that," I confessed.

"I can't speak to what you should have done. But I know you weren't trying to use what happened. You were trying to make the best of a bad situation. Capture the evidence needed to put a permanent stop to it. You can't help anyone if you piss Joe off and get yourself kicked out of the camp," Jake said. He talked me down with more patience than I would have managed in his shoes.

"It would have stopped him from touching Finn," I said, dour.

"You didn't know he would do that," Jake sighed. "And you aren't responsible for his actions, Aaron. The important thing is that you intervened, and you aren't disregarding or explaining away what you saw. Keep your eyes open. See if you can get the audio of Joe, or anyone else, trying to force the older teens into signing up with SPIRE. Pay particular attention to Finn and any other grade A's."

"I love you," I blurted, feeling more settled than I had all day. Jake's calm voice made me feel like together we could fix anything.

"I love you too, Aaron, but we need to focus on the task at hand for now. It wouldn't make sense for me to return after our fight, it might arouse suspicions since its well established I'm with SaFE. I am on site during daylight hours for the picket. We leave after dark for safety reasons, but during the day we can back you up, all right?"

"Okay. I miss you, I know it's stupid all things considered, but I miss you," I said.

"I miss you too, nothing stupid about that. The sooner we get hard evidence, the sooner we can be together again. What do you think?" Jake's question rang with false flippancy.

"I think I've got your hard evidence right here," I grumbled, looking around to make sure that there still weren't any teens in earshot. Then I sighed and added, "you're right, though. The campers must come first. Okay, I should get back. Goodnight, I'll be in touch."

"Goodnight, Aaron, stay safe," Jake said.

I hung up with a soft chuckle, stay safe or stay SaFE, doubtless he would say both if I asked which he meant. I hadn't been interested in SaFE before, they were too radical for my liking. Too willing to tear apart the establishment to get their way.

I had looked into them at Yale when I first found out that my career goals were not compatible with my psionic status. But I had convinced myself that they were taking things too far in the name of equality. Throwing the baby out with the bathwater. The more I saw though, I wondered if I had been wrong.

What was wrong with abolishing the registry? Psions were as worthy of dignity as norms. I believed that, so why had I lost sight of it? When had I let rhetoric about allaying norm fears and appeasing potential allies override the principle that psions should have the same civil rights as everyone else?

Were they even our allies if their support was conditional on submitting to restrictions on our liberties? Shouldn't an ally accept that psions are people too? That psions deserve peace of mind as much as norms. They labeled Jake, and all anchors, as potential predators. Or ostracized Finn for their PK.

Whose side I was on? The answer was obvious. I wanted to side with those fighting for my rights. The rights of people like me. Not those advancing reasonable-sounding arguments that hurt my community. Framed that way it was simpler. I could stand with my community, or I could stand with people who wanted us all thrown back in quarantine or worse.

They might choose easy targets at first, but thinking it would stop there was a pipedream. It was easy to vilify pyrokinetics. Just because they said the laws were about protecting norms didn't mean they were about anything other than taking away psion rights.

In light of what I had seen and heard today, it seemed foolish that I had ever felt any different. Jake had known all of that, he had fought for psions when I still trusted being a psion wasn't so bad. Because my experiences as a psion weren't that bad.

"Well, shit," I muttered because this new revelation sucked. And it meant that my views on SPIRE had been naïve at best. At a minimum, I needed to reevaluate without my preconceived notions.

I should return to the mess hall, but I wasn't ready yet. I needed time to cool off. So I did a lap around the outside of the mess hall.

I noticed the light was on in the little office Joe was using, just across from the mess hall kitchens. But I knew he kept the door locked since he kept the camp records, his computer and first aid supplies stored there. Not to mention the safe for valuables.

The office sat atop a small incline so the window was well above the ground. I peered inside out of curiosity, cursing my short stature since I only just cleared the sill on tiptoes. As justification for my snooping, I reasoned that the light might indicate campers getting into things they shouldn't. That was how I stumbled upon Joe Armstrong for the second time that day.

The first thing I noticed inside the room was Joe's back. I couldn't think of a reason he'd be working this late. But there he sat. Behind a desk, situated where he had a direct line of sight to anyone entering the office.

The arrangement put his back to the window, fortunate for me. I doubted that he would take finding me lurking outside of his office well. If

I got caught peering in through his window, it would only give him more cause to distrust me.

Joe had a clunky cell phone pressed to his ear. Of more interest, I noticed the faint glow of the camera in the upper right corner of the room. Angled to capture anyone who entered the office or accessed the safe to the left of the locked door.

I could use the setup, I was certain. After all, I had spent most of the day learning how to use my electrokinesis to activate the recording and transmission capabilities of my phone. How different could a security camera be?

A little nudge at the camera and, yeah, it was recording. Or at least there was power to the circuitry. Following the flow of power I discovered it was a closed circuit feed. I sensed the connection where it was transmitting the data to a server in the office. The office with an electronic lock. Physical access was out unless I wanted to risk discovery, but the device was wireless. So it didn't take much to get my phone to pick up the signal. I was sure I could manage the task without altering the data on the server.

To prevent Joe from hearing any suspicious sounds, I muted my phone and moved away from the window to avoid detection. Then I pulled up the video feed on my screen, I saw where Joe was in the frame's corner. I hoped that the file I saved to my device would have audio to go along with the video.

Nothing exciting happened as far as I could tell. Joe talked on the phone, hung up, slammed the receiver onto his desk with excessive force, typed something on his laptop. Then he closed the lights and locked up behind himself. To my chagrin, the camera did not capture the computer screen.

I could nudge it into a position that would include the laptop with ease using my TK since it was just a hair out of frame. That would risk giving myself away though, so I opted against it. I filed that option away to use as a last resort.

When I was sure Joe had left for the night, I saved the transmission and forwarded it to Jake. Then I went to ensure my team made it to their beds before lights out.

Chapter 23

Jake

I didn't expect to receive a video file from Aaron so soon after he called me. I was glad he had reached out to me though. Over the moon even, I had spent most of the time since I left him the previous afternoon moping about losing him yet again.

Caleb and Elliott welcomed me back, just holding me and petting me with gentle hands the first night back in the bed we shared. Em was understanding, but I could tell the lost opportunity to get inside information frustrated them. Aaron's change of heart would go a long way to mollify them though.

When Aaron had called, it was already getting dark. Caleb, Elliott and I were in our living room. We had picked up food on the way home, wraps from a vegan place Elliott liked. And Em and Jess had eaten with us before leaving. Another day picketing left us too tired and keyed up to cook.

The turnout was smaller today, closer to twenty than thirty, since it was a few days in with nothing to sustain interest. A small knot of counter-protesters from the Society for Safe Schools had held up signs calling for keeping psionic youth off public lands. Word of their involvement would boost our numbers for the next day. And I'd called my media contacts to make sure word would spread.

It had been a long day. The last thing I expected was the call from Aaron, not even after his vague apologetic text earlier in the day. And as much as I cared about him and hoped that we could repair our fractured relationship yet again, I was also wary.

Too much lay unresolved between us. The whole argument had driven home that the Aaron I had known had grown up. We both had. But he had done it without his family around him, without me.

And I had broken his trust. That wouldn't alter because we loved our memories of each other. No matter how much we might both wish otherwise. When I hung up, Caleb watched me, an unreadable expression on his face.

"You guys all good?" Caleb asked, tentative.

"I think we will be? We agreed to focus on the recruitment thing for now. I think Armstrong has him concerned about a camper."

"He has reason to worry," Elliott said, voice glum. Caleb slung an arm around Elliott to comfort him. An icy prickle of dread ran down my spine.

"What do you mean?" I asked.

"I lived at PYDC in Seattle, remember? Well, before it became PYDC if you want to get technical. But Joe was there already. Joe Armstrong never could keep his hands to himself, we called him Strongarm. He mostly left me alone; he likes the grade A's," Elliott said.

"If everybody knows about it then why is he still camp director?" I asked.

Elliott rolled his eyes, "yeah, because anyone would come forward? Did you forget that PYDC is the only home those kids have? It's a month in the summer where Joe works with the kids. The rest of the year he wasn't around much unless a teen expressed a specific interest in joining SPIRE. And he's not stupid. He keeps it to the oldest ones. Builds a rapport with them, and it never goes far enough he can't brush it off as normal link stuff. 'I was just consoling an upset teen,' you know how it goes."

"Do you think this is just him exploiting Finn then? Or do you think it goes deeper than that?" I asked.

"Who knows?" Elliott said. He sounded glum.

"Our best recourse is keeping the pressure on them with the protests. Without solid evidence no one will come forward, but if there is a credible video, that might change," Caleb suggested.

"It's possible? I'm not sure. The thing is, I was a grade C. And even though telepaths are less common, weak ones are still common enough not to waste effort on me once they realized how spotty my abilities are. SPIRE didn't want me. They wanted the powerful psions, or the ones with unusual abilities and those are the residents Joe targeted.

"So I can't say if it's a power thing he gets off on, or if it's a recruitment thing. Or some combination. He didn't target me for recruitment, once he realized I could barely get a proper reading with skin-to-skin contact," Elliott said, bitterness lacing the words.

I didn't know many details about the period of Elliott's life between aging out of the group home and UDub. Only that it was something he didn't talk about often. Caleb had his arms wrapped around Elliott and he shot me a warning look not to keep pushing.

"I'm sorry, El. This one must be hard for you. It hits close to home, huh?" I asked. I wanted to console him, but since my return from SPIRE, he'd shied away from my touch.

"It's all close to home," Elliott said with a little shudder. "Everything we've fought for, it's not abstract for us, you know? It's our lives."

"I know," I rushed to assure him. And I offered El my hand. To my surprise, he responded to the overture with a hard grip. More shocking, his aura reached for me. The way it always used to do. Like a kitten coiling around my ankles to demand attention, I wrapped our link around him, submitting to his wordless demand for affirmation. Had it really only been a week since he stopped touching me like this? It felt so much longer.

"Are you staying with us tonight?" Elliott asked. The question made him sound vulnerable. Raw.

"If it's not an imposition," I said, and I hoped he would say it wasn't because I didn't want to be alone. I wanted to be with he and Caleb.

"You are never an imposition, big guy, but we don't want to get between you and your new lover-boy," Caleb said, with forced levity. Elliott flinched at the mention of Aaron. I didn't regret being with Aaron, but I regretted how sudden it had been. How little time I'd given Elliott to consider. And the way it seemed to be affecting our already strained relationship.

"Aaron said he understands that I love you guys. And even if he didn't, he sent me away. Besides, we already discussed this, my relationship with him has no bearing on what the three of us have. But I'm not up for sex tonight," I said.

"Fair enough," Caleb agreed, "El, you good with that?"

Elliott shrugged, "I only want you both to hold me," he said. And he shivered again, spurring Caleb and I into responding to the raw need in his voice. I stroked my thumb over his hand and reached out along the link between us to offer comfort. For the first time in a while, Elliott's aura responded by coiling tighter into mine. An intentional reinforcing of our link. He gave a contented sigh.

Caleb shifted, so he was sitting behind Elliott, his chest to El's back. He rubbed his hands up and down Elliott's arms in a soothing repetitive motion. Elliott relaxed against Caleb, letting his head loll back onto Caleb's shoulder so he could look into Caleb's face.

"You haven't though. Wanted me to touch you I mean," I forced myself to put the problem into words.

"You prickled," Elliott said, tone sad. "I'm sorry."

"Do I prickle tonight?" I asked.

"No. Not since you got back," Elliott said, "You feel different though."

"I'm sorry I upset you. I didn't intend to spring Aaron on you, everything happened so fast, I never meant to hurt you."

"You didn't. I'm just…"

"You're having nightmares again?" I filled in for him when he didn't finish the sentence.

"Yeah."

"Do I make it worse?"

"No. But seeing Armstrong again did."

Just then my phone buzzed with a multimedia message from Aaron. It reminded me I needed to get him set up with the anonymous apps we used for communications related to SaFE. Any communication was better than none though.

"Is that Aaron?" Elliott asked. His demeanor shifted at the interruption. Tension returning to his body. I ached to soothe him. But we needed to deal with the message first. Our relationship troubles had to take a back seat.

"He sent a video," I said, showing the other two my phone. The momentary closeness with Elliott evaporated as he climbed off Caleb's lap to peer at my phone. Caleb crowded closer too, so we could all watch.

"That's Joe," Elliott pointed to the corner of the screen, all traces of vulnerability swept away at the hint of evidence we could use. "Turn up the volume?"

I obeyed and hit play. The images were grainy, and not much happened other than Joe talking and shifting the phone from one side to the other at one point. His words came through clear enough though.

"... four good candidates for this summer," Joe was saying at the start of the video. The other end of the conversation was inaudible, leaving a pause before Joe spoke again.

"I'm working on the pyrokinetic first. He has a little brother. So that gives us some leverage if nothing else," a pause and then, "I understand the laws in Washington state. I was here when they passed the registry decriminalization initiative," another pause, "I know how to do my job. I had the PK on the brink of lashing out at me earlier, but your new recruit interrupted us," another even longer pause. Joe sounded more frustrated when he got in his reply.

"Then keep your pet on a tighter leash! It's bad enough he's parading around with a radical pro-rights activist as an anchor," Joe said.

Joe flinched at the response to the outburst before saying in a more conciliatory tone, "no. Of course not... I understand... of course. Electrokinesis is a valuable skill... yes, I will get results soon," he said. He hung up and turned to his computer.

Joe spent a few minutes stabbing viciously at the keyboard as evidenced by the loud clacking of the keys. Then he stood and strode out of frame, the lights turned off and the image darkened and froze.

"That's the end," I observed. "This development will excite Em when we show them. He must have been talking to someone from SPIRE."

"He said nothing explicit though," Caleb said, his frustration clear. "It might convince those who already believe something shady is occurring. But he could say anyone was calling him."

"And he could twist it around. Say he meant he was helping the psion in question learn to control their abilities, the mention of leverage was a poor choice of words. He meant an incentive to try harder. Joe's a slippery one," Elliott said. He was right. I longed for the video to be enough, but it wasn't. Not alone.

"Tell your boy solid work, but we need more," Caleb said. And then peering at the screen he added, "and tell him to delete the convo stream and switch to a secure messaging app."

"The last thing he needs is Armstrong getting wind he is doing more than showing up at inconvenient times," Elliott agreed.

I texted Aaron back, thanking him and making the suggestions for future communications. Aaron did not respond right away. But he must be busy with the teens, so I tried not to imagine worst-case scenarios.

The three of us settled in to watch an action movie. Aaron's text had derailed any chance at further clearing the air with Elliott tonight. Elliott and Caleb snuggled together. They leaned into my side, both making a point of including me. I put my arm around them. Caleb and I both touching Elliott. And it was almost like old times between us.

We might not have resolved our problems, but we had taken a first tentative step in that direction. Elliott relaxed into me, his aura not pulling back for a change. Our link grew stronger for it. The familiarity was comforting.

I didn't hear from Aaron again for a few days. My life fell into an easy pattern. Picket during the day and then spend the evenings with Caleb and Elliott. I took comfort in snuggling into our bed with them. Elliott clung to me at night, wrapped around me like he used to before things turned sour between us. I was thankful that my weeklong exile to the guest room appeared to be at an end.

Elliott and Caleb acted subdued in the light of day though. Our usual easy touches throughout the day remained absent. Whether it was the protest or Aaron's sudden return to my life that catalyzed the change, it seemed like a cloud had descended over us.

As if they realized things were changing. The unspoken discontent was almost palpable between us and Elliott was still struggling with being face to face with PYDC and everything it represented to him.

The emotional distance I had been ignoring seemed almost insurmountable now. I understood I needed to talk to them about Aaron, beyond the barest details they already knew, but I feared their response. I didn't want to lose them as lovers, and I couldn't bear the thought of losing their friendship.

Caleb brought it up on the third night. We were all sitting on the couch, Elliott drowsing against my chest, his legs propped in Caleb's lap while Caleb rubbed his feet. El made an occasional contented sound as Caleb worked on his arches and those sounds went straight to my groin.

I felt conflicted about that. We hadn't broached the subject of sex in what felt like ages. And the situation with Aaron confused me. He had reached out, but did that mean he forgave me or just that we were working together on this issue? Did he still want to try dating?

And Caleb, Elliott and I hadn't resolved our issues. The distance I had felt between us of late persisted unabated. I wanted to reconnect, be absolved of my doubts. But with all the surrounding turmoil I wasn't certain how. And I had told no one that the offer to work for SPIRE was the only job offer I had received in months of fruitless searching for a path forward after graduation.

I figured we would just continue in the weird sexless space that had developed between us over the past few weeks for the indefinite future. At least until we uncovered what I was now certain was a widespread recruitment scandal. I thought Elliott was more than half-asleep when Caleb spoke.

"Are you and Aaron serious?" Caleb jumped in without preamble. I sputtered, trying to figure out where the question came from.

"I'm not sure where we stand," I admitted. "We talked about dating, before he figured out I agreed to join SPIRE to dig up dirt on the organization. He wanted to link bond, but he said I should keep seeing you two if I wanted."

"And do you?" Elliott inquired, more awake than I had thought. He shifted, his elbow digging into my side when he craned up to look at me.

"Of course I do! How can you even ask that? I love you," I said, more than a little hurt by the question.

"But you've been distant," Caleb pointed out. "It's a fair question."

"You're right, and I'm sorry," I muttered. "It seemed like with graduation and everything changing there wasn't time for me."

"Big guy, we will always make time for you. We love you, but we can't read your mind. If you're feeling left out or neglected, you have to tell us," Caleb patted my thigh with affection.

"I can read his mind, sometimes," El said. "But Caleb's point stands, I shouldn't have to, not if you're hurting."

We stared at each other over a drawn out silence. I could tell they were both waiting for me to break it.

"I mean, you guys are smart, pursuing fancy degrees, and I'm just a stupid jock. Not even that anymore. I figured I'll get a crappy office job and you guys will outgrow me, leave me behind. Except I haven't even managed that much."

"You're not stupid," Elliot said, smacking my arm in rebuke.

"I mean, maybe a little bit stupid, if you believe we want you out of our lives," Caleb teased. He pinched two fingers together to emphasize a little bit. I huffed, nudging Caleb with my foot. He snorted a laugh, and I chuckled too. Caleb resumed massaging Elliott's feet, the tension broken.

"Sorry, I guess it was a silly thought. And I let it consume me and then worrying about losing you guys made me push you away until I almost lost you. So, we can agree I'm a little stupid. I get you guys were giving me space. But I don't want space. I want what we've been building together. But I need to contribute, pull my weight."

"And you do, Jay. If it takes time for you to find a job, we won't kick you out over the rent. Take all the time you need."

"We'll even love you if you decide working for SPIRE is a good fit for you," Elliott teased, pressing a light kiss along my jaw.

"Thanks," I snorted. "So, are we good?"

"We're good," Elliott said. Caleb hummed, like he had something further to say, but he held his peace.

"El, you said you'd tell him," Caleb prompted after a long pause. "Now seems like a good time if we are clearing the air."

Elliott sighed and squeezed my hand.

"I told you I was all right with you and Aaron. And I meant it. But it makes me think… that maybe I'm not enough. I don't want him to take you away. And I feel selfish for even telling you this."

"It's not selfish, El," Caleb said, tightening his hold on Elliott until he squirmed to free his feet, and curled into my side. I looped my arms over his shoulders, my hold loose because he always got tense if he felt restrained. After years together, reading his body language was second nature.

"I'm glad you told me," I said. "How can I help you feel more secure?"

Elliott shrugged, "you can't. It isn't about you. It's about me. And my jealousy that Aaron gets a piece of you we can't share. It sort of helps knowing the reason your aura changed after graduation is that he is back in Seattle. That it's not something you asked for. I want things to return to normal. For you to fit with us the way you used to. A seamless part of us. But that isn't how life works. I don't want to lose you though."

"I promise you won't lose me, El. Not to Aaron. I promised to be your family when I moved in with you guys, and I meant it. I have no desire to go back on my word. What do you need to believe me?"

"Time I guess. To see it's true."

"Is this about Aaron, or you not trusting me to stick around?"

Elliott shook his head.

"El, hun, what's bothering you?" I implored.

"You've been pulling away for months." Elliott said, reluctance clear. I tried to sound patient and calm when I responded.

"You're the one who asked me to sleep in the guest room last week."

"Because you were already distancing yourself!"

"Oh. I didn't think you'd noticed," a silly thought, because Elliott couldn't avoid noticing. His ability to get a telepathic reading was amplified during sex. And he could always read me better than he could strangers.

"We noticed," Caleb interjected. "We wanted to give you space to figure out what you wanted to do with your future."

"But it hurt too much, to sleep beside you and pretend I didn't notice you slipping away. Didn't notice the way you stopped letting me in. How you wanted someone else."

"You told me my aura bothered you."

"It did. Because you wanted him, you were reaching for Aaron when we were right there beside you. I didn't realize what it was before. But the way your aura changed around him made it obvious. And you didn't reach back when I tried to reach out to you. You wanting someone else didn't bother me, as much. It was that you wanted someone else *instead* of me."

"That's not what I want."

"Are you sure?"

"Yes. Aaron was my first love. We were childhood sweethearts, sure. But I fell in love with you too, Elliott. Because of who you are. You have such a big heart, always trying to help everyone around you. Always trying to solve the world's problems, no matter how much it takes out of you.

You are facing down SPIRE and PYDC and your past to make a better future for kids you don't even know. And I couldn't be more proud of you.

"You make us a family, you get that, right? That Caleb and I adore you? The three of us have built something special, and you're at the center."

Elliott fixed me with a disbelieving stare, glancing between Caleb and I.

"He's right, El," Caleb said.

"So, what? If it weren't for me you two wouldn't be together?" Elliott said. He seemed wary, almost accusing.

"No," Caleb said, voice calm and even, "but we both want to give you the home and the family you deserve. We want to make you feel safe."

"I do. When I'm with you guys, I do. And I don't want you to leave, Jay. Please don't leave?"

"I'm not. I have to live on site for SPIRE training, but I'm not leaving you. I'll see you both as much as possible during training. After the training period we can work out an arrangement. If Aaron even wants to keep me as a partner. If we work things out. And that seems like a big if right now. Would getting to know him help or would that make it harder? Or do you need me to give him up? Because if you need me to, then I will, Elliott."

"No! I don't want you to resent me for keeping you apart."

"And I don't want to make you feel inadequate. Tell me what you need, hun."

Elliott took a deep breath, holding it until I thought he must be getting lightheaded, but he let it out in a long gust and nuzzled into my neck. He took a few more long inhalations, breathing me in. Then he returned his feet to Caleb's lap, nudging him to resume the foot rub. Caleb obliged.

"I need us to be a family. The way we were before you graduated. And if that means accepting Aaron as your lover, then I will. He can come to a family dinner on Sundays even. If he's part of you, then that makes him part of us too. You said you thought you had to leave us behind, to grow up or get a real job or whatever, but you don't. Please don't leave us behind, Jay?"

"I promise, El. I won't leave you behind. It seemed like we were drifting apart though. The prospect you might want me to leave scared me too much to say anything. I convinced myself it wasn't fair to ask for more from you guys when I'm not willing to let go of Aaron."

"We don't want you to let go of him," Caleb said. "If you want to date him, go for it. Hell, if he doesn't want you to sleep with us anymore, then we can live with that even, just don't cut us out. Talk to us."

"Mm," Elliot agreed, then he leaned up for a soft kiss, "you can't ditch us that easy. We never wanted you to stop being a part of us."

"You're stuck with us for as long as you want us, big guy," Caleb said. We sat together in silence for a while. Caleb still massaging Elliott's feet and Elliott tracing idle patterns onto the forearm I had looped across his chest.

"So, I feel like an idiot for not realizing how torn up you two were over the past few months, Caleb said. "I thought it was just a transition thing, Jake spreading his wings and exploring being a full-fledged adult or whatever. And Elliott stressed with stressed from his research. Elliott, I'm sorry I didn't listen better when you told me you were worried Jake was pushing us away. And Jake, I'm sorry we didn't clarify we still had a place for you no matter where your career takes you."

"Not your fault. I should have said something sooner. And I understand the timing sucks, with Aaron showing up."

"I'm glad he did though," Elliott said, to my complete surprise. "Seeing you with him made sense of the way your aura changed the last little while. It was never about me being enough. It was about you still loving him. I can live with that. With you loving us all. It's better than thinking we're just not enough for you.

"And, yeah the timing is awful. You were right, the past few days have been hard. The campers remind me of being in their shoes and I hate it. It brings up bad memories. And I wish the three of us weren't fighting, or whatever it is we've been dancing around. I miss you, and I need you, I need both of you to get through this."

"You've got us," I said, wholeheartedly.

"Both of us," Caleb agreed. He set Elliott's feet on the ground and crawled over us, kissing each of us. "Is Aaron all right with you still having sex with us, Jay?"

"He said he was," I said.

"Did he have any concerns we need to address?" Caleb asked.

"He wants to meet you both. I still love him, it's not more, but it's different with him."

"We get that, big guy, you can have both. If he's important to you then we want to meet him, right, El?"

"Yes," Elliott agreed.

"But if he runs off on you again, we might have to kick his ass," Caleb added with a playful smile to show he was joking.

"Thanks. I missed being close to you guys like this these last few months," I admitted.

"Then come to bed and let us show you how much we love you," Elliott offered. He got to his feet and sauntered down the hallway. Caleb hopped up after him, took my hand and led me after Elliott.

Elliott pounced on me as soon as I entered our bedroom. His kisses desperate and needy. His arms looped around my neck, pressing me close. He hooked one leg behind my knee, forcing it to buckle.

Caleb had to catch me, propping me up when I stumbled from the force of Elliott's ardor.

"Sorry," Elliott murmured against my lips, a faint smile curving his mouth. I returned the smile, dazed at the change in Elliott. His renewed openness with me as he hauled my shirt over my head and ran his hands along my torso. And with every touch the link between us strengthened, grew. The threads of his aura weaving with mine ever tighter.

"Missed you, so much. Missed this. Us," Elliott said.

El's hands never left my body, as he peppered kisses across my chest, working his way downward. I heard the whisper of cloth as Caleb undressed behind me, then his warmth enveloped me as he wrapped his arms around me. His hands joined Elliott's.

And I sensed the link to Caleb expand and grow too. The strands tying me to him renewed, twining with Elliott's link, separate yet inextricably connected. And running parallel to the familiar beloved connection to the men I had loved and lived with, the link to Aaron. New and perhaps fragile. But stronger than ever before. He was in my heart too.

All three of them were. Each had become a part of me that the others couldn't replace. They were everything. And we needed each other if we hoped to get through the coming days. Of that I was certain.

But tonight was for Caleb and Elliott and I. To rekindle what we had almost lost. Bolster the ties that bound us together. Relearn each other's bodies. Remind ourselves of our shared love. Reinvigorate our link.

Elliott sank to his knees in front of me, dispatching my pants while I reveled in the sense of being an anchor. Their anchor. He looked up at me now, my erection in his hand, his touch almost unbearably tender.

I knew they could feel what I was doing. That they noticed the way I shored up our links. And that the touches that threatened to overwhelm me with their intimacy were magnified to them, psionic senses dialing up their reactions to even a simple caress.

"You feel it? Feel our link? Our love."

"Yes, El, I feel it."

"Good," He said, and he lowered his mouth to taste me. His tongue teasing, each contact light, almost delicate, as he mouthed at my dick. And I froze, letting him explore at his own pace. Because while Caleb was all for having his face fucked, Elliott almost never offered to give head. It overwhelmed him too easily.

I understood it brought back bad memories without him saying anything. But right now I perceived the pulse of our bond like a separate heartbeat, thrumming between us. Strong, powerful. Because Elliott was trusting me and touching me and giving himself to me without reservation.

And I responded to that trust by wrapping him in the warmth and comfort of the bond.

He took the head of my dick into his mouth and for an instant a weak projection of his telepathy pushed into my mind. The sense of love, belonging and family he felt in that moment.

"Love you too, El. So much."

Caleb hadn't moved from behind me, but he must have used his TK to snag the lube from beside our bed. Because his hand slid from the base of my spine, moving lower to slide slippery fingers inside me. His other hand pinning me against him, holding me upright while he and Elliott worked me to the point of orgasm. Between the almost excruciatingly gentle suction of Elliott's mouth and Caleb's insistent strokes I would not last.

"El, gonna come, hun," I gasped out a warning. Elliott squeezed my ass shoving me further into his mouth at the same moment Caleb increased his tempo and I couldn't hold back a second longer. Elliott pulled off, but didn't move back, using his hand to stroke me through my orgasm, his cheek nestled against my thigh, breathing heavy.

When I recovered my senses, I stroked a hand through his hair.

"You with us, hun?" I asked, because sometimes he wasn't. No matter how much he wanted the sex, sometimes it was too much for him and he retreated from us in the aftermath. Tonight wasn't one of those nights though.

Elliott tipped his head up and smiled at me, present in the moment.

"You taste good," he said, with a dreamy expression.

"Yeah? Care to share?" I urged him to stand, kiss me. He came to his feet with a dancer's natural grace, kissing first me and then Caleb.

"You feel loved yet?" Caleb asked, a gentle tease in his voice.

"I want to feel more, I want you to fuck me. While Elliott fucks you."

"Yeah?" Caleb raised a brow.

"And I don't want to be careful. I want to feel you, Caleb. Please? I know you worry, but I want you with no barriers."

Caleb chewed his lip, "you're still on PrEP?"

"Yeah. And I know you got another test last week, that you're still undetectable, so please?"

Caleb considered, then nodded, "if you're sure that's what you want, Jay."

"It is."

"El, you okay with that too?"

"Mhm, I've got no problem with that plan. I don't need a condom for touch sensitivity with you guys. You know that. You're my links."

"Okay. Jay, you hop on the bed and finish prepping yourself," Caleb took charge, tossing me the bottle of lube. He and Elliott scrambled out of their remaining clothing. Then in a tangle of limbs and frantic movements they joined me. Caleb crawled over me, Elliott positioned at his back, working him open.

"Ready?"

"Yeah," I said. Caleb pushed into me, working his way deeper with slow shallow strokes. His hand on my dick, fondling me with lazy languid movements to help me stay hard. Once he was all the way inside, his mouth sought mine with bruising force.

Caleb's kisses distracted me from the fact he wasn't moving yet. Giving Elliott a chance to fuck into him. He moaned into our kiss when Elliott penetrated him. And then we were moving, Elliott setting a rhythm for us to follow, each thrust forcing Caleb deeper inside me. Like Elliott was fucking us both.

I allowed myself to get lost in the sensations. Caleb's body moving inside me sent sparks of pleasure building ever higher. His aura meshed with Elliott's until they almost seemed like one presence. Their auras wrapping around me and through me so I couldn't find the seams between the three of us.

We'd fucked before. Countless times. But it was still special, an expression of the bond between us. It transcended the physical, binding us together, driving our link bond to new heights of intimacy. And I was certain we all sensed it.

We all shared in long moments of pure bliss through our connection. I couldn't guess who climaxed first, but the other two followed close behind. Afterward we collapsed into a pile of sweaty, sticky contentment. And I had never felt more loved and accepted by them. I knew they felt it too.

Chapter 24

Jake

The next morning I got another video file from Aaron, just as Caleb, Elliott, and I were taking an early lunch break in the van. Elliott read the text notification from the passenger seat. I opened the attachment and held the phone above the console so we could all watch. Elliott and Caleb leaned in close to view the video.

I recognized the little room from the last video in the thumbnail before I hit play. This time when the video started, Joe was sitting on the edge of the desk. He loomed over a teen, presumably Finn, who slouched in a chair facing the desk.

"Come on, kid. You understand how this goes, right? You're strong, we aren't letting you walk away. If you cooperate, I can sweeten the deal," Joe's voice sounded tinny through my phone's speakers.

As we watched, Joe glanced up, into the camera before returning his focus to Finn. I could understand why Finn huddled into the chair, trying to make themselves as small as possible as Joe wheedled.

"We can help you get custody of Tim," Joe offered.

"PYDC is why I need to get custody," Finn snapped, their head jerking up to glare at Joe before they looked back at the ground.

"We always strive to keep kids with their families where possible," Joe said, sounding reasonable. "After what happened to your parents with the fire, you needed to be in a place that could bring your psionic abilities under control. PYDC was there to help you learn control. And we took in you and your brother when you had nowhere else to go."

"We had our aunt," Finn said, though the protest sounded weak, defeated.

"Social services didn't equip her to deal with two psionic teens," Joe insisted, "I have seen your files. Did you know your aunt suspected your involvement with the house fire that killed your parents? We offered her an option that allowed her to protect her nephews and her own family."

Finn bristled at that but they gritted out, "we are her family too."

"I don't presume to understand your family dynamics, but PYDC stepped in to help you when you had nowhere else to turn. Just think what would happen to Tim with his big brother in jail. Who'll look out for him without you around, Finn?"

"Sibling," Finn corrected. "I'm his big sibling. And I did nothing wrong."

"You didn't register him. I have the records. You were living in California when your brother had his emergence and you didn't register him until after the grace period."

"There was a filing error because our parents died around the same time and we got sent to live with our aunt up here. We filed for a waiver."

"And you falsified your registration Finn, that is a crime."

"We didn't realize it was pyrokinesis until after the grace period. I updated my registration as soon as my PK came in, we got a waiver for that too."

"It is still in your record though, you have a registry mark, who else will hire you? The law doesn't care about excuses. But SPIRE will overlook your past indiscretions if you agree to work for them."

"And if I don't?" Finn challenged.

"Then you and I might work out an alternative arrangement," Joe leaned closer so that his knees were touching Finn's legs. Finn's face snapped up, and they looked at Joe with fear.

"What are you suggesting?"

"You're smart, Finn, what do you think I'm suggesting?"

Finn's gaze darted around the room searching in vain for an escape route before settling back on Joe. "What are you going to do?" Their voice came out so soft it was a surprise the camera picked up the words. Joe leaned in closer. His hands on Finn's upper arms, Finn froze as Joe invaded their personal space. A flash of light washed out the image as something on the desk ignited and Joe jumped away from the teen.

"You assaulted me with your PK," Joe said, but the triumphant smile on his lips was at odds with his accusatory tone.

"I, uh, no, I wouldn't. You scared me, but I wouldn't hurt anyone," Finn protested.

Joe doused the flames with his suit jacket in a casual movement. He burnt his hands in the process if his body language was anything to go by. But his voice remained matter-of-fact as he said, "I have the proof right here. You scorched my desk, burned my hands, my jacket is cinders. What proof do you have?

"Who will believe the delinquent little pyro who burnt his own parents in their beds over the respected director of this camp? The authorities never charged you in their deaths, but if you try to fight assault charges now, it will come up in court."

Finn slumped their voice small and defeated. "What do you want me to do?"

"Sign the contract. Go where SPIRE tells you. Do what they tell you to do. Prove your loyalty and in a year we can discuss custody of your brother."

"A month, I need to know Tim is safe," Finn countered, voice fierce.

"Six months and you show me you can follow orders."

"He's my link, please?" Finn begged, the fight draining out of them. Joe took a moment, either considering the request, or drawing out the moment of his victory.

"Sign the papers. After you complete your SPIRE training requirements Tim can move in with you, conditional on your continued employment with SPIRE."

"And if I agree, you won't press charges?"

"I will have to file an incident report," Joe heaved a long-suffering sigh. "But as long as you cooperate this won't go any further than that."

"Ok. I'll sign," Finn acquiesced, reaching out a hand for the pen.

Joe handed over a clipboard and a pen. Then he stood behind Finn's chair leaning over them and putting an arm around the teen's shoulders. Joe pointed to show them where they needed to sign as they paged through the sheaf of papers on the clipboard.

The part of Finn's pixelated face in the camera frame showed no emotion as they signed everywhere Joe instructed. Joe's hands wandered more, while Finn sat silent, signing away their life.

After a few minutes of going through the paperwork Joe took the clipboard and set it on his desk. Then he caressed Finn's cheek as a knock sounded on the door. Joe jerked away from Finn, turning to the door.

"Who is it?"

"It's Aaron, I need the first aid kit again," Aaron's voice came through the door and Finn slumped in apparent relief. Joe moved to open the door and Aaron stepped inside, playing at blithe ignorance.

"Why is the door always locked? Shouldn't we have easier access to the first aid kits?"

"Because we store confidential files in this office too," Joe said through gritted teeth. He turned to grab a first aid kit from out of the camera frame. "If a camper was injured, you need to file an incident report," he chastised Aaron in a sharper tone than the circumstances dictated.

"Oh, no. I was just a klutz. Broke a light bulb in the restroom and cut open my hand trying to pick up the pieces," Aaron waved away the rebuke. He held up his bloody hand as proof. Joe seemed mollified by that, maneuvering around his desk to sit in his chair.

"Oh, hey, Finn, I didn't realize you were in here too, everything ok?" Aaron asked.

"I was just talking to Mr. Armstrong about enlisting with SPIRE," Finn said in a shaky voice.

"That's great! SPIRE does so much for the psion community, I recently enlisted too. I bet we'll be in the same training group, you turn eighteen soon, right? We should talk about it over lunch. Do you want to join me?"

"Um," Finn gave Joe a surreptitious look, seeking permission.

"Go ahead. We're done here, for now. Just remember what we talked about. About following orders."

The video ended with Aaron shepherding Finn out of the office.

"That was super uncomfortable to watch," Caleb commented. He was holding Elliott's hand tight. Elliott's return grip was white-knuckled. I patted his shoulder and Elliott leaned into the touch.

"Yeah," I agreed.

"So, I guess we give that to Em?" Elliott suggested. He flashed a weak, unconvincing smile at us.

"It's the proof we need, right?" Caleb looked at us in question.

"It proves that Joe is doing this. But it only implicates him. And what he did after they signed the papers gives the higher ups an easy out to say he was doing it for his own sick purposes," Elliott said, doleful.

"If it is widespread, then wouldn't there be similar cameras recording these exchanges at other facilities?" Caleb suggested. His brow furrowed.

"Aaron's text said the camera was off when he discovered the meeting. He turned it back on. And he had to turn off the led indicator. You saw the bit where Joe glanced at the camera? Checking that it wasn't recording," I reasoned out loud.

"So we need to get more proof?" Caleb's frustration was clear.

"Let's show Em and see what they say," Elliott suggested.

When we showed them, Em and Jess watched the video in silence. They stopped it before the end.

"Tell me this does not turn into a sex tape," Em demanded in a low growl.

"It's not, they get interrupted," Caleb said, voice grim.

"That does not help as much as you think it does," Jess was also spitting mad at that point.

"That video is as explicit an example of blackmail as possible. It would be better if we had more widespread evidence. Video from other camps, but maybe this, alongside statistical analysis, will encourage more victims to come forward." Em said. I thought their confidence in statistics to change minds might prove over optimistic. But we had to try.

"I will," I offered. "I was present when the local head of SPIRE pulled the same script with Aaron at their Seattle headquarters. They made him enlist in exchange for not prosecuting him over not knowing he had EK. Hell, they coerced me into signing on too. Two SPIRE agents stood in the room. One of them was chummy with us after, he might corroborate our story," I said.

"Will Aaron?" Caleb asked in a gentle tone.

"I don't know. At the time he dismissed any widespread sinister intent. He chalked it all up to some convoluted combination of misunderstanding and isolated bad actors. Now, I can't say. He seems to have a bond with Finn, so seeing the same thing happen to someone he feels responsible for might help him see it for what it was?" I mused.

"Ask him. No other way to be certain. Jake, you get in touch with Aaron and the SPIRE agent you mentioned. Try to bring them around. Then you can drum up interest in a scoop with the media, let them know there's a bigger story here. I need to call my contacts, but I think if we get this file into the right hands it might turn public opinion.

"The rest of you, hold the line with the protest, we need to keep the pressure on here. We can't tip our hand too soon. Once this hits the news, it should at least attract more interest in picketing. If we are here and visible, then that makes it easy for like-minded people to find us," Em laid out the plan.

"Right, back to the picket lines," Caleb agreed, but he didn't let go of Elliott who still looked off-kilter after watching the video. Caleb and I exchanged worried looks, and I was sure we were on the same page about keeping a close eye on Elliott until this was over.

"I'll reach out to our contacts with other pro-rights groups. The pro-reg side is out in force today, so this might be enough to get our less radical allies out here to support us?" Jess suggested.

"It's worth trying to get the word out, just stick to what is public knowledge, for now. Mention the counter-protesters as your reason for reaching out, that goes for you too, Jake, when you reach out to your media contacts," Em recommended

"Yes, Em," Jess said. It might have been my imagination, but I thought her words held a hint of uncharacteristic exasperation. Jess patted Em's shoulder before walking to the parked van for privacy to make her calls.

"I should go join her, but I wanted to check how you are holding up?" Em touched my elbow in a supportive gesture.

"I'm all right. Worried about Aaron. Not sure where things stand between us. I hope this evidence is enough to bring everything to light."

"I can't say for sure until I show my contacts, but it looks damning."

"Yeah. So, you and Jess are okay, right?"

"Yeah, why do you ask?"

"Things just seem off between you two, I guess."

"We had a fight, nothing serious."

"You sure?"

"I forgot our anniversary. It's been a hectic week."

"Nothing else going on?"

"Nothing that matters right now. I appreciate the concern though. We have calls to make, come on big guy, the sooner we bring PYDC down the sooner you get to reunite with lover-boy. And I can appease Jess."

"Yeah, there is that," I agreed, "and you'll have more time to plan a celebration for Jess when you aren't busy being the mastermind behind bringing down SPIRE."

"My thoughts exactly, brace yourself, Jake, this will be big," Em shot me a wolfish grin. They strode off after Jess, phone already to their ear.

I opted to contact Roy first. Since I was less invested in his cooperation than Aaron's. I sent a quick text to ask if he had time for a chat. A few moments later my phone rang.

"Hello, Jake, speaking," I answered.

"Hey, man, how are you?" Roy greeted me.

"Good, listen, you know how I told you about Aaron and I not working together anymore?"

"Yeah? I meant to contact you about that. You understand the deal he made is contingent on you both joining, right?"

"That deal is what I'm calling about. Um, is that a common recruitment technique?"

"Asking powerful psions to work with an anchor they already have an established link with?"

"Threatening to press charges if they don't enlist."

The line went dead for a minute, then Roy spoke with quiet urgency.

"It isn't the official protocol, no. SAC Smythe only gets involved with recruiting grade A psions. Those who prove less than amenable to joining of their own free will. And, according to Anna, Director Russell himself authorizes the protocols she uses."

"And your involvement with this?" Because that was the real question, whether I could trust someone complicit in the problem.

"Smythe recruited Anna and I too. We linked long before they changed the registry laws here. They recruited us the same way. And I keep my mouth shut and my head down because there isn't any proof, Smythe is careful about that."

"Do you know how widespread it is?"

"Anna and I don't work with the other regional offices much. She's a strong telepath, one of only a handful who can consistently read minds without skin-to-skin, so they like to keep us close to home.

"From what I gather, Smythe is the only one involved at the Seattle headquarters. Anna and I get called in to deal with grade A's who violate registry requirements.

"The two of us getting assigned to check out security at the camp Monday morning worked out. But someone would have called us in once Aaron zapped that news camera, regardless. We report to SAC Smythe. And she is not someone you want to cross without rock solid proof."

"What if I told you we have proof? Not of Smythe's involvement, but a video of someone affiliated with PYDC and running a SPIRE youth development summer camp using the same script."

"I can make discrete inquiries to some other agents, she has recruited a handful of grade A's. I can't promise they will come forward, but I can delve into who might be worth asking?" Roy offered.

"That sounds perfect. So you and Anna have seen her do this with some regularity?"

"Look, Anna will be a tough sell, being forced to enlist pissed her off to no end. But she came around to thinking the ends justifies the means. She and Aaron might get along given a chance. They both appear to be of the opinion SPIRE does enough good to balance out any harm it causes.

"In Anna's defense though, there are things she doesn't tell me. Things she learns with her abilities. So I can't say for certain she is wrong, and I trust her judgment. Or I wouldn't have gone along with it all these years.

"But if compelling evidence exists that the practice is more widespread than I thought, then yes, I will corroborate your account of what happened to Aaron. If that is what you are skirting around asking me. I think I can at least convince Anna not to comment if she won't corroborate your story," Roy offered.

"That's more than I expected, thanks. I'll owe you one if we can bring this to light."

"Sure, I'm not a fan of forcing people to join. It's not what SPIRE purports to be about, you know?"

"Yeah, I hear you. I need to talk to Aaron, so I'll be in touch. I'm not sure when this is going public, but I expect it will be soon."

"Yeah, I'm sure we will be in touch, take care, Jake."

"You too."

I ended the call and then stared at Aaron's contact information, nerving myself up before hitting the call button. It rang until I believed he would let my call go to voicemail. But at the last moment, he answered.

"Hey, sorry, I had to finish something, what's up?" Aaron sounded breathless.

"I got your video."

"Oh, yeah? That's good, I hope you liked it."

"Um, is everything okay there?"

"Yeah, just busy with the campers. Did you need something?" Aaron asked. His voice light and cheery, the way he always used to sound when he was pretending everything was fine.

"Right, so, you are somewhere you can't talk, but are you safe?"

"That about sums it up, yeah."

"Are you willing to go public about the similarities between your recruitment and what happened with Finn in the video?"

"I can do that."

"And I'm worried about Finn, can you keep a close eye on them? Because we got the video and we will get it into the public eye soon. I can't predict how Joe will react when it comes out, but regardless, that kid should not be alone with him."

"Yeah, I agree, but I need to let you go now. I'll talk to you later," Aaron said.

"Please be careful, Aaron, I love you," I told him. I tried not to let his attitude alarm me. He had to be practicing caution. No sense drawing attention to his change in loyalties.

"Me too, you take care."

Then Aaron ended the call. Leaving me to worry about him inside the campgrounds. Aaron was on his own. Without backup and shouldering the weight of responsibility for the kids in there with him. And no way to identify Joe's allies. I had to trust that Aaron could take care of himself and do my part to back him up if it came down to it.

Once this was over, Aaron and I might have a shot at seeing what was between us. After clearing the air with Elliott and Caleb I felt much more up to the task. But I had to keep my focus on the mission for now. Finn and the other campers depended on us to play our cards to maximum efficacy or they would be the ones to suffer the consequences. Time to get my head in the game.

I called around to my usual contacts and when I couldn't think of any others who would be useful, I joined the throng of protesters to keep the pressure on the summer camp. There wasn't a full news crew out here at present. The crowds on both sides were larger today, the counter-protesters had drawn more media attention which had increased interest on both sides.

A print journalist whom I recognized must have arrived while we were eating because he was chatting with Caleb. I waded in to make myself available for an interview. Doubtless, Caleb's mind wasn't on answering questions with El on the brink of falling apart.

I had to push aside my concerns about Elliott and Aaron. Caleb supported Elliott as best he could. And I sent as much warm acceptance through our link to Elliott as I could manage. But I couldn't protect Aaron. I needed the distraction, and I had a good rapport with the journalist in question so I jumped in to take over from Caleb answering questions.

It was going to be a tense afternoon, that was for sure.

Chapter 25

Aaron

Finn seemed shaken after what had happened in Joe's office. They didn't want to be alone and spent the rest of the lunch break sitting silent with my team. Tim picked up on their distress. But we didn't discuss the incident.

As a solution to keep them safe, I made arrangements with the other two TK counselors. Teams lime, blue and violet would work together that afternoon. The other counselors agreed with minimal convincing. A tenet of the camp was mentorship, so the older teens working with the younger met that goal.

My phone rang as we were heading to the skills course en masse. I excused myself from a chat with the other two counselors. Before answering Jake's call, I moved toward the edges of the group.

While we discussed what he planned to do with the video I sent him, all I could think was how sorry I was that he wasn't at my side. My self-recriminations knew no bounds. I should have listened to his concerns. I had been so naïve about SPIRE.

I had known there was never an innocent misunderstanding over my EK. With my parents being who they were, I learned early to analyze every offer of aid for hidden motives or manipulation.

I wasn't stupid. I understood Smythe had coerced me into enlisting from the start. However, I had wanted to believe better of SPIRE; I felt gullible for ever believing in the organization now.

Seeing the same tactic used on Finn crystalized things. This behavior was routine for SPIRE. The revelation called everything about SPIRE into question. Sure they helped psions, but only when it suited their own ends. I had been willfully obtuse about their machinations.

I couldn't help concluding Jake had made the best decision available when he resolved to make the most of a bad situation. And try to use his position on the inside to uncover the extent of the problem. So he and Elle were right. But even if the corruption reached all the way to the highest echelons of leadership, I could and would do my part to make SPIRE live up to my ideals for it. All too soon we had arrived at the obstacle course and I had to end the call.

I attempted to put the video of Finn and Joe—and what Jake planned to do with it—out of my mind. The campers in my care deserved my attention. It helped that coordinating the afternoon session was a ton of work.

Organized chaos reigned as the older teens each paired off with one of the younger ones. They set to work with the obstacles. Some hiccoughs occurred, but we got everyone squared away with no major incidents.

There wasn't enough training gear to go around, but we improvised. A shortage of anchors only exacerbated the problem with all the teens clamoring to practice at once. It kept the counselors busy pitching in to help out with stabilizing links and shuffling anchors to those with the greatest need. It proved an exhausting ordeal.

My mind kept wandering, though. The whole experience left me on edge. I couldn't keep an eye on all the teens for an entire month. I couldn't be everywhere that Joe was to prevent him from hurting the campers. And I couldn't risk tipping our hand when the stakes were so high.

If the blackmail effort was widespread, then acting alone might let the rest of the network continue undiscovered. It would be too easy for Joe Armstrong to take the fall. Any investigation now might not go further than implicating him for his abuses. I wouldn't allow that to happen.

The afternoon sped past and dragged on simultaneously. The joint exercise proved a huge success. Well worth the challenge of supervising so many teens working in tandem. And spending the time with Tim calmed Finn down considerably.

I was acutely aware that once the exercise ended, I wouldn't be able to keep tabs on Finn. I wasn't sure if the violet team counselor would be safe to tell. My gut said yes. But Finn knew them better and hadn't confided in them. So I didn't dare trust my gut.

It all came back to proof. If I hadn't amassed enough evidence yet, I would have to locate more. I reasoned that the best bet for finding further proof must lie within the locked office.

It seemed clear that I must act tonight, after Joe finished work for the evening. It would put Finn's wellbeing at risk to put it off any longer than that.

I only needed to get through the afternoon joint sessions, dinner and the evening free time for the campers. Then I could act. I would just have to hope that Joe didn't bother anyone else before I gathered the proof I needed. The time to figure out a more solid plan ran out, and we all packed it in for dinner.

"Hey, thanks for that," Finn found me in the crowd as we all went to eat.

"No problem, how are you holding up?" I asked. They looked less upset than they had been earlier.

"I don't think it has sunk in yet. That I have a plan for after July?" Finn said, a questioning lilt to their voice.

"You do?" Tim said. He had approached us unnoticed and must have overheard.

"Yeah, buddy, I do. I talked to some people, and it looks like if I make it through training, then SPIRE will help me get custody of you," they explained.

"Really? But what about the fire departments?" Tim said. Excitement and concern warred in his features and his tone of voice.

"I can do good work with SPIRE. And who else will hire me?" Finn reasoned.

"You aren't just doing it for me, right?" Tim accused, his insecurity about that clear.

"No way, buddy. I think it was the right choice for me, I was just talking to Aaron about it at lunch. He works there too," Finn assured their brother.

"I do," I agreed, with a healthy dose of false cheer. "I'd be happy to answer your questions over dinner, if I can."

"Okay," Tim said, mollified. If only it was that easy to allay my own concerns about what agreeing to work for SPIRE might entail.

Joe ended up taking a call on his cell soon after we cleared the dinner trays and the campers started their evening free time. I watched him have a brief phone conversation. After he hung up, he stood and left the building heading toward the protesters.

I wasn't sure what Joe intended. Or how long he would be gone, but I figured his absence afforded me the perfect opportunity to slip away to carry out my plans. I told my team I would be back and left them playing a card game with the pink team.

Harold had been sitting near Joe during the call so I sidled up to him.

"Hey, what was that about?" I asked. "Joe left in an awful hurry, I hope everything is okay."

"He said something about media. There are more reporters talking to the protesters, I think the higher-ups at PYDC want him to make a statement?" Harold shrugged it off, like it didn't make much difference to him.

"I'm just glad they're staying out in the parking lot. They upset my kids the other day when we got here," I confided. Harold nodded his agreement.

"Yeah, that sucked," he said. "I'll never understand these activists causing a nuisance like that. Wasn't your anchor one of them though?"

"Why do you think I sent him away?"

"Good call," Harold favored me with a grin. He slapped me on the back in a gesture of solidarity. "You dodged a bullet there, if you ask me. I have to say it surprised me though, you psions get so sentimental with linking. It's nice to meet one with some brains for once."

It took monumental effort not to bristle at his observations. It wasn't an uncommon assessment of psions. But it was an attitude I hated to find in anchors. I hummed a non-committal response though. And after a few beats of silence I brought up my request.

"Hey, listen, would you keep an eye on my kids for me for a while, I need a break. Radical activists notwithstanding, not having an anchor sucks," I said, I thought Harold would go along with the request.

"Sure, man. If you'll trade off when you get back. I need a smoke break."

"You're on," I clapped him on the back, giving an internal wince at the contact. At least now I understood why his aura felt so off. The man was downright unpleasant, even if he was a more than competent anchor. I left him sitting near my team. After a surreptitious check that no one was paying attention to my actions, I ducked outside to the office.

Joe had locked the door, as expected. It was an electric keypad though, so getting in was child's play for me now. As was neutralizing the camera. Logging onto his computer was more of an obstacle.

Joe had left his laptop unplugged. I gave the battery a quick jolt, improvising to test the bounds of my electrokinesis. The biometric lock might have stopped anyone else if it was any good. And SPIRE could afford the highest quality security, but I bypassed it by applying my EK to the relevant circuitry until the desktop loaded.

I didn't know what I was looking for though, so I called Jake. His friend Em sounded like they would know what would help. When the call connected, I didn't wait for Jake to say anything.

"Hey, if I had hypothetical access to a locked computer that may have incriminating files, where would I look for them?" I asked.

The clock was ticking, and every second risked discovery. I wasted no time in opening a folder from the desktop at random and found a bunch of promotional pictures of the campers. At a glance everything in there looked legit, so I closed it and tried another. That one contained liability paperwork and medical releases for all the campers and staff. I backed out of that one too.

"I'm not sure, try his emails? Just a second, let me give you to Em," Jake said.

Jake put Em on the phone while I navigated to an email client from Joe's bookmarks. A quick scan of the inbox showed a list of inane subject lines. Communications with vendors related to the camp, the rental agreement to use this campground, the food orders and so on.

I almost clicked out of his inbox, but the deleted folder caught my eye. It was full of messages. And one of those messages included a link to a shared spreadsheet titled 'recruitment'. The body of the message showed a reply from Joe chastising the sender for not using a secure messaging service or encryption.

For all that he had chewed out the other party regarding the security of the message, he hadn't handled the email properly on his end either. There it sat in his deleted email folder, just waiting to confirm all of my suspicions.

When I opened the file, it listed what I had to assume was every grade A psion at all SPIRE sponsored PYDC summer camps, nationwide. Along with their names, locations and classifications was a column listing whether they were amenable to recruitment. And those marked as uninterested or uncertain had an entry in a column marked 'leverage'. I found Finn's listing highlighted in green to show that he had signed papers.

"Nevermind, I think I found what we need," I said when Em picked up. "I'm sending it to Jake now, let me know if you need more? It's a spreadsheet listing the grade A's at every PYDC facility. The clincher is a column of blackmail material. Text me your email address real quick please."

"That sounds promising. Look for anything else incriminating in his emails. Check for any files in hidden folders, incriminating photos or video files. And see if you can find any financial records, he might have the login for his online banking saved?" Em suggested. "We might only get one crack at this information. The more evidence stacked against SPIRE and PYDC, the better."

"Yeah, I'll check," I agreed, "I'll forward whatever I find. But I should go. I don't want to get caught."

I hung up without waiting for a response. There were hundreds of entries on the spreadsheet, and there were tabs along the bottom labeled by year with similar spreadsheets going back years. My phone buzzed, indicating that I had the text with Jake's email.

I took screenshots and saved a pdf of the damning file to send to myself and Jake. Along with a screencap of the section listing who they had shared the file with. The list was lengthy and many of them were at government domains associated with SPIRE. I risked forwarding the email, with my evidence attached, to Jake and myself from Joe's email account.

I pulled up a new tab on the web browser and searched through Joe's history to find his online banking portal. And he had his information saved, he must trust the encryption on his computer. I was a little surprised to see how well his job apparently paid when it loaded.

I didn't know how much longer I would have, so I found the option to download bank statements. Hoping the last year would be enough to capture anything that Em needed, I attached the file to another email. Then I returned to skimming the deleted emails.

The buzz of my phone confirming that my emails from Joe's account were sitting in my inbox was a relief, and it meant Jake had the evidence too. I deleted the email from Joe's sent email folder. If I got caught at least it wouldn't be for nothing.

I was still going through all the deleted emails when I heard footsteps and hushed angry voices approaching. I ducked under the desk, powering off the computer by the simple expedient of cutting the flow of energy to the battery as I went.

As I released the stream of power a wave of exhaustion hit me. I was still adjusting to the EK and using so much of it in such a short span was hard. The lock disengaging sounded too loud from where I hid.

Well, that put paid to any hopes I harbored of going undetected. There would be no slipping away unobserved. I recognized Joe's voice barking out a command.

"Get in here."

Footsteps approached me, two sets. One sounded rushed and off balance, like someone was dragging them around, or pushing them, followed by a thump of someone hitting the desk over my head.

The lights were still off, thank god I didn't turn them on when I entered. It would have given my intrusion away. The muted glow of an outdoor floodlight through the window illuminated the room. That might allow me to avoid exposure, depending on how this played out, but I wasn't counting on it. I heard the door lock re-engaging and then Joe spoke again.

"What did I tell you about following orders?"

A gap of a few inches between the front of the desk and the floor gave me a limited view of what was happening. I saw two sets of feet. A pair of black loafers that must belong to Joe moved from the door to the desk. And a familiar pair of bright orange sneakers dangled just off the floor in front of the desk. Those were Finn's shoes.

"I'm sorry you're upset. But I had nothing to do with it, I swear. I know nothing about any reporters. I'll do what you say and keep my mouth shut. Tell them it was a big misunderstanding. Whatever you want, just please leave me and Tim out of it?" Finn's voice shook. There was a crack of sound, like a slap.

"Just shut up and let me think!"

It took everything I had to stay under that desk. I was uncertain what I could do at that point. Joe was a big guy, and his TK was powerful, grade B at least.

Finn and I together might overpower him, but if Finn resorted to using their PK again, it wouldn't help our case. I had no excuse for being in Joe's locked office. And hiding after being caught ruled out trying to talk my way out of the situation. Not that I believed I would keep getting away with that either.

"All right, prove that you can take orders, got it?"

"Prove it how?"

"I've got a problem with one of my counselors. Anderson is nosing around where he shouldn't. You will take care of him for me."

"I don't understand," Finn's voice shook.

I sensed them through the desk; the faint flickering pulse of their heart racing had an odd clarity to my taxed EK senses. Which meant that with a tiny push of my abilities I felt Joe's pulse too. And if I could feel it, then I could affect it. Stop it.

Kill him with my electrokinesis and it wouldn't just look like a heart attack, it would *be* a heart attack. Could I live with doing that? The real question was could I live with not doing it?

"Don't make me spell it out for you," Joe said his voice low and threatening. He shifted his weight closer to Finn. "You're a smart little pyro. Figure it out."

Finn's terror spiked.

And I knew I had to act now if I wanted to stop Joe.

I rolled out from under the desk to find Joe standing over Finn, pinning the teen in place. Blatantly invading their personal space. Finn shoved Joe off, taking advantage when he startled back at my sudden appearance.

"Anderson! What the hell are you doing in my office?"

"What are you doing to Finn?"

"Nevermind that, I'm dealing with you once and for all," Joe said. And I sensed the shift in his aura as he reached toward me with his TK. The power raw as it squeezed around my throat. I only had moments to respond before I lost consciousness. No way I could fight him off telekinetic to telekinetic. He was stronger than me.

I reached for my EK. Concentrated and sensed the flickering beat of Joe's heart. It turned frantic as I touched it with my abilities. Like I was holding something living in a physical sense.

It reminded me of the time Jake and I had found a baby bird in the woods as kids. We had returned it to the low tree branch it had fallen from. But I still remembered the way its tiny heart had hammered against my palm as the bird stilled in my grasp, frozen in terror.

I'd felt such power over that little bird. And with that power came an overwhelming sense of responsibility. The need to protect. And that impulse—not to cause harm—persisted. I had to push it aside.

I eased the frantic pulse down. Slower, slower, stop. Joe made a strange gasping sound and Finn scrambled back over the desk tumbling past the edge to hide behind me, trembling.

The grip on my windpipe faltered and then broke. Both Finn and I stared at Joe where he was grasping at his chest. His visage a mask of genuine panic.

It crossed my mind that I could still undo it, restart his heart, give him back the spark of life. But there was a scared kid trembling beside me. They clung to my arm, and god only knew how many other kids had been through worse at this camp under Joe's care.

Perhaps I should have trusted to the justice system to deal with him. But I didn't have the strength to do it and fight him off again. I couldn't force myself to do it. I let go of my EK, and we watched Joe gasp out his last breaths in eerie silence.

I reeled a little with an overuse headache that was building in my temples but I needed to make sure Finn was all right. We clutched at each other for comfort. The desk between Joe and us providing a barrier. Finn was afraid and in need of comfort and I was on my last legs.

I needed to do a lot more training with my new abilities. Each individual task had seemed small. But the accumulated effort overwhelmed me; too much tight control over too short a span. My new abilities felt erratic, on the brink of breaking free from my control. I ached, my head pounded. I needed Jake if I hoped to stay stable.

"You okay, Finn?" I gasped, petting the top of their head where it pressed against my shoulder. The teen trembled in my arms.

"Uh, I don't think so," Finn said, voice a bare whisper, and then they lunged for the trash bin and vomited. I followed and rubbed their back for them while they retched.

"You're safe now, all right?" I crooned, sinking down to sit beside Finn where they huddled over the trash bin. They slumped against me.

I called Jake again because I didn't think I could get myself out of the office at that point let alone both of us. And nothing would induce me to leave Finn alone with a corpse.

"Aaron?" Jake answered right away. "Are you okay?"

"Yeah."

"You are amazing, those files you sent will nail them."

I smiled a little at the praise, "glad to hear it—slight problem."

"What's wrong?" Jake asked. His tone instantly shifted from excited to concerned.

"Finn and I are in Joe's office—and Joe's dead."

"Dead how?"

"Not sure, he was very worked up, threatening Finn, and then he sort of dropped dead," I explained.

"Not fire though?"

"No, not fire. Finn didn't touch the bastard. I think he had a heart attack or something. He seemed wicked stressed, maybe he had an underlying condition," I reiterated.

This was the story I had committed to when I acted. No going back. Finn stared at me in a manner that made me think they knew what I had done. The pause before Jake responded alerted me he had his suspicions too.

"That must be it, an underlying condition," Jake stated in a flat tone. Then, sounding tentative, he added, "why are you calling me?"

"I, um, I think I might have overdone it with my EK," I admitted. My control slipping further even as I spoke. I shifted a little, leaning heavily on the desk. Finn scooted over to lean against my side, they were shivering still.

"I'll be right there, and I'll call 911 for Joe, okay?" Jake said.

"It's too late for him."

Jake paused again, and I was sure he had more than an inkling of my involvement now.

"We can't know that, Aaron. I'll call and be right there."

"Okay," I said. Jake hung up, presumably to call an ambulance. I let my phone drop and looked over at Finn. They made eye contact with me.

"Thank you," they said.

"Just doing my job, kiddo," I slurred my words and Finn shifted closer.

"Hey, stay with me," they said patting my cheek to focus me. "I know what you did. I won't say anything about it."

I glanced at the camera out of reflex to ensure that it was off. If Finn wanted to talk about this, we didn't need it caught on camera. I spared a trickle of EK to confirm that we remained unobserved. Finn bit their lip pensively before blurting out an admission of their own.

"I was home. The night the house burned down. I lied, and Tim lied for me but I was there."

"Oh," I said, and god, I just wanted to sleep, but that admission required a response. "Um, was it self-defense?"

"I don't remember much from that night. Just that I lost control of my abilities and the next thing I knew Tim and I were standing on the sidewalk watching the house burn. The only reason they didn't arrest me is that Tim told the first responders I had been out in the garage working on the family car when it happened. He told them it was an accident, that he knocked over a candle, and he was the one who started the fire."

"And they believed him?" I asked, incredulous.

"They didn't have much choice. They investigated, but the fire started where Tim said it did. And my abilities leave no evidence that the fire is anything other than natural. Our aunt suspected me, and when she found out Tim was a psion too she had us both packed off to PYDC."

"I'm sorry to hear that. Sounds like a shitty deal for you two," I said. It helped ground me, listening to Finn talk. And it seemed to help them remain calm and in control too.

"At least at the center we're with other psions. It was fine until they pushed the narrative I needed to join SPIRE. They want pyrokinetics to work with fire departments and I can't handle large fires like that. I keep seeing that night and I can't do anything to stop it. I don't think I could control my PK at a big fire like that. It makes me useless," Finn shrugged like it was no big deal, but I saw that it weighed on them more than they wanted to let on.

"You don't have to fight fires to be useful," I patted their hand in emphasis. It was hard to follow the conversation enough to respond coherently though.

"Not to them, to them, I'm just a pyro and if I refuse to use my abilities to help them, then I'm not useful at all. And now I've signed a contract, so it's all a moot point, anyway. If I thought finding a job outside of SPIRE as a pyro was hard before, it will be impossible if I get a registry mark for leaving now."

"Things will change now, Finn. You'll see," I said. I had confidence in that much. Jake would fix things for Finn.

"You think so?" Finn sounded guarded but hopeful.

"I do," I said with as much conviction as I could muster.

I understood why they told their story, and I wanted to reciprocate the shared trust. Because we had something in common. Strong abilities that left devastation in their wake with little to no evidence of our involvement. Finn offered solidarity. A way to assuage my guilt.

They were trying to make me feel better. Despite that being my proper role here. I was the adult in this situation, and they were old enough to understand what Joe had in store for them if I hadn't intervened. I wanted to offer reassurances.

Our conversation was cut short by the sounds of arguing outside the door though. Then someone opened the door. They flooded the office with light and activity.

"Aaron?" Jake called.

I perceived the warmth of his aura even before he entered the room. Controlled chaos erupted around us as Tim called to Finn and he and Jake rounded to desk. Other people came in too, and they fussed over Joe's body. From where Finn and I huddled together I glimpsed someone attempting CPR.

Then Jake was pulling me up off the floor. Everything would be all right now. Finn was safe. And Jake was with me. So I let myself drift off on the tidal wave of exhaustion that my conversation with Finn had been holding at bay. The last thing I was conscious of were Jake's strong arms lifting me off the ground.

Chapter 26

Jake

After the paramedics left with Joe's body, law enforcement officers and SPIRE agents crowded into Joe's office. They relocated Aaron and Finn to the mess hall where there was more room and treated them for shock. Once the first responders descended on the camp, they sent the other campers and their counselors off to their cabins with instructions to remain there for the night.

The explanation that Joe suffered a medical emergency was true enough. Everyone seemed to accept the news. The camp staffers were more than willing to stay out of the way while the authorities dealt with the incident.

I stayed in the mess hall with Aaron. The first officers on the scene permitted Tim to stay with Finn who the EMTs had draped in blankets and settled in a chair. Each of the teens held a large mug of hot cocoa despite the warmth of the evening. Finn still shivered. Everything that happened this week entitled the teen to recover in peace from the trauma of the evening.

Caleb maintained constant contact with me, texting back and forth to keep me apprised of events. Em went public with everything. And the media latched onto the narrative.

Elliott held it together through all the action, but Caleb planned to take him home soon. I told them to go ahead without me. Even though I wanted to be with them, Aaron needed me more tonight. It was not the time to introduce them yet either. I spoke to Elliott before they left though, to remind him I loved him, even if I couldn't be with him tonight. Caleb would be the rock Elliott needed. And I would support Aaron. Once we weathered the immediate storm, the three of them could get acquainted.

Aaron was resting, cuddled into my side. He had lost consciousness as I arrived on the scene. The paramedics confirmed that he was suffering from severe psionic overuse symptoms and an incipient hyper-gamma reaction. But he regained consciousness once I stabilized his brain waves through our link.

I might have also used our link to nudge him into a restful sleep, but he was stable now I had smoothed away the sharp spikes in his aura. So that was the important part. He had run himself ragged.

When I found him on the floor with Finn, it took a strong link and every bit of my skill to stabilize him. His role in the events surrounding Joe's death was harder to explain without incriminating him.

I told them a version of the truth. Aaron was adjusting to his electrokinesis. The stress of the situation without an anchor proved overwhelming. He came within a hair's breadth of hyper-gamma crisis.

The authorities determined that neither Aaron nor Finn had been in any shape to render aid to Joe. Both having suffered quite the shock. It helped that the other camp counselor who opened the locked door for me had also attested to that fact.

The officers questioned Aaron's presence in the office though. Despite circumstances forcing me to think on my feet, I thought the excuse I concocted would hold up to scrutiny. Aaron must have been doing work for Joe when he stumbled upon the emails by accident, I suggested.

I further explained that he had called me to ask what he should do with what he discovered. That was how I explained the files coming into my possession and then making their way to Em. The incriminating evidence hit the media while I was still dealing with the fallout of Joe's demise.

I also told the EMTs that Joe looked stressed when I saw him a few days ago, which was no less than the truth. As to my suspicions about Aaron's involvement, I kept my mouth shut tight.

My understanding was Finn did the same. I overheard them talking to the police. They alluded to the fact that Joe brought them to the office because he was angry about the video that had leaked earlier in the evening.

Finn assiduously avoided accusing the dead man of specific wrongdoing. Since they still looked shaky, the officers questioning them agreed to schedule an interview for another time to get more details. The EMT's pointed suggestion on the matter may have played a role in that decision.

After a few hours, the police finished their investigation of the office. As far as I could tell, they concluded there was no foul play involved with Joe's death. Though they warned us all not to leave town. I had every confidence the coroner would corroborate that Joe died of cardiac arrest though.

Roy and Davis were the ranking SPIRE agents on site. Davis seemed angry, but Roy came over to sit with me once he finished with the police officers.

"So, awful convenient, your boyfriend finding those records tonight, huh?" Roy drawled as he slumped into the seat across from me.

"Aaron was just doing his job."

"I'm sure. Same way he happened upon that video when the security footage in that room has more holes in it than swiss cheese."

"Good fortune, I guess."

"Well, the media are here in force. We've got local affiliates for all the national outlets clamoring for the big scoop. Your friends are giving interviews."

"Em must have gotten those files to the right people," I said, relieved that Aaron hadn't risked his safety for nothing.

"Seems that way. Time will tell if it makes a real difference. But the local police took the laptop since it contains evidence implicating SPIRE in a scandal. They were leery of leaving it in SPIRE's hands, for obvious reasons.

"However, this story is too huge to cover-up now. We can hope they get it into the hands of a tech expert. And turn over any other evidence Joe might have stored on his hard drive to the investigation into SPIRE. Looks like we might get to the bottom of this."

"We can hope."

I wished I shared his confidence that the recruitment scandal covered the extent of SPIRE's dirty dealings. That the scope of the corruption remained limited, and it did not involve the majority of the organization. But my gut told me otherwise.

If I knew Aaron, he would be even more optimistic about rehabilitating SPIRE than Roy was. So if I wanted Aaron, I would have to stick with SPIRE. And I'd signed that contract. For whatever it would be worth once the investigation brought everything to light.

I hoped that at least now Aaron wouldn't dismiss my concerns about the organization out of hand. Ignoring SPIRE wouldn't make their underhanded tactics disappear. Someone had to hold SPIRE accountable for its actions. Might as well be us.

I'd made my decision over the course of the long afternoon spent anticipating the final outcome here. The widespread nature of the recruitment issues convinced me the best place to find evidence of any future dirty dealings would be from the inside. That made deciding to work for SPIRE easier to swallow.

Elliott and Caleb didn't love the plan, but they understood my reasoning. Aaron and I would have to discuss it, the details might prove a challenge. But I was willing to put in the effort to make my relationships work regardless of where my career trajectory landed me. For now, it was all a waiting game to see how events unfolded.

Maybe SPIRE could become the beacon of psion rights and societal integration it claimed in its mission statement. It might live up to Aaron's high standards for it. And if not, we could always help to nudge it toward that path as needed.

The chance to keep Aaron safe and at my side was enough incentive to try. And with this whole ordeal behind us we had room to breathe—figure out our future together.

I was certain whatever came next, we could face it together.

Epilogue

4 Months Later

Aaron

Jake and I went to his family's cabin on the lake for our week of leave once we finished just over two months of SPIRE training. We had graduated to special agents now. All official and ready for field work.

After everything came out about PYDC's involvement in shady recruitment practices, they shut their summer camps down early to facilitate a full review. Jake and I got caught up in the fallout. We had to give statements and testify at hearings in Washington DC. It ended up being bigger than I suspected and smaller at the same time.

Once the public got wind of the PYDC scandal, there was a huge investigation and the company folded not long thereafter. PYDC went down hard. But SPIRE cast itself as another victim of PYDC's attempts to take advantage of grant money and game the system.

It turned out the owner of the company behind the PYDC network was a close friend of SPIRE Director Norman Russell. Robert Pederson, the man behind PYDC, killed himself before his trial.

Russell facilitated PYDC getting the contracts they used in their rapid expansion efforts. The evidence also implicated Russell in suspect grant funding allocation. The funding PYDC used to become the single largest provider of care and housing for psion youth nationwide. I thought he and his friend were in it up to their eyeballs.

PYDC had also taken aggressive steps to gain custody of those psionically gifted wards of the state unable to find other placements in the foster care system. SPIRE awarded them the contracts for their summer camp program. And in return PYDC funneled the teens with the strongest and rarest abilities to SPIRE. But SPIRE's involvement was harder to prove.

The biggest surprise had been the efforts PYDC made to get custody of strong psions through state foster care programs. A search through the registry revealed there were even cases of grade A psions being taken from their families on unsubstantiated charges. Similar to the tactics used to get the teens to enlist with SPIRE once they were under PYDC's care.

The higher-ups at PYDC were facing serious jail time. The company itself disbanded. Their assets seized and put into a fund to help local agencies fill the gap in care for the kids in the system. The outcome satisfied me. As far as it concerned me, the people behind exploiting vulnerable teenagers deserved whatever punishment they got. The legal experts settled on an arrangement to make money available to the youth affected.

The biggest problem, at least to my way of thinking, was that PYDC was the largest provider to the point of forcing smaller providers to close their doors. In the wake of PYDC's disbandment, a scramble to fill the void ensued.

I called my old social worker friend at the PYDC shelter in Connecticut when they announced the settlement. It heartened me to learn that—at least for her location—a local non-profit stepped in to keep the center running after PYDC failed.

Eagle House was under new management. The residents appeared to handle the transition well. To my relief, my mentor, Mrs. England, had no involvement in the scandal. But hundreds of others did.

As to SPIRE, the organization passed most of the blame for the policy to PYDC. They were the ones running the summer camp program after all. The investigation into SPIRE's involvement stalled when Director Russell resigned. I forced myself to listen to his speech.

It was a long-winded, rambling piece of theatrics—Director Russell claimed to be unaware of what was going on under his nose. But as the director, he took full responsibility. He made a big production of being appalled at Robert Pederson's—someone he knew and trusted—involvement in the debacle.

I was not at all convinced of Russell's innocence, but at least he wasn't leading SPIRE anymore. That would be the former Assistant Director, now Acting Director, Lisa Nelson.

Through the whole process, Jake exercised dogged determination in making sure that our story got told in front of the committees investigating SPIRE. Even after the information we acquired brought the whole thing down, he persisted. We even went on a circuit of morning talk shows with our sordid tale along with Finn.

Roy and some other agents stepped forward with their stories too. It upended the leadership at a number of field offices. Few regional SACs escaped unscathed. A handful of their immediate underlings also resigned. Or were forced into early retirements, Anna Davis among them. Roy was vague on the details. My understanding was she leveraged her knowledge to negotiate an easy out for herself. Roy opted to stay on and take a new partner.

We would still work with him out of Seattle headquarters. That he came forward as a whistle-blower improved my opinion of him. They still busted him back to special agent for his involvement in covering the scandal up over the years though.

In exchange for the restructuring and resignations, SPIRE dodged any criminal charges. Jake was livid about that. SPIRE's involvement got minimized and brushed aside. The official story made it clear PYDC was behind the widespread abuses. Those in power knew better at least.

Behind closed doors, congress put a program in place to help the victims of the recruitment scandal. A new oversight committee formed. There was even a council set up to help victims of the coercive enlistments get out of their contracts with generous severance packages and aid with job retraining and placement.

We met with the new acting director of the agency while we were in DC after the hearings. Jake and I received a commendation before we even became full agents.

Lisa Nelson was a slim no-nonsense woman. I never saw her looking anything other than impeccable, blond hair in a tight chignon and rocking a power suit. I didn't quite trust her, but Anna said she wasn't lying about not being aware of Russell's plans. Or the scandal so we had to take her word as a grade A telepath for gospel.

I was uncertain how to feel about the way everything shook out. It was a relief to know the summer camp I trusted was no longer being used to coerce teens into enlisting with SPIRE. Even if it meant the program was on hold for the summer.

Next summer, the plan was to restructure it back into a SPIRE run camp instead of contracting it out through a third party. I still believed SPIRE could live up to its mission to benefit psions and build inroads between psions and norms out in the community. And so far working with Jake lived up to my aspirations.

After we finished giving our testimony, we returned home to Seattle. The new regional leadership whisked us off to the SPIRE equivalent of basic training at the tower. It took time to get used to the way everything glowed to my electrokinetic senses with all the electricity flowing through the downtown core. But I enjoyed living downtown. Seattle was home.

The training itself was fine, honing my electrokinesis and deepening my link-bond with Jake was not my idea of a hardship. I liked the tower and the other agents we met there. Jake begrudgingly admitted that it wasn't all bad. He and Roy struck up a close friendship, which I gave my wholehearted endorsement since the agent was fun to flirt with.

Roy didn't take it seriously and Jake only rolled his eyes in exasperation when I pushed too far. I considered it only fair since he had his relationship with Caleb and Elliott. Going into my first meeting with them I'd been full of trepidation. Jake spoke about them often, but I had been unsure of how warm a reception I would receive from his other boyfriends.

It surprised me how much I ended up liking them once we got to know each other though. I had expected to feel jealous of them. Especially when stories about their four years with Jake came up, but I found it an odd comfort.

I discovered that I liked sharing Jake with them. Like it made our relationship more somehow rather than taking away from it as I had initially feared. It was nice having more people I cared about, and who cared about me. They welcomed me into their family and I couldn't resent that.

Elliott and I got along well, much to Jake's surprise. He had expressed concern we wouldn't have much in common, but he needn't have worried. Though there were some missteps and hurt feelings along the way. El reminded me of the kids I'd been friends with at PYDC in Connecticut. He had that same guarded wariness around strangers.

Caleb and I hit it off from the start. Caleb had a wicked sense of humor, and he appreciated my sex puns. On one notable instance early in our relationship he and I spent an evening conversing through bad puns alone. It was epic. Jake and Elliott had left the room, unable to handle our sheer level of awesomeness.

When I agreed to see Jake while he continued to date Caleb and Elliott, I had assumed it would be two separate relationships. In some respects that was true. But I hadn't expected for Jake's lovers to become two of my closest friends over the past few months. They supported Jake dating me so that helped win me over.

An open relationship wasn't something I would have sought. And we were all still working out the details of how we fit together, but it was important to Jake and I found that it suited me too. I liked the way they felt like an extension of our family. I was coming to feel secure in my place with them.

I needed connections to other people. More so now I was a grade A. Jake, Elliott and Caleb provided that in spades. Our other friends helped too. And Jake and my relationship grew stronger because of the open communication that our unique relationship dynamic required to function. I still had some doubts, but I figured time would erase them.

As to our training program, it got intense. The initial training sessions lasted a month before we began field training alongside the other lessons. My SPIRE training certification and years of training in TK use leant me an advantage over the others in our training group. But it was still hard work.

It might have been too much to handle on top of getting reacquainted with Jake and figuring out how we fit together now. We got our nights to ourselves at least. To connect and recharge. It thrilled me to get to call Jake my boyfriend even if I wasn't his only boyfriend. And I was sure he would agree that our sex life was worth the wait.

The whole summer was a whirlwind though. Between dealing with all the fallout after what happened at the camp, forging a relationship with Caleb and Elliott and getting through our training I still hadn't made it out to see Jake's family yet.

I spoke with his mom every week, as I had done for years, but it had been ages since I had seen Sofia and Luca and I missed them. Now I felt entitled to be a part of Jake's family again, I wanted to surround myself with my loved ones.

And speaking of loved ones, I called my parents. In a moment of weakness, between television interviews and sworn affidavits and the minutiae of being a key witness in a huge scandal and attempted cover-up.

Mom told me she read about my affiliation with SaFE. She read me the riot act about my many failings as a son. How I disappointed her and my father by associating with radicals and flaunting my lifestyle in public. I hung up on her, then deleted her seldom-used number from my phone. No more letting her hurt me.

Afterward, I called the woman who had been my mom in every way that mattered. And Mrs. Moretti told me how proud she was of Jake and I and everything we were doing. So I still had a family. It didn't look the way I had expected, but that was fine. I was glad to have time to decompress with my loved ones at the lake before we got our first assignment in the field.

Roy planned to bring Finn and Tim out for the day on Saturday. Finn negotiated a deal to work with SPIRE contingent on not having to work fires. They ended up in the same training class as Jake and I. We bonded over the work, Finn gravitated toward me after everything that happened with Joe.

I suspected Finn had developed a puppy dog crush on me. But they would outgrow that, given time. And it turned out we worked well together so there was talk of us doing joint missions in the future.

The SaFE leadership team planned to join us too. Elliott and Caleb would spend most of the week with us. It would be a blast. It felt like Jake's family was giving us the big graduation party I never got back in high school or university, come to it. I felt all warm and fuzzy knowing so many people were in my corner these days.

I also had high hopes that Jake and I would have some alone time. But Jake's family should arrive for the weekend at any moment. The cabin had three bedrooms, so it would accommodate all the expected guests with enough creative shuffling.

I was happy, truly happy, for the first time in ages. Maybe ever. Content with my life. Being back in Seattle, having Jake as my partner and link, I had almost forgotten what it was like to have support and people who cared around me. It was nice to be reminded.

Jake

I exited my family's cabin to join Aaron on the narrow rocky shore where he worked to set up a fire. My arms were full of grocery bags, not that I hoped to surprise Aaron. He must suspect he would find the ingredients for s'mores inside, but I knew it would make him smile.

From the way he watched me I had a strong suspicion he was calculating whether there was time to make-out by the fire before my parents and siblings arrived. The crunch of tires on gravel, followed by slamming car doors dismissed that idea though. I set down my bags and watched as Luca and Sofia dashed around the side of the cabin.

"Hey!" Aaron cried, a gleeful grin on his face as my brother, a good foot taller than Aaron now, tackled him in a bear hug.

"We missed you!"

Sofia crashed into them next, almost toppling all three to the ground. I reached out to steady Aaron's shoulder. He flashed me a grateful smile.

"You can't disappear on us like that ever again," Sofia chastised, slugging Aaron in the arm, "I'm serious, bro, we missed you."

"Guys, maybe get off my boyfriend before you crush him?" I suggested hiding my amusement behind a mild tone. They backed off, albeit with reluctance.

"Tell us everything! What have you been up to? How did you like Connecticut? What's a fancy place like Yale do for graduation?" Sofia demanded.

"What's it like having superpowers?" Luca added to the barrage of questions.

Aaron laughed, ruffling Luca's hair. "I don't have superpowers. I'll show you pictures of the graduation ceremony later. Connecticut was great, just what I needed. Yale was hard, lots of pressure, lots of entitled asshole classmates who didn't like sharing space with psions. I missed you guys, so much. So, here I am, the prodigal returned home."

"And you're sticking around this time?" Luca asked.

"You are not breaking my brother's heart again, or you will have us to answer to, got it?" Sofia threatened.

I watched as the threat hit home. Aaron got choked up, and he looked at me with so much uncertainty it made me ache for him. I snaked an arm around his waist and tugged him into my side, dropping a kiss in his hair. I sent warm reassurances through our link. And shot my sister a dirty look.

"We broke each other's hearts. That's what happens when you're young and stupid and don't communicate, but it will not happen again, right, Aaron?" I answered for him. Sofia rolled her eyes, but I didn't care, because it was true.

"Yeah," Aaron beamed up at me.

I suppose my expression was just as sappy and besotted as Aaron's looked when our eyes met. Heedless of our audience, he squirmed around in my embrace, threw his arms around my neck and pulled me into a passionate kiss.

Mom clearing her throat brought us back to reality before we embarrassed ourselves by rutting against each other right there on the narrow rocky beach. I released my hold on Aaron. For a long moment, he only stared at Mom as she closed the distance between us. It was one thing to talk on the phone, but he seemed overwhelmed at seeing her again. I wondered what he was thinking.

Confronted with the sole connection to home he had allowed himself to preserve, he wavered. His uncertainty broke my heart. Sofia was right though, Aaron had hurt me and this was my mother, not his. I watched the realization dawning on him. But I knew my mom too.

No way would she turn her back on one of her own. And Aaron had been hers from the moment it became clear he needed her. I wasn't sure if he understood the full extent of her love for him. But that was fine. He had time to learn.

"Hey, Mom," I said, chagrined at being caught in a lip lock. She pulled me down to kiss my cheek and then turned to Aaron and opened her arms.

"*Caio, belli*! My beautiful boys. Do I get a hug from my long lost third son?" she asked, light and playful, and he threw himself into her embrace.

"Hi, Mo—I mean Mrs. Moretti," Aaron choked out through a throat tight with emotions.

"You know you can call me Mom too, Aaron, *caro mio*," she said, rocking him from side to side in a suffocating embrace.

"I missed you all so much." Aaron said, not moving to break the hug.

"We missed you too, *caro*."

"You sure you aren't just dating me to steal my family?" I teased.

I poked Aaron in the ribs using humor to break the emotional tension. He let go of Mom and stood beside her, a little awkward. Dad walked out the back door of the cabin then, turning on the outdoor lights flanking the door so we could find our way inside after our campfire.

"Don't be silly, Jacopo, Aaron is ours regardless of whether he dates you," Mom reached up to tousle my hair. "And we expect to see more of you both now you're done with your training."

"Aaron, Jake, good to see you boys," Dad greeted with warmth. "We're so glad our very own secret agents took the time to visit with us little people."

Dad stood next to Mom, slipping an arm around her waist.

"We're not secret agents, Dad," I said with a chuckle. "The correct title is special agent. Although Aaron turned a little rogue with his file stealing."

"I stumbled upon those files when I was ordering pancake mix. It made sense to look through the old invoices to ensure I got the right amount," Aaron said with false indignation. "Let me tell you, I was shocked to find something so scandalous, shocked!"

"I can't believe you pulled off that lie," I groaned.

"Excuse you," Aaron gave my arm a playful swat. "I am an excellent actor. And I had to work with your lies to begin with, if you'll recall. What did you think Joe would ask me to do on his computer?"

"I can't believe they made you a special agent, Jake," Sofia interjected. She flounced over to the circle of chairs set up around the little fire on the beach. "Didn't they ask for like, character references?"

"They did, and I passed all of my background checks. Even if I have activist tendencies."

I joined my sister, Aaron trailed after me, reaching for my hand. Soon we were all seated around the cozy little blaze.

Aaron plopped onto my lap with his usual disregard for propriety. I understood though, no matter what else he was still a psion, and he needed the closeness. No one batted an eye although Sofia snorted and made an under her breath suggestion we get a room. Dad reached for the bag I brought out earlier and handed out bottles of cold soda.

"Attending a protest is an activist tendency. Or going to a march. What you did, bringing down a government conspiracy is badass spy shit. You guys are freaking heroes," Luca enthused. He took the seat closest to us.

God, had he grown. The kid must have put on at least another couple of inches since I'd last seen him in June. I could only imagine Aaron's shock. He remembered Luca as a child. But in the last six years, Luca grew as tall as me. He wasn't as broad and muscular, being only a fifteen-year-old, though. Still, it was strange to see my baby brother growing up before my eyes.

Whatever Aaron was thinking put a dopey grin on his face.

"God, I love you," Aaron blurted out of nowhere. "You know I'm never letting you go again, right?"

The sentiment was mutual. Even if our relationship was nothing like we had envisioned at sixteen. I thought it was better than anything my teenage self could have imagined.

"Right back at you, babe," I smiled and kissed his temple.

Aaron squirmed, and I knew he could feel my dick hardening under his ass. I nudged him off of me, PDA was one thing, getting to second base with my family gathered around was a whole other matter.

"Why don't you grab the marshmallows out of the bag," I suggested. We couldn't act on our feelings at the moment, but we could re-enact the sweet perfection of the one part of our first date that had gone right. Chocolate and marshmallow flavored kisses sounded like heaven just then.

Aaron slid off my lap, crouched near the fire as he focused on making his s'more and I signalled Sofia. She messed with her phone. Luca chattered about being related to a spy. It was nice, being surrounded by family. I knew Aaron hadn't had this in years, sharing it with him made the moment sweeter.

Only having El and Caleb here to share it with us could have improved the moment. They were coming out tomorrow though. And they knew what I had planned for tonight. Understood why I was doing it and that it didn't change things between us. They both gave their blessing, so I intended to ask Aaron to be part of my family for keeps. Tonight was about the two of us. How that fit with Elliott and Caleb was an ongoing process, but we were all navigating it together.

"Can you get the chocolate ready for me?" Aaron directed. I reached for the bag to comply.

Turning to face me, Aaron pulled a perfectly toasted marshmallow out of the heat. He slid his gooey treat between the two pieces of graham cracker I held ready for him. He grinned at me before greedily snatching the finished product from my grasp and taking a big bite.

I almost laughed out loud. He had missed the small object I balanced on top of his treat. I think he might have swallowed it whole if he hadn't bitten down on the object in question. I made a strangled sound of horrified amusement. Luca snorted off to the side.

Aaron pulled the sticky chocolate covered ring out of his mouth. He scrutinized it a moment, eyes narrowing and then widening in surprise as he brushed away gooey crumbs. The metal glinted in the firelight.

"So, speaking of never letting you go, what do you say to making that sentiment official?"

Aaron stared at me for a long time, forgetting to chew his mouthful of marshmallow. My breathlessly silent family forgotten in the background. I squirmed as the silence stretched.

I thought Aaron needed this. Not marriage per se. But a tangible commitment. A family to call his own. The longer he took to respond though, the more doubt crept in that I had misread him. He swallowed so he could talk.

"Oh my god, hell yeah, babe. Yes! Sofia are you recording this? You all knew?" Aaron demanded. Sofia gave me a cheeky grin and Luca whooped.

"Congrats, bro," Luca offered me a fist bump.

"Can't believe he said yes," Sofia teased. "But I got your proof."

"We're happy for you both," Dad said.

"*Molti auguri di felicità a tutti e due.* And now you can be our official third son, *caro mio,*" Mom said.

"You need to kiss me now," Aaron said and then his lips were on mine.

I had a distant awareness of my family discreetly getting up and going inside to give us some privacy. But that kiss took most of my attention, it was everything I could have wanted.

Our auras entwined. I knew I glowed to his EK senses in the absence of all the electric noise of the city, a bright flame to rival our little campfire. I wanted to memorize this moment. The taste of my lover and chocolate, the smell of wood smoke and the sound of the lake lapping at the shore.

We could have been kids again, our love pure and innocent and our whole lives laid out ahead of us. But this was better. Our bond stronger for the years we spent apart. Our love had grown and matured with us. This time nothing would come between us, this time we would face whatever came at us together and I couldn't wait to see what our new beginning would hold.

About the Author

Alex Silver grew up mostly in Northern Maine and is now living in Canada with one spouse, two kids, and three birds. Alex is a trans guy who started writing fiction as a child and never stopped. Although there were detours through assisting on a farm and being a pharmacist along the way.

Visit Alex online at: http://alexsilverauthor.wordpress.com/

FB group: https://www.facebook.com/groups/PsionsofSPIREreaders/

Sign up for my newsletter for a free short featuring Aaron and Jake at: http://eepurl.com/dNcScQ

If you enjoyed this book, please consider leaving a review on the site where you purchased it. Reviews are vitally important to independent authors. Thank you.

Psions of SPIRE Series

Shelter *Novella 0.5*	February 2019
Bright Spark *Book 1*	February 2019
Bold Move *Novella 1.5*	February 2019
Keen Sense *Book 2*	April 2019
Weak Link *Novella 2.5*	June 2019
Quick Fire *Book 3*	July 2019
Clear Sight *Book 4*	Coming Soon

Shelter

Family is what you make it.

Former foster kid and abuse survivor, Elliott Sheffield, lost everything when he developed telepathy at twelve years old. He's used to not relying on anyone. There are worse things than being lonely and alone, even for a psion who craves closeness. He has plans for his life and nothing can distract him from proving that he can succeed. That will show everyone who cast him aside. Especially his former best friend Caleb Gaetz.

Pansexual, poly, psion, Caleb is comfortable with all of those labels. Life seems easy for Caleb. He has a supportive family and a vibrant social life. The future will figure itself out. For the present he plans to enjoy his university years to the fullest extent possible. He knows his hedonistic tendencies irritate his former best friend, Elliott, to no end. He just doesn't understand why Elliott takes Caleb's sex life so personally.

When life throws them both curve balls, they must adjust their visions for the future to one that will give them both a happily ever after, or risk their plans falling apart.

Contains an open M/M relationship, mention of past abuse, and positive HIV status. This is a prequel novella to the Psions of SPIRE series.

Bright Spark

Sometimes growing up means giving up your preconceptions.

Aaron Anderson and Jake Matthews were childhood sweethearts until Aaron developed psionic abilities that turned both of their worlds upside down and tore them apart.

Six years later they reconnect when Aaron returns home to work with a youth summer camp affiliated with SPIRE. Jake is at the same camp, along with his current partners, to protest the organization funding it. Sparks fly when the couple reunites and Aaron discovers hidden abilities that bring him to the attention of SPIRE.

Aaron and Jake have every intention of seizing their second chance at love. But once more, forces outside their control are at play. And the organization Aaron believes in is at the center of events targeting vulnerable youth.

This urban fantasy romance contains M/M and an open M/M/M relationship. This is book one of the Psions of SPIRE series.

Bold Move

Jake Moretti is putting a new spin on bringing his boyfriend home to meet the family.

When polyamorous Jake invites Aaron Anderson—his high school sweetheart and current lover—to meet his boyfriends, Caleb Gaetz and Elliott Sheffield, they all have some concerns.

Jake worries that the three men won't get along and he'll be forced to choose between the three men he loves. Aaron fears rejection from the two strangers who love the person who means the most to him.

Caleb frets over the logistics of it all. He is ready and willing to embrace Aaron as his metamour, but troubled over Elliott's negative reaction. Elliott fears the changes facing his family and resents Aaron as the catalyst of the unwelcome conflict.

The one thing Elliott, Aaron and Caleb can all agree on is that they love Jake, and he loves them. But sometimes love—and a relationship—is hard work.

This urban fantasy short story contains open M/M and M/M/M relationships and touches on issues of mental health including panic attacks and PTSD from past abuse. This is a companion novella to the Psions of SPIRE series.

Keen Sense

In the blink of an eye, everything can change.

That's what happened to Andrew James. One minute he was just an average IT guy, working for a large company. The next he was waking up in a hospital bed as a powerful psion. Learning to navigate the unfamiliar world of psions as an adult is a daunting prospect. And as Andrew's carefully constructed life falls apart around him, the only one helping him hold the pieces together is Oscar Watkins. The anchor from Mount Hope Hospital who saved his life.

Oscar has worked at Mount Hope for almost a decade. And not once has he experienced the deep connection to a patient he feels toward Andrew. While he finds his work rewarding, it's also demanding and emotionally exhausting. When Andrew arrives in a psionic crisis, it sets off a chain of events that changes everything for Oscar.

While Oscar struggles to find a balance between work and a personal life, Andrew struggles to rebuild his life. Andrew turns to SPIRE. But his new senses soon reveal that everything is not as it appears, leading him to wonder what SPIRE is hiding.

This urban fantasy M/M romance contains themes including a verbally abusive ex, medical drama, and a homophobic family of origin. It is book two of the Psions of SPIRE series.

Alex Silver

Weak Link

Anchors lie, it's in their nature.

Telekinetic, Marc Overton, learned that the hard way as a teen. Five years hasn't blunted the sharp edges of the lesson. So when Marc starts a fling with an anchor he knows better than to get attached.

Zane Parker might be fuzzy on the details, but Marc has obvious baggage and clear rules for their friends with benefits arrangement. The longer their agreement lasts, the more the lines between them blur.

This urban fantasy M/M romance contains mention of a past coercive relationship and alludes to dubious consent in that context. A companion novella in the Psions of SPIRE series.

Quick Fire

When you love your work, you never work a day—when you love your work partner, life gets complicated.

Finn Cooper is content to use their pyrokinesis fighting infernal forces on behalf of SPIRE. Their only problem is their lack of a psionic link to replace their little brother. And not having a dedicated anchor is taking a toll. Their struggle to control their abilities is impacting their job performance. And if they lose their job, that means they could lose custody of their little brother, Tim. Failure is not an option.

Oliver Hawkins wants to join SPIRE. Working with other psions appeals to him. He wants a job where his trans identity won't hold him back from his career goals. His plans hit a speed bump when he learns his psionic abilities are too weak to qualify him for fieldwork.

When a chance encounter brings the two of them together, Oliver's aura draws Finn to him. They devise a plan to solve each other's problems by forming a link bond. As Finn's link, Oliver can join SPIRE and in return he will stabilize Finn's volatile aura. That way Finn can regain control of their pyrokinesis and their life.

At first their solution seems perfect, but then work drama intrudes on the situation. Oliver suspects all is not as it seems with his new team and their mission. And when your work has fangs, claws, and venom, the drama can get intense. Throw in guardianship of a teenage math whiz and Finn's life is about to get hectic.

This is a queer (M/NB) urban fantasy romance featuring a trans man and an asexual non-binary person who is raising their teenage brother after they lost their parents. This is book three of the Psions of SPIRE series.

Clear Sight

When the slightest touch triggers visions of horror, you learn not to let anyone close.

After more than a decade hiding from society, Seth Albright is sheltered. His visions make it a necessary evil. After a precocious emergence as a seer when he was eight, his mother took him to live in the woods. To protect him.

When he can't take another day of isolation, Seth turns to SPIRE. There, he gets partnered with Roy Merchant as his anchor. Enough inexperienced psions have burned Roy by using him as a stepping stone to last a lifetime.

Roy has seen scandals come and go in his time with SPIRE. Seth has seen horrors most people couldn't imagine. But neither of them has seen anything like what's coming for them next.

This urban fantasy M/M romance is book four in the Psions of SPIRE series.

www.ingramcontent.com/pod-product-compliance
Lightning Source LLC
Chambersburg PA
CBHW030401180626
46812CB00005B/1885